Kate,

Thank you, thank you, thank you.
Times 1,000,000,000...000.
Your insights were beyond
invaluable. This ~~book~~ would not
have happened without your
~~feedback~~ ideas, and encouragement.

A Woman of Valor

Gary Corbin

This book is a work of fiction. Names, characters, businesses, incidents, and dialogue are either drawn from the author's imagination or are used fictitiously, and are not to be construed as real. Any resemblance to actual events or persons, living or dead, is entirely coincidental.

Copyright © 2019 Gary Corbin
Double Diamond Publishing, Camas, WA
All rights reserved.
ISBN: 0-9974967-9-7
ISBN-13: 978-0-9974967-9-6

To all those who could say #metoo

For all those who #fightback

For the allies who say, No More!

CONTENTS

Speak up for those who cannot speak for themselves,
    for the rights of all who are destitute.
Speak up and judge fairly;
    defend the rights of the poor and needy.

                                    - Proverbs 31:8-9

PART 1

A Woman With a Past

Chapter One

Valorie Dawes tiptoed to her roommate's bedroom door. She could never be sure if Beth had company, or if she'd pulled an all-nighter to study for exams and wanted to sleep all day, or both. Usually, Beth left some sort of signal in their tiny common living space if she didn't want Val to disturb her before 9:00 a.m. But during finals week, none of the usual rules applied, except one: waking her meant Val would have hell to pay.

She crept closer to the door, grimacing every time the old floorboards creaked, and listened. Nothing. Maybe Beth hadn't even come home.

Val waited another moment, pressing her ear to the door. A soft buzzing sound seemed to emerge from within. Snoring, or perhaps her morning alarm. Maybe if she brought coffee—

The door swung open, and Val jerked back in a panic. The five-foot seven, pear-shaped figure of her lifelong friend appeared in the darkened doorway, her eyes bleary between tousled locks of brown hair.

"What are you doing there?" Beth asked, striding past her toward the kitchen in a pale-yellow bathrobe. "And please, tell me there's caffeine. I've still got to cram for my Business Ethics final today."

"Fresh, dark, and strong," Val said, pausing for Beth's stock reply.

"Like my men," Beth said.

Val grinned with relief. Good old Beth.

Beth poured coffee into a tall ceramic mug and made a pouty face. "I hate that you're finishing a semester early. I'll never find a roommate as good as you." She searched the fridge and dumped a pint of creamer into her mug. "Oh, thanks for getting groceries. Otherwise we'd have starved today."

"I'll be out of here by dinner," Val said, "once I drop my application in the mail. I was hoping you'd look at it for me...?" She pointed to a stapled set of printouts on the kitchen table. "After you've had your coffee, of course."

"Dammit, Val, this makes me sad. It's the end of an era." Beth poured Val a mug of black coffee and they sat opposite each other at the table. They toasted each other with their mugs and took long sips of the tasty brew.

"It's just a few months," Val said. "We'll be roomies again once we're both back in Clayton. That's still the plan, right?"

Beth's gaze floated upward, over Val's shoulder. "Good morning, gorgeous," she said.

Val furrowed her eyebrows. What a curious thing to say. She started to reply, but something moved in her peripheral vision. No, not something. Someone. She turned, and the bare, muscular chest of a large, dark-haired man filled her vision. Close to her face. Close enough to smell his cheap cologne.

Cologne that brought her back to the worst day of her life—the day a man towered over her, dominated her, hurt her—

Val leaped out of her chair, hooked her right foot behind the dark-haired man's left leg, and pushed him to the floor. She stepped over him and spun around, crouched in a jiu jitsu fighter's stance, fingers curled and ready to strike.

"Val! What the hell?" Beth shouted, jumping to her feet. Her coffee had spilled all over her bathrobe, drenching her and the floor. "Geez, Rick, are you all right?"

Rick, who Val realized was Beth's latest conquest, picked his tall, muscular frame off the floor and wiped coffee off of his face. He wore only a set of red boxer shorts and a goofy smile. "I'm fine," he said, laughing. He glanced at Beth, then nodded to Val. "That's quite the security team you've got there. You must be Valorie." He opened his arms, reaching out to hug her. Val backed away.

"Val doesn't hug, Rick," Beth said. "Go put some clothes on."

Rick planted a long, wet kiss on Beth's lips, grinned at Val, and ambled back to the bedroom, shutting the door behind him.

"I've told you a thousand times, you need to warn me when you have guys over," Val said. "Where'd you find this one?"

"Never mind. He's temporary. Now, let me see this application." She picked up the stapled pages and read while refilling her coffee. Val busied herself with cleaning up the spill.

"It looks great," Beth said after a minute. "But Val, are you certain you want to do this? I mean, given what you've been through..."

"I've never wanted to do anything else," she said. "You know that."

"But why Clayton?" Beth sat down again. "With what happened to your uncle there, and to you—"

"That's why it has to be Clayton," Val said, tossing the soiled rag into the sink. "No place needs an infusion of justice more than our own hometown."

"That's what worries me." Beth set the application down on the table, careful to avoid the wet spots, and rested her chin on her hands. "It feels like—and please, don't take this the wrong way—maybe you're not seeking justice so much as revenge. For your uncle, and the whole Milt incident."

"Don't say his name," Val said, clenching her eyes shut. "And I'm fine. I've put all that behind me."

"Are you sure?" Beth stood and circled the table, placing her hand on Val's shoulder. "Val, what if your anger over your uncle's death, and for what Milt did, drives you to...I mean, what if you get into tough situations with bad guys, and, you know...it doesn't end well. For them, or for you."

Beth squeezed Val's shoulders and knelt to put her face level with Val's. "I'm afraid for what could happen to you."

"Nothing will happen to me," Val said in a voice more forceful than she'd intended. "I'm not out to punish other men for what those scumbags did to my family. I just don't want other scumbags doing it to other families, and to other thirteen-year-old girls. Or grown women. Or anyone." She locked eyes with her friend, softening her tone. "I promise. I'll be safe."

Beth's face crumpled into a sad smile. "I know you will." She gazed into Val's eyes for another moment, then looked away.

Val sighed. She might never convince her friend of how she felt. What unsettled her was that she hadn't yet convinced herself yet, either.

***

Valorie paused outside the open doorway of Lieutenant Laurence Gibson's cramped office, a shaded-glass enclosure trimmed with dark wood and beige government-issue metal chairs, desk, and filing cabinets. Gibson's bearlike figure seemed overly large for the room, and his dark brown skin, broad nose, bulbous eyes, and untamed salt-and-pepper hair exaggerated the effect.

"Come in, Ms. Dawes."

Val shut the door. The breeze of its motion caused papers to flutter, pinned to the walls or stuck to the filing cabinets with refrigerator magnets. A quick perusal told her where Gibson preferred to get his coffee, pizza, and sub sandwiches, and, like everyone else in Clayton, Connecticut, he rooted for the Boston Red Sox and New England Patriots.

"Thank you for meeting with me, Lieutenant."

Val sat in the worn, thinly padded metal framed guest chair. Gibson's desk towered in front of her, resting on cylindrical risers to accommodate his massive frame. At five-six, one twenty-five, she felt like a kid in the principal's office, rather than a 22-year-old who graduated a semester early from the University of Connecticut.

And that simply wouldn't do.

She stood and extended her hand across the lieutenant's enormous, cluttered desk, raising it uncomfortably high above the coffee cups and pencil holders stacked along its edge.

Gibson remained engrossed in a document pulled from a manila folder. Finally, he noticed her outstretched hand and took it briefly in his.

"Very impressive credentials." Gibson peered over his pince-nez glasses. "Criminology degree from UConn, graduated *cum laude*. Outstanding entry exam. Your essay on community policing was first-rate. And you're a bit of an athlete, aren't you?"

Val allowed a tiny smile. "I ran track in high school and college. I also played soccer."

"All-Metro midfielder in high school. Starter on the ACC championship team at UConn. More track ribbons than I could fit in this office. You've proved yourself a worthy competitor, Ms. Dawes." He glanced at her again. "You're a little small for a cop, but you've stayed in good shape. You should have no trouble passing the physical."

"Thank you, sir." Val blushed and held her breath. She should say more, but what? She had no idea. She kept her mouth shut.

He flipped through her application. "Have you ever shot a gun?"

She nodded. "My...uncle taught me." Dammit. She hadn't wanted his name to come up in this interview. But she smiled at the memory. Uncle Val's gift of firearms training for her tenth birthday had infuriated her parents, but only endeared him to her more.

Gibson set the application on his desk and removed his glasses. "I'll come straight to the point. The name Val Dawes carries a certain amount of, shall we say, *respect* around here."

Val sat upright and rigid in her chair. "I'm not trading on my uncle's repu—"

"You'd be crazy not to." Gibson sat back in his chair. "Valentin Dawes was a good man and a great cop. One of the best. Some of that must have rubbed off on you."

Val's face darkened, and she stared down at her hands. "I want to be considered on my own merits, sir. On my credentials, not his."

"We wouldn't have it any other way." Gibson put his glasses on and picked up her application again. "Your exam was among the best I've ever seen. Clearly you've prepared for this for some time."

"It's all I've ever wanted to do, sir. Since I was a child."

"Since your uncle—"

"Before that."

Gibson's eyes widened, and he gazed at her a moment. Val sat motionless in her chair, torn between regret over interrupting him and relief over derailing discussion of an emotional subject. Finally, Gibson gave her a closed-mouth smile and a curt nod. Good. He understood.

"As you may know," he said, "we're on a push to recruit more women and minority officers."

She shifted in her chair, and it scraped the floor with a harsh, raspy noise. "I don't want to be an affirmative-action hire. If I don't out-compete the men—"

"You do. Don't worry. That's not the point." Gibson pushed his glasses over the bridge of his nose. "Ms. Dawes, we have 335 sworn officers in the Clayton Police Department. Guess how many are female."

She shook her head. "Twenty percent?"

"Ha! I wish." He exhaled, the wind whistling through his teeth. "Less than thirty. Not percent. *Total.* That's even worse than the national average, which is pitiful." He sighed. "People say that police work is a man's game, Dawes. It attracts people who are a little more aggressive, controlling, and confident in their physical abilities. More often than not, those people are men. And a lot of men around here want to keep it that way."

"Do you?" The words escaped before she could stop them. "Um, I mean, do you, *sir?*"

"If I did, you wouldn't be here." He leaned back in his chair. "Unfortunately, the Neanderthals outnumber the ones who agree with me. And they can make life tough on a young woman, even one with your qualifications. But given your uncle's legacy—well, let's just say I'm hoping that slows them down a little."

"So, are you saying...?"

Gibson smiled. "We'd like you to start at the academy on the first of next month. Can you do that?"

Val's heart pounded, and she could not suppress a grin. "Yes, sir!"

"Very well." He stood and offered his hand. "Welcome to the Clayton, Connecticut Police Department, Officer Cadet Dawes."

Chapter Two

Val jogged to a stop ten feet from police academy trainer Sergeant Matt McKenzie, a side of beef with a razor-sharp silver crew cut and a jaw like a concrete block. First to finish their three-mile "warm-up run," she hurried to get ready for whatever drill he planned to push the cadets through next. Sergeant Mack, as he preferred to be called, barked orders like an army drill sergeant, and had no patience for cadets who wasted his precious time.

"Line up, lunkheads," Mack yelled, clapping his hands above his head. He glared at the twenty-six male cadets from around the state as they trickled in from the running track. "Come on, come on, double time!" He pushed the last few cadets into position with a rough shove around their shoulders. "You guys ought to be ashamed of yourselves, getting beaten that bad by a damned *girl!*" With that he cast a wicked grin at Val, and not a friendly one. Her cheeks burned, but she'd learned the hard way not to object aloud to Mack.

A lanky cadet with thick brown hair pushed into line next to Val. She sighed. Whenever Ben Peterson came near, things seemed to go wrong for her.

"Way to go, Dawes," Ben said in a low sneer. "Showing us up again. Can't you cut us some slack now and again?"

"If that's request number 206 for a date, the answer is still no," she murmured.

Mack glared and pointed a thick, gnarly finger at her. "You got something to share with us, Dawes?"

Val snapped to attention. "No, sir!"

"Then shut your trap." Mack paced in front of the group. "Gentlemen and ladies—*lady*—we have a special treat for you today. A guest instructor, here to school you on the finer points of hand-to-hand combat. Sergeant Brenda Petroni of Clayton P.D. Sergeant?"

Val's breath caught in her throat. After six weeks of men giving her nothing but grief and hostility, seeing a female instructor at the academy—from her own department, no less—seemed too good to be true. She glanced at Petroni, who, like Mack, wore a loose workout uniform and running shoes, despite the chilly morning air. About five-eight, with curly, dark brown hair and a sturdy build, the forty-something woman smiled at the cadets. Compared to Mack, she appeared relaxed, even downright friendly.

"Thanks, Mack. Cadets, I've taught you the basics of self-defense, but the rules of engagement out there are changing." She scanned the group and locked her gaze for a moment on Val. Her eyes sparkled and her smile seemed to sharpen—or did Val imagine that? Petroni gave her a slight nod, then continued. "To demonstrate, may I have a volunteer?"

For a few seconds, no hands rose. Long experience with Mack had ingrained in every cadet a grave fear of volunteering. Too often it involved pain, humiliation, or, at a minimum, extra work. But with Petroni, things might be different. For a woman, anyway. Val raised her hand, and two or three male hands followed.

"You, and you." She pointed at Val and Ben. Val gazed up at him in surprise. Ben never volunteered for *anything*.

He grinned. "I can't let you have all the glory."

They stepped forward, one on either side of Petroni. Behind them, Mack emitted a low chuckle. Damn. If he expected to be entertained by this, then volunteering was definitely a mistake.

"Mr. Peterson? Please demonstrate the proper method for restraining this perp, here." She indicated Val with an open palm and instructed them to face each other. "Ms. Dawes, try to escape your hypothetical crime scene by getting past Peterson."

Peterson grinned, then crouched. Val feinted left, then lunged right. Ben hooked his elbow and spun behind her, twisted her arm behind her back and forced Val to the ground. A sharp pain streaked up to her shoulder, and she howled. He dug his knee into her side and forced his arm around her neck, choking her.

"All right, let her up," Petroni said, sounding disgusted. "Okay, guys. What did you see here? Anyone?"

Ben started to help her up, but when Petroni's gaze turned away, he shoved her back onto the ground. His knee slammed into her upper thigh, pressing all two hundred pounds of his weight onto her. She grunted in pain again.

"You ladies done over there?" Mack said with a growl. Peterson scrambled off her, his face reddening. Val got up and dusted herself off. The other cadets stared at their feet.

Petroni shook her head at Peterson and turned toward the group. "Come on, speak up," she said. "What'd he do right? What'd he do wrong, according to your training?"

"Well," drawled a blond-haired cadet off to one side, "he could've broken her arm."

"And choked her to death," someone else said.

"Good, good," Petroni said. "Would you say he used excessive force?"

"For a girl that size? Sure," the blond said.

"But he doesn't know if she's got a gun, or knife, or what," said a muscular man with a dark crew cut.

Petroni nodded. "Good observations, everyone. Now, again, but reverse roles. Dawes, use appropriate levels of force." Their eyes locked, and Val detected a hint of a smile on the older woman's face.

Peterson faced her, hands out front, as if to grab her. Val got into a defensive crouch, her fingers curled, karate-style. Peterson lunged straight at her, grabbing her, pushing her to his left. She grabbed his upper arm and dropped into a tight roll, pulling Peterson along, using his own momentum against him. He landed on his back with an audible *whump*, followed by a groan. Val scrambled onto him, pinning both arms with her knees, her forearm pressed hard against his windpipe.

"Whoa!" "Holy cow!" "Did you see that?" Mumbling from the male cadets filled Val's ears.

"What did Ms. Dawes just demonstrate?" Petroni said, her eyes gleaming.

"That Peterson's a pussy," said someone at the far end of the line. A roar of laughter from the cadets followed.

Val stood and extended a hand to Peterson. Ben shook it off, rolling to his side, lifting himself to his hands and knees on the turf. "Where'd you learn that?" he asked between gasps.

"From my sensei, of course," she said. "Black belt, jiu jitsu. Perhaps I should have warned you."

"That would have been nice." Ben got to his feet and shuffled back into the line of cadets.

"What we're going to learn today—those of us who don't know already," Petroni said with a wink at Val, "is how to restrain a suspect with minimally necessary force, and the guidelines for doing so. Partner up. Try to find someone your own size. Dawes? You stay here with me." She said to Val, "I don't dare sic you loose on those guys. You could kill one of them."

"They've tempted me, more than once," Val said. "I'm sorry for ruining your demonstration, though. I should have taken it easy on him."

Petroni stepped closer. "Have they ever taken it easy on you?" she asked.

Val shook her head. "Unless you consider constant belittling and having your ass grabbed twice a day 'taking it easy'."

"Then don't you ever take it easy on them," Petroni said. "They'll never respect you if you do. And no need to apologize to me. I knew your martial arts abilities going into this drill. That little demo had a purpose. With luck, none of them will ever forget it."

"I hope we get to work together in Clayton," Val said, dumbstruck.

Petroni smiled. "Me too, Dawes." She blew into a whistle hanging from a leather string. "Listen up, cadets! It's time to learn how to defend yourselves out there!"

***

Two months later, Val stepped off a city bus in downtown Clayton, exchanging the bus's pungent aromas of stale sweat and diesel exhaust for the muggy heat of a late New England summer afternoon. She hustled across the street and climbed the wide, shallow steps leading to Central Police Headquarters. The aging, six-story block of brick, glass, and concrete looked like it might have been designed, built, and last maintained by Joseph Stalin.

Val pushed through the wide glass entry doors to the public lobby. Twin rows of pink granite pillars, three feet in diameter at the base, rose thirty feet from the white marble floors to the vaulted ceilings. Bronze chandeliers held dim bulbs too high off the ground to provide any real illumination. The air, a good ten or fifteen degrees cooler than outside, gave her goosebumps. "Chicken skin," as her uncle Val used to say.

She'd arrived a half hour early for her "entry interview," a series of administrative meetings with Human Resources staff and an evaluation by the department's psychiatrist. She hoped to finish by five. She and Beth planned to meet for drinks to celebrate the new job and their new shared apartment. But the receptionist delivered bad news: her first appointment would start twenty minutes late.

Too nervous to sit on the uncomfortable benches in the HR office, she toured the building's impressive lobby, absorbing the department's public relations efforts on display. Photos of City Council members, the police commission, and the top departmental brass took up most of one wall. Another summarized highlights of the city's history since its founding in the early 1800s, most of which she'd learned in grade school. A third exhibit, however, brought her browsing to an abrupt halt.

The Wall of Fallen Heroes consisted of photos and news stories commemorating the two dozen or so officers—all men—who'd given their lives in service to the city of Clayton. The first such incident dated back to 1831, taking the life of a 22-year-old—Val's own age—attempting to halt a bank robbery. Half of the fatal events occurred during the Civil War in efforts to aid the Underground Railroad. A handful had occurred since World War II.

The most recent, though, hit home to Val. The photo depicted a rugged, clean-shaven man with short brown hair. He resembled her older brother, except for his sparkling hazel eyes flecked with gold, like hers. A man she'd loved like a father, and the only man to whom she had entrusted her darkest, most horrible secret.

Detective Valentin Dawes, 1969-2008

She ran her fingers over the nameplate under the photo, a lump rising in her throat. She didn't need to spend time gazing at the giant image. She'd kept a copy of it on her dresser since her ninth birthday. Yet she couldn't help but read every headline from the many newspaper clippings framing it.

Shopping Mall Shooter Kills Officer, 4 Others

Officer Slain at Mall Saved 'Dozens,' Witnesses Say

Families, Fellow Officers Remember Val Dawes as Hero

Val's attempts to read the remaining news articles had to wait, as tears blurred her vision and forced her eyes closed.

***

Ten Years Earlier

Valorie approached the casket, her heart aching. Every step took longer than the one before. She couldn't see inside the coffin yet. It was open, but elevated on a viewing platform, putting the top edge a few inches higher than her wiry frame. Behind the casket, a photograph of Uncle Val rested on a tall easel, his friendly hazel eyes betraying the stern look he'd adopted for his official departmental head shot.

She had dressed entirely in black, but in slacks and a tight-fitting, short-sleeved top rather than a dress. Her father had argued with her about that, but at thirteen, she could choose her own clothes. Besides, Uncle Val would have wanted her to be comfortable and "ready for anything." Who could be ready for anything in a dress?

Besides, dresses only attracted the unwelcome attention of creepy old men like "Uncle" Milt, who preyed on innocent young girls. And thanks to Milt, she no longer thought of herself as "innocent."

She shuddered, pushing the awful memory out of her mind. Or tried to. Something that horrific, she would never forget. But next time, if there ever was a next time, she'd be ready.

Uncle Val had always been ready for anything and everything, until four days before, when a criminal's bullet cut him down in the line of duty. Forty-five-year-old Detective Valentin Dawes died a hero, not only in her adoring eyes, but in the eyes of the entire city. The long parade of strangers behind her waiting to view her uncle's open casket proved that.

Taking heavy breaths, she trudged up the dais steps, her eyes cast downward. Valorie wanted to see him all at once, at a moment of her choosing.

She shuffled over to the casket, eyes still on her feet. Another deep breath. Okay. Ready.

She studied his still figure, only visible from the shoulders up, pale and lifeless in the casket. Her first thought—Thank God they hadn't shot him in the head—made her angry at herself. Then, hot tears flowed down her face. This isn't Uncle Val, her heart raged. He was always so vivacious, so alive. This is someone else. It's not real!

She dried her tears with a tissue and stood tall in front of the casket. Uncle Val would not want her to cry. He would want her strong, remembering their special moments together, rather than mourning the ones they would never have. Thinking of the future, not the past. Of what she could become.

Uncle Val, she vowed, I will make you proud of me. I'll carry on your work, like we talked about. I'm going to be just like you, Uncle Val. Or at least, as good as I can be.

She stiffened her upper lip and tasted the salty tears flowing into the corners of her mouth. She peered at her uncle's lifeless form one more time, then turned and hurried off the dais.

Chapter Three

D r. Christopher Cyrus, PhD, considered the young female cadet before him. Twenty minutes into the interview and she had said nothing that indicated a lack of fitness for serving as a police officer for the Clayton police department.

But he knew something about this cadet. First off, he knew her uncle and near-namesake, Valentin Dawes. Who didn't? A local hero, a detective who'd cracked the most famous murder and kidnapping case in local history twenty years before. A man who'd taken three bullets over his career, the last one fatal, each time sacrificing himself for citizens who walked away without a scratch. A man whose funeral drew the attendance of over a thousand people, including Cyrus.

The funeral's attendees had also included the thirteen-year-old version of the cadet sitting in Cyrus's office with her hands folded on her lap. He remembered her much-younger face from that day, wet with tears, far more innocent and trusting of the world than the woman who smiled at him now. He sensed the anger inside her, in her terse, barely restrained responses to his questions. Given her family's history, he could hardly blame her.

But anger, justified or not, was not a quality sought in police cadets in Clayton, or anywhere else.

"Let's explore your past a bit more," he said, smoothing his salt-and-pepper beard with his fingers. "Specifically, your childhood." He smiled at her and adjusted his wire-rimmed glasses. He coughed into his hand, waiting.

"My...childhood?" She uncrossed her legs and smoothed her wrinkle-free black slacks. "Which part of my childhood?"

He noted the slowing of her enunciation, the way people

do when they're uncomfortable with a topic. "Yes," he said. "The period from when you were, say, twelve to fifteen."

She tensed, worry lines crowding her hazel, gold-specked eyes. "Oh, you mean, how have I dealt with the grief from my uncle's death?" She exhaled, tossed up her hands. "What would you like to know?"

"How do you feel about what happened to your uncle?" He watched her face, her hands. "Was justice served in his case?"

"The murderers were caught, convicted, and sentenced to life in prison," she said. "I couldn't ask for anything more."

Still relaxed. Had he missed the boat here? "Yes, that's true," he said, "but how do you feel about it? Do you ever wish, for example, that the people who shot him should have been punished more severely?"

She shrugged. "Sure. Lots more. But we've done away with the death penalty in Connecticut," she said, her voice growing more animated, "and rarely used it even when we had it. If child molesters don't get executed, why should cop killers?" She paused, took a breath. "I'm sorry. I get a little emotional about this topic."

He nodded. "Understandable. Ms. Dawes, we have a responsibility to ensure that our peace officers...how shall I say this? That they—"

"That they're not vigilantes? No kidding. Look, doc, I had three years of grief counseling after my uncle died, and I've talked this issue to death. The truth is," she said with a mischievous smile, "I know what kind of answers you want here, and I could give them to you all day. But here's the reality. My uncle was my inspiration to become a cop—before a couple of hostage-takers gunned him down at the shopping mall that day. We were close. It pissed me off that he died so young, and I'm super-pissed that he died the way he did. But I'm not becoming a cop to avenge his death. Okay? Straight-up, that's the God's-honest-truth."

He sat back in his chair, pushed there by the force of her words. She felt strongly about this, but he wouldn't say that her feelings or her reactions were in any way imbalanced or perversely motivated. Still, he was missing something.

"Ms. Dawes, if you found yourself in a similar situation,

do you think you could keep your personal feelings under control?" He fought for words. "Would you be able to restrain yourself from using deadly force, unless absolutely necessary?"

"I do, doctor." She grimaced. "I'll never forget my uncle, and I think about him every day. But not because I'm out to exact justice on his killers or their successors roaming Clayton streets. I miss him. I loved him. I've tried my whole life to live by his example—to put people first, exercise kindness, communicate, and strive for understanding. That's the kind of cop he was, and it's the kind of cop I'm going to be." She'd leaned forward during her speech, and Cyrus had to admit, her passion was infectious.

He had no reason not to believe that Valorie Dawes, like her uncle, would make a great cop. Still, something about her left him unsettled. Apprehensive, even. Nothing he could put his finger on. Just a feeling.

He gazed at the form in front of him, one that, with his signature, would arm this woman with deadly force and release her to the streets. Should he make the highly unusual move of rejecting her admittance to the police force, based on a feeling?

No, he should not.

He checked the box for "Approval," and signed the form.

***

"You must be Dawes."

Val turned to find the man with the baritone voice who had spoken to her. "G. Kryzinski" read the nameplate pinned to his chest, just below eye level for her, on his dark blue uniform. About six-two, with a build just to the husky side of athletic, he had ten or fifteen years on her. Not that it showed in his wavy, jet-black hair—not a gray speck there, nor in the five o'clock shadow darkening his high cheekbones and rugged jawline. Three chevrons adorned his sleeves. A sergeant.

"That's right. I'm Val." She extended her hand, grateful to have company in the briefing room. She felt like a complete geek showing up over an hour early for a 5:00 p.m. shift on her first day.

"I'm Gil. Welcome to Clayton P.D." He shook her hand,

nodded, and smiled. "Partner."

Val blinked. "You drew the short straw, eh?"

Gil's smile broadened. "I'd say not." He turned and walked toward the coffee urns at the side of the room. "Actually, I requested you. Can I buy you a drink?" A boyish smile revealed tiny laugh lines around his dark brown eyes.

"Sure, thanks. Black, one sugar. Um...why did you request me?" Please, she begged the universe. Not another Ben Peterson.

Gil poured the coffees and stirred sugar into one. "Your reputation. Outstanding cadet, family legacy, great athlete, big into community policing. I heard you even aced the marksmanship test."

Val nodded. "Fair enough. But you have me at a disadvantage. I know nothing about you." She sipped the coffee—piping hot, weak, and bitter.

"Eight years on the Clayton force. Just made sergeant. Refused a desk job. I want to stay on the streets, so they made me swing shift supervisor here at Liberty Heights. Essentially, the straw boss for the beat cops in that neighborhood—our neighborhood. Transferred in to get that, from South End."

"That's why you needed a partner?"

"Smart girl."

"Woman." She set her awful coffee down on the counter and met his gaze.

He nodded and surrendered another boyish grin. "I stand corrected."

"But why me?" she asked. "You could have chosen anyone, with your rank. Someone with experience."

Gil shook his head. "Nope. I wanted someone with a fresh perspective. And I wanted to train you—the right way."

Val nodded. "You had several newbies to choose from. Why the only woman?"

Gil sipped his coffee again and grimaced. "This stuff's awful, isn't it? First thing I'm gonna do is change the coffee service."

"Second," she said. "The first thing is, you'll level with your partner when she asks you a direct question." She met his surprised look with a steady stare.

"Once again, I stand corrected," he said. "And that fearlessness you just showed me fits your rep. That's why I chose you as my partner." He stepped away to toss his coffee into the sink.

She gave her own cup a disapproving stare, then focused back on him. "I hope I can live up to your expectations."

Gil nodded, and a smile curled at the corners of his lips. "You will, Dawes. Just do me one favor."

She cocked her head and looked at him with mock suspicion. "What's that?"

His smile fell into a line across his lips. "Be honest with me," he said. "Always. As I will be with you."

"I will."

He sat in the hard wooden chair next to her, putting their eyes on an even level. "This is important, Dawes. By being honest I don't mean just being truthful when asked. You need to feel you can talk to me. Anytime. About anything. Even if it means correcting my latent sexism." He smiled again in a self-deprecating way.

She nodded and turned aside. His words provoked memories she'd much rather suppress. She'd never shied away from stating her opinion or calling out bias. But she'd never excelled at opening up, not about herself.

"Dawes?"

His suspicious tone startled her back into the moment. "Uh, sorry," she said. "What's on our agenda?"

"Getting you to stay in the present, first off." He grinned at her. "Where'd you go just now?"

She hesitated and then regretted it. Recognition shone in his eyes. He knew she was hiding something, dammit. She shrugged and took a solemn breath. "I was remembering something from my childhood. Someone said something similar, and—well, it triggered a memory." She smiled. "Not in a bad way."

He cocked his head. "Your uncle?"

She shook her head. "No. My father. He was always getting into my business, you know? Until he began to ignore me." She clamped her mouth shut. She hadn't intended on revealing so much.

After a moment, his lips eased into another smile. "Fathers can be that way, can't they? So, did you ever tell him?"

"Tell who, what?" Her face grew warm.

"Your dad. Whatever he was asking about. Did you ever tell him?"

"Hell, no." She grimaced. "We, uh, didn't have the closest relationship. Still don't."

"Closer to your mom, then?" His tone seemed innocent enough, but his eyes bore into her with savage intensity. Nothing innocent or casual about this conversation.

She shook her head again. "Mom left when I was fourteen. Haven't seen her since. Things...weren't good at home."

"Ah. Well." His expression softened. Whatever he'd been looking for from her, he'd found it. "I'm sorry to hear that. Well, let's get going. We'll never catch any bad guys in here." He stood and gestured toward the door with his cap.

With a sigh of relief, Val stood and followed him out. That conversation had veered close to troubled waters— dangerously close. She'd trusted him right away, more than any man since Uncle Val. He had a way of putting her at ease while challenging her protective shell. Depending on the type of guy Gil was, that could spell trouble. She made a mental note of it.

***

"Where do you live, Val?" Gil guided their cruiser east on Albany Avenue. He had taken her out on patrol immediately after her new-employee orientation session ended—forty minutes of pep talks and PowerPoint presentations by desk jockeys. Probably the same people that made the coffee.

"Not far from here." She pointed out her passenger-side window. "Three blocks from that coffee shop, toward the cemetery. About a fifteen-minute walk from the precinct."

"Me too." He nodded. "We're practically neighbors."

"No kidding?" She turned toward him. "I thought you lived in South End."

He scoffed. "Hell no. On a cop's salary? I wish." He peered through the windshield at the group of African-American youths loitering outside a boarded-up pawn shop. "This spot's usually trouble," he said. "These kids have no jobs, nothing to do, no parents—or none paying attention, anyway. We have to keep an eye on them."

"What are their names?"

He gave her a quizzical, sideways stare. "Names?"

"Yeah. Like Gil, Valorie, John Doe. You know. Names."

"Don't be such a smartass." He almost suppressed a grin. "I don't know their real names. Just their nicknames. Well, for most of 'em." They passed the gang at low speed. "The tall one, he's called Pope. No idea where the nickname came from, but it fits. He's the leader. Whatever he says is Gospel to The Disciples."

"Disciples?"

"That's what they call themselves. The gang." He pointed to another member of the gang. "That one there, the little guy? Seems to be one of Pope's favorites. They call him Dog."

She laughed. "I don't recall any of the original twelve disciples being called 'Dog'."

"Historical accuracy ain't their thing. Ruling the streets, on the other hand..."

Val craned her neck to watch the group stare back at her as they passed. "Let's swing back around and talk to them."

"Later," Gil said. "If we go back now, they'll scatter, thinking we're gonna bust their asses for something. Not that we shouldn't. They're always up to something."

"You have quite the outlook on life." She turned back toward him. "So did you move to Liberty Heights when you transferred, or have you always lived here?"

"When I transferred. I lived in the Barry Square area before, east of Maple. Another lovely spot." He wagged his head and snorted. "Hell, I got robbed twice down there myself. Those bastards are nervy." He stopped at a light and checked something in the rear-view mirror.

"I'll say. Robbing a cop? Off-duty, I take it."

"Well, burgled, to be more precise. Ripped off my TV, stereo, and a couple hundred in cash. Even a gun, the first time."

"Service revolver?" Her eyes widened.

"No. Little .22 pistol I kept around. I've always had my own guns." The light changed. He put the car back in motion. "In this line of work, it pays to be familiar with a variety of weapons." He turned onto a side street and drove through the neighborhood.

"What do you mean?" She frowned. "The .38's they give us

pack plenty of pop, they're reliable, and accurate as pistols go. Why do you need a .22?"

He glanced at her out of the corner of his eyes, then shrugged. "I see Uncle Val didn't teach you all the inside dope on policing."

"N—no," she said. "Hey, take a right here."

His eyebrows shot up. "Okay. Why?" He slowed for the turn.

"I want to get back to Albany Avenue and walk around a little. Maybe meet the Pope and his Disciples."

"*Ay caramba*, you are persistent," he said. "In due time, and I'll warn you. They're gonna have fun with you."

"Because I'm a woman?"

"A woman with a gun. I can smell their pheromones from here."

Val sighed. "And you're one of the progressive men on the force?"

Gil grinned as he took another right, heading north toward Albany Avenue. "You wait. You're going to meet some guys that make me look like Hillary Clinton."

"Ew," she said.

Gil laughed. "I rest my case." He pulled the squad car over and parked. "Okay, Officer Dawes. Time to meet and greet. Your first hour of community policing has begun."

Chapter Four

The good old boys at the station rewarded Val for showing up early on her second day with donut duty. Rather than protesting, she took requests for special varieties and filed away the memory for her own first opportunity to haze new recruits. Juggling the donuts and a tray of coffees in one hand, she reached to lift the door handle of her cruiser with the other. A mocking male voice greeted her from behind.

"So this is the famous new police officer, the one and only Valorie Dawes."

Val's hand froze on the handle. She took a deep, calming breath and turned to face the sneering figure one car away in the parking lot. "Have we met?"

The man's tall, lanky body seemed a mismatch to the mocking baritone emanating from within. His dress shirt hung loose about his slender torso, and amber transition lenses shaded his dark eyes. Thick, brown waves of hair framed his long, angular head. "Val Dawes. Everyone knows *that* name. Clayton's hero. Do you hope to be a hero, too, *Miss* Dawes?" The final few words echoed off the buildings framing three sides of the urban parking lot.

Her face flushed and color rose from her neck to her cheeks. Less than two full days on the force, and already it had started. "I just want to be the best cop I can be, Mister...?"

Tall Boy extended his hand across his bright blue Subaru WRX. "Paul Peterson, Clayton Copwatch. I believe you've met my cousin Benjamin."

She shivered. Ben Peterson had once mentioned his cousin. Ben had described Paul as smart, tenacious, and arrogant—quite the combination, given Ben's own penchant for looking down his nose at the rest of humanity.

"Of course," she said. "Now I notice the resemblance." And she had to admit, his serpentine smile aside, Paul was far more handsome than Ben. She gave his hand a quick, polite shake. "Well, my partner's waiting for me. Better go."

"He lets you drive?" Peterson's tone grew even more derisive. "This department's going soft. First women cops. Now the rookies drive. What's next? Weekend retreats? Strategic planning meetings? 'Kumbaya, my lord! Kumbaya!'" Peterson's laughter drowned out the echoes of his booming singing voice.

"Don't give up the day job." Val hopped inside her cruiser before Peterson could respond. That idiot! She couldn't get away from him fast enough. She turned the key, shifted into reverse and, a moment before looking over her shoulder, jammed her foot on the gas.

Crunch! She heard her error before she felt it: the crumpling of metal and smashing of glass, universal sounds of the low-speed fender-bender. A quick glance behind her confirmed it. She'd hit another car passing in back of hers. And not just any car: a Clayton Police cruiser.

"Heroic move, Dawes!" Peterson grinned. "Take out two patrol cars in one blow, without even leaving your parking space. Did you learn that at the academy, or was this something your uncle taught you?"

She scrambled out of the vehicle. "Don't you have someplace to be? There must be a politician who needs investigating somewhere."

"Oh, I'm right where I'm supposed to be." He leaned on the other cruiser's hood. "After all, a witness should never leave the scene, now should he, *Officer* Dawes?"

"I've changed my mind," Val said, about ready to spit. "Go ahead and quit the day job."

"Strikes me," he said, his grin widening, "that's more your problem than mine."

The officer driving the impacted cruiser, a tall, overweight, middle-aged man with a thin crown of short brown hair, got out and inspected the damage: a dented and scratched passenger door on his car, a crumpled rear fender and smashed tail light on hers. "What the hell, Dawes?" he said.

"Don't they teach kids to drive these days?"

She noticed his three chevrons, read his nameplate. "A. Papadopoulos." She held up her hands in surrender. "Sorry, sir. My fault."

"No kidding," he said. "Holy cannoli, look at this mess." He walked around the vehicle to inspect more of the damage.

"Well, Ms. Dawes," Peterson said, "this all works out nicely for my next blog entry. Supports my theory, you know?"

"What theory? What story?" Val spun back to glare at him. "Are you kidding me? Is news so slow that you report on fender-benders in parking lots?"

"It appears to this reporter," he said, shaking his head in disdain, "that the rumors are true. You got hired because of your uncle's reputation, rather than any ability you might have. The great Val Dawes. What a tragic next chapter to his fine legacy."

"Did I do something to offend you?" Val said between clenched teeth. "Or does hatred of me run in your family?"

"Just keep in mind, Officer Dawes," Peterson said with contempt dripping in his voice, "that I'll be watching you. Like a hawk, Dawes. Like a hawk." With that, Peterson jumped in his Subaru and sped off, laughing.

***

Filing the accident report took nearly an hour, making Val late for her scheduled shift. She hitched a ride with another officer heading out on patrol and found Gil in a city-owned parking lot on Woodland Avenue. He sipped coffee from a paper cup and leaned against their replacement cruiser, the sun setting behind him.

"I heard about your driving skill demonstration," he said with a grin. "So, have we discovered your one weak spot— your skill behind the wheel?"

"*One* weak spot?" she said. "If you're making a list, you'd better have a lot of paper and pencils handy."

He laughed. "Ah, such modesty. Now, where are those donuts you promised?"

She slapped her forehead. "What an idiot! I left them at the precinct, along with two ice-cold cups of coffee." She buried her face in her hands. "What kind of cop can I be if I can't even do donuts right!"

"Yeah, you're doomed," Gil said in mock seriousness. "Bad driving and no donuts. That's two flaws discovered in one day. Not a good trend, Dawes."

They walked in silence along Woodland for a few blocks. Gil pointed to an apartment building looming ahead. "That's Clayton Heights. Public low-income housing. The few men that live there spend most of their days in jail and their nights running from us. We'll knock on a lot of doors in there."

She nodded. "Mmm." She examined the sorry-looking tower of brick and glass covered in graffiti, grime, and hopelessness. A series of fire escapes rusted in the moonlight. Maybe she could get Peterson to do a story on housing conditions. Anything to get him off her case.

"And over there, that convenience store?" Gil pointed to a brightly lit, squat square of concrete on the corner. "Guy named Taufiq runs it. He's a good guy. From Bangladesh, I think. Free coffee to men and women in blue, and he keeps his eyes and ears open."

"Taufiq. Okay, good to know." She rubbed her arms against the night chill, wondering if the department would dock her pay for the accident.

Gil eyed her with a curious stare. "Come on, Dawes. Shake it off. It's just donuts...oh, yeah, and a patrol car. We'll all have a good laugh over it in a week."

"It's not only that." She stopped walking, fighting for words, not sure how much she should tell Gil.

Hell, he was her partner. She had to trust him.

"I smashed that car—make that *cars*—right in front of that jerk who writes that awful cop-watch blog, Paul Peterson."

"Peterson?" Gil shook his head. "He's a nobody. Don't worry about him."

"I don't want to start out with some big exposé hanging over me and sullying my family's legacy," she said. "My uncle would roll over in his grave."

"Forget the press scum, and especially bloggers like Paul Peterson," Gil said. "Don't sink to his level."

"I don't think there's a chasm deep enough for me to get to his level," Val said, but she grinned. Gil's upbeat dismissal of Peterson was infectious.

"Don't let him get to you. He's a schmuck." Gill pulled her down the sidewalk by the arm. "Besides, we've got a big night planned. You're going to meet Pope."

She stepped ahead of Gil and spun around to face him, walking sideways down the street. "How do you know he'll be out tonight?"

"I just do. Trust me."

She made a sour face. "Gil, remember our talk yesterday, about being really open and honest with each other? If I'm going to be effective, you need to fill me in on how to reach these guys. If I don't—"

"Just trust me, okay?" Gil soft-punched her arm. "After you meet him, you can think about how to stay in touch. Or *if.* And it's not entirely up to you. He has a say in this too. In the meantime, watch and learn."

Val blew out a loud breath, turned forward, and fell into step next to Gil. They circled the block, back to where Gil had parked the patrol car. "Okay," she said. "Flip you for who's driving?"

"Flip me?" He grinned. "I'd never take a bet like that with someone who knows jiu jitsu." He handed her the keys. "When we see The Disciples, drop me off and circle the block, then look for my signal. If I wave, pick me up. If not, park and come join me."

"So mysterious." She clicked the remote to unlock the cruiser. "Why aren't we using our secret watch radios?"

"They're in the shop, with your car." Gil smirked and climbed into the cruiser.

She started the engine. "Is this standard protocol, you meeting with gang members alone?"

"Who writes protocols, Dawes?" he asked.

She bit her lip. "Bureaucrats?"

"And what do bureaucrats know about interacting with gangs?" he asked. "Nothing, that's what. Now drive."

He remained silent for the next few minutes. Maybe her driving made him nervous, after all. Then again, he never held back when he had something to say, particularly if it gave him an opportunity to tease her. She turned onto Albany Street and drove until they reached the spot where the gang usually congregated.

"They're not here." She slowed the car to a near-stop.

"Keep going," Gil said. "This isn't where we're meeting them."

"The mystery deepens." They passed another closed-up shop, then a second-run movie house.

"Pull up here," Gil said.

She shot him a quizzical glance, but did as she was told.

"Now, remember the plan. Circle once and look for me."

"Where?"

"Just keep your eyes open." He got out and walked to the corner of the building, a dimly lit area populated by trash dumpsters and the remains of a few locked-up bicycles. She drove off, shaking her head. While she shared his disdain for bureaucracy and ill-informed rules, leaving him alone there made her nervous.

It took several minutes to make the circuit. When she returned to the front of the theater, Gil stood in the center of a ring of black youths. He faced away from the street, but he turned and nodded when she passed.

She parked the cruiser in a convenience store lot around the block and jogged back to Gil and the gang. She paused when they came into view, waiting for a signal. Gil stood a few feet from the man he'd called Pope, a hulk of a man in his late twenties with a broad, expressionless face. Easily six-four, two-fifty, probably bigger, with a series of gold rings adorning each earlobe. Two shorter, bulkier giants stood on each side of him, the positions of rank in the gang, each with a smaller set of gold earrings. Several younger boys, none over the age of eighteen, spread out in either direction.

"Your girlfriend's here," one of the smaller boys on the fringe of the group said to Gil. With his skinny frame and girlish voice, he couldn't have been older than fourteen.

"Who's talking to you?" Gil spat, his back still to Val.

"Yeah. Keep your dumbass trap shut, Dog," one of the bigger guys next to Pope said, spitting at Dog's feet. Dog dodged the spit and pounded one fist on his chest, but said nothing.

"You got new pussy?" Pope grinned at Gil. Gil still hadn't turned to look at her.

Val's cheeks burned in the cool night air. There were no women in this group, not even the hookers and meth queens she'd expected to find. She slowed her pace.

"She's my partner. You should meet her." Gil waved one hand over his shoulder. "Come on, Dawes. Show the Disciples your pretty weapon."

"Woo!" the guys yelped. "Forget the gun," one of them added. "Show us your pretty little titties." Another Disciple slapped him a high-five and several of them laughed.

Warm-faced, Val strode into the circle, bumping Gil on purpose as she passed. She didn't turn to see his almost-certain glare. Two could play this game.

"You're The Pope?" She extended a hand.

The big man scowled and turned away from her offered handshake.

"Not 'The' Pope," one of his lieutenants said. "Just Pope."

She dropped her hand. "I stand corrected. Pope." She stood with her hands on her hips, feet spread shoulder width.

Pope spoke without looking at her. "You must be the new sister of Albany." He turned to Gil and grinned. "You getting nun?" The whoops from the Disciples clued Val into the pun. "Nun," not "None."

She spread her hands wide. "That makes you—what? The priests? Or the altar boys?"

"Ooh!"

"Stinger!"

"Nice."

Pope finally looked her way, the hint of a smile tugging at his lips. Gil stepped up next to her. "Pope, this is Val Dawes. You may recognize the name."

Pope scowled and spat. The spit landed within an inch of Val's foot. "That rotten motherfucker. You're his—what? Niece?"

"I sure ain't his nephew," Val said. "Got a problem with my uncle?"

"No, I ain't. That motherfucker had a problem with me. Locked me up two times for nothing. Got my ass fucked good the second time. I ever see his white ass out on the street I'll—"

"He's dead," Val said. "Get over it." Advice she could take herself.

"Dead?" Pope looked, and sounded, truly surprised.

"Ten years ago. It was in all the newspapers. Where've you been?"

Pope narrowed his eyes. "Not reading no motherfucking newspapers." The space around Val closed in with large, male bodies.

"Well," Gil said, "fun party, boys, but we have a busy social calendar. Gotta go. Lotta criminals to go catch."

The tall one on Pope's left snickered. "That's good, man, that's good. Criminals to catch." He stopped when Pope glared at him.

Pope locked eyes with Gil. "Next time, come alone to our party, or bring some pussy to share. Something worth eating."

Val took a step forward and pointed a finger a few inches from Pope's face. Disciples on both sides of him closed in. She raised her other hand, palm-out, and they stopped. "Listen, cocksucker. Let's get a few things straight. I'm in charge here, not you. You see me coming, you best go the other way. I know the shit you boys are up to. You stay clear of me and you're fine. But if I catch you, I make your life miserable, just like my uncle. Understood?"

Pope pursed his lips as if to spit again. He hooked his finger around hers in a tight grip, swaying it back and forth a few times. A crooked grin escaped his face. He let go and turned his back on her. "Disciples!" He raised both hands over his head. He sauntered off, a regal pace that reminded Val of a papal march. His gang followed, forming a V-wedge behind him, the bigger gang members closest and the smaller ones trailing behind.

Val turned to face Gil. "Thanks a whole fucking lot."

"You said you wanted to meet him," he said.

"Yeah, but not as 'your pussy.' What the hell was that about?" She stood on tiptoes and put her face inches from his, shaking his shoulders.

"I didn't call you that. He did." Gil shook himself free. "But you're right. I should have corrected him there. My bad, and I'm sorry."

She sighed, and tension flowed out of her. "Thanks. I appreciate that. I just wish that had gone better."

Gil smiled and led her back toward the parked cruiser.

"Welcome to community policing, Val. Not all of our clients are sweethearts. And not every day with your partner is peaches and cream."

She scoffed. "Peaches and cream? I'd settle for a good cup of coffee now and again."

"Need I remind you, it's still your turn to buy," he said. "Stale donuts at the precinct don't count."

"What, don't you at least buy a cup of coffee for your 'girlfriend'?" she said in a mocking tone.

"I would if you were," he said, smiling, then grew serious. "But you're not. What you are is my partner, and a rookie. The rookie part means, until you know what you're getting into, you *listen,* with your mouth shut, and your eyes and ears open. Okay?"

"And since I'm a woman, I bring you coffee? Is that it?" Anger seeped into her voice again.

He shook his head and smiled at her. "No, Val. We're partners. That means we take turns buying coffee. And I've changed my mind. It's my turn to buy." He held out an open hand. "Partner."

She accepted his outstretched hand, shook it once, and nodded. "I've got a lot to learn, don't I?"

He grinned. "We both do, Val. That part of the job never stops."

She nodded and realized how lucky she was to have drawn Gil as a partner. She could have done much worse.

Chapter Five

Val fired her final six rounds, all hits on the human-shaped target fifty feet away, and smiled. She loved the firing range, and not only because of her second-in-class marksmanship at the academy. With the noise-blocking earmuffs on and her eyes focused on the target, the rest of the world disappeared, leaving her to her own little world of concentration and skill. She yanked off the earmuffs and waited for the automatic pulley system to retrieve her results.

"Pretty impressive, cadet," came a sneer over her shoulder. "Think you can fire like that when it's a live body coming at you?"

Val glared at the tall, round-bellied man in uniform watching her from the next shooting lane. The bald dome of his scalp shone with sweat. She recognized him from her fender-bender a few days before: Alex "Pops" Papadopoulos, a twenty-year man with a reputation for laziness and opposition to anything resembling change.

She took a deep breath and choked back a sarcastic jibe about how easy a target Alex would be. Instead she forced a smile and said, "I hope I don't have to find out. But perhaps you have wisdom to share from your own experience, Sergeant?"

His cocky smile faded and he shifted his weight against the wall. "I've had to pull my weapon out a few times," he said, "but I've never had to shoot to kill."

"Lucky you." Val brushed past him toward the exit.

"Not lucky," Pops said behind her, his voice rising. "I've just never had to panic, or over-compensate for my weakness or size."

She whirled to face him. "What's that supposed to mean?"

Pops smirked and shrugged. "You're the college graduate, rookie. You figure it out."

She drew in a slow, deep breath, then exhaled just as slowly. "I'm here to learn, Pops. From my elders. Please share your knowledge with me." She tried, but failed, to keep the sarcasm out of her voice.

"I'm sure you're smart, Dawes. But I'd rather my potential partners are half a foot taller, have sixty pounds more muscle, and keep cool in a crisis. A lot of those guys applied for this job. Instead, we hired *you*." He sneered and selected a firing lane.

Val stepped toward him. "You think I'm too small to be a cop? That I'll panic in a crisis? Why would you think that, Pops? Because I'm a woman?"

Pops gazed down at her with a crooked smile. "No, *cadet*. Not just because you're a woman." He stepped closer, looming over her. "It's because someday, we might have to work together. And I'd rather have someone next to me who can help me survive the encounter, rather than someone I'd have to pull from the bottom of a scrum."

She laughed. "I can handle myself, Pops."

He scoffed. "Oh, really? What are you going to do, Dawes, when a 300-pounder gets the drop on you and you don't have time to reach for your gun? What if the best solution isn't deadly force, but clocking the S.O.B. and making him eat dirt? What if—"

His talking stopped and he howled in pain, his finger caught in her vise-like grip and twisted backwards towards his wrist.

"What if," she said, "that 300-pound guy underestimates his opponent?"

"Ow! Jesus! Let go! Let go!"

Releasing his finger, she hooked Alex's ankle with her own and pushed him by the shoulders onto on the floor. "Oops. Clumsy me. I guess I must have panicked."

She left the target practice room with a spring in her step. With her ear muffs back in place, she could barely hear Alex's cursing.

***

Val's work week began on Thursday evenings at 5:00,

which meant eating a light, early dinner before meeting Gil at the precinct station. In late October, that gave them an hour to walk the streets before sunset, with another hour of twilight before the streets got too scary for most ordinary citizens in the Abernethy neighborhood. During those two hours, Gil preferred to walk the main streets with Val, chatting with business owners before they closed up shop for the night. He also engaged with the "regulars," as he called them—people who had nothing better to do than hang out on the unseasonably warm evening. Adults smoked cigarettes on front stoops and bus benches. Young men and a few women played pickup games of half-court basketball in the park or soccer in the street. Teens and younger kids tore up the sidewalks and parking lots with their skateboards. Gang action, Gil explained, picked up after dark.

"Why don't the other cops walk their beats as often as you do?" Val asked Gil. They strolled up Woodland Avenue past storefronts housing quick takeout restaurants, cheap clothing, and fly-by-night check-cashing stations. "I don't think I've ever seen Alex Papadopoulos out of his car, except at the station or firing range."

Gil shook his head in disgust. "Pops is a Type Three cop," he said. "A clock-puncher. Don't be like him."

"What's a Type Three?" she asked. "And how many 'types' are there?"

They circumnavigated a small park, a patchwork of asphalt with basketball hoops that had lost their chain-link nets, and which the city had long ago given up trying to maintain. "Four," he said. "Haven't I told you about this yet?"

She searched her memory, but came up empty. "No, and I'd remember something like this. It sure didn't come up at Academy."

"Okay, here's the world according to Gil," he said with a laugh. "Keep in mind, this isn't 'official'. That's why you didn't hear about this at Academy."

She nodded. "They said we'd learn 'real police work' on the job. So, fill me in, boss."

His expression grew serious, and he faced straight ahead while they walked. "Type One is the Soldier, or what's known as a 'Cop's cop.' That's the kind we all say we want to be.

Soldiers have each other's back, no matter what. They'll put their own neck on the line for their brothers—and sisters—in any situation. You go into a situation with them, they'll have your back. You can trust them."

"Cops like you," she said with a smile.

He eyed her sideways. "Depends," he said. "Can you trust me? In any situation?"

"Absolutely," she said. "And by 'situation', I assume you mean, an interaction with a perp on the street?"

"I mean *any* situation," he said, and stopped her so they could face each other. "Everything from going in on an arrest or a raid to having each other's backs in a staff meeting or an internal investigation. Soldiers in blue stick together, no matter what the stakes."

"Got it," she said. "Then yes, I'd put you in that category."

"Good," he said.

They walked a little farther in silence, checking out the activity in the park. A foursome in shorts and loose-fitting T-shirts shouted smack-talk over a pickup game of basketball. A half-dozen younger kids played on a rusty swing set while their parents chatted on a park bench that needed a new coat of paint ten years ago. She resisted the urge to ask him what the other types were. She'd learned, in her few short weeks of training, that Gil spoke when good and ready, and not before.

Still, she had to ask.

"Am I a 'cop's cop'?" she asked when they reached the corner opposite the parents.

"Too soon to tell," he said. "And I suspect you might be a Type Two. Or, possibly, a Type Four."

"Is that bad?" she said, her heart rate spiking. "What's a Type Two?"

"Type Two is the 'Savior'—the victim's cop. Those cops put the safety and welfare of potential victims above all else—including fellow cops," he said. "Citizens want us all to be Twos."

"Can't you be a mix of Soldier and Savior?" she asked. "Or are they incompatible?"

"In most situations, you can," he said. "But in a life-and-death situation, you might have to choose who you'll save. Soldiers back up their comrades in blue. Saviors will sacrifice themselves, and their partners, to save a crying baby."

"And you think I'm one of those?" She winced, noting his condescending stare. "Sorry. I don't mean to sound defensive."

"I'm not saying one is better or worse than the other," he said, his expression serious. "We need some of each on the force. If we didn't, we'd either have a lot of dead cops, or a lot more dead citizens, and neither is acceptable. We need to know who we're with when we go into a life-threatening situation."

She nodded, absorbing the implications of Gil's words. He'd have her back, no matter what, but wouldn't necessarily trust she'd have his. But he'd know she would fight for the victim to the death. "Fair enough," she said. "Now, what's a Type Four?"

"Patience, young Jedi," he said with a smile. "Let's go in order, shall we? Type Three is the 'Survivor.' All they care about is making it through the day. They avoid any kind of risk or change and never step up to do anything outside of the bare minimum. That's Pops. All he wants to do is survive long enough to collect on his pension. Survivors view citizens, perps or otherwise, as obstacles to get around. They take shortcuts instead of putting in the hard work. Threes are the ones that give cops a bad name."

They walked on, circling behind the parents watching their kids and stepping over a few piles of dog poop that had long since dried up on the sidewalk. She spoke in a low voice to Gil. "So, Type Four is even worse, eh? Are those the ones that are all trigger-happy?"

Gil shrugged. "Survivors can get that way, too," he said. "Tasers and pistols are the lazy cop's answer to the hard job of police work. But yes, Fours can get that way. Fours I call 'Avengers.' They'll do anything to get their man. Or woman." He grinned. "Women commit crimes, too."

"Sounds like Avengers are the opposite of Survivors," she said. "How could I be both?"

He shook his head. "You're not both," he said. "I'm just undecided which one you are. I *hope* you're more of a Savior type."

"Why?" she said. "What's wrong with going all-out to nab

a perp on the run?"

"Avengers lose focus, and forget what's important," he said. "They get so gung-ho about finding their perp, they start to bend rules, and, like Survivors, take shortcuts, albeit for a different reason. Like Saviors, they're passionate about their work, but sometimes they get such tunnel vision, they even forget about their victims." He stood in front of her, blocking her path. "Avengers are the most dangerous, Val. Don't become an Avenger. If you must choose, be a Savior or a Soldier. Okay?"

She met his steady gaze, one devoid of his usual humor, and shrunk under its intense fire. "I'd rather be a Soldier," she said. "But you're probably right. In all likelihood, I'm a Savior. I hope to hell I'm not an Avenger."

"I hope so, too, Val," he said. "And I'll do whatever I can to keep that from happening."

They stared at each other a long moment, with a slight smile creasing Gil's face, and Val absorbing the implications of what he'd just told her. Would she sacrifice Gil's life for a child's if she had to choose, with no time to think? Or any other citizen? Her brother and his five-year-old daughter, yes, without a doubt. But what about a stranger?

She averted her eyes and focused on the neighborhood around her, taking in all that she saw. Two gray-haired men laughed at a joke one of them had just told. They looked kind—someone's grandpas or uncles. A delivery truck rumbled past, honking its horn at a driver trying to turn the wrong way on a one-way street, resulting in a tense exchange of shouts and middle fingers. Did they merit more protection than a fellow cop? What about the gang members like Pope and Dog?

The crackling of a woman's voice on their radios interrupted her reveries. "All units in the vicinity of Woodland Park," said the dispatcher. "Backup needed on a 10-16 on Greenfield and Woodland. All units in the vicinity, please respond."

"That's a domestic disturbance," Val said, her heart racing. "Aren't we close to that intersection?"

"Very," Gil said. He unclipped his radio. "Unit A-27, on our way to that 10-16," he said. "We're less than five minutes away on foot."

"Make that three," Val said, breaking into a run across the park. In a split second she reached sprinting speed, heading toward Woodland Avenue.

Chapter Six

Six blocks into her dash, Val passed a group of middle-aged Latinas huddled on the sidewalk. They shouted something about a man beating a woman and pointed in the direction she was running. She kicked it into high gear and reached the faded red-brick two-story Colonial seconds later. Bright lights shone from every front and side window, all curtainless, but no human figures appeared in any of them. No sign of another officer in the area. Whoever called for the assist must have already gone inside.

A row of mailboxes signaled that the house contained four separate apartments. She paused on the front porch to catch her breath and listened for the telltale loud noises of a domestic disturbance. At first, only the sounds of distant sirens, honking horns, and the buzzing of street lamps reached her. But after a few seconds, the muffled scream of a woman or a young girl emerged from the house. Then a man's voice: "Shut up, you stupid cunt, or I'll give you something to cry about."

More sounds: flesh hitting flesh. An unmuffled cry of pain—definitely a girl. Teenager, or younger. "Stop it," she yelled. Another scream followed.

Val ran across the porch toward the sound. This time a man stood in the first-floor window, his ruddy skin flushed against the yellowed fabric of a stained white tank top. A lit cigarette dangled between snarling lips. His left arm held something—or, someone—below him. His right arm rose above his head and arced downward. *Slap!* Skin pounded skin. The female voice yelped, and his hand rose again. "Shut up!" he yelled, and swung again. No slap. "Stay still, you little whore, or I'll break your goddamned neck. Worse than your fucking mother."

No time to wait for Gil or the other backup. Val pounded the window with her fist. "Police! Let her go and get your hands up where I can see them!"

The man stopped his punch, looked around, apparently unsure of the source of this interruption. She rapped on the window again and pulled her flashlight off her belt, flicked it on and pointed it at his face. He squinted and shielded his eyes with his free hand.

"Get away from the girl!" She kept the light in his eyes. Best he didn't see that Val was alone.

Without warning, the man lurched forward, as if pulled by something, nearly falling. "Get back here!" he yelled.

A door slammed, and moments later, a girl of eleven or twelve stumbled around the side of the house toward her, dressed only in a torn nightgown. Welts and bruises marked her arms, legs, and face, visible even in the dim light. One eye had swollen shut and blood seeped from her nose and lip. More blood dripped down both of her legs.

Val knew what that meant. She'd suffered the same injury, once.

"That bastard," she whispered. He'd pay for this. She slipped her jacket over the girl's thin shoulders. The girl hugged her, crying. Val held her, rocking left, right, whispering, "It's okay now. It'll all be okay." But she didn't believe it. She knew better.

She looked back down the street. Gil had tripped and fallen while trying to rush around the group of women, who helped him up, then clutched at him, chirping in high voices. He seemed unable to pull away from them. He waved at Val: *Go on ahead.*

Val looked back to the window. The man had disappeared. Shit! "Who is he?" she asked the girl, pointing at the house. "Is he your father?"

"His name is Mr. Harkins," the girl said between sobs, with a slight accent. Puerto Rican, Val guessed. "He's mama's boyfriend. She calls him Richard. He's drunk, and so mean..." She broke into sobs again. Val hugged her and fought back her own tears. That rotten prick could not get away with this.

"Where's your mom?" Val shook the girl by the shoulders

to regain her attention. Harder than she meant. She took a deep breath. Don't take it out on the girl. Save it for him.

At last the girl managed an answer. "Still inside. In the bedroom."

Gentler: "What's your name?"

"Antoinetta."

"Okay. Antoinetta. Is there someplace you can go right now?"

The girl shrugged, curled back into Val's hug. Not knowing what else to do, Val walked her toward the sidewalk in front of the house. "How about the neighbor's? Can you go there for a minute, at least, to get out of the cold?"

The girl sniffled, nodded, and pointed to the group of women down the street. "*Mi tia*, Camila."

"Okay," Val said. "Go. I'll wait here. Oh, one more thing. Is he armed? A gun, a knife, anything?"

The girl nodded. "My mom keeps a gun by her bed. He shot the..." She broke into sobs again, throwing her body against Val's and holding tight.

"He shot someone?" Val managed to slide down to eye level with the girl. "Antoinetta, I know this is hard, but it's important. Did he shoot someone?"

The girl nodded. "A...a policeman..."

Shit! No time to waste. Val gave the girl a gentle push toward the cluster of women still clutching at Gil. She unclipped her radio, pressed the Talk button. "Dispatch, this is Dawes. Location, 2916 Greenfield Street. Officer down, repeat, officer down. Suspect is armed. Requesting additional backup."

"Roger that, Dawes," the female voice crackled. "On its way."

She grimaced. The guy could escape long before help arrived. She waved at Gil, but he remained focused on the girl running toward him. Frustrated, she peered into a bedroom window on the far end of the porch. No sign of the man, the mother, or the downed cop.

Gil broke free of the women and hustled over to her. "Did I hear 'officer down'?" he asked, out of breath.

"And he has a hostage inside, the girl's mother," Val said. "We've got to get in there."

Another cruiser pulled up, lights flashing, and two

uniformed officers jumped out. "You two cover the front!" Gil yelled to them. "We're going around back."

They drew their .38s and discovered an open door in the back that led to a tiny kitchen. Val entered first, crouching low, greeted by a humid stench ten degrees warmer than the air outdoors. Dirty dishes crowded a tiny Formica-topped table. Empty beer and whiskey bottles littered the counter. Pots and pans sat on the stove with food dried in the bottom, and a litter box in the corner overflowed with turds. "Police!" she yelled. "Come out with your hands up. Into the kitchen. Now!"

"Get the hell out of my house or you'll end up like your friend here," the man said. "Dead!"

Val's blood went cold. The bastard killed a police officer. Based on what Gil had told her, she guessed her partner would kill Richard without asking any questions. Maybe he even deserved that. But her priority at the moment was Antoinetta's mom. Which, she guessed, made her a Savior Type in Gil's taxonomy. Whatever.

Sure enough, Gil crept forward, toward the arch separating the two rooms. He peered in and tapped his own badge, then grimaced and mouthed to Val: "I see him." The downed cop, she realized. Gil signaled for her to cover him. She crouched, her shaking hands gripping her service weapon.

Gil spun into the room, weapon drawn. An arm swung down behind him holding something dark and metallic, smashing it onto Gil's head. He went down in a heap, unconscious.

"You want some of this action, bitch?" the man yelled to her, laughing. "I mean you there in the kitchen, lady. Fucking pig!"

Val stared at Gil, lying motionless in the middle of the room. Another cop lay bleeding from a gunshot wound, and a woman remained in danger. Clearly the man didn't fear cops and could handle himself when attacked. She needed another approach.

"Richard," she said, forcing her voice to remain calm. "This will go a lot better if you let Antoinetta's mother go."

"Get lost," the man yelled. "And take that worthless kid

with you. Her mom wants to stay here with me. Don't you, Rosa?"

A woman whimpered. At least she was alive. But Gil was down, and the other officer could still be alive and bleeding out. Time to expedite the conversation.

"Come out where I can see you," she said. "We need to talk." She gripped her .38's handle with white knuckles.

"Fuck off," he yelled back. "I haven't done anything illegal."

Except shooting a cop and beating a child. Asshole. "I'm not saying you did," she said. "I just want to talk to you."

"Bullshit. Lying pig."

Deep breaths. Stay calm. "What happened here tonight?" Val asked. "How did Antoinetta get hurt?"

"How the fuck should I know? Stupid kid. Always getting into trouble."

"That's kids for ya." Yeah, always getting bruised and beaten in their nightgowns by themselves, somehow without the knowledge of a drunk, sadistic bastard. She fought to keep the anger out of her voice. "What did she do tonight? What was she up to?" Val crept through the kitchen and pressed herself against the wall next to the doorway to the living room. "Did she misbehave?"

Derisive laughter. "Oh, yes. She was a *very* bad girl. Are you a bad girl, copper?"

"You rotten shit," Val said under her breath. Her stomach turned, and she needed to spit. She took a step to the sink, gagged at the sight of crusty dishes and standing water, and discharged the ball of mucus and hot bile that had collected in her mouth. She returned to the edge of the doorway.

"I didn't hear your answer, pig. Are you a bad girl?"

"No, dipshit, I'm not," she said. Okay, Val, keep the nasty out of your voice. "Nor was Antoinetta. But it sounds like you might have been a bad boy tonight. Are you a bad boy, Richard?"

That awful laugh again. "Is that what she said? That lying little weasel. Fucking *chingadera*." He laughed again.

Val gritted her teeth. *Stop it!* she wanted to shout. "Had a few drinks tonight, Richard?" Static on the radio. No news. No help yet. What the hell was taking the others so long?

"Nothing illegal about that, is there?"

"No, not at all. So long as you didn't give any to the girl."

Where's that backup?

Laughter again, setting Val's teeth on edge. "As if I could stop her. You should see her with the rum. Little drunken fucking *chingadera*." Loud, angry laughs, almost a cough, even more grating. "You know, when they get drunk, these little chicas, they can get pretty wild. Talk about ba-ad girls."

That bastard!

Blood pulsed in the veins at Val's temples. She shook her head, refusing to let him get under her skin. "Is that the best you can do, Richard? Underage girls, too young and small to say no to you?" Her voice quavered, and nausea stirred in her gut. She tightened her grip on her weapon, but the sweat on her palms made it slippery.

Floorboards creaked, in the next room or beyond, followed by his horrible laughter again, a little louder, a little closer. It sounded forced. Of course! He was "laughing" to cover up the noise he was making as he moved into position to escape—or, attack.

"Where are you now, Richard?"

Hoarse laughter, grating to the ear. "Let's play tag, like me and your buddy did. You're it, pig. Come and find me."

"I don't think so. You come out here and let's talk."

"We're talking just fine." Another creak.

A static-laden voice blared from her radio. Dammit! Something about a burglary in progress in Frog Hollow. No mention of her backup. She gripped her gun with both hands. Sweat collected on her upper lip, and she licked it off. Her mouth had gotten very dry. He didn't answer. Another creak—

"Talk to me, Richard. Let me know what you're d—"

A white blob flashed in the doorway. He came at her, his head ducked low, like a football player going in for a tackle. She swung her arms toward him, but he moved too fast. He crashed into her, knocking her backwards. Her back slammed into the cabinets, and her head thumped against the edge of the counter. She saw stars for a moment, then the floor rushed up at her face. Her forehead thumped onto the linoleum, and she collapsed face-first onto the floor. Dizzy, she tried to get up, but the world spun around her. Sharp pain jabbed her side. The bastard had kicked her! She rolled away, somehow, and sat up against the cabinet. The man stood before her, his fist arcing toward her. She dodged the punch, and a loud crack filled her ears. He howled in pain, holding his right hand in his left, swore, and dashed out the back door of the house.

Val rolled onto all fours, gasping for breath. She tried to stand, but the pain in her side made her cry out, and she leaned against the cabinets for support. He'd kicked her in the crease between her Kevlar vest and belt, a soft spot, and hard. She'd have a nasty bruise, if not internal organ damage. Shit, this hurt. On top of that, her dizziness returned, along with overwhelming nausea.

She cradled her radio to her ear. "Unit A-27...reporting. Suspect...in 10-16 on Greenfield...escaping on foot. White male, forty, six foot, two-fifty, light brown hair."

"Roger that," the dispatcher responded. "Backup units less than one minute from your location."

"One minute...is too late," Val said. Damn, this hurt.

"Checking," Dispatch said. "Status of officer reported down on that scene?"

"Two officers. Investigating." Val holstered her weapon and radio, then pressed her hands on the countertop and pulled herself to her feet. She ignored the pain in her side enough to walk a few steps on her own. A pair of sirens blared outside, one the unmistakable wail of the local ambulance company. She stumbled into the living room and checked Gil first. Breathing, with a steady pulse. She sighed with relief, then scanned the room and spotted the blue-uniformed man curled up in the corner in a growing pool of blood. She scrambled to him, turned his body toward her. Her own pain disappeared as adrenaline surged through her. She didn't recognize the officer, a 30-ish white man with short, brown hair and a stocky build. His face had gone pale—he'd lost a lot of blood. She checked his breathing and pulse, found both. He was alive, but unconscious.

"Get those medics in here!" she shouted into her radio.

"What's the situation inside the house?" Dispatch responded. "Are all suspects—"

"Clear!" she shouted back. "Get those damned medics in here!"

She spotted another officer lying face-down at the end of

the hallway and rushed to him. Also unconscious from a blow to the head, but alive. *R. Lopez*, read his nameplate. She returned to the living room and grabbed a man's shirt off the floor, pressing it onto the other officer's wound to stem the bleeding. She spotted his nameplate. "Hold on, Samuels," she said. "We'll get you out of here." Her head felt light, and dizziness washed over her again, but she kept the pressure on the wound. Where were those damned medics?

Moments later, footsteps pounded around her. A lanky African American man with close-cropped curls and a young dark-haired Latina, both dressed in blue scrubs, rushed into the room. The man tapped her on the shoulder. "We've got this, officer," he said.

She leaned against the wall, breathing hard. "I checked his vitals," Val said. "He's alive. Gunshot to the midsection."

"Let's move him out!" the male paramedic said. In seconds they'd secured him to a stretcher that appeared as if by magic, and they carried him out the front door of the house.

"You okay?" A familiar voice. Who? When had she closed her eyes? "Dawes? Are you awake?" Rough hands shook her.

She opened her eyes. Gil's face appeared, close enough to smell his after-shave. Dried blood formed a winding river down his forehead and cheeks. Lopez stood behind him, rubbing blood off of his own face. "The guy...where is he?" She groaned and held her side. Damn, it hurt.

"We'll catch him," Gil said.

Val closed her eyes again. Dammit. The son of a bitch shot a cop, raped a twelve-year-old girl, kicked her in the kidneys, and then he got away.

After all of her training, all of her preparation, spending all of her life dreaming about delivering justice to creeps like that, in her first big confrontation with a real-life criminal, she'd failed. Failed the community, failed Uncle Val, failed everybody.

Most of all, she'd failed herself.

Gil was saying something, but she couldn't hear him anymore. Her head swam, and she lay down on her back. Consciousness drained away from her, replaced by the image of the man she most despised: an untried, unpunished criminal. The man who had done to her what Richard

Harkins had done to Antoinetta.

The face of "Uncle" Milt.

***

Ten Years Earlier

Bedtime. Lights-out time, to be precise. Even though she'd turn thirteen in a few weeks, Mom and Dad still enforced her curfew. She closed her book, turned off her reading lamp, and set Mulligan, the stuffed bear with the little bell around his neck, against the door. Uncle Val gave the old bear to her when she turned six, promising that Mulligan would warn her if any monsters ever tried to hurt her. She'd long ago stopped believing in monsters, but as Dad often joked, never argue with success.

Her parents' voices rose above the rumbling of the TV downstairs, then "Uncle" Milt's, followed by raucous laughter. Her mother said, "Milt, that's terrible!" But she laughed along with the men.

Uncle Milt was telling his dirty jokes again. Once he'd even told a few in front of Valorie and Chad, until Mom put a stop to it. Valorie hadn't gotten the joke, but Chad had. He was sixteen, so he knew more about such things.

After witnessing Mom's reaction to the joke, Valorie didn't want to know about those things. Any of it.

They called him "Uncle" Milt, but Valorie had learned months before that he wasn't related to Mom after all. In fact, he was only about ten years older than Mom, but she'd always treated him like family, inviting him to holiday dinners and such. He'd served with Grandpa in the military or something, a long time ago. Milt had no family of his own, at least not anymore. He seemed sad to Valorie, despite his boisterous manner and bawdy humor. Maybe that's why Mom kept inviting him over—she felt sorry for him.

Chad found Milt funny and even looked up to him. From the racket raised downstairs, Valorie guessed Chad was showing off one of his latest jiu jitsu moves again to impress the old fart.

But then came the awful crash, Chad's yelp of pain, and Mom's cry of "Oh, no!" and Dad's "Chad, are you all right?" She hadn't needed to hear the muffled answer.

Minutes later, Mom knocked on her door. "Honey, your brother's broken his arm," Mom said. "We're taking him to the emergency room. Uncle Milt will stay with you while we're gone."

"Why can't Milt drive him?" Valorie asked, her heart pounding. Please, please, don't leave me alone with Milt.

"He's had too much to drink," Mom said in a low voice. "Anyway, we can't leave you here alone at night."

Downstairs, Milt said something like "I'm fine, really," and Valorie hoped he'd convince them to let him go.

"Nothing doing," Dad said over Milt's protests, and Valorie knew that battle was lost.

"I'll go with you to the hospital," she said, sitting up in bed.

"No, it's too late. You have school tomorrow." She used that insistent, commanding tone that told Val two things: first, that Mom had gotten drunk too, and second, she'd better not argue. Mom's footsteps faded down the hall, heavy and uneven.

Valorie sighed and crawled under her covers. "Mulligan, you guard the door," she whispered. He smiled back. Mulligan always smiled and always kept her safe.

Downstairs, Dad mentioned the guest room. Crap! The room right next to Valorie's. Milt probably snored really loud, too.

The front door slammed shut, the car pulled away, and she could hear only the blaring of the television.

Then footsteps, plodding on the stairs...

A thin crease of light crept under her door from the hall. The toilet flushed, and the light grew brighter and dimmer again. Quiet reigned for several seconds. Then, footsteps again.

*Too many footsteps. Six, seven, eight. But the guest
room was only three or four steps from the bathroom.*

*A shadow appeared outside her door. Two shadows,
actually. Feet. She shut her eyes, pulled up her
covers—*

*A tiny bell rang. Valorie's eyes sprang open. The
door swung wide. A large shadow filled the doorway,
framed by the dim glow of the ceiling lamp from down
the hall. The shadow became the figure of a man, six
feet tall, heavy, with a fringe of hair around his balding
head.*

*"Milt?" She shivered under her blanket. "I think
you're in the wrong place. The guest room is—"*

*"My dear Valley Girl," he said. "I'm so glad you're
still awake."*

Chapter Seven

Val stiffened at the touch of the doctor's ice-cold stethoscope on her skin, her gasp audible enough to elicit a comforting smile from the young nurse recording her vitals on an iPad. Val inched away from her on the examination table, crinkling its paper cover loud enough to drown out the hum of the nearby stack of computers and monitors.

"Are you experiencing pain there?" asked Dr. Kim, a forty-something Asian woman whose tortoise-shell glasses seemed to hold her long, silver-speckled hair in place behind her ears. "I tried to avoid the obvious bruises, but they don't always show."

"No, no," Val said. "It's just a little cold. Can I put my clothes back on?" She pulled the paper-thin gown closer and hugged herself for warmth. Why doctors always kept examination rooms so frigid, she'd never understand.

"We're almost done." Dr. Kim gave her a polite smile. "Breathe deeply for me, slowly. That's good." She jotted down another note, set her clipboard aside, and removed her glasses, letting them rest against her chest. "Based on what I've seen, I don't think you've suffered any serious internal injuries," Dr. Kim said, "but we'll take some X-rays to make sure. I think a CAT scan might also help us out here. You may have a concussion from that blow to your head, so we'll want to keep an eye on that for a few days. I'll write up a work release that you can give to your superiors."

Val's mood brightened. "So I can return to work tomorrow?" she said.

The nurse, a young Latina with bright red lipstick that contrasted with her light brown skin, laughed out loud this time, earning her a stern glance from Dr. Kim. The nurse took a step away from Val and busied herself with her iPad.

"A work release means you can take time off," Dr. Kim said with a smile, this time a genuine one. She stood only a hair over five feet tall, if that, and had to look up to meet Val's eyes. "So you can heal before returning to duty."

"So, it's optional?" Val asked. "I'd rather just go back to work, if it's up to me."

Dr. Kim and the nurse exchanged puzzled glances, then the doctor returned her attention to Val. "It's up to you, of course," she said. "Why don't we see what the X-rays and CAT scan tell us?"

Val sighed. If only her doctors had been this thorough when she'd needed them to be, ten years earlier. "Fine," she said. "Let's get this over with." She followed the nurse down the hall. They passed a waiting room filled with clusters of people standing and staring at mute TV screens.

"Look!" A boy of about twelve pointed at Val. "It's her!"

Val glanced back at the boy, giving him a quizzical look. The boy grinned and pointed to the TV screen above his head, which displayed two faces, side by side: Brian Samuels, the policeman who had been shot—and Val's. The caption on the screen read, "Clayton police injured in domestic violence response."

A girl standing next to the boy, a few years younger and bearing a family resemblance, ran up to Val. "Can I have your autograph?" she asked in a meek voice, holding out a coloring book and a crayon.

Val took the book from her, warmth flushing her skin. Protocol probably forbade such gestures, but she couldn't bring herself to say no. "What's your name?" she asked the girl.

"Autumn," the girl said. She took the signed book back from Val and hugged it close to her chest. "I want to be a policewoman when I'm old enough, just like you!" She skipped back to her family, showing off her new prize.

Val lowered her head and followed her nurse down the hall. Maybe a day off wouldn't be a bad idea.

A few steps before they entered the radiology lab, the familiar face of a young girl burst from another examination room, accompanied by an African-American woman in scrubs and a nameplate reading, "Dr. T. Phillips."

"Antoinetta!" Val rushed toward her. A sad smile broke

across the girl's tear-streaked face. She threw her arms around Val in a bone-crushing hug. Val grunted in pain, but the girl's grip only tightened. Maybe she *had* cracked a rib, after all.

"Are you okay?" Val asked her, breaking the embrace and cupping the girl's face in her hands. "Are they taking good care of you?"

Antoinetta's grin disappeared and her gaze fell to the floor. "*Sí*," Antoinetta said. "Can I go home now?" She teared up again and buried her face in Val's chest.

"Could I have a word with you, Officer?" Dr. Phillips asked, a worried expression on her face. She signaled to Val's nurse, who slid closer and wrapped an arm around Antoinetta's shoulders. Val gave Antoinetta another quick hug and followed the doctor across the hallway, out of earshot.

"Antoinetta is reluctant to let us administer the rape kit," Dr. Phillips said. "She keeps saying she did nothing wrong, which is true, but she has it in her head that we're blaming her for all of this."

"Did her mother give the okay?" Val asked.

"She did, but the patient also has to be willing," Dr. Phillips said. "But she respects you so much, so…"

"Give me a few minutes with her," Val said. She returned to Antoinetta and led her by the hand up the hallway to the waiting area. They sat facing each other on adjacent seats. "How are you feeling?" she asked.

"Okay," Antoinetta said in a dull voice. "But I want to go home."

"You will, soon," Val said. "The doctors need to check to make sure you're okay. They can't always tell just by looking at you." She spoke in a slow, measured pace. "They need to check your insides, too. It's standard procedure."

The girl's eyes welled with tears. "I didn't do anything *malo*, I swear."

"I know, honey," Val said. "But maybe Mr. Harkins did?"

Antoinetta stared at her, tears streaming from each eye, but said nothing.

"Don't you think we ought to find out?" Val asked.

Tears flowed like open faucets down the girl's face. She shook her head. "He…he told me…if I tell anyone…" She broke into sobs and pulled her hands free, covering her face.

Val's heart ached for the girl. She knew Antoinetta's feelings of fear and shame well. All too well.

***

"Say it!" the man said, his voice a nasty hiss, so harsh it made her jump. His hand pressed down on the back of her neck, gripping her with too much force. She shook her head.

"Out. Loud!" He pushed at her head. It hurt.

She tried to take a breath, but inhaled only pillow. She wheezed, an awful sound. He loosened his grip, and she gasped air into her lungs.

"I won't tell anyone," she said with a moan, choking on the words.

"Good girl," he said. "I know you won't. Because you don't want to get in trouble, do you? You know what people think about girls who do what you do."

***

"Antoinetta," Val said in a low voice, shaking off the ancient memory, "when I was a girl about your age, a man did something terrible to m—my *friend*," she said. "Someone I knew well. A terrible thing. And do you know what happened to that man?"

Antoinetta lifted her head, shook it.

"Nothing," Val said. "Because my friend was afraid to tell anyone. Her family, her friends, anyone. She wouldn't even admit it to me." Her voice caught on this truth, one she'd feared admitting all of her life. "Not for a long time, anyway. And when she did tell the people close to her, it was too late. The police could no longer collect the evidence, and the man went free."

Antoinetta blinked tears from her eyes. "Did they ever catch him?" she asked.

Val's shoulders trembled. "No," she said, her voice barely a whisper. "They never did. They never punished the man for what he did to...my friend."

Antoinetta lowered her own voice. "What happened to the girl?" she asked. "Is she all right?"

Air whooshed from Val's lips. "She suffered," she said, "for the rest of her life. She always wished she'd said something sooner, so the police could have caught and punished the man, and made sure he never came near her again."

The girl's eyes widened. "Do you think...Señor Harkins might come back?"

"Maybe." Val choked on the reality of her answer. "Unless we can prove what he did. Which is what the doctors want to help us do."

A long moment passed. Antoinetta's tears stopped, and a look of steely resolve swept over her face. "If you catch him," she said, "what will you do to him?"

Val squeezed her hand. "We'll prosecute him and put him in prison for a long time."

Antoinetta's face curled into an angry snarl. "Just prison?" she said. "*Eso es todo?*"

"I'm afraid so," Val said, her heart sinking. "But prison is an awful—"

"If you catch him and he tried to get away," Antoinetta said, "can't you shoot him, like they do on TV?"

Val's breath caught in her throat. "What you see on TV is not always what happens in real life," she said. "We try not to shoot people unless they're threatening the lives of others."

"What if he runs away?" the girl asked.

"Well...sometimes, but—"

"I hope," Antoinetta said in a menacing voice, "that when you find him, he tries to get away. And when he does, I hope you shoot off his little *bicho!*" She left a stunned Val seated on the bench and returned to Dr. Phillips, nodding in response to the doctor's question. She gave Val a thumbs-up and disappeared with the doctor into an examination room.

***

Radiology showed no cracked ribs or internal organ damage. Gil met her in the waiting room and spread his arms for a hug, but she grabbed his hands and squeezed them instead.

"Still sore," she said, averting her eyes. "Have you been waiting here all this time?"

He nodded, with what she interpreted as a slight pout on his face. "I wasn't going to let my partner walk out of a cold hospital without an escort," he said. "What's the prognosis?"

She grimaced. "I'll live. They wanted me to take time off, but I, uh, misplaced the doctor's note already. How's Samuels doing?"

Gil's face turned grave. "He's still in surgery. The doc was hopeful, though. Nothing major got hit, but he lost a fair amount of blood." His expression brightened. "You saved his life, Val. So far, anyway."

Her face grew warm and she shook her head, strolling toward the exit. "The medics saved him. What's the word on Harkins?"

"He's still on the run. But we'll get him." Gil put his hand on her shoulder and turned her toward him. "Val, I'm serious. You did impressive work at that scene tonight. I've seen those standoffs go on for hours. Had that happened, Samuels would be at the morgue instead of ER."

"Not such good work," she said. "Harkins got away."

"We'll get him," Gil said. "Stop changing the subject. I'm putting you in for a commendation and a medal—no, don't interrupt me. You earned it. Okay?"

The warmth in her face turned to fire. "Anyone would have done the same."

He gripped her shoulders, forcing her to stop walking and face him. "Not everyone, Val. And even if everyone did, it's still amazing and brave stuff. Look, the work we do is hard and dangerous, and we don't get thanked very often for it. That'll wear on you after a while, trust me. So when you do get a little recognition, don't spit on it, okay? Learn to take it and appreciate it."

He drove her home in silence. Val's mind raced from Antoinetta to Harkins and back to Gil's comments. They arrived at her apartment a few minutes before three in the morning, the end of their shift. Gil parked the cruiser in front of her building, turned off the engine, and looked toward her. She stared straight ahead, through the windshield, her side still aching from the bruises Harkins had dealt her. He exhaled loudly, his hands still on the wheel, waiting. A car droned by, and a light sprinkle of rain drizzled the windshield. Static buzzed on the radio, its sound turned low. The cruiser's headlights stayed on, shining bright circles of yellow light on the road.

She turned toward him and found his dark brown eyes gazing upon her. How long he'd been staring, she had no idea. At first he looked fierce, with his square jaw, stubbly beard, and slight frown. But his expression softened into a reassuring smile, and he kept his hands to himself, unlike most guys who'd gotten her alone in cars at night.

She should say something, she supposed.

"Thank you for the ride," she said. "And for your support, and...well, everything."

His smiled broadened. "Anytime, partner."

Another car swished by, kicking up the moisture from the wet pavement.

"Well, I...guess I'll see you tomorrow," she said, grabbing the door handle.

He shook his head. "Stay home tomorrow. You've earned a day off."

"Pfft! I took worse blows from clumsy soccer players and stayed in the game. I won't let this slow me down."

Gil laughed. "You're something else, you know that?" He shook his head and stared at the steering wheel, fumbling with the keys in the ignition. Then he looked up. "Okay, I tell you what. I'll recommend a few days of light duty for you. It'll give you a chance to catch up on paperwork and maybe do some digging on this perp, Harkins. We need to track him down, and we're not going to do it by looking in every low-income apartment building in the city. Sound fair?"

She considered it. She'd always done well with research projects. Anything that helped get a child molester off the streets sounded worthwhile. "Okay, partner. You've got a deal."

She tiptoed through her apartment so as to not wake Beth and plopped onto her bed, only to bounce back up, howling in pain. She'd already forgotten about the bruises. Damn that pervert Harkins!

For the next hour, she lay in bed, waiting for the painkillers to kick in. She vowed to find the man who'd hurt that little girl, and make him pay for what he'd done.

Chapter Eight

Val entered Friendly's, a tiny coffee-and-sandwich shop on Edgewood Drive across from City Park, and searched for Brenda Petroni, the self-defense trainer from the academy. Before she'd finished scanning the room, a tall, willowy blonde jumped up from a corner booth. "Shannon O'Reilly," the blonde said, her hand outstretched. "Brenda invited me to join you both for lunch today. You're Val Dawes, right?"

"How is it that everyone seems to know who I am?" Val accepted the handshake, but stood rooted in place. "Did somebody put a 'rookie female cop' sign on my back?"

Shannon laughed. "I knew your uncle," she said. "We worked on a few cases together before I made detective and moved downtown to Missing Persons. He kept a picture of you on his desk."

Val's eyes opened wider. Shannon didn't look old enough to have served with Uncle Val. Lean and fair-skinned, she had no wrinkles on her face, even around her eyes or mouth.

Shannon laughed again. "I'm thirty-five, in case you're wondering," she said. "And yes, I still get carded."

"Lucky you." Val waved at Brenda walking in the door. Dressed in street clothes, she appeared even stockier than when in uniform.

"It's less of an advantage than you'd think in our line of work," Shannon said, once they'd located a booth away from the hordes of screaming children. "It's hard enough for most women to get taken seriously as a cop. When you look twenty-one, you might as well wear a dunce cap all day. Oh, and did you somehow miss the blonde hair?"

"That's reassuring to hear," Val said. "I was beginning to think they saved it all for me."

"Honey, welcome to the party-crashers at the old boys club," Brenda said with a sneer. "Most of these guys think we should all be home raising babies and cooking meatloaf for our hard-working, brave husbands in uniform."

"It's even worse when a woman makes sergeant, like Brenda here." Shannon thanked the waiter for their coffees. "It's bad enough we're taking their jobs, as they see it, and 'pretending' to be their equals. When they actually have to follow orders from us, forget it. The shit you take from your peers on patrol will seem like a celebration in your honor by comparison."

"Ugh." Val fought down the image of her fellow academy cadets' sneering faces and could barely sip her coffee. But then she considered Gil and shook her head. "That doesn't translate into a lack of backup on the street, does it? I mean, if you're in a dangerous situation—"

"No, then it's the reverse. Totally patronizing," Brenda said. "They never let a woman take the lead and they're always trying to shield us from difficult situations. Half the time I was on patrol, they treated me like I was in their way. There are exceptions, like your uncle, your partner Kryzinski, and a few others. But out of 300 men on the force, you'll be lucky to find two dozen who will treat you as an equal."

"That may be a little harsh," Shannon said, "but it's close. The main point is, we have to prove ourselves every day on the job to these guys. Are we good enough? Tough enough? Smart enough?"

"And it's not like they're physical specimens or Mensa geniuses themselves," Brenda said. "Half of them got their jobs by having a brother or uncle on the force. No offense," she said to Val. "And I'm no better. My father, my uncles, even my grandfather was a Clayton cop."

"None taken," Val said. Brenda's admission buoyed her spirits. By comparison, the Dawes family was the new bunch on the block. "I think in my case, having a legacy makes it harder to live up to expectations."

"You have big shoes to fill," Shannon said. "Speaking of filling up, what are you gals going to eat? I'm starved."

Over lunch, Shannon and Brenda gave Val an earful. She had a tough road ahead as a female recruit. By the end of

the meal, she felt utterly depressed. "That's crazy," she kept
saying in response to the reality they painted for her:
promotion rates half those of the men. Lower pay. Longer
stints in undesirable shifts and precincts. Less desirable
assignments overall, and a greater likelihood of getting stuck
behind a desk or a phone. "And don't let your partner stick
you with all the paperwork," Brenda said. "They'll say it's
seniority, but that's bunk. With male recruits, they take
turns, and everyone pulls his own weight. After an
appropriate break-in period, of course."

"Gil's been good about that," Val said. "Are you gals getting
dessert?"

"Are you kidding? Why else come to Friendly's?" Shannon
grinned. "Ice cream all around."

"After this lunch, I need something sweet," Val said.

"Don't let it get you down," Brenda said, still cheerful
despite all the horror stories. "I tell you what, Val. Any time
you want, you call me. Any of these guys give you shit, I've
got your back."

"Me, too," Shannon said.

"Thanks." Val smiled. At last, she'd made a few friends in
the department, other than her partner. "This has been a big
help."

"Okay, enough talk," Brenda said. "Let's get ice cream."

***

Val ended up taking one day off, spending most of it in bed
in a painkiller-induced haze, eating nothing until Beth shook
her awake at seven o'clock.

"I picked up Korean barbecue on the way home from
work," Beth called from her adjacent bedroom while she
changed clothes. "And a six-pack. Let's party!"

"I thought you were going out tonight." Val blinked her
eyes and watched the ceiling swirl overhead. Or was the bed
swirling?

"I had a date with Victor, but the jerk-off canceled at the
last minute. Probably found a blonde with bigger tits who'll
go to bed with him on the first date."

Val sat up, trying to imagine a woman with looser dating
standards than Beth. "I'm not sure that barbecue is a good
idea," she said. "My stomach's still queasy from the

painkillers."

"That's because you took them on an empty stomach." Beth appeared in her bedroom doorway, buttoning the waist of her unzipped jeans and pulling on a New York Giants jersey. The shirt got stuck on her head. For a moment, only a bush of blonde-streaked brown hair poked through the opening on top as Beth struggled to yank it onto her pear-shaped torso.

Val glanced away, not wanting to stare at the bronze spare tire overlapping Beth's waistline, nor at the expanse of white padded bra that made her already large boobs seem enormous. Voluptuous women made Val feel tiny in her slender, athletic frame. "I'll pass on the beer, but I am hungry," she said, and pushed herself off of the bed.

Beth threw an arm around her and helped Val stumble into the kitchen. Val had to hold her breath to suppress the nausea bubbling up in her stomach, stimulated by the excessive scent of lavender emanating from Beth's neck. The girl never understood the concept of moderation in perfume, food, or men.

"Who is this Victor guy, anyway?" Val swallowed a tangy, spicy, melt-in-your-mouth bite of pork. "Have I met him?"

"He's the mechanic who replaced the starter in my Mustang last week," Beth said. "He just moved here from Arizona, and I promised him a drive through the fall foliage with the top down. I think he wanted *my* top down instead." She cupped her boobs, squeezed them once, and laughed. "Girl, your face is so red right now!"

True enough, Val's entire head felt hot, and not from the spicy pork. "I thought you were still dating Justin," she said. "What happened with him?"

"Justin's boring," Beth said. "And not only in bed. All the guy wants to do is play video games with his friends. How about you? You must be rolling in offers from all those hot men in uniform. Anything promising?"

Val shook her head, her face warming again, and she fished another rib out of the takeout box. "There's a strict policy against dating other cops, honored mostly in the breach, of course. Not that any of them seem interested. I think I threaten them."

"Introduce me, then," Beth said with a laugh. "I have no such policy." She bit into a juicy piece of meat. "Mm. So good. Hey, who was the good-looking guy who dropped you off last night?"

Val set down her half-eaten rib, irritation rising. "You spied on us?"

"I peeked out the window for a moment. It was a cop car, why shouldn't I be curious?" She swallowed another bite of barbecue. "So, are you interested in him?"

"No. Haven't I explained this?" Val picked up the rib again, then sighed and dropped it again. She still had no appetite. "Department policy aside, he's fifteen years older than me."

"Ah." Beth paused, a sad expression on her face. "I didn't realize."

"Realize what?" Val moped, staring at her plate.

Beth made a face. "With what you've been through, I know that older guys—"

"He's not *that* old," Val snapped, then regretted it. She registered the hurt expression on Beth's face and shook her head. Neither of them needed to mention Uncle Milt's name. His memory haunted every conversation they ever had about Val's relationships with men. "I mean, I'd rather meet someone closer to our age, if anyone."

Beth brightened and held up one finger. "Hey! That reminds me. I met these two guys at the Flag and Gauntlet Tavern a few weeks ago. One of them seemed interested, but he didn't want to abandon his friend. I could call them, set something up." Her face lit up with her gigantic trademark smile, so infectious that Val almost wanted to say yes.

Almost. Val couldn't remember the last time she had fun on a date. In fact, she couldn't even remember going on one since her second year of college, with a friend of Beth's that spent the entire evening hinting about the size of his penis. "I don't think so," Val said. "I'm busy with work, and I need time to recover, and—"

"Enough lame excuses," Beth said. "All you do is work. Besides, I need your help. I really want to meet this guy, and he won't do it unless I find a date for his friend."

"I work evening shifts," Val said. "My schedule doesn't leave much room for dating."

Beth's grin faded. "Come on, Val," she said. "Get back on

that horse. Give it another try. Not *all* men are creeps."

"I'm not saying they are. I just..." Her voice trailed off as Beth's face fell. Guilt swept over her. She and Beth had shared every important moment of growing up—every crush (mostly Beth's), first kiss (again, Beth's), every struggle with dumb teachers and crazy parents. Beth was the only one that Val had confided in after the incident with Uncle Milt. The only one she trusted with her horrible secret.

Gazing at her friend, Val knew she'd lose this battle of wills. And she owed her. The woman had fed her, for God's sake.

"All right," she said, and even as Beth celebrated by cheering and covering her head with hugs and kisses, Val knew she was making a mistake.

***

Lieutenant Gibson took Gil's recommendation and put Val on desk duty for the next several days: answering phones, running license plates and criminal records for patrol officers involved in traffic stops, and filing reports. It allowed her to research Richard Harkins, though, and what she found chilled her.

Harkins had been arrested multiple times in the past decade, but had yet to go to trial for any charges. His rap sheet included domestic disturbance complaints with three different women. In two cases, the complaint included allegations of child abuse. At least one girl intimated that she'd been abused, or at least touched inappropriately, but she later recanted her story. Without corroborating evidence, Harkins walked on all charges.

Val wondered how many other incidents had gone unreported. His record also included public drunkenness, giving alcohol to a minor (again, an underage girl), and a bar fight. No shootings, much less of a cop, but the guy represented trouble wherever he went.

And he went everywhere. Going back to age 16, she found prior arrests in Georgia, Utah, and California, plus temporary addresses and employment records in Oregon, Indiana, and Tennessee. He'd attended public school in Massachusetts and had family in Torrington and New Haven.

He'd spent time in Florida, where he picked up an illegal firearms charge, but once again, he somehow skated away from any real punishment.

Despite the all-points bulletin and aggressive manhunt launched by the department, though, Harkins appeared to have disappeared. Her guess was that he might have fled to another state.

But he wouldn't be gone forever. And when he returned, she'd find him.

***

After a few days, Val resumed her street duties and the evening shift with Gil. He greeted her with a wide grin and open arms, but when she hesitated, he dropped the hug and offered an enthusiastic handshake. "Glad to have you back, partner," he said. "They had me working with Pops while you were out. I'd have been better off working alone."

"I wouldn't wish that guy as partner on anyone," Val said. She regretted rebuffing Gil's hug, but too late now. "I'm glad I got you instead of him."

"That's what I like to hear." Gil clapped her on the back, harder than she would have liked, but she didn't complain. They rode out in their patrol car and parked in the lot of a small shopping center to start their walking rounds. She briefed him on her research on Harkins while they walked.

"Doesn't surprise me," Gil said. "Guys like that don't start out by shooting cops. They escalate, and after a while, they think they're invulnerable. Samuels, unfortunately, was his latest victim."

"How is Samuels doing?" Guilt washed over her. She hadn't even thought of her fellow soldier in blue since the night of the shooting. She should have visited him while she'd been on light duty.

"Better," Gil said. "They sent him home from the hospital yesterday. He's off for at least six weeks, though—if he comes back at all."

They fell into a somber silence, matching each other's pace while they walked. The air cooled as the sun descended toward the roofs of the shops and apartment buildings lining the busy street. Neon lights flickered in the windows of cheap watering holes blaring pop hits from ten years before. They turned a corner, and Val realized where they were. She faced Gil, excited.

"Let's head this way," she said, pointing to her right.

"That's not our usual beat," he said, his brow furrowing. Then recognition dawned on his face. "Woodland Avenue," he said. "The scene of the crime. You really want to go there?"

"I want to see what people know about Harkins," she said. "Try to get a lead on where he's hiding out."

"The detectives have done that," he said. "You think you'll find out something they missed?"

She nodded. "Who would you rather talk to? A stranger in a suit, or someone who walks your neighborhood every night?" She didn't wait for his answer, striding forward at a fast pace. He caught up to her after a few moments, breathing hard, but gave her a thumbs-up.

She stopped first in a corner convenience store on Woodland and Greenfield and approached the brown-skinned, dark-haired man behind the counter. She pegged his age as late twenties or early thirties. "I'm Val Dawes," she said. "I believe you know my partner, Gil Kryzinski. Do you have a moment?"

"Good evening," the man said. "I am Taufiq Sharkar. I always have a moment for the brave officers protecting us from the criminal filth who prey on our citizens. Would you like some coffee? On the house. Please."

She stole a look at Gil and mouthed, *Is that okay?* Gil nodded and strolled over to the coffee counter.

Val remained with Taufiq. "What do you know about this man?" She showed him a picture of Harkins. "Does he come in here often?"

Taufiq made a face, as if wanting to spit. "He used to." He pointed to a rack of hard liquor, cigarettes, and porn magazines behind him. "A man in search of trash, if you ask me."

"What else?" she asked. "Has he ever given you trouble?"

Taufiq shook his head. "No, but he has been in here with Rosa—his, well, girlfriend, I guess you'd call her—and her daughter. He does not treat them well. He always curses at them and calls them names. Once I saw him slap the girl, Antoinetta, just for asking him to buy her something. The man is a pig."

"When did you last see him?" she asked.

"Not since that night. But..." He fumbled for words, fingers fidgeting. "Rosa is not the only woman he has abused. He lived here several years ago, when I first came to Clayton. I saw him with two or three other women—sometimes one, then the other. Often they had bruises, and they always seemed sad and afraid when they were with him."

Gil returned with the coffee and handed a cup to Val. Still uncertain, she fumbled with her wallet.

"No, please, it is free, with many thanks," Taufiq said. "I insist."

Gil shrugged at her, then nodded once. "Thank you," he said.

"My pleasure."

They walked toward Rosa and Antoinetta's Colonial, asking everyone they passed about Harkins. Most shook their heads and denied knowing him, but a few did so with fear on their faces—especially the women. When they reached the small apartment building a few doors away from the Colonial, a woman emerged, wearing a long, flowing dress and scarf, calling Gil's name.

"That's Camila, Antoinetta's aunt," Gil said. He greeted her with a smile and wave, which she returned, exclaiming something in Spanish.

"She says Antoinetta's doing great," Gil said, "and, thank you." He pointed to Val. "She's the one you should be thanking, Camila."

"Gracias, gracias!" Camila said, shaking Val's hands with both of hers. Meanwhile, a door slammed, and Antoinetta raced down the street toward them.

"We thank you so much!" Antoinetta said, crushing Val in a tight hug. "You saved our lives!"

"Has Mr. Harkins been back since that night?" Val asked her after escaping the hug. "Have you seen him?"

Antoinetta's eyes widened and she shook her head. "My mother said he might be in Louisiana," she said. "He has a cousin there."

Camila erupted into a torrent of invective in Spanish, gesturing and spitting and stomping her feet. Val looked to Antoinetta, who grinned.

"She says she is not a cousin, but another girlfriend that he beats and cheats on," Antoinetta said. She asked Camila something in Spanish, sending the older woman into another angry tirade. "Or he could be in Georgia or Florida, also with women he beats."

Gil frowned. "Have you told the detectives this?"

Camila ranted again in angry Spanish. "She says, what detectives?" Antoinetta said. "The police only come here to arrest us, never to ask us anything. Other than you, she means."

Val sighed, anger building within her. So typical of Clayton! Of course the department would focus on the Samuels shooting. But it made no sense to ignore the rape of a young girl, even if she lived in the "wrong" neighborhood, not least because they might share clues to help find him.

Let the department work its agenda. Val had her own priorities.

She stepped closer to Antoinetta, put her face close to the girl's, and spoke in a low voice. "When he lived with you, did he...I mean, this was not the first time he..."

Antoinetta shook her head, tears streaming down her face, and buried her face in Val's chest. "Many times," she said, her voice breaking. Sobs wracked her body, and Val held her, rocking the girl side to side, soothing her.

"Did you ever report him?" Gil asked.

Val turned toward Gil and shook her head. She pulled Antoinetta closer, murmuring reassuring sounds, absorbing the girl's sobs into her chest.

"I'm just trying to—"

"Sh!" Val glared at him.

Gil stared at her, blinking, until Camila wrapped her own arms around him in a swaying, tearful hug. There the four of them stood, with Val fighting back her own tears, holding onto a girl who reminded her far too much of her own, younger self.

Chapter Nine

Gil and Val interviewed several other neighbors on Woodland and nearby streets, all of whom echoed what Taufiq had told them. Many had seen Harkins with a series of women, each of whom sported bruises and black eyes after a short time with him. In a few cases, the women's young daughters shared the bruised bodies and downcast expressions of their mothers. The women themselves had all left the city, most without filing police complaints.

"I think we get the picture," Gil said a few hours later. They headed back toward the main drag, each sipping a fresh cup of Dunkin' Donuts coffee. "It might be moot, though. The guy's in the wind. Without federal help, we're unlikely to find him."

"Unless he comes back," Val said. "If history is any guide, he will."

"I agree," Gil said. "He doesn't exactly keep a low profile when he's here. He must think he's invincible. Why don't these women report his ass?"

Val shook her head, her temperature rising. "Only a man could ask that question. Come on, let's hit Upper Abernethy. I bet he grabs a lot of asses in those bars, and we're sure to find someone willing to file a complaint."

Gil stopped walking, arms crossed. "We're going about this wrong."

"How so?" She stopped, waiting for him. "I thought our job was to scour the neighborhood, looking for any sign of him, to share with the detectives."

"We can't do this ourselves," he said, "and we can't do it piecemeal. We need organized help."

She laughed. "Who? You got a union of journeyman

fugitive hunters to call on?"

Gil smiled, a thin line with no teeth. "As a matter of fact, I do."

***

Several minutes later, they arrived at the corner of Albany and MLK Jr. Boulevard on foot. Val recognized the random assortment of broken-down bicycles and garbage dumpsters strewn around the parking lot next to the old, abandoned theater. A circle of black youths warmed their hands over flickering flames darting up from a metal barrel.

"The Disciples?" She shook her head. "That's your union of fugitive hunters?"

"Can you think of anyone who knows the streets better?" Gil leaned closer and lowered his voice. "Keep a low profile this time. I'm not altogether sure they'll help, but they sure as hell won't if you show them up again."

"I didn't show—"

"Just let me do the talking."

They approached the group, Gil taking the lead, and stopped at the edge of the empty lot. A few of the youths glanced their way, but otherwise they gave no sign of acknowledging the presence of the two cops.

"Good evening, gentlemen," Gil called out to them. None of them responded, although a few guys, huddled together on the outer circle on the far side of the fire, laughed among themselves.

"I said *good evening, gentlemen,*" Gil called out again.

This time one of the inner circle glanced over his shoulder at Gil. Three gold earrings sparkled in the reflected light of the fire. "We don't want any," he said, and gazed back at the fire.

Gil nodded once to Val and took a few steps toward the group. She followed. They both stopped when four of the youths—the oldest couldn't have been more than seventeen—formed a shoulder-to-shoulder wall between Gil and the gang. The smallest, whom Val recognized as the boy named Dog, flanked the left side of the wall.

"State your business," the seventeen-year-old said. His ears sported two gold rings each and a diamond post on the right side. The other three had no bling.

"Looking for Pope," Gil said.

"He's not here," said the seventeen-year-old.

"Who's in charge tonight?" Gil asked.

"That'd be me." Three-rings stood behind the seventeen-year-old, and the wall parted to expose his massive frame. Six-four and three hundred pounds of muscle, he looked like a defensive lineman Val had once tutored at UConn. He wore a short-sleeved vest over a dark, long-sleeved T-shirt and baggy pants that billowed in the soft breeze.

"Cardinal Thomas. Good to see you." Gil extended a hand. Thomas ignored it.

"Copsky, wassup?"

Val glanced at Gil, but could only see part of his face. He didn't react to being called "Copsky," but dropped his proffered handshake and crossed his arms.

"I have a business proposition for you," Gil said.

The youths muttered to each other, mostly unintelligible. Val made out a few phrases: "Ain't trucking no business with cops." "Pope gonna kick his ass, he says yay." Thomas, the acting leader, scoffed. "What kind of *business*?"

"Honest work," Gil said, and the group burst into laughter. Except Thomas. "Go on."

Gil winked at Val, then dug in the gravel with his toe, staring downward. "We're looking for a guy. White dude," he added before Thomas could respond.

Thomas grinned, his gold fillings glinting in the dim light of the street. "You see any white dudes here?" He spread his arms wide and turned from side to side. "Aside from you, I mean."

Gil, nonplussed, handed Thomas a copy of the Harkins photo. "You recognize him?"

Thomas glanced at the photo. "He looks like a thousand guys I see every day. You know, all those white guys that come pray at our black church."

Several members of the group giggled. "All look the same to me, you know?" one of them joked.

Gil shook the picture in his hand. "All the same, I'd appreciate it if you'd keep an eye out. Hundred bucks for any leads that work out." He offered the picture again.

Thomas laughed. "A hundred bucks! What am I gonna do

with that, buy a dime bag? Man, I thought you were talking *money*." He turned his back and faced the fire. The wall closed behind him.

"Hundred fucking cheetos, man," one of the gang said in a derisive tone, laughing. "We gonna be rich!"

Gil sighed, glanced at Val. Gestured with his head: *Let's go.* He turned to leave.

Val stared at him, then at the gang, her heart sinking. She'd been so impressed with the brassiness of Gil's idea and the fearless way he'd approached them, but now it appeared he'd already given up. Where was his resolve? Where was the patience he always counseled her to have? Anger and frustration boiled up inside her.

"Five hundred!" The words escaped Val's mouth before she could entertain any second thoughts. Gil froze in his tracks, and Cardinal Thomas pushed his giant frame through his bodyguard's human wall. He stared at her in amazement and whispered something to Dog, who dashed off down the street.

Val stayed put, ignoring Gil's hostile glare. Her knees shook, and her arms would have, had she not pressed them tight to her body under each armpit. Queasiness stirred in her gut. She'd intervened in Gil's negotiation when he'd told her to keep her mouth shut. Now a gang of toughs who probably hated everything she stood for—her uniform, her race, her sex—surrounded her, their muscles rippling under tight T-shirts.

Not to mention that she'd offered more than a week's take-home pay for clues to catching a white guy they didn't even know.

She cleared her throat, tightening with sudden dryness. "If you'd rather not—"

"Wait." Thomas held up one hand. Gil turned to face Thomas, then Val. His face registered surprise mixed with irritation. He raised an eyebrow, as if to say: *Your game, now.* He stood next to her, facing the group.

A minute ticked by, then another. The gang resumed its hand-warming, other than Thomas and his bodyguard. Cars grunted past, many of them needing mufflers or new timing belts. Their radios, set to low volume, burped static.

After several minutes, someone in the group turned to the

side, followed by the others. A large black man with seven gold rings in each ear stepped into the circle, trailed by Dog. Thomas gave way, and the new man stood in front of Val.

"I understand," said Pope, "that you have a business proposition for us."

Gil nodded to Val, said nothing.

Val cleared her throat again. "We're looking for a guy." She nodded to Gil, who offered up the picture of Harkins again. "We'll pay you five hundred dollars if you find him."

Pope glanced at the picture. "What you got on him?"

Val looked to Gil for support, got a blank expression in return. She took a deep breath. "He's wanted for beating his girlfriend and raping a little girl, over on Woodland Avenue."

Pope's eyes narrowed, and he nodded to Thomas, who held out an open palm. Gil handed him the picture. Thomas held it up for Pope to see. Pope nodded, and Thomas passed the picture around to the group behind him. "Motherfucker," Pope said in a low voice.

"We have more copies if you need," Gil said.

Pope shook his head. "You can take that one back when we're done. Come back in a couple of days. We'll let you know what we've got."

"I could return tomorrow," Val said. "In case—"

"Couple of days, I said," Pope said, his voice full of steel. "Bring cash. Twenties and fives."

Val found a card and offered it to Pope. "If you find anything sooner—"

Pope smacked the card to the ground and ground it under his heel. He leaned in closer to Val, putting his eyes directly in front of hers. "I don't call the cops. For *anything*." He poked a finger into her breastbone, hard enough for her to feel it through her Kevlar vest.

She took another deep breath, exhaled. "Got it. I'll come back in a few days." She took a step backward.

Pope smiled and followed her, wrapping an arm around her shoulder and walking with her toward the curb. "Look," he said. "I know you think you tough. But a little white girl like you gotta be careful." He glanced back at the gang, all of whom fixed their stares on him. He leaned close and whispered in her ear. "Pretty white girls tend to get hurt out here on the street. I don't want that to happen." He grinned.

"At least not 'til payday. Dig?"

He released his grip on her shoulder and returned to the group. Val stood at the edge of the lot, waiting for Gil, her body shaking.

***

Val's body continued shaking, long after they left the Disciples far behind them. Not helping matters, Gil refused to speak until they'd walked several blocks, his mouth set in a stern line.

"Please, say something!" she said for the tenth time after they ordered coffee in Taufiq's convenience store. "Yell at me, fire me, tell me I'm an ass, whatever. Just speak!"

"What the hell possessed you to jump in like that?" Gil said between clenched teeth. "And you're buying coffee, since you have so much cash to give away. Sorry, Taufiq. Today it ain't free."

She paid a smiling Taufiq and led Gil outside. "I thought we needed to up the ante. They clearly weren't going to take you up on an offer of a measly hundred bucks."

"Of course they would have," Gil said. "Have you forgotten who has a history with these guys? We were negotiating. Something you clearly suck at."

"How do you know?" Val sipped her coffee, the cup shaking in her hand. Her shoulder still tingled where Pope's fingers had dug in.

"Because I've done this before," Gil said, exasperated. "Well, don't expect me to bail you out of this. You'll need to come up with the cash yourself. Good thing we get paid tomorrow."

Val shuddered out another deep breath. Gil, of course, was right. She'd stepped in where he'd told her not to. She needed to listen to him more and learn from him. "I'm sorry."

"Forget about it. Call it a five hundred dollar lesson in street training." He took a deep slug of coffee and tossed his empty cup into a trash can. "I'll give you credit for how you handled Pope, though. That was great."

"Handled *him*? He terrified me!" She sipped her coffee, burned her lips. How could Gil gulp it down so fast?

"He terrifies me, too. But you pushed his buttons. I was

guessing he'd demand a grand. Instead he caved at the five Franklins." Gil smiled at her. "You got him in his soft spot."

"Which is?"

Gil clapped a hand on her shoulder, re-igniting the tingling sensation from Pope's earlier squeeze. "Cecily."

She squinted at him. "Who the hell is Cecily?"

Gil smiled. "His little sister. Pope's very protective of her. The moment you mentioned Harkin's abuse of Antoinetta, you had him."

"Did something happen to his sister?" Val asked.

Gil's face darkened. "Word is, their old man molested her when she was seven or eight. Then he just...*disappeared*." His eyes widened. "Pope was thirteen at the time, but already a big, tough kid. If you know what I mean."

"You think he killed his father?"

Gil shrugged. "No body, no murder. And let me put it this way: nobody's filed a missing persons complaint, either. Least of all, Pope's mother."

Val's heart pounded. She'd have bet every one of her track trophies that she shared nothing in common with Pope. Yet clearly they shared a connection she'd never have guessed.

She looked back at Gil, who had a stupid grin plastered all over his face. "What's so funny?" she asked.

Gil wiped the grin off—almost. "The fact that you offered Pope five hundred bucks for something that, in retrospect, he'd probably have done for free."

She finished her coffee and glared at Gil. "Next time," she said, "would you please share information like that *before* I offer up next month's rent?" She stalked off, pretending not to hear his laughter.

***

The rest of their shift dragged on, a slow night in the city. Val stewed over the incident with The Disciples most of the night, her emotions in turmoil. Pope's warning about how she could get hurt nagged at her. Her first instinct—to ignore it as an empty warning from a street thug working an advantage over her—failed, serving only to preoccupy her more. She wanted to pry some insight out of Gil, but his teasing her over the $500 offer pissed her off, and he couldn't resist making cracks about once an hour about how much money she had to burn. As the night wore on, worry that Pope may have intended his warning as a threat took over. On top of that, she pictured Cecily, whose older brother led one of the most feared gangs in the city—and still some sick asshole abused the poor child. That thought depressed her.

It also reminded her of Antoinetta, and in turn Officer Brian Samuels, still recuperating at home from his injuries. That made her blush, which only brought back the anger. The press, the public, and even other cops—even Gil, for God's sake—made her out to be a hero, when she'd just done her job. The title felt cheap, unearned—a mere label. Her Uncle Val had *earned* that title, taking bullets to save innocent lives. Multiple times. *That's* what she called a hero.

A half hour before quitting time, they returned for their final pass on Abernethy, still barely speaking to one another. Approaching the convenience store, Gil tapped her on the shoulder. "Coffee time," he said. "I'll buy."

"No coffee for me, or I won't sleep," she said. "But make it a hot cocoa, and I'm all ears."

Taufiq greeted them inside the door with a wide grin. "My favorite policemen—er, and women," he said. "Please, have a coffee on the house."

While Gil fixed himself a fresh cup, Val slouched against the check-out counter. She entered "Clayton police shooting Samuels" into the Google search app on her phone. She tapped on the top result, a story headlined "Local Hero Recovers After Saving Girl," accompanied by a photo of a smiling Samuels in uniform.

"See?" Val said. "At least *Clayton Copwatch* understands who made the real sacrifice in this incident."

Taufiq's ever-present grin faded, and he busied himself with something behind the counter, his head bowed.

"What's the matter?" she asked him.

Taufiq didn't answer.

Val moved closer to Taufiq and pointed to the picture of Samuels. "Taufiq? Why does this upset you?"

Taufiq forced a smile. "Please, let me buy that cocoa for you." He brushed her phone aside and refused to look at her.

Val gave him a quizzical stare. "Taufiq, what's gotten into you?" she asked.

Taufiq blanched and took a step away from the counter, saying nothing.

Gil finished fixing his coffee and came up behind Val, peeking over her shoulder. A moment later he let out a low whistle. "You'll regret reading that crap," he said. "I recommend you close that now."

"Why?" Val glanced at Gil, then Taufiq, both wearing sour expressions. Curiosity took over and she skimmed through the article until she spotted her own name. What she saw made her blood boil.

> Despite the fact that Clayton P.D. had Officer Samuels' assailant surrounded, the suspect remains at large. This raises serious questions, chief among them: why did Clayton P.D. allow a rookie police officer to take the lead in the suspect's attempted—and bungled—arrest?
>
> Copwatch has also learned that the department has not disciplined the officer, Valorie Dawes, for her failures in the case. Worse, the department has recommended her for decoration and honors.
>
> Confidential sources have informed Copwatch that such cases usually result in harsh sanctions such as demotion or suspension. But Dawes's namesake uncle is a well-known local hero. Could her celebrity status be the reason for her special treatment?

"Special treatment?" Val's shriek bounced off the walls. She slammed her phone onto the counter and spun around to face Gil, bumping into him and spilling his coffee onto the floor. "I *told* you not to recommend me for that damned medal!"

Gil shook hot liquid off his fingers and swore, then moved aside so Taufiq could mop up the mess. "I told you not to pay attention to what this idiot Paul Peterson writes," he said. "That damned muckraker. He knows nothing."

"He knows I'm not a hero, and I agree with him." Val wiped the counter with a handful of napkins from the donut rack. "But saying I let that son of a bitch get away—that I'm responsible—that—"

She squeezed the wet napkins in her fist, and coffee ran over her hands back onto the counter she'd just cleaned. She stared up at Gil, then at Taufiq, both frozen in front of her.

Staring at her, open-mouthed, as if in disbelief.

Their disbelief crept over her, and she realized that the blogger had it right. She *had* let Harkins get away. And the article's criticisms skewed not only her, but also Gil, if not the entire department.

"The next time I see Paul Peterson," she said through ragged breaths, "I'm going to break him in half."

Chapter Ten

Val picked at her salad, a gourmet mish-mash of unrecognizable greens, three different colors of beets, and some sort of under-cooked grain. She searched, without success, for another few drops of the sweet red dressing that made the mixture tolerable. Beth and their two male companions had long ago finished theirs, gushing about how "inventive" and "adventurous" it was. They gobbled an entire basket of tooth-shattering breadsticks they dipped in a bowl of so-called aioli, which tasted like store-bought mayonnaise and smelled like pickled garlic. Give her a hearty pasta with red sauce or a thick, juicy cheeseburger any day over this nouveau crap.

The white-shirted waiter offered to top off her wine from the bottle chilling on the stand at her elbow, but she declined with a quiet smile. He nodded and refilled Beth's glass, then emptied the bottle with a splash in each of the two men's glasses. "Another?" he asked.

"Definitely!" said Val's date, a thick-necked jock named Brent with curly hair and the uneven skin of a long-ago battle with acne. Brent laughed and half-pretended to pour some of his wine into her glass, but she snatched it away in time. He laughed again, a braying sound that reminded her of George Bailey's goofy friend Sam Wainwright in that old Christmas movie, *It's a Wonderful Life.* Brent laughed at everything, especially his own jokes. He probably laughed during sex. Something she never wanted to confirm.

"You'd better get drinking, if you're going to keep up with us," said Beth's date, a 30-ish rake with a dark shadow of a beard and an easy smile. Joshua's bright green eyes and tousled mop of light brown hair reminded her of the actor Bradley Cooper, but without the muscles or the charm. He smiled non-stop, probably to show off his perfect teeth, which at the moment were bright red from the beets in the salad, or the wine, or from sucking someone's blood. Both men creeped Val out, though she couldn't put her finger on why.

"No thank you," Val said. "I have to work tomorrow."

"Not until five o'clock," Beth said. She gulped her own wine and waved to the waiter, already returning with a fresh bottle. "Come on, Val. Live a little."

"If I were a cop, I'd drink non-stop!" Brent's crazy laugh echoed off the walls.

Val cringed. If people like Brent became cops, she'd stay drunk all the time, too.

Then again, too many guys like Brent *did* become Clayton cops. Why weren't more of them polite, self-reflective, and respectful, like Gil?

She blushed. How inappropriate! Gil was her partner and mentor, and *maybe* friend, not someone to think about on a date with someone else.

"So, you're not going to answer me?" Brent said. "Too personal a question?"

Val blushed again. She had no idea what he'd said. "I'm sorry," she said. "What was the question?"

"Do you ever take a nip of something before work, to help you get through the stress?" Brent said. "You know, to take the edge off?"

"Of course not." What an idiot. "Strictly against policy."

"Lots of cops break the rules," Josh said. "I mean, don't they all?"

"Not Val," Beth said, drawing Josh's face close for a sloppy kiss. Val cringed. A display like that would be inappropriate at the humblest of burger joints. In a place this fancy, they could get thrown out. "Val's a good girl," Beth said. "She never breaks the rules."

"Never?" Brent said. "You wouldn't even, say, take a free meal, or fix a traffic ticket for someone?"

"Can't we talk about something else?" Val said.

"Of course," Brent said. He rested his hand on Val's thigh. She brushed it away and crossed her legs, shuddering. He frowned at her, then issued another donkey-laugh. "I guess it's a good thing we have more wine!"

The main course arrived, and the conversation shifted to how amazing everything tasted and smelled. Val's own dish, a thick, juicy slice of filet mignon, dripped brown *au jus* onto her roasted red potatoes. A trio of asparagus stalks rimmed the edges of her plate like a green frame. A light scent of garlic and green herbs mingled with the savory aromas of the charred beef. She dove in with relish, the meat melting on her tongue.

"Try mine!" Brent shoved a fork loaded with lobster, dripping with butter, near her face. "I want to try yours, too."

She shook her head, still chewing a mouthful of her filet, but Brent pushed his fork closer, poking her lips. She waved her free hand to brush it away, but she slapped the fork too hard, and the chunk of lobster landed on Joshua's lap.

"I'm so sorry!" Val grabbed her napkin and dipped it in water, offering it to Josh.

"I'll get it," Beth said, rubbing Josh's leg with her own wet napkin.

Josh grinned and spread his legs wider. "Clean me, baby!" he said, way too loud.

"Lucky dog!" Brent said, braying again. He leered at Val. "Hey, baby, why don't you knock some food my way next time? I'll get the napkin ready for you!"

Val sank into her chair. No way she'd make it through dessert.

***

On the drive home, Val squished herself into the corner behind the driver and placed her purse on the center of the back seat of Josh's car. She hoped that would create a physical barrier large enough to discourage Brent from attempting physical contact. She regretted wearing a skirt, especially without leggings, but the unseasonably warm night convinced her to go bare-legged. Jeans, or stainless-steel armor, would have worked even better.

Sure enough, Brent disappointed her once again, grabbing her thigh and leering at her. She shuddered, failing to suppress the memory of creepy Uncle Milt grabbing at her body, grinning at her. No, *no, NO*—

Val pushed Brent's hand away, but he seized the

opportunity to hold her hand in his large, clammy paw. She pushed the vomit back down her throat—luckily she hadn't eaten much at dinner—and forced a weak smile before wiggling her hand free. He grabbed her leg again, this time higher up her thigh. Dammit! She wiggled her hand under his, pushing it to the seat, but he took it as a sign that she wanted to hold hands, and wrapped his big mitt around hers. She sighed, considered pulling away again, but at least this way he wouldn't keep grabbing at her. Instead, she held on to his hand for dear life, pressing it into the seat several inches from her knee. She stared out the window, plotting her escape from the inevitable goodnight kiss.

"Dinner was amazing, wasn't it?" Beth said from the front seat when they stopped at a red light. "What's next? Music and dancing?"

"Hell yeah!" Josh said, and their lips locked yet again in a wet, sloppy smooch. Val gagged and pushed Brent away from a similar attempt. Her heart raced, and the car grew stuffy. She lowered the window a notch.

"I love the night air, too," Brent said, his face still too close to Val's. His breath reeked of garlic and beets. "Maybe we can take a walk after Josh drops us off."

"You need to buckle your seat belt." She pushed him away. "And I'm sorry, but I need to call it a night. I have to work tomorrow."

"Once a cop, always a cop, eh?" Brent said with another one of his braying laughs, but it lacked enthusiasm, and hurt showed in his eyes.

"Come on, Val," Beth said over Josh's shoulder. "Don't kill the buzz. We're all having fun here." They returned to making out, like horny teenagers.

"I'd really like to get to know you a little better." Brent freed his hand and explored her leg again.

She found her purse and set it on top of his wandering digits and wondered what species of octopus he descended from. "Perhaps we can *talk* on the drive home," she said.

"Great idea," Beth said. "Let's go to our place. I've got a great bottle of wine I've been meaning to crack open, and—"

"I'm sorry, guys, but I have a splitting headache, and I need to sleep." Val frowned at Beth, who returned an angry sneer. Too bad. Val needed out of this car and out of this date more than Beth needed another quick lay. Besides, she'd said the code words, "splitting headache," that they'd long ago established as meaning "I need out!" The two friends had *always* respected each other's needs in that department. No exceptions.

Beth sighed and patted Josh's shoulder, nodding. "I guess we need to save it for another night. Val's migraines are not a pretty sight."

Good. Val didn't get migraines, but it meant Beth heard and understood the message.

Beth and Josh chatted in quiet voices during the drive home. Val and Brent remained quiet, although he cast a few longing glances her way, and after rebuffing a few more leg-grabs, she let him hold her hand out of self-defense, fighting her revulsion.

"Here we are," Josh said, parking a half-block away. "You guys go on ahead."

Shit! "Aren't you guys coming too?"

Beth glared at her. "Josh and I need a moment to, ah, *talk*." She giggled. Josh grinned like a wolf. They'd be making out before the doors even closed.

Val sighed. Fine. It was only half a block. How much harm could he do? She kept her distance as Brent walked her to the door.

"I enjoyed meeting you tonight," Brent said. "I hope we can get together again sometime."

"We'll see." Val stopped on the dark front steps, already out of view of Josh and Beth, and wished the landlord had replaced the burnt-out bulb in the lamp. Or at least trimmed the hedges. She felt hemmed in by his size and the tight space. "I work nights...and I try to visit my niece on my off days, and...well, it was nice meeting you, too, Brent." She forced a smile and braced herself for the inevitable move.

Sure enough, the moment she dipped her hand into her purse for her keys, he wrapped his long arms around her and pulled her in close. He cocked his head to move in for a kiss, but she worked her arms inside and kept him at a harmless distance.

"I'm sorry," she lied. "My head really hurts."

He stepped back, holding her hand, and gave her a long

look. "Yeah. I'm sorry too." He leaned in closer and spoke in a whisper. "Even with migraines, I think you're a pretty sight."

She smiled at him. "Thanks," she said, patting his chest. "That's sweet of—"

And then she couldn't breathe, because he crushed her in a tight embrace, and his mouth smothered hers, his tongue slathering her lips and reeking of vinegar. She gasped for air, but that only egged him on more. He pushed her against the door, pinning her arms, grinding his body against hers. Panic rose inside her. His size, his strength, his weight, forcing himself on her, refusing to take no for an answer—

Then her training kicked in, and muscle memory took over. Her knee shot into his groin, and she freed one hand. She drove two stiff fingers into his throat, and he tumbled backwards off the steps, landing hard on the ground. Val pushed her key into the lock before he could stand. She ducked inside, but he slipped his foot inside the door before she closed it. It bounced open, and he lunged. She stepped aside and gave his back a one-handed push. He crashed face-first onto the floor, howling in pain. She landed another kick to the groin, and his howl turned into a hollow groan.

"What the fuck?" he said between gasps.

"If you aren't gone from here in two seconds, I'm calling the cops," she said, spittle spewing onto his chest. "And if you have any doubts as to what my fellow officers in blue would do to protect one of their own, please, hang out and let me educate you."

Brent's eyes widened, and he scrambled on all fours out the door.

Chapter Eleven

V al welcomed the sight of Gil the next evening, his warm smile and calm demeanor a welcome change from the poor examples of manhood she'd witnessed the night before. Her lingering soreness at him over the "$500 incident," as they called it, evaporated with his polite and non-intrusive inquiries about her days off. Gil didn't exploit their small talk to invade her space, he listened to her, he asked intelligent questions, and perhaps most important, he kept his distance from her. Handshakes and claps on the shoulder, just like with their male colleagues. Like...friends.

She could use a few friends.

"We might run into The Disciples tonight," Gil said once they'd hit the pavement to start their rounds. "Did you bring cash for Pope, in case he finds something?"

"Crap, I forgot about that." She dug into the wallet tucked inside her belt and found $50. "I need to find an ATM."

"There's one in the Quick Mart," Gil said. "And I could use some coffee."

Taufiq greeted them with warm smiles and an offer of free coffee and donuts. They followed their usual protocol of accepting only the complimentary drinks, per department policy. Gil poured while Val slid her debit card into the ATM at the back of the store.

"Dammit," she said. "I was afraid of this." She waved Gil over and showed him the screen. "The machine limits me to a $250 withdrawal. Can you lend me the difference?"

Gil laughed and brandished his own card. "I'll split the bounty with you. I insist."

She wondered if he'd noticed the low balance on the screen before he offered, and guessed not. Would Brent have been so gracious? Only if it meant getting her in the sack. Gil offered out of genuine kindness. She owed him, big time.

And not just cash. He took care of her, as a rookie trainee and as a person. A wave of gratitude washed over her. She should do something, show him how she felt. That's what a normal person would do.

Val edged toward him, but something stopped her. Wouldn't let her get closer to him. Wouldn't let her do what anyone else in her position would do: smile at him, touch him, maybe even hug him, tell him thanks.

He waited, his head cocked, as if wondering what the hell was taking her so long. "Is something wrong?" he asked.

"No, no," she said. "I, uh...forgot my PIN for a moment." She touched the screen, and it beeped at her. Dammit! In her flustered state of mind, she'd pressed the wrong button, and canceled the transaction. She groaned and went through the process again, then stepped aside to let Gil use the machine.

The bells on the store's front door jingled. The aisles screened her view, so she leaned around the well-stocked shelves to peek. A short, wiry black teen approached the counter, turning his head from side to side. She couldn't see his entire face, but he looked familiar. The young man said something to Taufiq. Taufiq nodded, rang up a purchase—and disappeared from view with a crash. The teen grabbed at the register.

"Shit!" She pulled her club from her belt. "The kid's robbing the store!"

Val dashed up the aisle, but the youth ran through the door before she reached him. She followed him out the door. Fifteen yards ahead of her, he sprinted at top speed toward the street.

"Stop! Police! Hands up!" she shouted and ran after him, but the young man ignored her, and gained another few steps on her in a matter of seconds. Val's legs churned, but he maintained his lead on her, racing down the sidewalk. She contemplated pulling out her firearm, but a half-dozen people dotted the sidewalks and traffic clogged the busy street. Too risky, and drawing the weapon would only slow her down. She ran on, hoping her conditioning would give her an advantage. But the kid was fast, and her bulky uniform and gear weighed her down.

He reached the corner and dashed into the intersection. Tires squealed, horns blared, and two cars swerved in opposite directions. Their tail-ends collided with a loud bang, spewing glass and chrome onto the street. Locked together by their rear fenders, they blocked the young man's path, and he had to run around them. Val reached them moments later and, with an athletic leap, scrambled over their hoods, landing a few steps behind the youth. She flipped her baton forward. It got tangled between his legs, and he landed on the sidewalk, hard. Bills of various denominations littered the pavement.

Val grabbed his arms and yanked them behind his back before he could recover and lifted him to his feet, surprised at how light he was. She pushed him against the brick wall of the adjacent building, cuffed him, and spun him around to see his face.

Her heart sank when she recognized him. "Dog!" she shouted over heavy breaths. "What in the hell do you think you're doing, robbing a place with two cops *inside the store*?"

Dog's eyes widened. Recognition dawned, and his head drooped. "Damn, man, I didn't see ya'll in there." He glanced up. "The money's all getting away."

Val stole a quick glance around. Sure enough, a light breeze had picked up, scattering the bills further up the street. Footsteps thudded toward her from the other direction, followed by Gil's voice, shouting something she couldn't make out.

She glared at Dog, cowering against the wall. "You stay put," she said.

Dog nodded, dropped to his knees, and folded his hands behind his neck. Val shook her head. The kid knew arrest procedure better than she did.

She gathered up her baton and as many of the loose bills as she could. Gil arrived moments later and stood guard over Dog while a few passersby helped retrieve the money.

"How in the hell did you ever catch him?" Gil asked when they'd finished.

"I got lucky," Val said. "Dog didn't count on there being traffic."

She marched Dog and the cash back to the Quick Mart while Gil tended to the two drivers who'd collided.

"Thank you, Officer Valorie!" Taufiq said when they returned. "You have rescued my store!"

"What happened?" she asked.

"He pushed me, I fell against the wall," Taufiq said. A dozen packages of cigarettes remained scattered on the floor behind the counter. "Then he grabbed the money and ran."

They counted the cash, a little over $200. "You're lucky," she said to Dog. "You're under the felony threshold. But you assaulted Mr. Sharkar. He's within his rights to press charges against you."

Dog hung his head, tears streaming down his cheeks. "I don't understand," he said. "I didn't use no gun or nothing."

"You think that makes it all right?" Val shook her head. "What were you thinking, Dog?"

He shrugged. "I don't know. I never done this before." He scraped his toe on the floor. "I'm just trying to make Deacon."

"Deacon?" Val lifted his chin and met his eyes, read the fear and confusion there. His meaning dawned on her. "It's a rank, right? In The Disciples?"

Dog nodded and sniffled.

"It's part of your initiation?" she asked in a soft voice.

Dog nodded again. "Gotta make a grand against The Man."

She exchanged glances with Taufiq. "Does Mr. Sharkar look like The Man to you?"

Dog looked at Taufiq and toed the floor again. "I shouldn'a told you that. Pope gonna *kill* me."

"For telling me your initiation rules?"

Dog nodded, a nervous, vigorous twitch of the head.

An idea dawned. She should run it past Gil, but he hadn't returned from the fender-bender yet. She pulled Taufiq aside. "You okay? You're not hurt?"

Taufiq shook his head. "Startled, but I am fine."

"And you got your money back." Another nod. "Listen. You're within your rights to file a complaint, but we could do some good here—for the neighborhood, and for you. If we charge him, your store will remain a target. But if we work this right, The Disciples could become allies—for both of us. Are you willing to give it a try?"

Taufiq thought a moment, then nodded. "If it works, it will

be worthwhile," he said. "And I trust you."

"Am I going to jail?" Dog asked when she returned to him.

"There might be another option," she said, "if you'll help us."

Dog's eyes widened. "What I gotta do?"

She leaned closer. "Pope and I need to talk."

***

Gil pushed a still-cuffed Dog into the back seat of their cruiser outside the store and shut the door behind him. "Come on, get in," he said to Val, standing next to him. "We need to get him booked. Did Taufiq give you a statement?"

Val shook her head. "Let me drive," she said in a low voice.

"Sure." Gil tossed her the keys, crossed his arms, and squinted at her. "You're up to something."

She leaned closer. "My own version of community policing." She filled him in on the conversation they'd had in the store.

"You're crazy," he said when she finished. "We can't let him walk. Gibson will have your ass in a sling if he finds out."

She opened the driver's side door. "Just trust me, okay?"

Gil scowled, but he slid in on the passenger's side. He picked up the radio mic. "I told HQ that we were bringing him in. I'd better alert them to the change in plans."

"Not yet," Val said. "Wait until after we meet with Pope."

Gil smiled. "Ah, so some version of sanity prevails." He replaced the mic in its holder.

They reached The Disciples' corner two minutes later. As usual, a trash barrel provided warmth to a small circle of men. Gil and Val escorted Dog to the edge of the lot, each holding one arm by the biceps.

Cardinal Thomas greeted them with a humorless smile. "Returning our lost pet? We hadn't even gotten around to posting signs in the neighborhood." He reached for Dog, but the two cops pulled him back a step.

"We need to talk to Pope," Val said.

The Cardinal's eyes widened. "Cops don't usually hold hostages," he said, "except in jail cells."

"First time for everything," Gil said. "Come on, where's your boss?"

Cardinal Thomas's nose flared, but he kept his voice even.

"Pope's got an appointment."

"Fine," Val said, exchanging glances with Gil. "He can make another appointment to visit Dog downtown sometime." They tugged Dog back toward their cruiser.

"Wait." Thomas signaled to a young runner with a single gold loop earring, and the kid disappeared into a dark alley at the back of the lot.

"You have two minutes," Gil said without breaking stride. "Then we drive."

"What the fuck?" Thomas stepped toward them. "You think we just wait around here for you to show up so we can have a damned meeting? We got shit to do too, you know."

"Yeah, you guys are crazy busy today," Val said, waving toward the group warming their hands.

"You either produce Pope in two minutes, or Dog spends the rest of his teen years getting ass-fucked by guys your size," Gil said. "Your call."

"Hey, say what?" Dog said, almost a yelp.

Val leaned over to Gil. "Was that really necessary?" she said in a whisper. He shrugged in response.

Thomas fumed a moment, then held up one finger. He stepped away and made a quick call on his cell phone in a low voice. Ninety seconds later, a car pulled up behind the cruiser. Pope emerged from the passenger side, sat on the hood, and lit a cigarette.

"There's your meeting," Thomas said, disgust in his voice.

Gil shook his head. "He ain't *here* yet." He checked his watch. "Twenty seconds."

"Gil," Val said. "Come on. We can meet them partway."

"But we can't—"

"Gil, dammit, don't fuck this up for me!"

He glared at her, then let go of Dog. "Fine. Your circus, your clowns." He followed Val and Dog toward Pope.

When they got to ten feet away, Pope stood and crushed the cigarette under his heel. "S'up, Dog? Copsky?" He paused and grinned at Val. "And Copette?"

"Your boy screwed up," Val said. "Tried to relieve my friend Taufiq's Quick Mart of two hundred bucks. Didn't spot us hanging around in back. Right, Dog?"

Dog hung his head, toeing the pavement.

Pope scowled at him. "Dumbass," he said. "You know better'n that."

"Dog's going down for robbery and aggravated assault," Val said. "Unless..."

Pope smiled. "Ah. Now we get to the point. What's the deal?"

"Two things," Val said. "One. You owe us some information."

Pope shrugged. "What's the other thing?"

Val checked in with Gil, who lifted his shoulders an inch and let them fall. *Your circus, your clowns.* She took a deep breath. "I want you to protect Taufiq's store. In fact, nobody pulls crap like this in the entire neighborhood. Anyone tries, they catch hell from you."

"From *us?*" Pope laughed. "You want us to do cop work?"

"If you want to call it that."

"That's a good one." Pope shook his head. "It don't add up. You know we got, ah, *business* to do."

"Yeah, yeah," Val said. "So change your business model. No more knocking off convenience stores or roughing up the neighbors to earn an earring. Find something else that doesn't scare the entire neighborhood from walking on their own street."

Pope huffed. "Bullshit."

"Fine," Val said. "Come on, Dog. Let's go find you a public defender." She pushed him toward the cruiser.

"Wait, wait." Pope rubbed his chin and glanced at Thomas, who had edged closer, with a small crowd of Disciples behind him. "You're saying you'll let Dog walk on this if we help you?"

Val tugged Dog to a stop. "This one time, yes."

Pope signaled to Cardinal, and the two conferred a moment in low voices. Cardinal Thomas shook his head, arms crossed, anger lining his face. "I get it," Pope said at one point, "but dude, this is Dog we're talking about." Thomas reacted with more angry shakes of his head, but his body language signaled defeat. Finally, the two man-hugged and approached the cruiser together. "Deal," Pope said, reaching for Dog.

Val stepped between them. "First, the information on Richard Harkins."

"On who?"

"The guy we showed you a picture of the other day." She handed him another copy. "Any leads on him?"

Pope tapped the picture. "This white boy's gone, man. High-tailed it down to Alabama or one of them redneck places. Nobody's seen him in almost a week."

"Which redneck place, specifically?" Val asked.

Pope shrugged and lit another cigarette. "I'm working on it."

Gil stepped forward next to Val, dragging Dog along with him. "And you'll tell us the moment you find out? *Without* us having to chase you down and set up a damned appointment?"

Pope gazed at Dog through a cloud of blue smoke. Dog glanced up once and resumed his toe-digging in the gravel. Pope blew a hole in the fog and nodded. "Word." He waved a Disciple over wearing a single gold earring. "Gunner. Where's that cousin of yours live, the dancer?"

"Bay Saint Louis. In Mississippi."

Pope inhaled on his butt again. "She seen him there once before. She's looking for him. If she sees him, you'll know."

Val side-eyed Gil, who tilted his head down once. She unlocked Dog's cuffs, her heart pounding. Gibson might give her a tongue-lashing or worse, but she had to trust her instincts.

"Gentlemen," she said, "we have a deal."

Chapter Twelve

The next evening, as Val dressed in the women's locker room, Brenda Petroni tapped her on the shoulder. "Travis wants to jaw at ya," she said, pulling off her own Kevlar vest.

"Sergeant Blake?" Val paused while buttoning up her blues. "What about?"

"You tell me," Brenda said. "You in trouble for some reason?" she asked.

"Not that I know of," Val said, but doubt crept into her voice.

"Hey, how about drinks tomorrow with Shannon?" Brenda said. "We haven't talked in a while."

"You got it." Val tugged on her shoes, her mind racing. As squad commander, Travis Blake served as Gibson's right-hand man at the precinct, dealing with staff assignments and discipline. Had Gil ratted her out on the Dog situation? Her fingers shook, unable to create a knot in the laces.

She knocked on Blake's open office door moments later and spied him cramming a thick file into the top drawer of a tall metal cabinet. Sergeant Travis Blake was a heap of a man, generous in all proportions. He stood at least 6'5" even when he slouched, which was rare. His body resembled a whiskey barrel, and he had arms and legs like an elephant, with ham-like fists. Even his eyes and nose were large. He stared at Val, his gray eyes matching the curly swatch closely cropped to his watermelon-sized head.

"Close the door and have a seat," he said in a gravelly voice.

She did as he ordered and waited, hands folded on her lap. He sat behind his own desk, his eyebrows arched, a frown on his face.

"So, we got a citizen complaint," he said, and took a deep breath. He bent one leg and rested his ankle on his knee, tapped his thumb, waiting.

"About me?" she said when she couldn't bear the silence any longer. Such a brilliant deduction. At least it wasn't from Gil. Her mind raced, inventorying names of people who may have complained. Not Dog, but maybe one of The Disciples? Antoinetta? Her mother, or her aunt? God forbid, Taufiq might have changed his mind, and reneged on the deal. Gil's warning of what Gibson would do if he found out echoed in her head, and her heart pounded. "From whom?" she asked after an eternity.

"You know a guy named Davenport?" Blake asked. Tapping, tapping.

Davenport? Definitely a last name, but not Taufiq's or Antoinetta's, and probably not Dog's. But it sounded familiar. She'd heard it recently...where? "Should I?" she asked.

Blake harrumphed, unbent his knee, and let it drop to the floor with a thump as he leaned over his desk. "Don't you learn the last names of the men you date?"

"Oh, crap." Her body went limp in the chair. Not *that* jerk. "Brent Davenport complained about our date to you?"

"He said you threatened him and used excessive force in response to a 'friendly gesture,' which I take to mean an attempted goodnight kiss," Blake said. "Did you really kick him in the nuts for that?"

Unbelievable. For a moment, she regretted not kicking him harder. "It was more than a peck on the cheek." Val's face grew hot and her voice more animated. "He crushed my body against the wall and tried to break into my house. But what the hell? Why is this any of the department's business?"

"It's not, if that's what happened," Blake said. "But if a citizen complains, we have to investigate." He scribbled on a form, folded it in half, and shoved it inside a folder. "Consider it investigated."

"Thank you, sir." Val stood and headed toward the door.

"Dawes?"

Val paused and caught Blake's glance. "Yes, sir?"

Blake cocked his head with a sigh and a lazy half-smile.

"Try not to beat anyone up today, okay?"

"Yes, sir," she said. "I'll try."

"I mean it, Dawes," he said. "I'd hate to see the good work you're doing out there get screwed up over some ass-grabbing punk."

Heat flooded her face again. She took a deep breath and stepped closer to the sergeant. "Are you saying I should turn the other cheek?" she said. "No pun intended."

Travis smothered a smirk. "How about we put this *behind* you?" he quipped and burst out laughing. "Sorry, I couldn't resist."

Val, despite herself, chuckled along with him, but her mirth quickly subsided. Try as she might, she couldn't let this pass. "So, Sarge. Is the department saying women's bodies are fair game, and that we have to put up with this crap from whatever bozo can't keep his hands to himself?"

Blake started to respond, then shook his head. "I get your point, Dawes. Just...keep your responses in proportion to the crime, okay?"

Val smiled. "That, Sergeant, is exactly what I've been doing." She slipped through the door before Blake could respond.

***

Gil stood waiting for her at their cruiser in the parking garage, leaning against the driver's door with his arms folded. "I want to discuss something with you," he said when she got within earshot.

"Not you, too," she said.

He cocked his head in surprise, then moved closer and lowered his voice. "Something you want to tell me?"

She exhaled a heavy breath, tossed her hands in the air. "Blake called me in for getting too rough with that Brent guy I told you about. It appears the creepy mouth-breather filed a formal complaint."

"Why?" Gil asked in mock innocence. "The little shit doesn't enjoy getting kicked in the balls?" He shook his head and clapped his hands on her shoulders. "The punk had it coming. And if you need me to talk to Travis about it—"

"No," she said, wiggling out of the near-embrace, "but thanks. What've you got?"

Gil kept his hands spread at her sides for a moment, as if wondering what to do with them, then re-crossed his arms. "We're not covering much ground, walking the neighborhood together," he said. "I think we need a change of tactics."

Val's face fell, along with her heart. "You mean driving? I thought the whole point was to mix it up, be present on the street, build relationships. How can we—"

"No, no," Gil said, laughing. "Slow down. I suggest we split the beat. That way, we can cover twice as much territory."

She considered the idea and didn't like it much. "Aren't you're supposed to be training me? How can we do that if we're in different places?"

He waved at the air, as if swatting a fly. "You've shown me everything I need to see. You know procedure, you have good instincts, and you relate to the community better than I do. But I get your point. How about we try it for two hours, then get together for coffee and share notes? Any questions you have, you can ask me then. I'm sure there'll be some 'teachable moments', as they say."

"I thought policy was to work in pairs," she said. "For safety reasons."

"My plan was, we'd patrol parallel streets, a few blocks apart. Stay in touch by radio. Any weird things come up, we'll be close enough to help each other."

"Well, it will help us maintain a broader presence in more places." She smiled at him. "Why not? What could go wrong?"

Gil smiled and tapped her on the bicep. "That's the spirit."

As they drove to their usual parking spot, they discussed which streets each one would cover. Something about this new arrangement bothered her, but she couldn't put her finger on it. She shrugged it off as a matter of being over-cautious and did her best to put on a cheerful face for Gil.

***

Gil and Val settled into a booth at a pastry shop a few hours later. Heavenly aromas of baking confections and fresh-brewed coffee filled the air. Val finally understood why so many people believed cops spent all their waking hours in places like this.

"So, did you miss me?" Gil asked her with a slight smile.

Val dunked a half-crescent of powdered goodness into her light-brown brew and swooned, her free hand on her heart. "I can't stand being so alone!" she said in mock despair. "Thank you for rescuing me, oh knight in shining armor!"

Gil laughed and stole the other half of her pastry. "That's my reward," he said when she protested. "Besides, I have more places I can hide these calories." He patted his belly.

Val snorted. "I have more body fat in my little finger than you carry on your whole body. Give me that cinnamon twist!" She snagged a chunk of the golden-brown confection from his napkin and shoved it into her mouth. "Fair's fair," she tried to say, but it came out as "frumphs furmng." Or something like that.

"Anyway," he said, guarding the rest of his food, "I think that splitting up worked well. Don't you agree?"

She sipped her coffee, finally able to swallow. "Some people asked if you were sick or something."

"You set them straight, I take it?" He blew on his coffee.

She nodded. "I told them you had a mistress. They were horrified that you'd cheat on your wife *and* me."

His eyes widened in mock horror. "I would *never* cheat on my wife," he said.

"Only because you don't ha—wait. So you *would* cheat on me?" She swatted him on the arm with a playful punch. "Brat."

"Val, I have to confess." His shoulders sagged. "I...I *have* been seeing other policemen."

"Say it isn't so!" she said in a Southern accent.

"It'll never happen again," he said. "Until tomorrow."

"That settles it. I'm never leaving your side again." She scooted around and sat on the bench next to Gil, pressing him into the corner. Confusion crossed his face, and his arm hung in the air over her shoulders, as if he couldn't figure out where to put it.

Then Val realized what she'd done, and how things would look to a casual observer: a young female cop cozying up to her partner in a tiny booth. The touch of his leg and body against hers sent shudders down her spine. She coughed, paused, and snagged the final bite of his donut, and scooted back to her side of the table.

Gil remained in the corner, still frozen in place, staring at her while she devoured his treat. He relaxed and slid back to the center of his bench, shaking his body like a dog shedding water.

"So, I guess we'll, ah, continue to split the beat?" he asked.

"Yes, yeah, you bet," Val said with a little too much enthusiasm. "Let's go." She grabbed her coffee and scooted out the door, not waiting for him to follow.

She walked down Abernethy, her leg still tingling where it had pressed against Gil's.

Tingled, in a good way.

A way she rarely—if ever—had felt before with a man.

***

Val sipped her almost-untouched Chardonnay and wondered why she'd ordered the same damned wine again that, in truth, she didn't care for. It tasted bitter and musty, like an old oak barrel that had sat out in the rain for several years. She made a mental note to ask for something different next time. If the waiter ever returned to her booth.

She pushed the wine aside and checked the time. Shannon and Brenda must have gotten caught in traffic. She opened her news browser and scanned the headlines. Her finger hovered over the "Close" button, but a headline link at the bottom of her screen gave her pause.

Sex Offender Continues to Elude Clayton's Finest

Her blood pressure rose. She knew she shouldn't give in to the click-bait story title, but on the off chance it might contain new information the department hadn't uncovered, she had to check. She clicked on the link, hoping against hope that she was wrong about the writer's identity.

The byline appeared on screen and she sighed. No such luck. This was the "work," if she could call it that, of Paul Peterson of Clayton Copwatch.

She scanned the piece, a rehash of facts cherry-picked from old news reports to make Clayton P.D. look bad. Toward the bottom, under a section entitled "Analysis," she read:

> Clayton police continue to be stymied in their search for the suspect, identified by confidential sources as Richard Harkins, a

vicious thug reputed to have victimized several women and young girls in the city, particularly in the Abernethy District.

Critics say it's easy to see why. "Not when they put rookie cops on the case," said a source who asked to remain anonymous. "CPD sent a woman half his size in to arrest him. What were they thinking?"

Val scrolled down to read the comments. Big mistake.

What, indeed?
- **ClaytonLifer**

Yah they send a teeny woman cop in to defend us but the South End gets big guys. No surprise who gets more crime.
- **WrongSideofTrax**

If Herkns was raping men they'd have the best and britest on the case beleeve you me.
- **DancesWithBoys**

Val seethed and slammed her phone onto the table. She grabbed her wine glass and chugged its contents, choking on its bitter aftertaste. Definitely needed to switch to red.

"The Sisterhood of the Traveling Gunbelt is here!" Brenda Petroni appeared at the end of the booth, dressed in a dark blue blazer, a pastel blue button-down blouse, and black slacks. Behind her, Shannon O'Reilly appeared, her strawberry blonde hair looking wind-blown, her cheeks red, and a motorbike helmet under one arm. Brenda signaled to the waiter and the two women slid into the booth across from Val.

"Bad day at the office?" Shannon asked, pointing at Val's empty glass. "Or are we that late?"

Val tapped her phone. "I went browsing where I shouldn't have again, and I don't mean porn sites," she said.

"Not that blogger again," Shannon said.

"We warned you not to pay any attention to that idiot," Brenda said. She called out to the waiter, "Two merlots over here, please."

"Three." Val pushed her wine glass to the end of the table. "Sorry, I can't help it. I'm like a moth drawn to flame. I can't resist."

"More like a train wreck," Shannon said. "Believe me, that Peterson jerk sheds no light on anything."

"I don't understand where he gets his information," Val said. "Who feeds him this crap?"

"Let me see it," Brenda said. She scanned the article on Val's phone and tsk'd. "The old boys' network is up to their tricks again." She showed it to Shannon, who cursed.

"They did the same thing when I came in," Shannon said. "Certain men in the department get bent out of shape at the prospect of women moving up in the ranks—or even women getting hired as patrol officers. It's a constant battle."

"You're saying he's getting this misinformation from within the department?" Val asked. Color drained from her face. She'd assumed Peterson got his made-up facts from know-nothings on the street, or from his imagination. She'd never considered that her own comrades in blue would undermine her.

"Be careful who you talk to," Brenda said, thanking the waiter for their fresh round of wine. She passed a glass to each of her companions and raised her own in a toast: "To cops we can trust."

"AKA, women," Shannon said, and they clinked their glasses together.

The merlot tasted chocolaty and smooth, far better than the fruity Chardonnay. "I hope we can trust more than just each other," Val said, feeling the wine's warmth in her throat. "I'd like to think I can trust my partner."

"Gil's one of the best you'll find," Brenda said. "At the opposite end of the spectrum, Pops is an antique. We should have put him out to pasture a century ago. Gibson is all right, but no saint. Blake too—wait, why that face?"

Val blushed and tried to hide behind her wine glass. "Travis didn't impress me as the most progressive of men in our last conversation," she said, and recounted their recent meeting.

At the end of the story, Shannon shrugged. "That almost qualifies him as a feminist in this department," she said. "My sergeant asked me out a dozen times in my first year—and he was married. I had to wear Kevlar in my pants to stop him from grabbing my ass all the time."

"At least Travis took your side on the complaint," Brenda said. "That's more than most would have done."

"But who's talking to Peterson?" Val sipped her merlot again. She'd definitely stick to reds from now on. "I can't imagine it's the detectives on the case. They came off looking pretty bad."

"You can eliminate them, and the women in the department," Shannon said, twirling the stem of her wine glass on the table. "That narrows it down to...oh, three hundred people."

"The bottom line is, you can't worry about what the idiots in the press say, especially on the Internet," Brenda said. "Nobody reads their stuff anyway."

"But someone in the department is trying to discredit me," Val said. "Shouldn't I be worried about that?"

Shannon and Brenda exchanged glances. "All I can tell you," Brenda said, "is to trust few, and talk even less. And..." She and Shannon raised their half-empty glasses, waiting for Val to follow suit. "When in doubt, come to us. We're always here for you."

"Hear, hear," Shannon said.

"Likewise," Val said. "I've got your backs, too." They clinked glasses and downed the rest of their drinks in unison.

Chapter Thirteen

Two nights later, Val hurried along the boarded-up storefronts of Jacobs Street. She apologized mentally to the various regulars that, tonight, she didn't have time to stop and chat up. She should have walked this stretch over an hour ago. Not that anyone kept her on a clock, and Gil had warned her not to get too "regular" on her beat or she'd lose the element of surprise. But on this warm Indian summer night in late October, people came out in numbers. She'd made several stops and spoken longer than usual with "the clientele" on both sides of the trouble coin: shopkeepers, tavern bouncers, loitering teens, street musicians, and homeless old men carrying hand-drawn cardboard signs pitching for money. All part of good community policing.

"How goes it?" Gil's voice crackled over the radio.

"I'm a little behind," Val said. "Lots of people out. You?"

"Slow over here. I'm jealous. Coffee in fifteen?"

Before she could respond, a noise about 100 feet away interrupted her. A woman's voice, or a young girl's, leaked out of an apartment window of a mixed-use building, two stories above a street-level grocery. "Stop, please! You're hurting me!"

"Shut up, bitch!" a man's voice replied. Next came the sound of skin slapping skin, and a cry of pain. Definitely a young girl.

"You need help up there?" Val's hand rested on her baton, her other hand on the radio mic.

No response. A light flickered on. Glass shattered, and the light blinked off. "Where the fuck do you think *you're* going, bitch?" a man snarled. Another scream, this time, muffled.

"What's going on?" Val's heart raced. "Come to the window, mister. Let me see you. And her."

The silhouetted figure of a man darkened the opening for a moment, then darted away. "Shh!" someone said from inside. "See what you've done?" The man's voice.

"Bring the girl to the window." The pounding in Val's chest made it hard to hear. "I want to make sure she's all right."

Again, no response. Val moved closer.

"Leave me al—mmph!" The girl's shout disappeared, as if swallowed up by a blanket.

"Suspected 428 on Jacobs and Leach," Val barked into her microphone. "Backup requested. Gil, how close are you?" Val hustled to the entrance of the apartment building, a solid metal door next to an electronic security panel. No way to bust in there. She pushed several call buttons, but no one picked up or buzzed her in. Candy wrappers fluttered on top of a pile of cigarette butts in the corner of the entryway.

"I'll be there in less than five," Gil said over the radio. "Is that the Jacobs Arms?"

Val read the nameplate over the security panel. "Affirmative. You know it?"

"There's a rear exit and a fire escape," he said, out of breath. "We'll need to cover the exits. Dispatch, where's that backup?"

Another scream erupted from the third floor, along with the sound of fabric tearing. Val moved away from the building to get a better view. Shadows flitted across the window, including what looked like a man pulling the hair of a much smaller girl, then pushing her down.

"Leave her alone!" Val shouted.

The man's response: More yelling. Another scream, from the girl.

Val's blood boiled. Jesus, this guy had balls.

But he wouldn't when she got done with him.

"Hello?" An old woman's voice crackled over the speaker. "Is someone there?

"Police!" Val shouted. "Responding to a domestic disturbance. Please, buzz me in!"

The lock clicked, and Val yanked open the door. Odors of stale tobacco smoke, spicy food, and urine seared her eyes and made her gag. Fighting for breath, she raced up the stairs two at a time. She arrived at the third-floor landing in time to spot a dark-haired man in a yellow tank top and jeans emerging from a doorway midway down the hall.

"Stop! Police!" Val shouted, reaching for her weapon. The man glanced at Val and ran the opposite direction, disappearing down a staircase at the other end of the hall. He carried an object in his right hand—something dark and metallic.

She broke into a run, heading toward the stairs he'd descended. A girl of eleven or twelve stuck her head out the door he'd just exited. Tears streamed down her cheeks, and her dark, tangled hair draped over her torn blue blouse. The girl wiped blood from her lip. "He—he has a gun," she said, sniffling.

"Are you all right?" Val slowed up as she approached the door.

The girl broke into tears. "He...tried to..." She pulled the door part way closed and tugged her blouse down to hide her underwear. "I didn't let him, and he...got mad." More sobs.

Val's muscles tensed, and her whole body shook. *Another one!* "Stay inside!" she shouted and pulled the door shut. She dashed to the stairs, following the man down. He had already passed the second floor, on his way to the first. "Freeze!" she shouted.

The man looked up at her—a mistake. He stumbled, missed the last few stairs, and tumbled to the landing between floors. He lurched back onto his feet and continued down the final flight of steps. Val gained ground on him, but not before he burst through the heavy metal door into the alley behind the building.

"Stop! Police!" she yelled after him. The man ran through the alley toward Jacobs Street. She grabbed her radio off her belt. "In pursuit of 428 suspect fleeing southbound from the Jacobs Arms," she puffed into the mike. "Suspect is Asian male in his thirties, five-eight to five-ten, one-sixty to one-eighty, and armed. Request backup, stat! Gil, where are you?"

She clipped the radio onto her belt. Calling in had slowed her, and the suspect had gained ground. She gritted her teeth, put her head down, and charged harder. Even harder than when she'd run to Antoinetta's, or when she'd chased Dog. Her heart pounded, but she felt good. It had been a long time since she'd run this hard. Not since the 440 relay at the regional meet a year ago. Her lungs ached, sucking in air.

The suspect looked over his shoulder and right-angled across the street, dodging cars. She followed on a diagonal, closing the gap to fifty feet, then forty. The man turned onto a side street. She followed. Thirty feet. He had to make choices. That slowed him down. All she had to do was run.

He turned again. She recognized the street. An alley—a dead end. Apartments with locked, secured entry doors loomed over street-level shops, all closed. He had trapped himself.

She followed him part way into the alley and hit a tidal wave of unwelcome scents emanating from dumpsters lining the walls on all three sides. She halted twenty feet from him, unholstered her revolver, and flicked off the safety. "Freeze!" she yelled. "Hands up! Now!"

He stopped, still facing away from her. As if in slow motion, his left hand drifted to his side. His right remained shielded from her.

"Turn around! Face me!" She edged closer, her weapon aimed at the center of his body mass.

His body twisted, achingly slow, counter-clockwise, his hands spread wide. For a moment his right hand ducked out of view. When it came back into view, it held something dark. His arm jerked forward, supported by his left. Something whizzed past her head just before the loud "pop" reached her ears. A memory from academy training flashed in her mind: *Bullets travel faster than sound.*

Instinct, training, and reflexes kicked in. She dropped to one knee, still aiming, both hands steady, supporting the weapon. He moved his arm, following her path, pointed again at her—

She fired.

A red blotch appeared in the center of his chest. Redness sprayed the dumpsters along the brick wall behind him. His body slammed into the dumpster, his arms wide, his feet forward but his weight supported by the metal wall behind him. He stared at her a moment, shock fading from his eyes. His head lolled to one side, his legs buckled, and he tumbled face-down onto the street.

And he stayed there.

Val remained in her crouch for two or three seconds, still holding her right arm in position with her left, both hands shaking. Voices murmured somewhere in the background. "Did she just shoot that guy?" said a man's voice. "Is he dead?" asked someone else. The voices seemed far away. Recorded, like in a movie.

A woman's voice above her broke her frozen stance. "You got him!" the woman yelled. "Good shot!"

She spotted the aging matron two stories up. "I saw the whole thing!" the woman yelled. "He shot at you first. I'll testify!"

Val gave her a slow wave with her left hand and lowered her gun toward the fallen man. She stood, gravity tugging at her body, numbness washing over her. More voices, words she could not recognize.

Sirens wailed, and grew louder. Val trudged toward him. She knew before checking his pulse that he was dead.

She took a deep breath. Siren-blaring cruisers pulled up, doors opened and slammed shut. Shouting voices, most of them male. Gil's among them, asking if she was all right.

She felt more than all right. She reholstered her weapon, staring at the man's lifeless body. The pervert who'd attacked a young, helpless girl. He'd tried to rape her, and would have had Val not happened by. *Fucking child molester.*

She tried, and failed, to suppress the exhilaration swelling in her chest.

Got the bastard.

It felt good.

Too good.

PART 2

Harsh Reality

Chapter Fourteen

Val sat through endless hours of grilling under the command post canopy set up at the scene of the shooting with detectives, Internal Affairs representatives, and police union stewards. She ignored the shouted questions from reporters who snuck in too close when the officers securing the area let their guard down. She recognized few faces or voices, from the police side or the press. In particular, she did not spot the unwelcome presence of Paul Peterson.

Val sat numb throughout, repeating the same phrases to nearly identical questions: yes, he was armed, and shot at her first. No, she saw no other way to subdue him. Yes, she followed him alone, without backup. Yes, she and Gil had split up for a bit. No, she hadn't met the man before.

Gil remained absent from the command post for the initial two hours. During a brief break, he sat by her, and set a cup of coffee on a nearby folding table.

"Can't we do this at the precinct?" she asked.

Gil shook his head in sympathy. "Trust me," he said, waving off the plainclothes detectives standing a few feet away. "There'll be more discussion there, and a mountain of paperwork. But don't worry. I'll help you as best I can."

"More?" Her head ached, like someone had split it open with an ax. "By my count, everyone in the department has asked me the same questions at least twice. Who's left?"

Gil frowned and counted off on his fingers. "Gibson for one, and Travis, for sure. And probably half the guys who've already talked to you."

"Why?" Her head weighed a hundred pounds. She could barely support it, even with her elbows on the table.

"First, politics," Gil said. "They have to put on a circus

here to show the public how much grief you're going through. Clayton's come under fire in recent years for police-involved shootings, and the press is hungry for drama."

"Yikes. What's the other reason?"

"To see if your story stays consistent, and that it lines up with mine," Gil said. "That's why I they haven't allowed me in here. They want to make sure we're not colluding."

"Why would I lie about this?" She sipped the bitter, lukewarm coffee and winced. Still, she needed the caffeine. "I mean, for God's sake. I could have gotten killed."

Gil sighed. "Not every shooting is as clean as this one," he said. "Don't worry. You'll be fine."

"When you tell me not to worry, I worry more," she said. At least she hoped that's what she said. She could barely hear her own voice with the incessant blaring of sirens every time a cruiser, ambulance, or first responder vehicle moved more than a foot in any direction.

"You didn't have dinner," he said. "I'll get you something."

"No, I'm fine." Val finished her coffee, and her stomach boiled. Maybe she'd turned down Gil's kindness too soon. "Unless you're getting a bite for yourself...?"

"I'm starved," he said, nodding. "I'll pick us up a couple of meatball subs." He stood to leave.

She held up her hand to stop his exit, leaned closer to him, and spoke in a whisper. "Gil," she asked, "am I in trouble?"

Gil wagged his head sideways and exhaled a noisy breath. He spoke full voice and seemed unconcerned that the detectives might overhear. "Shootings are always a big deal, but particularly for a rookie who hasn't finished her training period. One damn week later and we'd have at least cleared that milestone." He lowered his voice and spoke through still lips. "Plus, there's that Davenport complaint."

"What does that have to do with anything?" she said, her heart racing.

Gil pretended to sip his coffee and murmured, "Another violent incident...doesn't look good." He spoke louder. "We'll take care of the paperwork later, at the station. Someone from IA will help you with it."

"Thanks." She glanced at the plainclothes cops, who chatted amongst themselves. "What about the Dog thing?" she said. "Doesn't that show I'm not violent by nature?"

"Ix-nay on the og-Day." He glanced around and raised his voice. "Looks like the next member of the Spanish Inquisition is coming. I'll get you that sandwich." He stood and reached out his right hand to her.

She met his gaze and accepted the handshake. He held on an extra moment, and a boatload of tension flowed out of her. She clasped harder and pleaded with her eyes: Please stay.

He shook his head, his mouth in a line. Squeezed her hand again. Then he left her to her thoughts.

When the interviews finally ended around 10:00 p.m., a plainclothes officer from Internal Affairs drove her to the station. She'd expected another grilling from him, but he maintained his silence, and she gave silent thanks for that. She'd hoped Gil could drive her, but understood why they wouldn't allow it.

As Gil predicted, Lieutenant Gibson and Sergeant Blake were waiting for her at the precinct, both looking like they hadn't slept in weeks.

"How are you feeling, Dawes?" Gibson asked after they'd taken seats around the small table in his office.

"Like shit," she said. "Begging the Lieutenant's pardon for my language."

Gibson smiled and waved it off. "I expected worse, given the circumstances. Are you injured?"

Val shook her head, surrendering a weak smile. "Physically I'm fine, but my heart and soul are on fire. I can't believe this happened."

"What did happen?" Blake said. "I mean, we know you chased and shot the perp. From all accounts it appears to be a clean killing. But walk us through this. What got this whole thing started?"

"I heard a woman—a girl—screaming for help in the Jacobs Arms," she said. "I yelled up to ask what was wrong, and the man—"

"Alfred Takura," Blake said.

"Excuse me?"

"Takura. That's the perp's name," Blake said. "You'll want to start using it when you talk to people. It makes you appear less...impersonal."

"Right. Mr. Takura—"

"Did you know him?" Gibson asked.

Val took a breath, counted to three. How was she supposed to tell her story if they kept interrupting? "No, not before...no. I didn't."

"Go on," Gibson said.

"Mr. Takura claimed to be her father and was punishing her for misbehaving. The girl contradicted him, saying she wasn't his daughter. I heard her scream and say he was hurting her."

"So, you went inside? Without calling for backup?" Blake asked, exchanging glances with Gibson. "Where was your partner?"

Val's heart pounded in her ears, and she had trouble drawing a breath. "We—he was a few blocks away. We were splitting up the beat—"

"Aren't you still in training?" Gibson asked in a sharp voice. He turned to Blake. "Is this standard procedure in your shop? Because if so—"

"Absolutely not," Blake said. "I'll talk to Kryzinski. Go on, Dawes."

Val's hands shook, and she folded them together in front of her to still them. "Where was I?"

"You entered the building, alone," Gibson said. "Then what happened?"

Val took a deep breath, gathering her thoughts. "Mr. Takura ran for it before I reached the apartment—"

"You were certain you had the right apartment?" Gibson asked in an even tone. Not accusing. Just asking.

"I—well—I was at the time," Val said. "Anyway, the girl stuck her head out the door and said he'd tried to rape her, and that he had a gun. He—"

"She said that? In so many words?" Blake asked. More accusingly.

Val sighed, fought to remember what she'd said. "Maybe not in those exact words," she said. "But her blouse was torn, and—well, I'm a hundred percent sure about the gun, and that it was the right apartment. What does any of that matter?"

"Just answer the questions, Dawes," Blake said. Gibson frowned at him, gave his head a subtle shake. Blake shifted in his seat, his face flushed, and softened his tone. "So you chased him?"

"Yes. He ran out of the building and into a dead-end alley. I ordered him to freeze, but he got a shot off. After that, I just...reacted, I guess."

"Did they find Takura's gun on the scene?" Gibson asked.

Blake nodded. "It's being analyzed. Pretty sure it was fired."

Gibson reached both hands across the table to Val. She hesitated, then took his hands in hers. Blake added his to the mix a moment later.

"You need to file some reports," Gibson said. "Travis will help you. Tell the story just like you did here. Got it?"

Val nodded.

"For now," he said, "I'll put you on paid leave, pending the outcome of the investigation. IA will interview you, probably a dozen more times, or so it will seem. Don't worry—tell them the truth. Don't try to protect anyone, including yourself, or your partner. You don't *need* to, okay? Are we clear?"

Val stared at him, cowering under the intense glare of his pitch-black eyes. "Will I—or Gil—are we—"

"You're fine, Dawes. You're going to be fine." Gibson squeezed her hands again. "Really."

She exhaled, nodding. Because that's what they wanted her to do.

But she didn't feel fine.

***

With Blake's guidance, Val filled out a series of forms and reports over the next few hours, detailing the key facts of the incident, the circumstances behind her pulling and discharging her weapon, and a tortured explanation of why she and Gil had split the beat. The clock ticked toward 4:00 a.m. by the time they'd finished.

"I'll get these filed right away," Blake said with a loud yawn, tossing his paper coffee cup into the trash can. "You need to go downtown and chat with I.A. They're waiting for you."

"Now?" She hadn't meant to shriek, and it revived her headache with a vengeance.

"Got to do it while the memories are fresh, they say. I'll

have a patrolman drive you over."

"Travis," Val said as the sergeant stood to leave, "how bad is this?"

"For you? Not so bad, I don't think. I.A. might make noise about that citizen complaint, but I'll back you up there. Then it'll come down to the psych eval."

Val nodded. "How long will that take?"

"The whole process usually takes a few weeks." Blake smiled again. "Enjoy your time off."

"Sarge," she said, "the psych part. Is it that same guy...what's his name...?"

"Chris Cyrus?" Blake said. "Yup. He's our man. Don't worry. He doesn't go on any witch hunts. Just be yourself, and you'll get through it fine."

"Thanks, Sarge."

Ten minutes later, Val waited outside the front door for a driver to take her to the downtown precinct. Light peeked over the buildings on the east side of town, and a damp chill enveloped her. With the warmth of the previous evening, she hadn't worn an overcoat. After a few minutes, Gil strolled up, street-side.

"Are you my ride?" she asked, relief flowing over her.

He shook his head. "Sorry. Listen, I only have a minute. I'm not supposed to be talking with you, but, hell...Dawes, are you okay?"

She blew into her hands, turning numb in the cold air. "I guess. It's such a whirlwind, I haven't had time to think, or feel, much of anything."

Gil glanced around and stood close to her. "Val, one thing I need to emphasize. Don't mention that thing with Dog where we let him go. I know you think it helps show you're not a violent maniac, but Dawes, listen. We never reported that, and we didn't follow proper procedure. If you bring it up now, it'll only make things worse for yourself. Okay? You understand?"

She nodded, her mood souring. She wanted to cry, but then again, she really did not want to cry. "Gil...I'm sorry. I made a mess for you tonight, didn't I? The whole splitting the beat thing—"

He waved her off. "Don't worry about that. We have bigger fish to fry. Just remember—the Dog thing did not happen.

Okay?"

"Yes. I understand. But...I feel bad that I'm getting you into trouble."

Gil shrugged. "Thanks. I'll deal with it. Worst case, they bust me back to street cop. But I'm happiest there anyway." He ducked his head to get eye-level with her. "You need anything—anything at all—you call me, okay?"

She nodded. A moment later, a police cruiser emerged from the garage and turned toward them. Gil hustled away, leaving Val to stew over the mess she'd made of her life and career—and probably his.

***

Late the next morning, Val revived her body and spirit with a feta cheese omelet and a pumpkin latte at The Claytown Cafe, a neighborhood diner she'd often passed on her walk to work. After spotting the headlines in the *Clayton Courant* sitting on the counter, she bought a copy and sat down to read.

OFFICER FATALLY SHOOTS MOB LEADER

Clayton-area man Alfred Takura, 35, died of gunshot wounds after an exchange of gunfire with local police in the Upper Abernethy neighborhood last night. The shooting occurred after an on-foot chase led to a confrontation in an alley off of Jacobs Street, according to Sgt. Travis Blake of Clayton Police Department. The suspect died at the scene.

Witnesses said that the suspect fired first at Officer Valorie Dawes, who returned fire, fatally wounding Mr. Takura with a single shot.

Takura has been linked to the Setting Sun street gang, an affiliate of the Tokyo-based Nakaguchi crime syndicate. Police suspect the Setting Sun is responsible for several shootings, robberies, and teen kidnappings in western Connecticut over the past decade, according to a Department spokesman.

The FBI lists Nakaguchi as one of the ten most dangerous crime syndicates in the U.S., with links to drug traffic, prostitution, and child abduction networks.

"Your espresso, ma'am?" The slender, pink-haired woman

who'd taken Val's order placed a large, steaming mug in front of her. She glanced at Val and gasped, revealing a tongue piercing that matched her nose ring. "You're *her*, aren't you?"

Val froze in mid-reach for her espresso. "Her, who?" she asked, dreading the answer.

"Her, who!" The pink-haired woman pointed to a TV perched over the service counter, displaying news footage from the crime scene of the night before. Takura's face appeared on the upper left of the screen. Val's department-issue head shot appeared below Takura's.

Dammit! She'd hoped that going to a new place might spare her from scenes like this. She gripped her coffee mug with both hands, but they shook too much to dare trying to lift it to her mouth. "Yes, that's me," she sighed.

"Did he, like, really shoot at you?" Pinkie asked.

After a moment, Val nodded, still too numbed by the experience to think about it.

"That's so freaky," the girl said. "Well, I'm, like, totally glad he didn't get you. That would suck a bagga-you-know-what, right?"

"Definitely," Val said, not really sure what the woman meant.

"My girlfriend is Japanese, and she hates those mofo fofos," Pinkie said. "They almost grabbed her sister one time. So her sister says. Annie's a bit of a drama llama, though. That's the sister, not my girlfriend." Pinkie whipped out her phone and scrolled through it, then showed it to Val. "There she is. Isn't she beautiful?"

Val glanced at the photo, relieved that it looked nothing like the girl Takura had abused in the Jacobs Arms. "Gorgeous. Um...what's the status of my omelet?"

"Oh, right on. It'll be up in a sec. Hey, let me buy you breakfast, okay? I mean, dude. I don't get to meet heroes very often." The woman dashed off to the kitchen, oblivious to Val's protests.

Val sighed. If she wanted to avoid the spotlight and media noise, she'd have to work a lot harder.

Chapter Fifteen

C had enveloped Val in a tight embrace just inside her apartment door, squeezing hard enough to push all the air out of her lungs. "I came as soon as I heard. How are you feeling?"

"Kind of numb." She patted his back, and they swayed from side to side. "I guess it hasn't fully sunk in yet. I mean, I killed a man yesterday. But it's weird. I don't feel—well, anything."

He gave her another long, tight squeeze. They stepped inside, and Val pointed her free hand to the couch. "Beth's here."

Chad smiled. "Hi, Beth. Looking good, as always." He gave Beth a quick hug. She received him with a loose embrace, as if uncomfortable with it. Chad stepped back from her. For a few seconds, they all stood in awkward silence.

"Can I get you something to drink, Chad?" Val asked.

"I'd love a cup of coffee," he said.

"Cream, two sugars?"

"Just one," Chad and Beth said at the same time. They exchanged a quick glance.

Val turned her gaze away from them. "Beth? Coffee for you?" Beth shook her head. Val cleared her throat. "Okay, I'll be right back."

"Let me get it for you," Beth said. "You and your brother should spend a few minutes alone." She rushed into the kitchen.

Val and Chad sat on the couch. If Chad ever realized the impact he'd had on her friend, returning home from college to take Beth to her senior prom, he never acknowledged it. Beth had talked on and on for weeks before and after the event, convinced they'd live a long, happy life together. For Chad it was a crazy lark, a way to hang out with his kid sister on a platonic double-date.

At least, Val's remained platonic. With Beth, no dates stayed platonic for long.

"Sorry," she said, "I should have told you she would be here."

Chad shrugged. "Of course she'd be here. She's your best friend and roommate." He wrapped a reassuring arm around her. "Besides, I'm happily married and a father now. Anyway, this is about you. Tell me what you're feeling."

"Numb," she said. "Part of it is, the guy pointed his gun at me. For that brief instant, I was afraid of—of *dying*. After that, instinct and training took over."

"Academy training? Jiu jitsu? Or Uncle Val's 'special lessons'?"

She shrugged. "Impossible to say. It's ingrained now." She described the sequence of events in detail. Beth returned with Chad's coffee. When she handed it to him, her hand touched his and lingered for a moment. Chad winced, but said nothing, and Beth took a seat in the chair across from the couch.

"So now there will be an investigation, and in the meantime, anywhere from ten to thirty days, I'll be on paid leave," she said.

"Are they providing counseling?" Chad blew on his coffee before taking a sip.

"Mandatory." Val shrugged. "At least two or three sessions, starting tomorrow. He has to sign off before I can return to work."

The doorbell rang. Beth jumped to her feet. "I'll get it."

"No more visitors," Val said. "I got all the peeps I need right here already." Chad gave her a sad smile, and his eyes followed hers to Uncle Val's photo perched atop the table at the end of the couch.

"Flowers!" Beth held a bouquet in her arms when she returned to the seating area. "From the guys at the station."

Val's teeth clenched. Beth and Chad exchanged an uncertain glance.

"Shall I put these in a vase for you?" Beth asked.

"Yes, please." Val's voice dropped to a low register, stone

cold. Beth disappeared into the kitchen.

"Val, what's the matter?" Chad patted her shoulder. "Is it just starting to sink in?"

"It's not that." Val shrugged his hand away. "Would they send a *man* flowers?"

Chad blew air out through his lips and clasped his hands together. "Oh, *that*." He shook his head, took another sip. "Maybe. You'd have to ask them."

"Yeah, well. I doubt it."

"Val, look. Take it for what it is. A nice gesture of support from your colleagues. A symbol. A demonstration that they care."

"A reminder that I'm a woman in a man's world."

Chad slapped both palms on his thighs and sighed. "Dammit, Val, you *are* a woman in a man's world," he said. "You understood that going in. It's one of the things you keep talking about, what you wanted to change, remember?"

"Yeah, well, it's not changing. Hell, Chad. I just killed a man. What do they think, I'm sitting at home crying?"

"How the hell am I supposed to know what they're thinking?" Chad said, almost a shout, then calmed himself. "You're the cop. You work with these guys. You tell me."

Beth re-entered with the bouquet-filled vase. "I understand Val's point." She set the flowers on the coffee table and joined them on the couch next to Val. She'd brought herself a cup of coffee after all and sipped on it while they talked. "They do little things that diminish her. Men do this all the time. Not so much you, Chad," she added before he could interrupt. "But a lot of guys. Especially the more traditional, conservative guys. And there's a tendency for cops to be, well, more conservative."

"Well, that's such a broad generalization," Chad said. "Aren't most of them college graduates? I mean, isn't that changing?"

"Slowly," Val said. "And I realize they're trying to be nice, as best they know how. I just haven't finished educating them how to do it better."

Chad smiled and threw an arm across her shoulder. "That's my girl," Chad said. "Now, do you have any beer in this place, or is buying drinks still the man's job?"

"That's still the man's job," Val and Beth said in unison, laughing.

They talked for hours, about everything but the shooting. Val had to admit that it helped to have both of them there, particularly Chad, who always knew what to say—and when to shut the hell up. He crashed on the couch around midnight, despite Beth's inappropriate suggestion that he sleep in her bed, never quite clarifying whether she'd still be in it.

But when Val shut her bedroom door for the night, loneliness swept over her. She considered waking her brother again, but he needed to get on the road early, back to his wife, kids, and work in Danbury. Beth would love to make it a slumber party, but she'd never quit with her questions. Val had never been good about accepting help or sharing her innermost feelings, even with her closest friend.

Not since right before her thirteenth birthday, anyway.

***

Valorie dragged her spoon across the bottom of the squat paper bowl that once held twin scoops of chocolate-chunk cherry ice cream, now a soupy brown mess. Her unfocused eyes gazed past the antiseptic white service counter crowded with customers ordering their favorite cones and sundaes. She leaned against Uncle Val, seated next to her on the bench along the glass wall.

"He's going to hurt me now, isn't he, Uncle Val?" She stared into her melting ice cream, stirred it in the cup.

"No, honey. He will never hurt you again. I can guarantee that." Uncle Val wrapped his arm around her, squeezed.

"Are you going to arrest him?" she asked.

Uncle Val's voice grew hard and raspy. "If he's lucky, that's all that'll happen to him."

She stared up at him. "Are—are you going to shoot him?"

Uncle Val smiled, a sad smile. "Probably not. They don't let us do that unless they're attacking somebody."

She moped and stared back at her ice cream bowl. "I wish he would attack somebody else so you could shoot him." But she couldn't think of anyone she'd want him to attack.

"People like him are too careful." He cradled her in his beefy arms and spoke in a deep, low voice. "Valorie, have you told anyone else about this?"

Tears streamed down her face, as they had for the past twenty minutes. Her voice had never risen above a dull monotone while relating the story of that incident. "Just Chad," she said. "A little. Not everything. He made me tell you." She sniffled, wiped her nose with her finger, dried it on her jeans.

"Not your Mom and Dad?"

She shook her head, again.

"Do you want to tell them, or should I?" He kept his voice gentle and squeezed her into a tighter hug.

"No!" She pulled away from his embrace and glared at him. "Why do they have to know?"

"They're your parents, Valorie. They care about you."

"Ha." She faced forward again and pressed her head against his side. "Not like you do."

"Aw, Valorie. You know they love you. A lot." Tears leaked from his eyes, too. He bit his lower lip, suppressing a sob.

"They don't care. They don't even take me to soccer anymore. I get a ride from you or Beth's mom."

He hugged her again and rocked with her from side to side on the bench. "My girl," he said, "people have different ways of showing love."

"I like your way better, Uncle Val."

They were quiet a while—the graying, overweight cop and his twelve-year-old niece—lost in their own tears and thoughts. Customers came and went, ordering ice cream at the counter, but one and all keeping their distance from the odd couple in the back corner.

"It hurts still, doesn't it?" he asked.

"Not like it did that night."

He wiped a fresh supply of tears away from his cheeks with a napkin. "But it feels...icky. Doesn't it?"

"Yes. Very."

"Does talking to me help?"

"Yeah. A little." She hugged him tighter, too. "More than a little. A lot."

"You can always talk to me. About this, or anything. Any time."

"Thank you, Uncle Val. I will."

His body shuddered as he exhaled a deep breath. It took him a moment to come up with words.

"It would be good if you could talk to a doctor," Uncle Val said. "They can help you with the hurting."

"But it doesn't hurt any more. Not in that way."

"There are doctors who can help with all kinds of hurting, including the kind that hurts deep inside when you think about things."

She thought about that a moment. "I like talking to you better."

He nodded. "Me, too. But I can only do so much. The doctors can help you in ways that I can't."

"The doctors can't shoot him, either."

Uncle Val laughed, a soft chuckle, and hugged her close again. "What Milt did to you was a terrible, horrible thing. It's a crime and he should go to prison for it. But more important is what happens to you. What he did will haunt you for a long time. You feel ashamed. Dirty. Like you did something wrong. Right?"

She nodded. Uncle Val understood. He cared.

"But you didn't do anything wrong. And those doctors—they'll be able to help you get those feelings out of you so you can feel good again. Don't you want that?"

She held him hard against her. Her throat hurt so much, too much to speak. Instead, she nodded her head against his chest, and disappeared inside his bear hug.

***

Dr. Cyrus relaxed in his chair, a thick padded leather recliner. A few feet away sat Valorie Dawes, the rookie policewoman he'd met once before. A tough customer, he recalled. Not very forthcoming. Untrusting. A little angry, though he couldn't piece together why.

Dawes leaned forward in her upholstered chair, elbows digging into her thighs, hands clasped into a tight ball. Cyrus relaxed his own body as best he could, hoping it might relax her. He ran his hand through the black, bushy hair still covering his scalp, thanks to the finest product money could buy. He adjusted his black-rimmed glasses and glanced at the neat, printed notes on the pad resting on an end table next to him, then smiled at her.

"How are you today, Officer Dawes?"

Her clenched hands bobbed in front of her. "Fine, considering." A light sheen of sweat dampened her cheeks and forehead, and her breathing came in shallow, staccato bursts.

He cleared his throat. "How are you sleeping?"

"Not much."

Cyrus nodded again. The dark circles under her eyes gave that away. At least she didn't lie about it, like so many do. "It's natural for people in your position to—"

"In my *position*?" She stared at him and shook her head.

Cyrus's words stuck in his throat. Her anger leaked out of every pore, fueling her attacks on him. Her fierce sarcasm challenged his considerable patience. Still, he had a job to do. He willed himself to remain calm, and to reflect it in his voice.

"You understand why we're here today?" he asked her.

Dawes shrugged. "To see if I'm too crazy and trigger-happy to return to the streets. Or, just crazy enough to want to go back. Right?"

Not even a hint of a smile creased her lips or lit her eyes. Cyrus cleared this throat. "My charge," he said, "is to determine whether you're exhibiting any disturbing violent tendencies, anger issues, depression, or anything else that might affect your ability to perform your duties. Officers who have experienced an encounter similar to yours often suffer ill effects—"

"Encounter?" She exhaled and shook her head again. "You kill me, doc. Ill effects? Damn straight there are. I shot a man. He's dead. Gone. His family misses him. They'll bury him in a day or two because of me. *Shouldn't I* suffer from 'ill effects'?" She sat back in the chair, pressing her body against the cushions, arms anchored on the armrests.

Cyrus jotted down some notes, a million voices in his head screaming at him to take it slow with this one. Dawes seemed ready to explode, though her body remained motionless—rigid, even. Still, he had a process. He would follow it until it failed him. Thus far, it had not.

He forced another smile and waited for her to look at him. "Please explain in your own words. Why did you shoot Mr. Takura?"

She sighed and focused on a spot somewhere over his head. "It was self-defense. He shot at me. My life was in danger. I followed procedure and training and protected myself from harm." She returned her gaze to him, her eyes narrowing.

That squared with the brief background the department had supplied him. "You had no alternative to shooting him, is that right?"

"Of course." Her expression softened. "Doc, I have to ask you something."

Cyrus nodded and waited.

"Is everything I tell you here confidential? Doctor-patient privilege and all that?"

Uh-oh. Questions of that kind usually preceded an unfortunate revelation. Unfortunate, but almost always important. "Of course."

Dawes pointed to his notepad. "But you will write a report to the department about me."

He thought a moment. "I'll inform them of your mental fitness for duty," he said. "But no specifics of what you tell me."

She stood and took a few steps away from him, staring at his diplomas on the wall, hands clasped behind her. "Well, less than six weeks on the job, I shot a man and killed him. Kicked another guy in the nuts for trying to rape me on a date. Is that a 'violent tendency'?"

Cyrus frowned. "That's all...relevant information." He made a note to follow up on the date rape story.

Dawes sighed and sat again in her chair.

Cyrus cleared his throat. "So. The man you shot threatened you with a weapon and fired at you. You then returned his fire and shot him fatally, according to your incident report. Do I have that right?"

She swallowed hard and examined the pattern in the carpet at her feet. "Yes. My life was at risk."

"How do you feel about the incident now?"

At the word "incident," she covered her mouth and held her abdomen, as if fighting nausea. "Horrible."

A fitting response. "Horrible as in guilty? Depressed? Angry?"

Her voice remained steady, quiet. "Sure. All of that. I ask myself: isn't there any other way I could have handled the situation? Shot him non-fatally, or used pepper spray, clubbed him maybe—any other choice but the gun? I don't know. It all happened too fast."

"It's natural to second-guess yourself. That's a good sign. It shows you have a strong, ethical conscience. I'd be more worried if you didn't feel that way." He smiled at her, hoping it didn't appear fake.

"I'm relieved." Sarcasm filled in her voice. He'd have to work on that smile.

Cyrus checked his notes again. "I want to get back to your sleep issues. How much are you getting per night?"

"An hour or two, perhaps. But it's only been a few days."

He frowned. "That's not healthy. Would you like me to prescribe something?"

"No. Not yet anyway."

"Are you eating?"

"My appetite's a little down, but I could stand to lose a few pounds." She patted her stomach, which looked flat and washboard-hard to Cyrus.

"Headaches, nausea, anything else?"

Shrug.

He sighed. "I can't help you if you won't talk to me."

"I'm not sure how much you can help me, anyway. Other than reassuring the department I'm not a savage, bloodthirsty killer."

Cyrus regarded her for several seconds, his pen resting on his notepad. "Do you have anyone else you can confide in? Family, friends, your partner?"

"I've talked to my brother. It helps."

He made a note on his pad, then looked back at her. "Very well. I'd like to see you again next week. I'm recommending more time off for you, or at most, light duty. You're not ready for the stresses of patrol yet."

"Doctor, I—"

"I also recommend you undertake a mental exercise for me," Cyrus said over her objection. "Imagine yourself meeting with the victim's family, and what you might say to them."

"What? No. That's crazy."

"Perhaps. But it might help you process this."

Perspiration dotted her forehead and dampened her collar. She fidgeted with her hands, shuffled her feet on the floor beneath her seat. "I don't think I want to do this."

Cyrus smiled. "Of course you don't. Who would? But it will help you confront your guilt and get it behind you. Perhaps you'd imagine yourself apologizing—"

"*Apologize?*" Dawes stood, her skin flushed. "To a man who tried to kill me?"

"—to the family. And understand their anguish." He spoke in his most calming voice. "That will help you ground your own pain and put a human face on it. Then you'll be able to process your feelings of guilt much more effectively."

She shook her head and turned away from him. "It seems stupid."

"Trust me." He forced gentleness into his voice, tried to make it sound less officious and analytical. "It will help."

She barked out a sharp laugh. "I stopped trusting middle-aged men long ago."

Cyrus sighed and made a note of that comment. Something to come back to. "Shall we meet on Tuesday at nine, then?" He flipped through his appointment book, pen in hand.

"Sure. Whatever." She turned to leave.

Cyrus stood and smiled. "Valorie, you're a strong, smart woman. I'm sure, with time, we'll be able to put this incident behind you."

Dawes stiffened again, and for a moment something flickered in her eyes—a look of loathing, and of fear. Then her eyes darkened, and she nodded. "Tuesday at nine, then."

Chapter Sixteen

The grilling at the hands of Internal Affairs came to a sudden halt when the lead detective announced in an abrupt phone call that she "wouldn't be needed" for the next several days.

"So they'll just make up their own minds about the situation?" she asked Travis Blake in his office. "My input doesn't count?"

Blake grimaced and shook his head. "Dawes, I understand. This feels like we're putting you through the wringer. But it's all routine, and I'm confident they'll clear you of any wrongdoing. You'll probably get another commendation, even. Relax."

"Easier said than done," she replied. "What do I do in the meantime?"

He shrugged. "Take a few days off. You've earned it. Spend some time with your family."

That appealed to her, if for no other reason than to escape the apartment. With her nights free, Beth hounded her to go on yet another double date with her and Josh, who spent the night with disturbing frequency—and reminded Val too much of that idiot Brent Davenport. She needed a getaway, and could think of none better than a ninety-minute drive to her brother's place in Danbury.

But first she had to retrieve her car.

Uncle Val had promised her his old Honda Civic long before she'd learned to drive, telling her she'd need it for college. Turns out she didn't, and still didn't when she returned, as she lived close enough to walk to work. Instead, she'd asked Chad to garage it at her father's place for her.

Her father's place. Not "home." It stopped being home the moment she walked out the door to go to college. And not

"Mom and Dad's." Mom left a few months after Val's fourteenth birthday, a year after Mom and Dad stopped talking, and two years since either of them had remained sober for over three days in a row. Mom blamed her leaving on Dad, the drinking, and everything except what mattered: the travesty that had befallen them—*her*—at the hands of "Uncle" Milt. A few weeks after she left, the phone calls stopped, then the letters, and then Mom simply disappeared.

Dad had remained—in body, if not in spirit. The whole ordeal broke him, and he slid into a walking coma of alcohol, anger, and denial. If not for Chad, he'd have drunk himself to death years ago. Long before he should have, at age sixteen, Chad became the family's caretaker. How he'd done it, Val could not fathom.

Val couldn't remember when it happened, but somewhere along the way, she and her father ceased communicating. Even living in the same house, they rarely spoke. What did they have to discuss? Nothing, until he stopped repeating the lies that Milt had spun about the incident. She understood now, after years of counseling, that Dad believed Milt's version of the story because he had to. The fantasy to which he clung—along with the constant drinking—brought him comfort, and accepting the truth was too horrible of an alternative. Then Val had gone away to college, and not talking became second nature.

But now, far more than her need to maintain radio silence with her father, she needed the car.

She considered renting one and sparing herself the grief, but she couldn't afford it, and most rental companies wouldn't lease to someone under 25. Or borrowing one, but the only person in town who trusted her enough was Beth, and she needed hers for work.

So she took a city bus to her old westside suburban neighborhood and walked up the cul-de-sac to her childhood home. The modest two-story Cape Cod blended in among a dozen more carbon copies of it on 70-foot tree-lined lots. She paused at the driveway that led to the closed garage, which she and Chad had converted to a gym, her private escape during her teen years. She'd moved out of her bedroom—too many awful memories associated with that space—and often slept on a cot in the garage. Now, her car slept there.

Val glanced at her surroundings. Nobody had mowed the grass in months. Large blotches of gray leaked through on the siding where the old blue paint had flaked off. Clumps of moss curled the charcoal-colored asphalt shingles on the roof. At least a week's worth of bills and catalogs clogged the mailbox.

She trudged up to the front door and pressed the doorbell. Listened for the twin four-note bars of the traditional singsong greeting to play.

Seconds passed. Nothing.

She pressed again. Still no sound. Dammit. She rapped her knuckles on the glass pane of the old aluminum storm door. It rattled open with a painful squeak. She pushed it aside and knocked on the white metal-clad door. Waited.

Nothing.

Val sighed. She fished out her keys, found the right one, inserted it into the lock. It still worked. She pushed open the door.

"Dad? You home?"

No sound.

She sighed in relief. Maybe he was away, and she wouldn't have to face him after all.

She stepped inside. The place smelled of mildew and rotting fruit, and dust tickled her nostrils. The old sofa remained in front of the picture window, facing the 40-inch flat-screen TV, the only thing close to new in the place. Chairs that used to match the sofa had disappeared. Empty Pabst Blue Ribbon cans lay scattered around an overflowing ashtray on the battered coffee table, along with a closed pizza box. She lifted the cover. Hawaiian pizza, cold and stale. Might have been last night's dinner. Or last Friday's breakfast. Hard to tell.

Val wandered into the kitchen, unsurprised by the mess she found there, or the smell, twice as pungent and eye-searing as in the living room. She scanned the kitschy plaque on the wall that sported four hooks, each labeled with one family member's name. Chad had made it in shop class, a place for everyone to hang their keys.

Empty.

She pulled on the handle to the junk drawer. Halfway

open, it got stuck, rattled with a metallic clash, and bounced back shut. She tugged it open part way and worked her hand inside to push aside whatever kitchen implement blocked the damned thing from opening—

"Well, look what the cat dragged in."

Val froze at the sound of her father's scratchy voice, at first not wanting to turn to see him. Then she chided herself for being childish and summoned up the most enthusiastic smile possible, under the circumstances. She freed her hand from the drawer and faced him.

The man slumping his round, stooped body in the doorway looked nothing like the father she pictured in her memory. Wearing baggy pants and a wife-beater T-shirt, Michael David Dawes bore no resemblance to the tall, athletic, well-dressed businessman, brimming with the confidence she remembered from her youth. Nor even the gaunt figure of her teen years. His hair, always black and cut in a conservative over-the-ears 1950s style, now streamed out in dry, white bursts as if he'd been electrocuted. Angry red blotches dappled his tanned skin, and his dark brown eyes seemed lost inside their deep sockets.

The voice, however, she recognized. It belonged to the former vice-president of Ashford Machine and Dye, who doubled as soccer coach and scout leader, and who'd once attempted to raise her.

"Dad. I meant to call, but—"

"But you knew I wouldn't answer." He coughed, not bothering to cover his mouth, and the aroma of cheap bourbon overpowered the stench of the dishes rotting in the sink. "Well, come here. Aren't you going to give me a hug, after all these years?"

Her stomach lurched, and her muscles tightened in recoil. He couldn't be serious. Could he?

Dad stepped toward her, arms wide. Dammit. She held her breath and kept her arms by her side, letting him wrap her up for a moment. Then she wiggled free.

"I came to get the Honda," she said, not making eye contact. "I'm going to visit Chad in Danbury."

"Assuming it still runs. Yeah, I figured you weren't here to see me." He stumbled over to another cabinet and pulled open a drawer. "I think the keys are in here." He rummaged through, stealing a glance at her after a moment. "That drawer's broken."

"I, uh...Dad, it's not like we've kept in close touch, right? I graduated from UConn, by the way." The words rushed out of her, faster than she could think.

"Good for you. About time. Chad told me you got a job." He stopped rummaging and glared at her, his eyes glowing. "On Clayton P.D." Suddenly he seemed alert, almost sober.

Like he always did when he was angry. When he accused her of lying, or holding back information. Like every time they ever discussed what had happened with Milt.

Goose bumps spread over her skin, and she rubbed her bare arms for warmth. Stepped away from him, for safety. "Th-that's right. I always said I would."

Bang! The drawer crashed shut, and her father's face lurched to within inches of hers. "Are you fucking crazy?" he seethed, spittle spewing from his clenched teeth. "It's not enough they killed my brother? You've got to go join those stupid sons-of-bitches too? What are you trying to do, kill *me*?" He slammed his fist on the counter, sending dishes and silverware flying.

Val dodged a fork that flew by her nose, just in time, and stepped out from under his hot gaze. She kept her hands in front of her, her voice calm, and focused on him while speaking. "I didn't do it to hurt you. It's what I've always—"

"Because you think you can find all the big bad bogeymen who scared you as a little girl, and what? Lock them all up? Kill them? Is that what you want to do?" He lurched toward her again, grabbing her by the shoulders and shaking her. "Yeah, I heard the news reports about what you did. Killed a man. Are you proud of yourself now?"

"I acted in self-def—"

"Hah! I've got half a mind to call them and tell them what your agenda is. Maybe that'll convince them you have no business being a goddamned cop. Putting a gun in your hands and a badge on your chest has to be the craziest goddamned thing this city has ever done!" He gave her a final shake and pushed himself away, supporting himself with stiff arms planted on the filthy counter, his body shaking, wracked with sobs.

Val stood there, watching him cry, not knowing what else to do. Her father's anger stunned her, and his threats frightened her. Would he do such a thing? He seemed crazed enough to try. But how would the department react if he did?

Fear soon gave way as a familiar ache crept up inside her. She'd only seen Dad cry twice before. The last time was when Mom had left. He'd sobbed, like he did now, his whole body expressing sadness, the grief taking over, crushing him. The all-encompassing nature of his despair had surprised her, and the violence of it had alarmed her.

The first time was after she told them both what Milt had done.

No sobbing then, though. More quiet and stoic, just shedding of a few tears. Since she'd never seen him cry before that—or any other grown man—she assumed that's how men wept. Thought nothing of it.

Funny. She remembered Dad crying, but not Mom. Surely she must have—

"Well," he said with startling abruptness, standing erect for the first time, "I guess I'd better find you those keys."

"Dad, I—"

"No, fuck it. Take the car. Go on, get out of here." He fished around in the drawer again, the one that opened, and tossed her a key chain with the familiar black fob, sporting the stylized "H" in bas-relief. He stared at the floor, sniffled, wiped his nose with his finger.

She took a breath and steadied her voice. "I'm sorry that I haven't visited. I just—"

"Valorie, don't, okay? Just go. Please." He waved at the air, shooing her.

"No. Dad, listen. I should have called more. I admit—"

"More? Try *ever.*"

Val clenched her fist, shutting her eyes for the count of three, then opened them again. "I invited you to my graduation. Left you a voice-mail. You didn't respond, and you didn't come."

"I wasn't feeling good." He coughed again.

"Yeah. I figured." She sighed. "You can call me, too, you know."

"I don't even know your number," he said, his voice harsh. "Where you live. Nothing. I know nothing about you, except that you're trying to get yourself killed. Well, if that's what you want, go ahead. I won't stop you."

She shook her head, fighting the angry words bubbling up inside. "I'll call you when I get back in town—"

"Spare me the lies, okay? Just go off to your broth—"

"Spare *you*? Jesus!" With that, her restraints dissolved, overcoming the discipline she'd fought to maintain. "You have a lot of nerve. Who's the one who refused to believe what that asshole 'family friend' did to me? Who told people that the reason I had to stay home from school, and go to the hospital, is that I had the mumps—the fucking *mumps*!" Her breathing grew ragged, her voice shrieking.

"Stop it!" he yelled, hands over his ears. "Shut the hell up!"

Val raged on, barely cognizant of his interruption. "Who refused to call the cops on a goddamned child molester who raped your own fucking daughter? Who's the goddamned liar? Huh? Is that me, Dad, or am I describing you?"

She glared into his eyes, which she suddenly realized were only inches from her own. She let go of him, not having been fully aware that she'd grabbed *him* by the shoulders, had shaken *him* in teeth-rattling fashion. Had overpowered *him*—her own father. Her once big, strong, confident father.

Who now collapsed, mouth agape, his back against the wall, sliding to the floor, tears once again wetting his cheeks. "Get the fuck out of here," he said, and closed his eyes.

Chapter Seventeen

Val's hands stopped shaking only after she pulled into Chad's driveway. Her tension melted away to zero when she spotted her pig-tailed five-year-old niece bouncing into view through the picture window of the sprawling 1980s-era ranch house. Alison's muffled shouts escaped the closed doors and windows. "Mommy! Mommy! Auntie Val is here!"

Val waved to her niece from the driveway. Ali had grown so much. Val needed to visit more often.

The door opened before Val reached the front door. Kendra, Chad's auburn-haired wife of seven years and Val's personal nominee for sainthood, met her with a warm hug. "Your brother's still at the office, trying to finish up his monthly billings," Kendra said. "Come on in, I've warmed up a pot of fresh apple cider."

"My favorite!" Val followed her inside, shaking her head in admiration of Kendra. Her spotless house, beautiful children, and perfect skin alone could get her woman of the year. Plus her career as a violinist heralded increasing local acclaim, even occasional mentions in the New York papers. She raised Ali while Chad had attended law school and maintained a model-slim figure even after two pregnancies. Val doubted there was anything she couldn't do.

Ali squeezed one leg of each woman. "Pick me up!" she squealed. Val scooped Ali into her arms.

"Ali, get down," Kendra said. "You're too big for Auntie Val to be carrying you."

"Auntie Val is *strong!*" Ali said. "Me too, Auntie Val. Look! Watch me!" She jumped to the floor and counted off push-ups. "One, two, three..." She made it to ten before rolling exhausted onto her back. "I did twelve yesterday. Robert

Keene can only do seven!"

"My little athlete." Kendra rolled her eyes and grabbed Val's suitcase. "Chad told her about your track medals and ever since, all she wants to do is beat the boys at *everything*. Ali, honey, why don't you show Auntie Val the guest room while I check on the baby?"

Val followed the bouncing child down the hallway, laughing at the five-year-old's boundless energy. She longed to collapse onto the guest bed and kick off her shoes, but Ali tugged at her arm as soon as Val's suitcase hit the floor. "Auntie Val, do you want to see my room?" Ali said.

"Sure." Val let Ali drag her farther down the hall.

She wasn't prepared for the scene that greeted her there. Instead of Barbies, stuffed animals and pastel pinks, Ali had packed the room with action hero figures and posters from cop movies and TV shows she could never have watched. Val's academy graduation picture took prominence on her dresser. Right behind it, Uncle Val's smile gazed out in uniform from a silver frame. A toy water rifle lay on the floor at the end of her bed.

"Oh, my God," Val whispered.

"Look what Mommy and Daddy gave me to wear for Halloween!" Ali pulled a dark blue vest from her closet with a silver badge pinned to the chest. "Daddy said it's just like the one you wear!"

"I see you've gotten the tour." Kendra stood at Val's elbow, holding Darwin, their six-month-old, in a bundle of pale blue blankets against her chest. "Here's the little rascal that made me miss your UConn graduation." Kendra had suffered complications while carrying him and spent much of her pregnancy bedridden. Dar entered the world at ten pounds, three ounces, and twenty-three inches long—tall, like his mother. "Almost ready to break your track records," Chad had joked to Val at the time.

"He's beautiful," Val said to Kendra. "I love those clear blue eyes. And he's gotten so big in the last two months!"

"Pkew! Pkew!" Ali pointed her water gun at the baby, pretending to fire on him. "Got ya!"

"*Ali.*" Kendra's voice grew stern, but no louder. "What have I told you about pointing guns at people? Please put that away."

"But all police ladies have guns," Ali said. "Don't they, Auntie Val?"

Val squatted down to Ali's eye level. "Only after a lot, lot, *lot* of training and passing very hard tests," she said. "Have you taken your water rifle safety test yet?"

Shaking her head, her lips set in a dramatic pout, Ali set the gun on her toy chest. "Will you play with me?" she asked.

"Of course," Val said. "In a little while."

"Let Auntie Val rest a bit," Kendra said. "Why don't you read one of your picture books?"

"I want to play cops and robbers in my new Halloween costume!" Ali tugged on Val's leg. "Can I be the cop and you be the robber?"

Val laughed. "Sure," she said. "I could use a little role reversal."

"Yay!" Ali ran in tight circles around the two women, flapping her arms in excitement. "Okay, you hide outside, and I'll come find you. Don't run away, or I'll have to shoot. Just like on TV!" She dashed out of the room, singing unintelligible words from what Val guessed was a cop show theme song.

Val stared after her, not knowing whether to laugh, cry, or pass out.

***

To give Kendra some relief, Val sprung for pizza for dinner, to Alison's delight. It arrived a few minutes after Chad did. Kendra and Ali fetched plates, silverware, drinks and napkins while Val and Chad caught up in the living room.

"How are you feeling?" he said. "About...everything?"

"Still numb," Val said, taking a seat on the sofa. "Part of me can't believe I took away a man's life. It's such an awful power we have, and I'm not even used to the idea of having it yet. Another part of me is still getting over the fact that he shot at me—tried to kill *me*. If he...I could be dead." Her throat grew dry, and she sipped her tea for comfort.

"It worries me," Chad said, sitting next to her. "The risks of your job, I mean."

"You know," Val said, "I always wanted to be a cop. I never thought about what it would be like to have—done this." She paused and glanced at Ali, now dressed in her little police officer uniform, helping set the table.

"Well, I hope we can help you forget about it for a night," Chad said. "I see you had no trouble getting the car out of Dad's garage."

"Not exactly," she said in a low voice. "Dad didn't fight me over the car, but he did on everything else. Even on my choice of becoming a cop, which I've talked about my whole life."

"I'm sorry," Chad said. "I guess I can take the blame for him bringing that up."

"That wasn't the worst of it." She stared at her feet and lowered her voice. "We got into it over...what happened ten years ago. The stupid cover stories, the lies, all of it."

"Holy cannoli," he said. "The first time you two have spoken in five years—and *that's* what you talk about?"

"I wouldn't say we 'talked' much," Val said. "Shouted and cried, mostly."

"I don't know what amazes me more—that Dad talked about it, or that you did," Chad said. "He spent so long denying it ever happened. *You* told no one about it for weeks afterwards, and after it all blew up, you—"

"Sh!" Val said, spotting Ali returning to the living room with an armload of napkins and a liter bottle of Coke. "Later."

"That's what I'm talking about, Val." Chad shook his head. "There's always a reason not to discuss it."

"Discuss what?" Ali set the Coke and napkins on the coffee table and pried open the pizza box. "Daddy, can I have your extra cheese and pepperoni?"

"Of course," Chad said. "Go wash your hands before dinner."

"I already did!" Ali grabbed a piece of pizza and the toppings from a second slice. Chad rolled his eyes and set the naked slice on a napkin. Alison sat next to Val, munching her pizza sandwich and making moon eyes at her favorite aunt.

Kendra entered with Dar in one arm, and glasses, silverware, and paper plates in the other. "Started without me, I see. Val, thank *you* for waiting, at least."

Val slid a cheesy slice onto a plate for Kendra, then herself. After taking a bite, she took a long sip of Coke, and pretended not to catch Alison stealing her toppings to construct a three-layer munch.

"Auntie Val, when you go back to work, will you shoot any criminals?" Alison asked.

Cold soda blasted up through Val's nostrils.

"Ali! What a question!" Kendra said.

"My kindergarten teacher brought us to the arcade, and I played this game where you draw your gun against the bad guy. I got him every time except one," Ali said.

Val recovered from choking on her soft drink and drew a deep breath. "We try *not* to use our guns. It's not like on TV."

"I know," Alison said. "You know what, Auntie Val? I want to be a policewoman when I grow up, just like you."

Kendra covered her mouth, but tears gathered on the edge of her eyelids. Chad patted her arm and swallowed hard.

Val put her arm around her niece, hugging her tight. "I'm sure you'd be an excellent police officer," Val said. "But maybe you'd be an even better lawyer, like your dad?"

"No way," Alison said. "Most lawyers are crooks and S.O.B.'s, right Mom? Auntie Val, what's an 'S.O.B.'?"

"Alison!" Chad glared at her. Kendra's face turned beet red, and the two of them exchanged open-mouthed glances. Val, to avoid laughing, pretended to choke on her pizza.

"Where did you hear anyone say such a thing?" Kendra asked at last.

"On TV," Ali said.

"Someone needs to change the Etflix-Nay, ogin-lay again," Kendra sang around a bite of pizza.

"And to remember to log out when he's done," Chad sang back in the same tune. He sighed and snagged a new slice, this one with toppings.

"After dinner, can we watch a movie?" Ali asked, gazing up at Val. "We have *Captain Underpants* on DVD. I'll go plug it in!"

"*Captain Underpants* would be great," Val said. Anything but a cop show.

***

Dr. Cyrus waited for his patient to get comfortable, reviewing his notes for the hundredth time. Perhaps some small talk would ease their way into the conversation and put Ms. Dawes in a more forthcoming frame of mind.

"How was your weekend?" he asked her. "Did you do anything for Halloween?"

She exhaled a noisy breath and smiled. "Sure. It was great. My niece dressed up as me and shot the neighborhood boys with Pez candy. Apparently, sugar is more fatal than we thought."

He chuckled and nodded. "How old is she?"

"Five, going on thirty."

"My granddaughter is six," he said. "They sound like twins. Did you talk at all with your brother?"

She sighed. "*You* and *he* could be twins. Neither of you is very subtle. Yes, we talked a fair amount. But I'm sure if you ask him, he'd email you a detailed set of notes, complete with a list of unanswered questions from my teen years."

Cyrus grinned. Dawes seemed to be in a positive, if feisty, mood. Maybe she'd volunteer more of her feelings this time. "I'd like to follow up on something you mentioned the last time we met," he said. "You said a man attempted to rape you on a recent date?"

Dawes stiffened and her body hunched forward, her shoulders curled inward, arms crossed. Cyrus winced. Perhaps he'd waded into this topic too soon. Ah, well. What's done is done.

"I can see it was a mistake to mention that," she said in a low voice.

"No," he said in a reassuring tone. "You were right to do so. You never want to surprise your shrink, right?" He chuckled, hoping to relax her. He hated using words like "shrink," but speaking in the vernacular seemed to put patients at ease.

Not Dawes. "So, what about it?"

"Well," he said, nervous heat rising in his ears, "how recent was this attempted rape? I found no police report on the matter."

"I didn't report it," she said. "As I said, I kicked him in the nuts, pushed him out the door, and the whole incident was over in ten seconds."

"So, you acted in self-defense?" Cyrus jotted down a few notes.

"It was a matter of possibly getting raped, or defending myself. So, yes. And there was a report. The jerk had the nerve to file a complaint against me."

Cyrus stopped writing, glancing at her over the rim of his glasses. He'd seen no complaint in her file. "How do you feel about this incident?" he asked her. Again she reacted to the word "incident."

"I won't be going on any blind dates again for a decade or two," Dawes said. "To be honest, I'm angr—er, *frustrated* that he had the nerve to file a complaint against *me*, and I had to defend myself against him. The system is pretty fu—er, screwed up, if you ask me."

He sighed in agreement. A woman should be able to defend herself, police officer or not. He wrote "resolved" next to that item on his list of questions. "Now, I understand you had another recent violent encounter on the job. A similar situation, of sorts. A man abusing a child and her mother–"

"Richard Harkins. Yes. Unfortunately, he got away."

"Yes." Cyrus nodded. At first he sought a delicate way to ask this. But given her blunt nature, he opted for the direct approach. "Do you think you might harbor any anger or resentment against Mr. Harkins, anything that might carry into your job on a day-to-day basis?"

Dawes shrugged. "You mean, am I pissed off at myself for letting Harkins get away, and am I taking it out on the Kenny Takuras of the world? No, Dr. Cyrus. I encounter criminals and potential criminals every day of the week on my job. I wouldn't last long if I let every one of them get to me."

He nodded and gestured agreement with a sweep of his open palm. He'd heard a dozen cops make the same claim, nearly verbatim. There must be a class on that in the academy. "I'm, ah, glad to hear you've given some thought to this," he said.

Dawes made a wry face, like he'd reminded her of some unpleasant inside joke. Cyrus let it pass. He had to pick his battles. "How are you doing with your health? Eating, sleeping, exercising?"

"Yes, yes, and yes."

"When you sleep, do you make it through the night?"

"Except when I have to pee."

"No nightmares?"

She shrugged. "I don't remember my dreams." Her voice grew distant, as if fading into a long-forgotten memory.

During their first session, she'd claimed to have reached peace with the punishment meted out to her uncle's killer. She'd denied becoming a cop to avenge his death. Perhaps a little too quickly. Perhaps she protested the idea too much.

But he'd approved her entry into the force less than two months before, knowing about the issue then. If he flagged the issue now, this might all blow up on him.

Dawes was probably fine, anyway. Other than a little frustration with the whole psychological evaluation process, she *seemed* fine. As balanced and in control of her anger as any other cop that had gone through such an event. Perhaps more so.

But he was missing something, still. It bothered him that he couldn't identify it.

Cyrus realized with embarrassment they'd been silent for some time. He pretended to study his notes another moment, then glanced up at her. "What else can you tell me right now?" he asked. God, what a dumb question. She knew it, too, and it showed on her face. No poker player, this one.

"I really would like to get back to work," she said.

He sighed. Not one of his best interviews. "I'll be writing up my recommendation to the department within the next couple of days," he said.

"What will you recommend?" she asked.

"I won't reach a decision until I review your entire case file," he said. "But the options I'm considering are either to reinstate you, or to recommend further counseling."

She sighed. "Right. Well then, I guess I'll expect to see you next week." She stood and marched out of his office.

He couldn't decide whether she was right or wrong about that.

Chapter Eighteen

Val counted off the last three reps of her bicep curls with audible grunts, then dropped the twenty-pound dumbbell on the floor with a thud. She sat up and scanned the police gym, almost empty at mid-morning. Almost. A sweaty figure approached her, a barrel-shaped man with legs like an elephant's and fists like sides of ham.

"Dawes," he said. "I was hoping to find you here."

"What can I do for you, Sergeant Blake?" Val forced her breaths back into a regular, slower rhythm.

Blake scanned the rack of dumbbells and selected a pair of 50-pounders. "Just wondering how you're doing," Blake said. He flexed each arm, testing the weight, and sat on an empty lifting bench. Red, loose-fitting shorts flapped around his thighs, and a gray "Property of CPD" T-shirt absorbed a ring of sweat around his midsection and armpits. His strong, musky scent preceded him by six feet.

"Doing okay." She replaced her own weights, selecting a longer, heavier bar for a set of bench presses. "Thanks for asking."

"Have you talked to the shrink?" He started a set of reps with his right arm, with slow, steady arcs, up and down.

Val nodded. "Twice. I prefer to get the mandatory stuff out of the way." She placed the barbell on the bench rack and stretched her arms and shoulders.

Blake scowled. "Don't just treat it as a mandatory thing to get your badge back. Sometimes these things can haunt you."

Her ears perked up. Lieutenant Gibson trusted Travis more than any of his other sergeants. If Blake thought she presented a risk, so would Gibson. She softened her tone. "I'm okay."

He grunted and finished his first set, started with his left arm. "Have you caught up with your paperwork?"

"Completely." She lifted her arms to the barbell and glanced over at him. He stared back at her, even as he continued his workout. "Is there a particular reason for your interest in me today, Sarge?"

Blake nodded, a slight smile creasing his face. "Lieutenant Gibson wants a recommendation from me regarding your reinstatement. Gil, as your partner, is too close to you to be objective. I need to make sure you're ready to come back before I put you out on the street." He completed his set and placed the dumbbells on the floor.

"I'm ready whenever you are." Two weeks had passed since the shooting. But Cyrus hadn't asked for a new appointment, which she'd taken as more bureaucratic foot-dragging.

Val nodded once to her barbell. "Give me a spot?"

Blake stepped over and rested his hands underneath her barbell. She took the weight in her arms, brought it down to her chest. Up, slowly. Then down.

"Dawes, in some departments, when a cop says 'I'm ready' after a shooting, that's good enough," Blake said. "Not in Clayton."

"We have a higher standard?" She continued her steady movements, felt the strain in her arms and chest. Her breathing grew labored. Nine reps, ten. End of the first set.

"We do." Blake helped guide the barbell back to the rack. "You may have noticed, your perp was a person of color."

She took deep breaths, rested her arms on her abdomen. "Yes, Takura was Japanese-American, to be precise."

"And," he said, "whites make up less than forty percent of Clayton's population, but continue to dominate city government—including, Gibson notwithstanding, the top management of C.P.D." He nodded to her again, indicating the barbell.

She began her second set of reps, but at a slower pace, her heart pounding. From the exercise, she hoped. "Remember, I'm from here. I live ten blocks from where the shooting took place. My graduating class was less than half white. Almost a mirror image of the city population as a whole. So?"

He grunted. "Ever since Ferguson and Minneapolis, we've become much more sensitive to community perceptions about police use of force. That's why all the 'grilling', as you put it, after your shooting."

"So, everybody gets the same treatment?" she said with a wry grin. "I'm not special?" Five reps. Six.

Blake choked out a laugh. "Look, in vice, you plug a guy, the paperwork's just a formality. Here, in the precincts, the neighbors have to trust that you're not going to gun people down for stealing a donut."

Val grunted. Seven. "I don't think that's a problem here."

"I don't either," Blake said. "But they need to be sure. More sure than me, even."

"Give them the shrink's report." Eight, nine.

Blake shook his head. "You know how that comes across. 'She's one of us; she's fine.' Put yourself in the shoes of the neighbors, The Disciples, anyone out there. Would you buy it?"

She finished the set, pushed the bar back toward the rack. "Probably not."

"More important," Blake said, again guiding her bar onto the rack, "are *you* ready? Will you be able to draw your weapon to defend yourself, your partner, or a citizen? Will you know when not to? Or, are you too spooked still to make a quick, rational choice?"

Val glared at him. "I didn't intend to draw my gun this time, but I did what I had to do," she said. "To survive."

Blake returned to his own bench and resumed his right arm curls. "Good answer." He counted off six reps, then switched arms. She waited, hoping he'd return to spot for her again. Instead, he finished the set and wiped his watermelon-sized face with a towel, soaking it instantly. He stared off into the distance, steadying his breathing. "We had a Richard Harkins sighting yesterday," he said.

Her mouth gaped open, and she sat up on the bench. "No shit? Was it The Disciples?" She panicked for a moment, wondering if she had the five hundred bucks she'd promised Pope.

He shook his head. "Nope. One of the neighbors. What was the young girl's name that he abused? Anita?"

"Antoinetta?"

Blake nodded. "Her aunt. She doesn't think he saw her, but seeing him scared the shit out of her."

Val's heart pounded. "Guy's got balls. He doesn't expect we'll catch up to him?"

Blake laughed. "I guess not. But he's wrong about that." He reached into his fanny pack on the floor and opened his massive fist in front of her. A shiny object filled his palm.

Her badge.

"Your gun's in my office. Stop by when you're done." He stood and sauntered off to the water fountain.

Val grinned and bench-pressed another set. This time she didn't need anyone to spot her.

***

Gil greeted Val outside the locker room five minutes before their shift started, his big paw extended in a warm handshake. She welcomed his friendly smile and noticed his five-o'clock shadow seemed more subdued than usual. Like he'd actually paid attention to how his ruggedly handsome face would look with a clean shave.

"Welcome back, partner," he said. "Are you ready to resume your training?"

She gave his hand a vigorous shake and grinned. "Like nobody's business! Let's hit the streets." She headed toward the garage exit, but Gil beat her to the door and grabbed her arm. Instinctively, she shook it free. Maybe a little harder than necessary.

He furrowed his brow. "What's eating you?"

"Nothing." Her face warmed. "What's up?"

His voice took on a wary tone. "Let's take a walk before we head out," he said. "I want to talk to you."

"What about?" she asked, but followed in silence to the street exit.

"First, you're going to get another frigging medal," he said. "Pretty soon you won't have room on your chest for a badge."

"I'll hide it in my underwear drawer, with the other one." She glanced down at her chest, self-conscious. She wondered if Gil ever looked there. Probably not, since the damn Kevlar hid what little she had. Then she chided herself for thinking that way about him, again. Her partner. Boss. A man almost fifteen years older, that she'd just pushed away, for God's sake.

"Whatever. You earned it." He popped a hard candy into his mouth and crunched it in his teeth. "Second," he said, most decidedly *not* looking at her chest, "things are going to be different."

"I kind of figured we'd have to patrol together again for a while," she said. "I hope you didn't get in trouble for that."

Gil shrugged. "I'll live. But it's not only that." He turned down a side street, and after she followed, he stopped and stepped in close enough that she could smell peppermint on his breath. She took a nervous half-step back. He didn't seem to notice.

"Listen," he said in a low voice, and jerked a thumb over his shoulder. "On a good day, most people either love us or hate us. There isn't much that we can do to change their minds. It's based mostly on what sort of experiences they've had with cops in the past."

"Makes sense." Val nodded. "So, is this a good day?"

"Don't make light of this," he said. "There's been a ton of media attention to the Takura thing, most of it positive. Some people are even calling you a hero." He fixed her with a fierce gaze. "Don't listen to them."

Numbness swept over her. "I don't understand. You just said you thought I earned a medal. Now—"

"You swept some scumbag off the street, and a lot of people wish you'd do the same to the rest," he said. "They don't have much use for courts, trials, or people's rights. We can't buy into that. Understand? Don't let this go to your head. It'll ruin you."

"I would never—"

"None of us ever expect we will. But it's hard to resist. Tell me, how have you been feeling these past few weeks since the shooting?"

Her eyes found an interesting shiny spot on the pavement. "Like crap."

"Do you feel good about shooting that guy?"

"What? No, of course not!"

"Good." Gil lifted her chin with one finger, then placed gentle hands on her shoulders. She fought the urge to knock them off, and, this time, succeeded. He waited until her eyes met his to speak again. "That's the feeling I want you to hold on to. You know why?"

Val shook her head, fighting nervous tears, willing them to stay in her eye sockets. Do. Not. Show. Weakness.

"Because," he said in a soft voice, "that's your humanity talking to you. That's what keeps us on the right side of the thin line between good and evil out here. That's what separates the good cops from the bad. And, Val, you're a good cop. A damned good cop already, and you're going to be a *great* cop."

Her vision blurred, but by some miracle, the tears stayed off her cheeks. "Thanks, Gil." After a long moment of hesitation, she patted his hands with her own. "That means a lot, coming from you."

"Now, the other half of them," he said, waving one hand in the general direction of the world, "will say you've already crossed the line. Any time a cop pulls out a gun, we're abusing our power, no matter what the circumstances. Even in self-defense. By saving your own skin, you've only given them more proof of how terrible we are. Don't listen to them either."

She shook her head and sniffled. Her nose had gotten wet. So much for holding back the tears. Dammit.

"So who do I listen to?" she asked.

Gil smiled. "Tune into that little voice inside you, the same one that's guided you all along." His smile turned into a grin. "And, of course, listen to me. *Always* listen to me."

She shuddered out a laugh, tension draining from her. "As long as you believe in me, Gil," she said, "I will. That, I promise."

He squeezed her shoulders again, and this time it didn't feel weird. In fact, in that moment, all felt right in the world.

***

Gil said he needed to check in with someone before hitting the streets, so they returned to the precinct building. While she waited, Travis Blake flagged her down outside of his office. He waved her inside and handed her a large yellow mailer envelope, addressed to her. Per department practice, the package had been opened.

"This came for you," Blake said. "From 'Anonymous.' Take a peek."

She glimpsed inside. The mailer contained a black box, about eight inches long. The kind jewelry came in from chain stores. She slid the box out onto the table. "Is it safe to open?"

Blake shrugged. "It's not going to explode, or anything. At least, that's what Security concluded."

Val opened the box and lifted out the contents. A small pendant swayed from a thin gold chain.

"You can't keep it, of course," he said. "But we thought you ought to see it."

"I don't understand," she said. "Why would someone send me cheap jewelry? Wasn't there a note, or anything?"

He took the envelope and shook it over the desk. A small card fluttered out.

Val she caught the card in the air, flipped it over and read it. "What the...? *'Officer Dawes. May this ever remind you of the "good" you're doing. — An Admirer.'* They put 'good' in quotes." She shook her head and sighed. "Not very subtle, are they?"

Travis snorted. "That's for damn sure. Take a closer look."

She held the necklace closer and examined it: a simple, thin gold chain with a tiny pendant.

In the shape of a revolver.

She slammed the chain back in the box and threw the entire container into Blake's garbage can. "Is this someone's idea of a joke? Because it's pretty damned sick, if it is!"

He wagged his head in disgust and retrieved the package from the trash can. "Hey, that's city property now. Any idea of who might have sent it?"

Val's mind raced. Half the world would hate her, Gil had warned. A disproportionate number of them, she added to herself, wore blue uniforms like hers. "No," she said, seething, "but whoever it is better hope I never find out."

She stomped out of Blake's office, right past a very surprised Gil Kryzinski.

Chapter Nineteen

Walking the beat calmed Val, as did Gil's soothing baritone voice and his steady demeanor. "It's just some asshole's idea of a prank," he said. "Forget it. You have way bigger fish to fry out here." He returned a stray basketball to a group of neighborhood kids on a street-side court, and they waved back in thanks. Other neighbors came out on their front stoops to watch them stroll by, some waving, others staring in stony silence.

"I'm hungry," Val said when she spotted Taufiq's Quick Mart on the next corner. "Let's make a stop."

Gil pushed the door open and held it for her. She scooted inside and smiled when she saw her friend at the cash register.

"Welcome back, Officer Valorie!" Taufiq opened his arms wide and rushed around the counter and embraced her in a long, tight hug. "So good of you to come in. I have missed you!"

Val's body trembled a bit in the embrace, and she signaled her partner for a rescue. Gil smirked and pretended to take an interest in a rack of Little Debbie cakes.

"Uh, thanks, Taufiq." The unexpected hug had not only unnerved her, but pushed most of the air out of her lungs. She wiggled free after a few uncomfortable moments and nudged Taufiq back toward his station behind the counter. "I just need a quick bite and wanted to see how you're doing. Are the neighborhood kids giving you any trouble?"

"The teenagers," Taufiq said with a sad grin, "prefer the tricks to the treats this Halloween."

"I'll talk to them." She stepped aside as Gil returned with their coffees and set two snack cakes on the counter. Val reached into her pocket.

"Oh, no. Your money is no good here," Taufiq said. "You come by any time."

"I can't accept that," Val said, with another "Please help me!" look at Gil.

Gil smiled and held his arms out wide. "As much as we'd love to, as underpaid and under-appreciated public servants, we can't," he said. "Department policy says nothing more than a cup of regular coffee."

"Besides," Val said, "you have a business to run. You're not going to make any money if you give all your profits to the cops."

"Not to all cops," Taufiq said. "Just you, Officer Valorie, and Sergeant K. It is a thank-you for making our neighborhood safer."

"We all work together on that." She dropped cash on the counter and sipped her coffee. "But thank you for the kind words. By the way, this coffee is excellent."

He grinned. "Thank you, Officer Valorie."

Neighbors greeted her with a mix of reactions along their walking route that night—some with scowls, but most with smiles and waves. Universally, though, business owners showed support. Shop owners offered thanks, congratulations, even gifts that she politely declined. "You look cold," a sporting goods shop owner said, offering her a New England Patriots skull cap. She almost accepted that—after all, it *was* freezing out, typical of early November. A clothing store offered her a parka. Others offered DVD's, food, a lifetime membership to a yoga studio—all turned down, with sincere thanks.

"See? Like I said. They love you!" Gil said when they took another coffee break in McDonald's around 8:00 p.m.

"That's not what you said!" She laughed when she realized he was teasing. "I only wish we could have spoken to Antoinetta's Aunt Camila. I really wanted to get a lead on Harkins."

"Let the suits handle the detective work." Gil stirred a packet of sugar into his coffee. "Focus on your job: policing the beat and engaging with the neighbors. Which you're doing very well, I might add."

"Are they being genuine, or putting up a front?" she asked. "I expected more negative reactions, after your warning earlier."

"Their reactions are far more positive than I expected." He sipped his coffee. "Most of them do seem to love you."

"Because I plugged a guy?" Val sat next to him at the counter overlooking the street through wall-to-ceiling glass. "That doesn't seem right. At least, it's not very consistent with community policing."

Gil shook his head. "Not only that. You're doing what nobody else has done around here in years: paying attention to them. They feel empowered and listened to."

"It does feel good," she admitted, and grew excited. "We need to tap into this somehow, get them more involved. If we could do that, we could clean up this area, make it livable again." She sipped on her coffee. It scalded the roof of her mouth.

"Now don't get all touchy-feely on me here." Gil scowled. "They're not excited about democratic participation and liberty, Val. They're happy that you wiped one of the dirt-bags off the street who's been making their lives miserable. That's why they think you're listening. But they don't want to become cops. They just want you to keep on doing it."

She swirled her coffee, blowing on it again. "Maybe, after what we saw tonight, we have an opportunity to change things."

"You got a plan?" he asked.

She shook her head. "Not yet. But I will. And soon."

Gil clapped his hand on hers, clutching it in a rough embrace. "You do that," he said. "And when you do, I'll back you, a hundred percent. And who knows? Maybe it'll help us track down guys like Harkins. Anyway, I gotta hit the men's. I'll be right back." He pulled back his hand, gulped his still-scalding coffee, and ambled off to the restroom.

Val stared at her hand, still tingling where his fingers had touched hers. Normally she'd brush away contact of that sort. This time, her instinctive reaction to the friendly gesture remained dormant, for some reason. The touch felt almost...*good*.

Maybe she was healing.

Maybe.

***

Seated at a small table in The Claytown Cafe the next morning, she jotted ideas on a pocket-sized notepad, focusing on her community policing idea. If she could engage the neighbors to be more proactive and make them think it was their own idea—

"Bang! Bang! Hey, there, Annie Oakley. Looks like I got the drop on you this time."

Val jumped at the sound of Paul Peterson's grating voice. The ball of her pen jabbed a hole into the sheet of paper in front of her, clear through to the chipped Formica. She gripped it and took a deep breath.

"Don't you have some other place you need to be?" she said without looking up. "Say, Afghanistan?"

"Aw, c'mon there, Officer Dawes." Peterson sat his lanky frame across from her. "Where's your sense of humor? Anyway, I meant it as a compliment."

"A compliment?" That made her look up. She shook her head in wonder. "You've got a funny way of making a girl feel good, Mr. Peterson."

"Leave my sex life out of this," he said with a smart-assed grin. He'd grown a wispy mustache in recent weeks, and it made his pointed, thin face resemble a rat's. "And please, call me Paul."

"Fine. *Paul.* I'm very busy, so if there's nothing else..."

"You know, Dawes, you truly are impressive," Peterson said. "You've been on the job what, six weeks? Already the bodies are falling."

"Get the hell out of here, Peterson." Val searched the room for someone who could remove him, found no one. Not even the pink-haired waitress.

"You're on quite a pace," Peterson said. "And not a scratch on you. Like in that movie *Tombstone.* Maybe we ought to call you Val Kilmer instead of Val Dawes?"

"You'd be happier if he had shot me instead?" she asked through gritted teeth.

"No, no." Peterson leaned back in his chair and held his hands out in front of him. "Believe me, Dawes. Nobody wants to read a blog about the scum you lock up every day. But a free-shooting rookie cop attracts a whole slew of readers. My numbers are *way* up."

"Count me among those who have unsubscribed." Val

returned to her notepad.

"In all seriousness, Dawes, I am impressed. You're a fabulous shot. Just like Ben said you were."

Val closed her eyes, drawing in and exhaling a slow, noisy breath. She'd forgotten about Ben, who had hit on her a few times in the Academy. She drew upon the one factoid she remembered him mentioning during an otherwise stultifying night of group socializing with her fellow cadets: Paul's hated nickname.

"I'm busy...*Paulie.*" Childish, but she had nothing else at the moment.

Peterson stiffened at the diminutive, then chuckled and shook his head. "See? So serious. All business. But I tell you what, I'm glad we're on the same team, *Valley Girl.*"

Val froze, and the world froze with her. That horrible nickname from her past, the one she'd hoped to have left behind forever, echoed in her ears. The man's tenor voice transformed with each echo, deepening, slurring, taking on the nails-on-the-chalkboard rasp that her tormentor had long ago used, fooling her parents into thinking of Milt as a kind old uncle instead of the child rapist that he was—

With an angry roar rising from somewhere within, her finger shot up to within an inch of the man's eyes. "*Don't call me that!*"

His face blanched, and Milt's visage morphed back into the smirking Paul Peterson. He pushed back, hands raised, the legs of his chair scraping on the linoleum floor. "Whoa, whoa, whoa. Sorry. Dawes. Jeez, I'm just glad that finger wasn't loaded."

"Argh!" Val stood and grabbed for his throat, but couldn't reach. "You rotten shit! Get out of here!" Her breathing came hard, her face hot.

Peterson jumped away from the table. He stared at her a moment and forced a hollow laugh. "Fine," he said. "I have other things to do. I don't need to hang around trying to see where you've hidden your sense of humor." He stood, took a few steps, then turned. "But, Dawes?" A sardonic smile creased his face, making him appear even more repulsive.

"Yeah?" She calmed a bit with his retreat. This was *not* Milt. Just a slimy blogger with an ax to grind. Her breathing slowed.

He hedged, cleared his throat. "I've, ah, kept my silence on this latest incident of yours out of respect for the victim's family—"

"*Victim's?*"

"But I'm not done with you. You'll be seeing your name in the headlines of my publication again very soon."

"Your *publication* is a heaping, online pile of click-bait, and I told you, I've unsubscribed!"

"Heh. You'll be back. Your type, you glory-seeking heroes, you can't resist seeing your names in print."

"Don't flatter yourself."

Anger flattened Peterson's condescending smile for a moment. Then, as if a light blinked on, his face brightened, and the snarling smile returned. "What's that, Dawes?" he said in a loud voice so that everyone in the place could hear. "You want me to buy you breakfast? Why, doesn't that violate your department's policy on gifts and bribes? Especially to a member of the press?"

"I wouldn't accept a 'gift' from you to save my damned life!"

A cruel smile crossed Peterson's face. "Now, what sort of gift might save a rookie policewoman's life?" he asked. "Or, more important, her career? Say, a gun, planted on an innocent victim of a police shooting?" The cruel smile hardened. "Read my blog, Dawes." He turned and strolled out of the restaurant.

***

"How many times have I told you to ignore that Peterson creep?" Gil said with a shake of his head as they walked down Albany Street the next evening. "He's just trying to stir the pot and get under your skin. Don't let him."

"My head agrees with you," Val said, waving at a group of kids gathering at the basketball court. They ignored her and continued choosing teams. "But my heart disagrees with my head on this one."

"Listen to your head, then," Gil said with a grin. "Trust that amazing intelligence of yours."

Val scoffed but said nothing.

They walked along in silence for a block or two. Gil threw her a few skeptical glances, then sighed. "You're still thinking about it."

Val sighed. "One thing he said sticks with me," she said. "That whole thing about planting guns. I've heard about that, but how common a practice is it?"

Gil frowned and scanned the area. "Let's not discuss that out on the street," he said in a low voice.

Val stopped walking, stunned. "In other words, it's common," she said.

"Not here," Gil said. "Listen, police don't shoot people that often in Clayton. Before yours, the last one was nine months ago. The most we've had in a single year is four, and that was the year your uncle—." He stopped, covering his mouth. "I'm sorry. I'm an idiot."

Val's head felt light, and she steadied herself by leaning against the chain-link fence abutting the sidewalk. She fought to catch her breath, and the only sound she could hear was the pounding of her own heartbeat.

"Are you all right?" Gil asked.

Val glanced at him, nodded her head. "It's okay," she said. "I need to get over my uncle's death...one of these days." She sucked in deep gulps of air and fanned herself. Despite the chilly November night, her head and neck felt as hot as a cup of Dunkin' Donuts coffee.

"We all do," Gil said. "His death was a great loss to everyone in the department. Not that our grief compares to what you and your family went through." He set his hand on her shoulder. "And I didn't mean to say that what you did–"

"It's okay, dammit." She pushed his hand off and twisted away from him. "I'll be fine."

After a moment, Gil sighed. "Okay, partner. You say so."

They resumed their beat-walking, stopping to chat with shopkeepers and neighbors from time to time. Val showed them a picture of Harkins, but nobody had seen any sign of him.

A short while after darkness fell, they reached the theater parking lot at the corner of Albany and MLK, Jr. Boulevard, the place Val thought of as The Disciples' headquarters. They didn't get far before a few Disciples, each sporting one or more gold loops in each ear, formed a human blockade. Cardinal Thomas, who wore three rings, stood cross-armed in the center of the group.

"S'up, Copsky?" Thomas asked.

"Not much," Gil said. "Slow night, hoping to keep it that way. You?"

"Nothing happening here." He glared at Val. "Yet."

"Yet doesn't sound so good," Gil said. "So, you're saying we should stay awhile to make sure things stay quiet?"

Thomas shrugged and spit at Val's feet. "You can. As long as *she* don't."

Val exchanged puzzled looks with Gil and took a step toward Thomas. "You got a problem with me?"

Thomas glared at her, let out a puff of exhaust. "You could say that."

"Yeah, well, as officers of the law, we can go wherever we damn well please," Gil said. "Including her. Including right in the middle of this parking lot, which, I remind you, is private property, not owned by any of you."

The men on either side of Cardinal Thomas grumbled in low voices. Val could make out the occasional word: "our damn space," "ain't doing nothing," and all too clearly, "fucking white-girl cops." Then: "See what *Pope* has to say."

Thomas held up one hand, and the grumbling stopped. "We don't need to find out what Pope has to say," Thomas said. "I know what Pope thinks about this."

"Do you now?" Pope pushed through the line of men, with Dog trailing behind him. "I don't recall ever needing anyone to do my talking for me."

Thomas seemed to shrink in the shadow of Pope, his face downcast. "I'm just doing what you told me to do," he said. "I ain't—"

"Don't worry about it." Pope waved the group back, stepped forward, and leaned in toward Val. "You the one that shot that Asian dude." A statement, not a question.

Val shuddered, hoping it didn't show. Putting on a brave face, she said, "I am. He was breaking the law and evading justice. Not to mention, *he shot at me.*" Her voice grew heated, something she'd tried to avoid.

Pope stared at her a long moment. "So you say," he said at last. "So cops always say. 'He had a gun.' Bunch of bullshit."

"There were witnesses," Gil said. "Lots of them."

"White people," Pope said.

"And black, and Latino, and Asian," Gil said.

Pope sneered at them. "Bunch of cop-loving pussies. They just trying to get on your good side. Ain't none of them seen nothing."

"You're calling them all liars?" Gil said. "You know these people?"

"I don't need to," Pope said. "I know cops and how much they love they guns. What else I gotta know?"

An idea popped into Val's head, something she remembered Gil telling her about Pope, about his little sister. "Maybe you might want to know what he was doing," she said, "that caused me to chase after him."

Pope cocked his head. "What the fuck that got to do with anything?" But doubt had crept into his voice. Gil smiled at her, gave her a subtle thumbs-up.

"He was abusing a little girl," she said. "Or trying to. I happened by and heard the ruckus. When I went up to stop him, he ran."

Pope gave her a long look, rubbing his chin. "For real?" He shook his head. "You making that up."

"No, she ain't," someone said behind Pope. Dog slipped around the larger man and stood in front of him. "This is the lady cop that let me go that night. She's straight up, Pope. She says something, I believe her."

"Do you, now?" Pope grabbed Dog by the shirt and pulled him close to his own face, glaring into the young boy's eyes. "Why you fucking sticking up for a goddamned cop? Is this part of your deal, why she let you go? You sucking her ass now?"

Trembling, Dog shook his head. "N-no, Pope. I ain't made no deal. I'm just saying. She coulda rung me up. Most cops would've. She didn't. She different, that's all I'm saying."

Pope glared at Dog another long moment, then pushed him to the ground. "Fine. So maybe the guy deserved it. This time." He stepped toward Val, poking his finger at her. "But here's what I know. Once a cop pulls the trigger, they start liking it. And then things get a whole lot worse for people like me."

Val took a deep breath, forcing herself to stay calm. She

rubbed her hands together, as much to keep them away from her weapons as for warmth. "I will tell you, flat-out, that I didn't enjoy shooting that man. I'm not that kind of cop, and I never will be."

Pope sneered again. "Bullshit. You just like your uncle. Damn dude killed what, five, six people? Shee-it. It's in your genes, girl."

Heat rose in Val's face, her heart pounding. "First off, I am not my uncle. There are days I wish I was half the person he was, but I'm not. And second, he shot those people in self-defense. And third, one of them *killed HIM!*"

Her body shook, her face inches from Pope's. The big man's eyes grew wide, and he backed away, holding his hands out in front of him. The other Disciples backed up with Pope, widening their circle. Tense silence filled the air.

Finally, Gil spoke. "This meeting's gone on long enough." He tipped his cap at Pope and pulled Val back a step. "Good chat, boys," he said to the group. "See you tomorrow and we'll pick this up where we left off." He pulled Val back to the sidewalk.

Val stared at the group, retreating to the center of the lot where their usual trash-can fire burned. She followed Gil down the block, then grabbed his arm. "I screwed up back there, didn't I?" she said.

Gil smiled and shook his head. "Not at all. You stood your ground and made them think. A good middle-ground choice. Had you gone to either extreme—backed down or lost your temper—*that* would have been a mistake."

She shook her body loose, letting the tension flow out of her. "I guess that's part of that 'other half' you were talking about," she said.

Gil laughed. "Let's just say, we shouldn't expect them at any Neighborhood Watch meetings."

Val saw the humor and wanted to laugh with him, but she couldn't. She had far too much work to do, and a lot more to learn about becoming the type of cop that would make her uncle proud.

Chapter Twenty

After their break, Gil and Val prioritized how they'd cover the rest of their beat that night. "You probably don't want to go anywhere near the Jacobs Arms," he said, "but it's on the way to Antoinetta's. I was hoping we could catch up with her aunt before bedtime, see if she's heard anything else about Harkins."

Val shuddered at the mention of the building where she'd first encountered Takura, but shook it off. "Agreed," she said. "I haven't seen Antoinetta in weeks. I'd love to check in on her, too."

Fewer neighbors waved friendly greetings as they walked the sketchier side of their beat. Young Asian men made themselves scarce whenever they spied the two officers coming. A nightclub bouncer bobbed his head, expressionless, and an old Hispanic man sniffed in disapproval while they waited for a walk signal to change. Otherwise they could have been invisible.

They turned onto Greenfield Street and spotted a small group of Latino boys smoking cigarettes under a street lamp, chattering in Spanish. Gil picked up the pace and headed straight for them. Val caught up after a few steps. "Do you know these guys?" she asked in a low voice.

"Not yet," Gil said. He smiled at the boys. "*Hola, amigos. ¿Sabes dónde vive Camila Martinez?*"

The boys glanced at each other, then laughed, coughing blue smoke and wheezing. "Speak English, man," the tallest of them said. "So it don't hurt so much."

Val smirked, but Gil scowled. "In English, then. Do you know where she lives?"

"Maybe," said the tall one, a dark-haired, thin boy with the faint beginnings of unkempt facial hair. All of them wore dark leather or faux-leather jackets, not nearly warm enough for the chill of the evening. The tall kid stomped out his cigarette and peered out through long black bangs. "You arresting someone for something?"

"We just want to talk to her," Val said.

"Yeah, right," one of the boys said. The others muttered agreement. "Buncha bullshit," another one said.

Val stepped in front of Gil. "Do you guys remember the night a few weeks back, when we chased the white dude out of Antoinetta's house? Do you know Antoinetta?"

A few of the kids nodded.

"Well," she said, "we're the cops who chased him out. Have you seen him?"

"Carlos?" A woman's voice emerged from the front porch of a small ranch house behind the two officers. With her porch light out, Val couldn't see her face. "Are you in trouble again?"

"No, Mama," he said. "These cops here want to talk to you."

"Camila?" Gil called to her. "*Señora* Martinez?"

"Yes?" She ambled down the steps, pulling a button-down sweater tight around her shoulders. She smiled when she got closer to them. "Ah, *Señor* Officer K," she said in a thick Mexican accent. "And *Señorita* Dawes! I have been hoping to speak with you. Please, come inside, where it is warm." Without waiting, she shuffled back to her porch and held open the door.

Gil gave the boys one last disapproving glare, then he and Val joined Camila at her kitchen table, where she poured them mugs of hot tea.

"As I told your detectives, *Señor* Harkins came by here a week or so ago, looking for my sister," Camila said in response to Gil's questioning. "He threatened to hurt me if I did not tell him where she was, but I shooed him off my porch with this." She held up a stout deck broom with long, stiff bristles, its handle sharpened like a spear tip. "Antoinetta, she say, he got my point. Ha ha! Funny girl." She chuckled and sipped her tea.

"Where does he stay when he's not at your sister's?" Val asked.

"My sister does not believe this, but he has another girl in

Hartford," Camila said. "An Anglo with fake red hair and fake you-know-what's." She cupped her hands a foot from her chest. "*Pechos*. You know? Boobies." She cackled and shook her head. "My good-for-nothing ex-husband has seen her dance at the Silver Fox strip club."

"What's her name?" Gil asked. Val buried a laugh behind a cough and covered her mouth. A person could interpret that question the wrong way.

Camila cast him a withering gaze in response. Gil retreated, frowning.

"Has Mr. Harkins been back since then?" Val asked.

"If he comes back, he will feel my point again," Camila said, grabbing the broom handle.

"It might be better if you call us," Gil said, sliding a business card across the table. "Or 9-1-1."

She glanced at the card. "You will not be here as fast as my broom," she said.

"*Señora* Martinez, we very much want to find Mr. Harkins," Val said. "He's a fugitive from justice. Not only did he harm Antoinetta, but he shot one of our officers. He—"

"Ah, of course. I did not believe that you would care so much about him, just for hurting my sister and *sobrina*." Camila tsk'd and sipped her tea. "But he hurt one of you, so yes, you must find him."

"Ms. Martinez," Gil said, his voice rising, "I don't care what you—"

"In fact, Camila," Val said, almost shouting to drown out Gil, "I care very much about what he did to Antoinetta. Perhaps because I know what she has been through."

Gil stared at her, a puzzled frown on his face.

"Mr. Harkins hurt you, too?" Camila asked.

"Mr. Harkins attacked me, but that's not what I mean," Val said. "Another man did...uh, a similar thing to me, when I was about her age..." Her voice trailed off. Suddenly it became very difficult to talk about it—as usual. The words that had flowed out in the passion of the moment fell to their usual silent death once she realized what she was saying.

Gil stared at her now, open-mouthed. Val's face flushed, heat flooding her cheeks and forehead. She hadn't intended to share this with him. Not this way, anyway. What had gotten into her?

Camila set down her tea and sat up straight in her chair. She looked at Val, then Gil, then back to Val. She nodded. "I will help you," she said to Val. "You. Okay? Because you know." She cast a glance over Gil's head, her chin held high, and sniffed at him. Then back to Val. "You give me *your* phone number," she said. "I only want to call you."

Outside a minute later, Gil turned toward her. "Val. I had no idea. I'm so sorry to hear that you—"

"Forget about that, okay?" Val stomped past him. "It got us what we wanted. Let's get going. We have a lot more ground to cover tonight."

She walked on, not waiting for him to follow. He wanted to talk to her about it, of course. But that was the last thing she wanted to share with him.

***

Ten Years Earlier

Valorie lay on her bed, her back to Uncle Milt while he zipped up and fumbled with his belt. Pain and shame and fear competed for attention inside her, each taking turns winning the battle. His noisy breaths, the rattling belt clasp, and the suffocating aroma of tobacco, whiskey, and sweat informed her that this had not yet ended. Hot tears stung her cheeks. She dared not let him see that. For some reason, it made her feel even more ashamed. More...weak. Pathetic. Open to another attack. That danger lurked as long as he stayed, and she couldn't force him out. He was too big, too powerful.

Surely, he would leave soon.

A heavy weight pressed down on the bed. Her insides turned into heavy mush. God, he couldn't possibly want to hurt her again, could he? So soon?

His hand rested on her shoulder. Valorie jerked away, pressed herself against the wall.

"Now, don't be like that," Uncle Milt said. "We're friends, right, Valley Girl?"

The contents of Valorie's stomach bubbled up into her throat. She swallowed the hot, acidic goo, somehow, but it burned her throat. She coughed, and gagged on the awful taste. "Please go," she said, and a sob escaped her. That only made her angrier, and she wanted to curse, but she didn't like to curse. She had the urge to punch something. Milt, to be specific. Probably not a safe move. Her frustration doubled, and another sob escaped.

"Please, don't cry," Milt said.

Suddenly she couldn't control the crying. It poured out of her, hot, painful, shameful, unstoppable. She buried her face in her pillow—

"I said DON'T CRY!"

The shock of his loud voice, of his anger, took away her breath, halted the tears, stopped her heart from beating. Her body stiffened, frozen in her awkward pose. No sound escaped her. No movement. No tears.

"That's better," Uncle Milt said, his voice gentle again. "You're a big girl, now, Valley Girl. You don't need to cry. Right?"

Valorie nodded, still not facing him.

His weight lifted off the bed. When Milt spoke again, he seemed farther away. "Now," he said, "neither of us tells anyone what we did here tonight. No one ever needs to know. Right, Valorie?"

She buried her face deeper into her pillow, tears again soaking through the pillowcase. Go away, Milt. Just. Go.

"Friends like us, we can keep secrets, right?" he said. He rested his arm on her back. She shook it off, rolled away from him, sobbing.

"Come on, Valley Girl. I need to hear you say it," he said. "I'll never tell anyone. Say it."

Valorie pressed the pillow against each side of her head. Please, God. Make him go away.

"Say it!" he said, his voice a nasty hiss, so harsh it made her jump. Milt's hand pressed down on the back of her neck, gripping her with too much force. She shook her head.

"Out. Loud!" He pushed at her head. It hurt.

She tried to take a breath, but inhaled only pillow.

She wheezed, an awful sound. He loosened his grip, and she gasped air into her lungs.

"I won't tell anyone," Valorie said with a moan, choking on the words.

"Good girl," he said. "I know you won't. Because you don't want to get in trouble, do you? You know what people think about girls who do what you did."

What she did? She hadn't done anything! But if she objected, he would grab her neck again. She shook her head, then nodded, and the tears flowed like an open spigot from her eyes.

"We don't want people to think that about you, do we, Valorie?"

She shook her head again, her eyes closed tight.

"I didn't think so." His weight lifted off the bed, and he pulled the covers over her. From the corner of her eye she saw him stumble toward her bedroom door. He stood by the doorway and gazed back at her.

"Good night, Valley Girl," he said.

Valorie moaned and turned away.

"Say goodnight!" he said in a commanding tone. Then, more softly: "Please."

"Good...g'nite...Unc... Milt."

Her door closed, and the long dark night of remembering began.

***

Val and Gil barely spoke for the rest of the shift beyond the perfunctory and logistical necessities of navigating a shared beat. Gil remarked once or twice on their conversation with Camila, but she steered all responses—brief as they were—back to work topics with ruthless efficiency. She realized she was acting like an ass, but she was in no mood for light banter or personal revelations, and work was a safe middle ground.

Toward 3:00 a.m., with minutes to go on their shift, Gil parked the cruiser behind a shady all-night bar with no windows, few customers, and too many neon signs advertising video poker. Two of the lot's four floodlights had burned out, including the one that would have illuminated their parking spot.

Alarms rang in Val's mind. She'd been stuck alone too many times in situations like this with handsy men. Her breath grew short, her face warm. She fumbled with the door handle, but it was locked. Shit shit shit—

"Oh, sorry," Gil said, clicking the door locks open. "Yeah, let's get out of this stinking car." He pushed his door open and got out.

She waited a moment, collected her thoughts, and let her breathing return to normal before joining him at the rear of the cruiser. He stretched out his hand toward her shoulder, and she jumped back.

"Hey, sorry about that," he said. "I keep forgetting you're not comfortable with casual touch."

Val let out a noisy breath. "It's not about you. It's...a thing with me." She looked away. She never could bring herself to explain this.

Gil waited for her to look back at him and kept his voice soft. "I get it. And I'm a hugger by nature. Men, women, everyone. I'll keep it in check."

"Thanks." She exhaled a heavy breath. "So, why are we here?"

He shrugged. "One of the neighbors said he used to hang out here. I suggest we poke around a little. By the time they serve us anything, we'll be off shift. And I need a beer." He pulled open the heavy metal door and waved her inside.

She stopped a few steps past the door, letting her eyes adjust to the dim lighting, shed mostly by neon signs advertising cheap beer and terrible whiskey. A wooden bar absorbed most of the back wall, and men of various ages occupied three of the spinner stools fixed to the floor, with a half-dozen or more seats between them. U-shaped booths padded with ripped red-vinyl seat covers lined the walls on either side. Spent peanut shells crunched beneath the feet of a couple of old gents heading toward the men's room. The whole bar reeked of grease, stale tobacco smoke, and spilled beer.

Gil leaned over the bar and conversed with the bartender in a low voice. After a few moments, the bartender shook his head and pointed to one of the vacant booths. They slid in moments later.

"What did he say about Harkins?" she asked.

"Nobody's seen him lately, but he was a regular until a few weeks ago," Gil said. "My guess is he's in Hartford now, like Camila suggested."

The bartender brought two sleeves of yellow, fizzy beer and a bowl of peanuts in the shell. Gil held up his beer in a toast. "To catching Harkins," he said.

Val wasn't sure if their shift had officially ended yet, but she had to drink to that. She clinked his glass, sipped, and grimaced. Cold, bitter, and otherwise tasteless, like all beer in her experience. She shoved it aside.

"I loved what you did out there tonight," he said. "The work you did with Pope, Dog, and Camila—it's nothing short of amazing. You have a knack for this." Under the table, his foot bumped hers. She moved hers away from him. "I never could have gotten that info out of Camila," he went on. "Only by you sharing your own personal experience—"

"Which I didn't mean to do," she said. "It just kind of slipped out."

Gil smiled. "I could tell by the way you blew me off afterwards," he said. "Which is fine. It's your own business, not mine."

She paused, took a breath. "Thanks," she said. An awkward moment passed. She should tell him the rest, but...

"You bring a whole new approach to things," he said. "It's creative, energetic, and exciting to be around." He smiled at her, a wistful smile. "Old-timers like me," he said, "we get too jaded and lose sight of what it means to be a cop."

Val sipped her beer again. It didn't taste as awful this time. "You're no old-timer," she said. "You have, what is it? Eight years on the force?"

"Eight in Clayton. I was in New Haven for eight years before that," Gil said. "What a hellhole."

"Hellholes need good police protection as much as Clayton. Maybe even more so." She stretched her legs out and this time she bumped his foot. He didn't react, and she curled her feet back under her seat. "Not that anyone has to be stuck their whole career in a hell hole to be a good cop," she continued, her words rushed. "But those are the people that resonate with me—the ones who feel stuck, or powerless." She slowed her speech, and words came out sounding slurred. What a lightweight. Slow down, girl. Shut up.

"There's that idealistic enthusiasm of yours again." Gil smiled and patted her hand, then frowned and pulled it away. "Sorry," he said. Her hand tingled. Damn, what was he doing to her?

Her stomach growled, and she chuckled in relief for the distraction. She tipped her glass at him and sipped again. "Shall we get something greasy to wash down with this witches' brew? Some Cajun fries?"

He grinned. "Girl after my own heart." Her face warmed. Was she sending signals she didn't intend?

Gil seemed not to notice and turned to wave at the barkeep. "Cajuns?" he said, just loud enough, and the bartender nodded. He turned back toward her. "Those fries are salty, greasy heaven."

"Friend of yours?" she asked.

"Friendly enough that we're safe to spend the last five minutes of our shift here."

Val set her half-empty glass on the wooden table, right over where someone had carved their initials into it. The beer was going down much too fast. She needed to slow down, keep her wits about her.

Silence lingered. Neon flashes reflected in Gil's dark eyes, dancing with humor. She noticed the strength of his square jaw, the coarseness of individual whiskers in his five o'clock shadow. He ran his hand through his thick, wavy black hair, now a few inches longer than the military cut he'd sported when they met seven weeks before.

She realized with a start that she was *admiring* him. His looks, for God's sake.

"So, why did you leave New Haven?" she asked after an eternity.

"I needed a change," Gil said, glancing away. He drank most of the rest of his beer and set the glass on the table, scooted deeper into the "U" of the seat, and lowered his voice. "After five years on the force, I met the woman of my dreams, I thought. We dated a few years, got engaged, and moved in together. But she discovered, luckily before we tied the knot, that she couldn't live the life of worry that comes with marrying a cop, and broke it off. I needed a change of scenery, and Clayton was hiring."

Finding it difficult to hear him, Val edged deeper into the "U" as well. They now sat at a 45-degree angle. She cleared her throat, searching for something appropriate to say. "So, you never married?"

Oh, how stupid stupid stupid—

"No," he said with an easy smile. "The experience with Jessica made me realize that only another cop would understand the life we lead. And you may have noticed, there aren't many of women on the force my age. One, to be exact, and Shannon O'Reilly's married."

"What constitutes 'your age'?" The words left her mouth before she could stop them, and she reddened.

"Plus or minus five years, so, roughly, a woman in her thirties. Don't worry, you're safe," he said, laughing. "By, what, seven or eight years?"

"Seven, in a few weeks," she said, with a nervous laugh not matching his in energy. "My birthday is in December."

"Noted. Mine was October 14."

"Why didn't you tell me? I would have—"

"Birthdays are for kids. No offense." He spun his beer glass on the table between his hands and laughed again.

She joined him this time for real. She hadn't celebrated a birthday in years. Not since—

Val's laughter died as if someone had hit a "mute" button on her face. The last time she celebrated a birthday, her twelfth, Uncle Val had given her a brand-new *gi* to wear to her jiu jitsu classes. On her thirteenth...she shook away the awful memory.

The fries arrived, as did Gil's second beer. Gil dove in with enthusiasm, while she picked at the fries, too nervous to eat much. He saved her the final handful, after which they leaned back in their seats. Val noticed that they'd moved close together on the seat, both at the short end of the "U," facing the same direction. Close enough that a casual observer might mistake them for a romantic couple. Which neither of them wanted. She should move away.

She almost did, too. But what message would that send? That she thought he'd moved too close, that he was some sort of creep? They weren't touching or anything, although they sat close enough that they could.

But they weren't. And they wouldn't. Because he was a good guy.

"Gil," she said, "I'm sorry I didn't trust you before. With my story, I mean."

"No apology needed," he said. "I haven't earned your trust yet. I'm okay with that."

"No, that's not right," she said. "You *have* earned it. You've been nothing short of amazing as a partner—and as a friend. And I want you to understand."

He bowed his head in a slow nod. "When you're ready to talk, I'm ready to listen."

She sipped her beer.   "I'm...almost ready." She surrendered a sad smile and turned toward him. He turned, too, and their bent knees touched on the seat. She jerked it away, then hung her head, blowing air out between her lips. "And, yeah...I'm such a goddamned liar."

Gil laughed. "4;00 a.m. isn't the time to start a long life story anyway. You can tell me about it on the drive to Hartford."

"Okay, I—what? What drive to Hartford? When?"

"On our next day off, we're going to the Silver Fox to find Richard Harkins, or at least his dancer girlfriend," he said. "Unless you don't want to go."

"Of course I want to go! But didn't you say we should leave that to the detectives?"

He shrugged. "I think it's time we do a little poking around on our own. Unofficially, of course. I have a buddy on the Hartford P.D. who owes me one. I thought we'd hit him up first, find out what he knows, then lurk around the nightclub and track down the dancer Camila mentioned, see where that leads us."

"You're amazing!" Val raised her nearly empty glass and toasted him. "I never thought I'd say this, but I can't wait to go to Hartford."

Chapter Twenty-One

Val dragged her sorry ass out of bed well past 1:00 p.m. the next day. She found Beth busying herself in the kitchen, preparing a platter of Buffalo wings and nachos big enough for an army. Which meant, of course, she'd stashed Josh in the bedroom again.

"What are you doing home this time of day?" Val asked.

"Watching football. It's Saturday," she said. "UConn plays UMass today. Want to watch with us?"

Val shook her head and opened an overhead cupboard, then wondered why. Her brain would not wake up. She should never drink after 3:00 a.m.

"We're out of coffee," Beth said. "I can send my boy out to get some."

"He'd do that?" Val raked through the fridge to find something easier on the stomach than Cajun fries for breakfast.

"For me, yes." Beth jiggled her boobs and laughed. "For these, I mean."

"Ask him to get eggs, too, then," Val said. "And aspirin."

Minutes later, a 30-ish rake with the dark shadow of a beard and an easy smile emerged from the bedroom, dressed in a UConn sweatshirt and matching sweatpants. Joshua's tousled mop of light brown hair seemed even more unruly than usual. He held his phone out to Val. "Hey, do you know this guy?"

Val squinted at the palm-sized screen and read the first few lines of the article before recognizing the truth-slashing style of Paul Peterson. "Yeah, sort of," she said. "He's a muckraker. I ignore him."

"Okay," Josh said with an easy grin. "You say so." He pulled on a jacket. "So, coffee, eggs, and aspirin? Anything else? Beer?"

"God, no," Val said.

"Guns and drugs?" Josh said, laughing.

"What? No, of course not," Val said. "What the hell?"

Josh pointed at his phone and shoved it into his pocket. "I guess you can't believe everything you read, then." He whistled tuneless noise and ambled out the door, landing a wet smooch on Beth's smiling face on the way.

"What do you see in him?" Val plopped onto the sofa.

Beth laughed and her eyes focused on a far-distant place. "It's not what I see in him," she said, "although his eyes are dreamy. It's what I feel in me...if you catch my drift." She giggled and flicked on the TV.

Val leaned back on the sofa and tried to rest, but Josh's words bounced around in her head. She sighed and tapped her own phone's browser, finding Peterson's blog. She groaned.

Crooked Cops Corrupt Clayton

Clayton residents once could rest assured that the unsavory practices often featured on late-night cop shows would never infect our safe little town. But what we have learned suggests that such assurances are no longer warranted.

Our sources (who wish to remain anonymous) indicate that the worst imaginable police tactics are as common in Clayton as they are in New York, Los Angeles, and Chicago—even the TV versions of those cities.

Not only do our men—*and women!*—in blue terrorize and shoot innocent citizens. But, our sources say, police regularly plant evidence such as drugs, guns, and stolen goods on suspects to create false justifications for their illegal acts.

Almost as bad, rumors persist that police routinely accept bribes—free food and drinks, valuable gifts such as jewelry and tickets to local events, and cash—to look the other way when local "businesses" (crime syndicates) are involved.

I wish I could say that this net of corruption snares only the jaded old-timers on the force. But the truth is much uglier. Even rookie police men—*and women!*—are apparently on the take.

Val's hands shook so hard, she dropped the phone before she could finish reading the article. How could this moron get away with posting such trash? Libel laws must apply, somehow. She considered phoning the department, but the lawyers wouldn't do anything about it until Monday, at the earliest. She still had a pair of nine-hour shifts ahead of her before Monday morning rolled around.

Val re-read the article's outrageous claims and got ripping mad again. She'd never met a single cop in her short career who'd even consider planting guns or evidence on suspects, much less taking bribes. She doubted that even Alex Papadopoulos would cross that line.

And Peterson calling out "rookie women"—of which Clayton had exactly one—amounted to a personal attack. Without a shred of evidence. That lying, scheming ass!

She calmed after a few minutes, listening to Beth cheer the home team for something awesome they did. The calming helped clarify her thinking, and she checked the article again. Sure enough, it alluded to gifts of "jewelry." She recalled the necklace with the gun pendant. Would this be one of those "gifts?" If so, she wondered how Peterson found out about it. He'd mentioned it in the coffee shop that day...the day he'd called her "Valley Girl," just to get under her skin. How had he discovered that as well?

***

The following Tuesday, Val followed Gil inside the Dutch Door, a 50s-style throwback diner on the street level of a three-story, mixed-use brick building in southeast Hartford. A brisk wind pushed the door shut behind them, but not before blowing in a few stray grocery sacks, empty potato chip wrappers, and brown oak leaves. The sounds of clanking dishes, steaming pots, and shouting kitchen workers filled the overheated air, lit by dim, low-slung light fixtures overhanging each table from twelve-foot ceilings.

"I love this place," Gil said. He took a deep whiff of the humid air, saturated with the aromas of coffee, stale grease, and frying bacon, and patted his stomach. "Food for kings."

Val stared at him, wide-eyed. "I can feel my arteries hardening just standing here. Have they even heard of salad?"

Gil led her to a booth in the back. "Let's get a head start on coffee while we wait for them." He waved down their waiter, a burly man whose five-o'clock shadow belied his obnoxious cologne, something Val described to herself as *eau de cigarette*. He delivered an insulated carafe of weak coffee and disappeared into the kitchen.

"Tell me about this guy, Jalen Marshall," Val said. "You used to work with him?"

Gil nodded, stirring four teaspoons of sugar into his mug. "Jalen and I went to the Academy together. He's the one that recruited me to Clayton, but he moved here when Hartford made a big push for diversity in their detective ranks. A good cop. As in, really good. Gibson nearly had a heart attack when he left. So did Pops."

"Why Pops?" Val followed Gil's lead, dumping what the Surgeon General would describe as three days' worth of sugar into her coffee, and an equal measure of cream. With all that, the stuff almost became drinkable.

Gil scanned the room and lowered his voice. "Pops was Jalen's first partner at Clayton. Just between us, that's a big reason he left. Jalen is a cop's cop, and he couldn't trust Pops to have his back." He leaned back. "But you never heard that from me, right?"

"My lips are sealed—oh, shit!" She ducked low in the booth, hiding behind Gil's large frame from the lanky man in his early twenties who'd just entered the front door. With his short brown hair and that awful smirk he always wore, Ben Peterson resembled his journalist cousin Paul far too much for comfort. Only his attire—a blue-gray police uniform with a silver badge and a bright yellow shoulder patch—set him apart from his muck-raking relation. "What the hell's he doing here?"

"Who?" Gil turned, then stood and waved at the tall, husky African American officer entering the diner behind Ben. He gestured again, and the man said something to Ben, then pointed at Gil. They approached the table together.

"Oh, no," Val said. "Please, tell me this isn't happening."

"What's your problem?" Gil asked, but the two men arrived before Val could answer.

Jalen removed his hat, revealing short, curly black hair

parted around his shiny, ebony dome. "Gil, you old dog," he said with a grin, and the two men embraced, pounding each other's backs. "It's been too long." He turned and gestured to Ben. "This is my new partner I'm training. Ben Peterson, meet Gil Kryzinski. And you are...?" He smiled at Val.

"I can help you out with that," Ben said, sliding into the booth next to Val. "Dawes and I went to Academy together." He gave Val a quick tap on the shoulder. Like he would for a man. Sort of. She slid away from him in the booth.

"So did we!" Jalen laughed. "What are the odds of that? Jeez, this is old home week!"

"Any relation to that asshole blogger, Paul Peterson?" Gil asked Ben.

Ben cleared his throat. "Cousins. But let me tell you, Paul and I have very different views on things. Very different."

Val's mind raced. Ben and Paulie may not agree on much, but clearly they talked on occasion, as Paul had mentioned Ben at their first run-in. And if he worked with Jalen Marshall, who used to work with Pops...the small-town connections bled with possibilities.

"What's Paul's frigging problem?" Gil asked him. "What'd we ever do to deserve his wrath?"

Ben winced. "Paul got busted in college once for possession. He got off with a slap on the wrist, but ever since, he's been on the warpath." He looked away, tight-lipped. "Not our family's proudest moment."

"How about you?" Jalen sat next to Gil and directed his question at Val. "Any relation to the late great Detective Valentin Dawes?"

"My uncle," Val said. "Did you know him?"

"He trained me at Clayton," Marshall said. "A good man. One of the best." Marshall helped himself to coffee from the pot. He drank it straight, to Val's amazement. "So you two are looking for a maggot who rapes kids? What else do you know about him?"

"Apparently he's hooked up with a dancer at the Silver Fox," Gil said. "Red hair, big boobs. Know her?"

Marshall scoffed. "Never been there, but that place is a well-known dipshit den. Fights, drugs, you name it. What about the guy? Is he a pimp, a beater, or a Methican American?" he asked.

Val looked for clues in Gil's face to decipher Jalen's lingo, but her partner was too engaged with his old pal to notice. She glanced at Ben, who waved one hand, as if to say, *I have no idea, either.*

"Probably all of the above," Gil said. "He gets around. We had rumors of him floating down south for a while, but he was spotted in Clayton a week ago." Gil half-smiled and sipped his coffee. "The name we have for him is Harkins, but he may go by a different name in every city. One for each girlfriend."

"Physical?"

Gil nodded to Val. "This one's yours."

"White male, about forty, dirty blonde or light brown hair. Six feet tall, two-fifty," she said, reciting from memory. "A few complaints on file, but no arrests."

Jalen and Ben exchanged glances. "That describes half of Hartford," Jalen said. "Ben, what do you know?"

Ben cleared his throat and sipped his coffee. "I, uh, might have seen him...on a stakeout," he said.

"You put your rookies on strip club stakeouts here?" Gil asked, amused. "We usually reserve that for old, useless farts who can't get dates."

"Sounds like Ben, except for the 'old' part," Val murmured.

"You want help or don't you, Dawes?" Ben said.

"Sorry," she said, but Jalen and Gil grinned.

"Let's keep our eyes on the prize here," Jalen said. "Catching a bad guy, right, Ben?"

"We have our hands full here in Hartford. What makes this creep so special?" Ben said, defiant.

Marshall glared at him. "When you have a nine-year-old girl of your own, and a wife who's been hurt by dickheads like Harkins too many times, you come back and tell me you're okay with abusers running free in your community," he said, his voice rising with anger. He set his mouth in a line and blew air out through his nose. Quiet tension reigned.

"I'm not saying we should let him go," Ben said, defeat in his voice. "I'm just saying...hell, I don't know what I'm saying." He scowled at Val and slouched down in his seat, arms crossed.

"Peterson will show you where we stake them out,"

Marshall said. "I'll run him through the system, see what the computer coughs up. Don't worry, Gil. We'll nail this guy. And I hope I get to be the one who drags his sorry ass into jail."

Val smiled. She and Detective Jalen Marshall had a lot in common.

Chapter Twenty-Two

Val had always envisioned stakeouts as tense, nerve-rattling activities, the glorious work of detectives high on the police food chain. Her debut experience at the Silver Fox did not disappoint.

Ben Peterson kept Jalen's promise and showed them a discreet location in the back of the club's parking lot where Gil and Val could keep an eye on the comings and goings of the front door. The location also allowed them to monitor the employee entrance in the dimly lit rear of the club. A third exit, marked for emergencies only, lay between the two. Gil scouted the interior and reported that clear warnings marked the emergency exit, with alarms to alert them if Harkins tried escaping through it. "I wouldn't want to piss those bouncers off," Gil said when he returned to the car with sandwiches for himself and Val. "Judging from their size and sheer number of tattoos, they've spent more time in prison than out, and neither one knows how to smile."

"Any sign of our dancer?" she asked around a bite of her sandwich.

"Yes, she just showed up for work." Gil unwrapped his own dinner. "I gave the bouncers a heads-up we're looking for Harkins, and they claimed not to know him. But they know her. Candy Sweet is her stage name."

"Gee, I wonder how her mother came up with that," Val said. "You think they'll cooperate?"

"Fifty bucks each says they will."

She took another bite of her sandwich and savored the spicy salami, pastrami, and banana peppers layered on top of cheese, shredded lettuce, and sliced tomatoes. The bread, fresh and warm, dripped with a heavy dose of pungent vinegar. "Thank you for dinner," she said, chewing. "This grinder's delicious."

"You can thank Jalen for that," Gil said. "His recommendation. He and Peterson are due back any minute with intel. That might be them now."

A brown Crown Victoria with far too many antennae parked a few spots away from them. Moments later, Jalen Marshall approached, now dressed in jeans and a leather jacket over a dark gray sweater, with an ascot cap atop his head. Gil lowered the driver's side window and waved.

"I'm feeling lucky tonight," Jalen said, leaning over to peer inside Gil's Ford Explorer. "Word is, our boy's a regular on weeknights, and Ben says he hasn't been by the last few nights. He's due."

"Where is Peterson?" Gil asked.

Jalen harrumphed. "The hell out of the way, that's where. Staking out the dancer's house in East Hartford. Hopefully he won't fuck that up."

"Any luck finding an address?" Gil asked.

Jalen shook his head. "Not for him. If Harkins shows up at the girl's house, we'll surround the place with cruisers, and we could be there in under twenty minutes." He handed Gil a sheaf of pages stapled together, thick with black type. "Read up. This is everything we've got on her, him, and this club. That ought to help you pass the time." He smirked at Val. "Having fun yet?"

"Just how I wanted to spend my day off." She held up half of her sandwich. "Have you eaten?"

"I've got leftovers in the car. Let's check in an hour from now." Something buzzed, and Jalen pulled a phone out of his jacket pocket. "Hey, Ben. Sup?...Okay, good to know...What? No, you asshole. Mind your damned business." He shook his head and put the phone away. "Stupid kid. These recruits, Gil, they get worse every year. Present company excepted, of course. I wish you'd have applied in Hartford, Dawes. Gil tells me you're a rock star."

Val ducked her head and blushed. "Thanks." She bit into her sandwich. She wondered how prevalent attitudes like Marshall's were toward new recruits, or whether Peterson had turned out as bad as she'd expected at the academy.

"What'd the kid have to say?" Gil asked. His sandwich remained uneaten in the open wrapper on his lap.

"The neighbors said Harkins hasn't been around since early this morning," Jalen said. "He drives a blue Impala, ten or fifteen years old, with Louisiana plates and a dent in the passenger side door. Should be easy to spot."

Gil held his sandwich at the ready, but still hadn't bitten into it. "Sounds like useful info. Why'd you call the kid an asshole?"

Jalen squinted at Val, then gazed off into the distance. "You don't want to know."

"I do," Val said, her suspicions climbing. "Did he say something about me?"

Jalen glanced at her again, a guilty expression on his face. "You two have bad blood, eh?"

"You could say that." She considered taking another bite, but her appetite had disappeared. "He hasn't gotten over being told 'no,' I guess. So what'd he say?"

Jalen sighed. "He made a smart-assed, inappropriate remark about you two being parked here in a dark spot, if you catch my drift." He shook his head. "Some people can't accept that women and men can do good police work together without jumping each other's bones. Hell. I can't wait to get my old partner back and dump this guy off on some other poor schmuck." He wandered off to his car, muttering to himself.

"Sorry about that," Gil said. "Jalen's a straight shooter. If you ask him a question, he'll give you an honest answer."

"I like that." Val wondered about Ben's comment, though. Was he seeing something romantic in the way they interacted, or was he acting on his own prejudices? She decided on the latter—it fit her view of the entire family of Petersons, not to mention her own preferred, platonic take on her relationship with her partner.

With that, her appetite returned, and she bit into her sandwich again. "Come on, man, eat," she said to Gil. "This stuff's delicious."

Gil grinned and tore into his grinder with gusto, finishing half before she swallowed two more bites. They spent the next hour reading the data sheets Jalen Marshall had provided. Unlike Harkins, Candy had a long rap sheet, with several arrests for prostitution, petty theft, and drug possession.

"I don't get why they're together," Val said in wonder. "He's almost twice her age."

"He probably feeds her habit, and provides protection from the pimps," Gil said. "Meanwhile, she gives him sex and a place to crash. He probably has ten more just like her, and vice versa."

"She's been in the hospital twice this year, according to this," Val said. "Claims that customers beat her up a half-dozen times. Twice in the past month." She set the pages on her lap, and blood drained from her face. "Since Harkins disappeared from Clayton."

Gil nodded and grimaced. "Fits the pattern. So much for the rumor he went down south."

Val shuddered at the thought of being with a man like Harkins. She felt sorry for Candy and the awful life she had to live. She scanned the page and chuckled. "I understand why she calls herself Candy. With a birth name like Eleonora Tagliaferro, it must take her an hour to fill out a change of address form."

Several minutes later, a blue Impala with a dent in the passenger side pulled into the lot. "That's him!" Val said in a whisper. "Let's go!"

Gil's phone buzzed. "Wait a sec," he said. "Jalen said Peterson will be here any second. Stupid kid forgot to call until a minute ago. He's calling for more backup now."

Val's heart pounded, blood racing in her ears. She couldn't believe it. Capturing Harkins would be the highlight of her short police career so far. While too many more like him remained, at least one child-abusing, woman-beating scumbag would be off the streets.

The Impala parked in a spot halfway across the lot, and a large, middle-aged white male got out of the car.

"Is that him?" Gil asked.

"I can't see his face," Val said. "Should I follow him?"

He eyed her with a quizzical look. "You want to go inside this place?"

She laughed. "Not really."

He reached across her and opened his glove box. A small pistol reflected the dim light of the lot. Gil checked it and stuffed it into his jacket pocket. "You brought a weapon, too,

I hope?"

"N-no," she said. "I didn't know we'd be doing a stake-out." Her eyes widened. "That didn't look like a service revolver."

He shook his head. "Nope. It's a Ruger Mark. Shoots .22s. But it'll do. You should get yourself one, if you don't have something already. They come in handy for moments like this."

"Why not your department-issue?" Her heart raced even faster. She didn't like this. At all.

"In case you've forgotten, we're not on official business." He gazed out at the man who'd exited the Impala. "But that doesn't mean we can't protect ourselves. Here, I brought a spare." He popped the glove box open again, pulled out a smaller, black weapon, and handed it to her. "My emergency backup. Ammo's in the box. I'd better get going. You go stake out his car in case he tries to make a run for it."

He got out of the car and signaled Marshall, then ambled toward the front door. Another unmarked Crown Vic with four antennae pulled in and parked on the edge of the lot. Peterson climbed out and hustled over to his partner's vehicle.

Val took deep, calming breaths while loading the snub-nosed pistol, a Walther .22, with ten rounds, its maximum. Her fingers shook. She hadn't fired a weapon since the Takura incident, except on the range, and never anything this small. Street thugs favored this type of weapon for its small size, low cost, and rapid trigger. Not very accurate, but at close range, with a ten-shot capacity, most gang-bangers found it adequate. Plus, it had threads in the barrel, to accommodate a silencer. A so-called "Saturday Night Special."

She felt ill at ease, and not only because of the street nature of the weapon in her hand. The idea of having to draw on another suspect so soon after Takura alarmed her. And she was off duty. What were the rules? How much trouble could they get into for this? Could they get suspended, or even fired? Or worse?

Gil seemed to have no second thoughts. But that didn't mean he knew what he was doing.

Val closed her eyes a moment, found her center. Pictured

Harkins in her mind. Officer Brian Samuels, bleeding on the living room floor of Antoinetta's house. Antoinetta, crying, bruised, and bleeding, having just been raped by Harkins.

She could do this. She had to. For Antoinetta.

She got out of the Explorer and walked toward the Impala. Her legs trembled beneath her. Please be him please be him please—

Sure enough, the Impala's plates matched the ones in Jalen's report. She took a position between the Impala and the strip club's front door where she could keep an eye on both through the windows of a large SUV.

The bouncers earned their fifty bucks. They delayed the man at the door long enough for Gil to get close, and their conversation grew animated and loud. "I come here all the time!" the man shouted at the bouncers, who continued to block the doorway and shake their heads at him.

"Forget it, pal," one bouncer said. "You ain't getting in here tonight."

"Screw you guys!" The man tried to push past them, but the bouncers blocked his path, standing shoulder to shoulder in front of the door.

"Last warning," one of them said. "Scram!"

"This is bullshit!" The man made one last attempt to push past, then collapsed to the ground, groaning and clutching his groin. "I'll sue you bastards for assault and battery!" he yelled around painful grunts. "I'll call the fucking cops on you!"

"No need." Gil walked over and grabbed the man, pulling him to his feet. "We're already here."

Without hesitation, Harkins shoved Gil into the two bouncers. He moved with surprising agility for his size and injured state, running away from the door, into the parking lot toward his car.

Toward Val.

The calm she felt in that moment surprised her. She slid the safety of the pistol forward, stepped into the open lane of the parking lot, and walked toward Harkins. He continued running toward her, glancing back at the doorway. Gil untangled himself from the bouncers and got to his feet. Harkins turned back toward Val and skidded to a stop, halfway between Gil and her.

"Freeze!" she said, feeling lame because he'd already stopped. She aimed her weapon with both hands at Harkins. "You're under arrest—"

Harkins dove to his left, hitting the ground with a grunt. She scooted toward him, following him with the nose of her gun, trigger finger at the ready. Her arms trembled, but she held her aim steady.

Movement behind Harkins caught her eye. Ben Peterson raced down the drive lane toward them. Harkins got up on all fours and scooted across the lane, toward a pair of pickup trucks—directly across Val's line of sight, in front of Peterson. Val cursed and relaxed the ready pressure on the trigger. She didn't dare fire when a miss might hit a fellow man in blue. Even a jerk like Ben Peterson.

Harkins ducked between the trucks, still crawling on all fours. Val ran into the line of cars, several spots away, parallel to Harkins' path. Footsteps crunched on the pavement behind her. She hoped that was Jalen, but dared not look away from Harkins' trajectory among the cars. Scuffling footsteps coming from the tangle of cars in front of her offered some idea of his location.

She crossed through the rows of cars to the Impala. She searched where she'd last heard movement. Nothing.

"Where the hell is he?" Peterson yelled from in front of her.

"Somewhere between us, in the lot," Val shouted back. "Where's our backup?"

"Coming," Jalen said from behind her, without conviction. "Secure the vehicle. I'll search underneath, row by row. Gil, you take the other side. Peterson, hang back in case he runs. We'll nail his ass!"

All went quiet, save for Jalen and Gil's footsteps padding between the cars, and their occasional grunts when they stood or crouched. A few would-be bar patrons stopped to watch by the bar's front door. Apparently, Hartford police put on a better show than Candy Sweet.

Minutes ticked by. Val's palms grew sweaty and her arms tired from holding her pistol at the ready. Her breath clouded in front of her face every time she exhaled, and the chilly air pinched at her nose and cheeks.

"Where the fuck is this guy?" Jalen said several minutes

later. "Dawes, are you sure you saw him?"

"Positive," she said. "He couldn't have gotten far." As soon as she said it, though, she realized it wasn't true. The lot stretched for a hundred feet in every direction. Poorly lit, it had no fence blocking escape on three sides, adjoining busy city streets. Harkins could be anywhere.

Two cruisers appeared, each containing two veteran cops in uniform. One parked behind Harkins' Impala, blocking it in, and freeing up Val to help with the search. But even with eight officers scouring the lot for the better part of an hour, Harkins could not be found.

"How the hell did he get away from us?" Jalen said when they gathered by the Impala. "We had him dead to rights."

"Who last saw him?" one of the veteran cops asked.

"I did," Val said, reddening. "He ducked into the lot—"

"Well then, there's your answer," Peterson said with a sneer. "A rookie mistake."

"You're one to talk!" Jalen turned to Val. "You couldn't get a shot off?"

Peterson stared at the ground, said nothing.

"I...no," Val said. "He—"

"Ben and I were behind her line of fire," Gil said, glaring at Peterson. "As were the security guys. Any stray shot, we'd have had casualties. Dawes did the right thing in not shooting."

Peterson scoffed. "You say so."

"Put a plug in it, Ben," Jalen said with a growl. "If you'd have given us a heads-up like you were supposed to, we would have had backup here in time, as planned. As it is, she probably saved your ass from getting shot."

Ben scowled at Val, his arms crossed. "Are we done here? Because I'm four hours deep into overtime, and unlike the rest of you, I haven't had dinner."

Jalen jerked a thumb over his shoulder. "Get the hell out of here, rookie." Peterson burned rubber leaving the lot moments later.

While Jalen supervised a tow truck called in to haul away the Impala, Val and Gil walked back to Gil's Explorer. "I'm sorry, Gil. I let you down," she said.

He waved it off. "You did the right thing. Don't worry, we'll catch him. He has no car and we know where he lives. He won't get far."

Val exhaled, her shoulders quaking with the release of tension. "What do we do now?"

Gil shrugged. "We go back to Clayton and let the Hartford P.D. do their jobs. Don't worry. They'll find him."

She climbed in Gil's Explorer, thinking of Ben Peterson's blundering moves and finger-pointing. Somehow, she didn't share Gil's confidence.

Chapter Twenty-Three

The moment Harkins saw the gun, he hit the ground, landing on his fingers and toes the way his wrestling coach taught him twenty-five years before. He scrambled into the haphazard rows of cars surrounding the Silver Fox and rolled underneath an oversized pickup truck jacked up way the hell too high. He continued rolling, finding darker shelter under a black SUV. Shouts and loud footsteps filled the air nearby, but faded moments later, as if his pursuers had lost track of him for a moment and run in the wrong direction.

But they'd return. He needed to move. He had one chance—a long shot, but one worth taking.

Scooting to the far side of the SUV, his left shoe fell off. Rather than waste time lacing it back on, he kicked off the other one and shoved both into crevices in the SUV's underbelly. That would muffle his footsteps while the Keystone Kops figured out which end of their assholes to wipe. He peeked out and spotted a dented silver Jeep. Raven's. One of his favorite dancers and occasional rolls in the hay. If he could make it that far without the cops spotting him...

Harkins crab-crawled among the cars toward the Jeep, occasionally rolling underneath for extra cover. Those stupid cops kept yelling to one another, creating enough noise to drown out his muted footsteps, and most seemed to move farther away instead of closer. Idiots.

He recognized the woman as the one he'd overpowered at Rosa and Antoinetta's. Dawes. The press had gushed about her after she shot that gangster in Clayton. What in the hell was she doing in Hartford? No matter. Once again she'd missed her chance at him. Dawes was weak and indecisive.

Harkins was neither.

Lying under a Subaru Forester, he checked out Raven's Jeep. Good—she hadn't gotten around to repairing the rip in the rag top. As always, she'd backed into the spot, as Harkins had taught her. He'd snuck out of her apartment one night while she slept and learned the ins and outs of the vehicle—in particular, where she hid her drugs and weapons. This chick made more on the side than she ever did dancing at the Silver Fox.

He heard scuffling footsteps to his right. The young skinny cop came into view, pointing a flashlight under the carriage of each vehicle in the line of cars leading up to the Forester. Harkins rolled, positioning himself behind the rear passenger side wheel. A beam of light cast long shadows on either side of the car, then swept past. He crawled around and suspended his body between the front of the Forester and the vehicle parked nose-to-nose with it, his ass pushed up against the other car's grille. If the cop looked closely, he'd be caught. But with luck, the darkness would provide sufficient cover.

The kid's footsteps crunched closer. Harkins controlled his breathing and kept his body still, his fingers aching from gripping the irregular shapes of the car's front end, his back and ass stinging from the sharp edges of the other vehicle's grille. Come on, kid. Hustle.

The footsteps got louder for several seconds, then stopped. The light flickered underneath the Forester, then through the windows of the adjacent vehicle. It stayed fixed on one spot, the beam flowing inches over his shoulder, for an eternity.

Radio static startled Harkins, and his hand slipped off the grille. Unable to support his weight one-handed, his body sagged toward the ground. His hand darted downward, landing flat-palmed on the rough pavement. A sharp pebble dug into the pad of his palm, and Harkins nearly yelped in pain. But fear of death smothered his scream.

"Peterson here," the kid said. The radio chirped static again. "Roger that," the kid said in response to the static. The flashlight flickered out, and the kid's footsteps grew softer again.

Harkins waited an extra ten seconds after the footsteps

faded away to silence, then eased himself to the ground. He crawled around the Forester to peek out behind the rear wheel. No sign of the kid. Without waiting, he dashed across the lane to the back of Raven's Jeep. He forced his body through the rip in the rag top, landing on an immense pile of laundry. He lifted the handle to the trunk compartment, scooped out the guns and drugs, and hid them under the laundry. He squeezed inside, shutting the lid behind him.

He lay there an hour or two. The air grew stuffy and hot, and his muscles ached from having to curl into a donut shape to fit in the compartment. At least three times, voices and footsteps sounded awfully close, and Harkins wished he'd kept one of Raven's guns handy. But, so far as he could tell, no one opened the vehicle.

He waited longer. The beeping and commotion of a tow truck filled the night air for a while. He assumed the worst, that they'd towed his Impala. Assholes. They'd pay for that.

The tow truck left, and another silent hour went by. He dozed off, waking some time later when he realized the car was moving.

***

Gil reassured Val a dozen times on the drive home that she'd performed "beyond expectations" on the Silver Fox stakeout, but doubts nagged at her the entire trip. He never changed his tune, though, even as he pulled up in front of her apartment to drop her off.

"Shit happens," he said. "The vast majority of perps walk scot-free. Most crimes don't even get reported. It's a miracle that we ever catch any perps."

"But we were so close." Val's chest grew heavy, and every breath seemed a chore.

Gil smiled. "And next time, we'll get him. I know we will."

She surrendered a morose smile of her own. "You're so full of shit, your eyes are brown."

"Shit floats," he said with a grin.

Val laughed. "You've got an answer for everything, don't you?"

Gil's smile sank to form a thin, horizontal line. "For everything except you," he said. "You, I think, will take a lifetime to understand. But, hey, I'm up for it." He paused a moment. "Gives me something to think about at night, instead of lousy street thugs."

Val's response caught in her throat. She swallowed, but the lump in her windpipe wouldn't subside. "Damn, you say sweet things, right when I least expect it." She sighed and stared at her fingernails, which needed serious work. According to Beth, anyway.

He said nothing back, instead sharing an enigmatic smile before gazing out the driver's side window. "This *is* your place, right?"

"Yeah. I should go." But she didn't. Her fingernails fascinated her all of a sudden. Next time she'd use something other than clear polish. Not pink, but maybe a dark red. Or something radical. Police blue, or—

Gil turned off the engine and drummed on the steering wheel. "I'll walk you up."

"No!" The word shot out before she could think, and Val covered her mouth. "Sorry. I mean, I'm fine. You don't have to."

One shoulder rose and fell. "I'll at least wait here, make sure you get inside."

"It's plenty safe." Still she sat in the seat, fussing with her fingernails, picking off the perfectly good polish. Dammit.

A car passed on the right, rolled to the end of the block, and turned. Leafless branches swayed in a sudden swift breeze. Gil's dashboard clock ticked to 11:49.

"So, in eleven minutes, do you turn into a pump—"

"I was raped two weeks before my thirteenth birthday."

Val's head spun at how suddenly the words spilled out of her, unrehearsed, unplanned, unpaced. A rush of syllables, revealing an inner truth she'd hated to admit to anyone her entire life. In so many words, she'd told exactly three people before: Beth, Uncle Val, and her first shrink. Not her parents. Not her brother. Not her first and only boyfriend in college, a boy who gave up after twelve weeks of dating with not even a hint of getting to second base. Not even the doctor who examined her, a middle-aged woman who diagnosed the situation in less than five minutes and threatened to tell Mom and Dad if Val didn't.

But now, Gil. Her mentor, partner, and—apparently—

trusted friend.

He locked eyes with her, lips sealed but downturned, like his unblinking eyes. Waiting.

"It was a friend of the family, a guy who used to bring toys and gifts to Chad and me...but mostly me," Val said, her eyes welling with tears. "And one night, my parents trusted him alone with me, and he...took advantage."

Gil squeezed the steering wheel with both hands, knuckles whitening. "I'm sorry, Val."

She shuddered out a noisy breath. "He never went to jail. I waited so long to tell anyone that there wasn't any physical evidence. By then I thought nobody would believe me, and convinced myself it was my fault anyway, and..."

Gil shook his head, but said nothing.

Val wrapped her arms around herself, shivering. "I felt so dirty, so guilty all the time. For the longest time I couldn't stand to be around boys of any kind—not my brother, my father, anyone. Except Uncle Val. He...I don't know...protected me, I guess. Believed me. Never judged me, just loved me for who I was. Then he died, and..." No more words would come. Only tears, and choked-back sobs, and a sharp ache in the center of her chest.

She opened her eyes, not sure when she'd closed them, and noticed Gil's open hand, reaching out to her. Still offering solace, no matter her response. Even if she never responded, Gil's helping hand would remain open to her.

Val took a deep, steadying breath and gathered his hand up in both of hers. Gripped it tight, felt its resolute strength, its warmth. She met his eyes, and blinked back tears, and discovered wet streaks lining his face.

"Why are *you* crying?" she said, choking over the words.

"Because," he said. "You're hurting."

"I was twelve," Val said. "That was a long—"

"You're still hurting," Gil said. "And, Officer Valorie Dawes, my friend and partner, who I've known for all of eight or nine weeks, I care about you. And I'll cry any damned time I want to." He finished with a wry smile and wiped tears off of his stubbled cheeks.

She laughed, a nervous release. "Okay. You hereby have the right to cry. This one time."

Gil smiled, then his face grew serious. "One thing I need

to ask you," he said. "Promise me something."

Val's heart raced. Oh, no. Now she'd done it. She'd known that telling him risked him wanting her to share even more, and he'd proven that in two minutes after—

"Promise me," he said, "that you'll never, ever tell me the name of the guy who did this to you."

She gawked at him, open-mouthed, and her tears stopped out of sheer shock. "Safe to say, that's not what I expected you to ask me."

Gil gripped her hands, still wrapped around his, and gave them a gentle shake. "Here's the thing," he said. "I'm a cop's cop. The moment I find out who hurt my partner...he's a dead man. And I'm not ready to quit police work over a silly little murder charge."

She laughed, so hard that it hurt her stomach. "Silly little...oh, man. Okay, you've got my word."

"And one more thing." Gil's eyes met hers, burning with intensity, and his voice shook when he spoke. "This was not. Your. Fault. Not one iota. Okay?"

"Okay." Val sniffled and wiped her face. They sat there a long while, long after the digits flipped over to 12:00 on the dash, looking at each other, hands locked. She took a deep breath. "Promise me something back."

He cocked his head. "Sure. Anything. What is it?"

She leveled a steady stare at him. "When we get Harkins—*when*—let me take that collar, okay?"

Gil smiled. "You've got it, partner. He's all yours."

Chapter Twenty-Four

Late November, ten years earlier

Valorie slumped in the back seat of the family station wagon on a raw, rainy Saturday morning, the day of her final 12-and-under soccer playoff. A win meant her team, The Wildcats, would raise the championship trophy at Pizza Hut later that afternoon. And with her thirteenth birthday coming up in two days, this would be her last game as a 12-year-old.

She didn't care.

The car progressed at a steady 30 miles-per-hour pace down the suburban boulevard next to the Clayton Youth Sports Complex. She stared at the streaks of water left by the constant drizzle on the windows, hoping the league would cancel the match due to rain. But no. When the fields came into view, girls and boys of various sizes, dressed in brightly colored uniforms, kicked wet balls to each other and rubbed their bare arms for warmth.

"Almost there," Dad said. "Look, we're not late after all. That's your team at the end, right?"

Valorie nodded. Kind of a jerk thing to do from the back seat, but Dad's eyes focused on her in the rear-view mirror, so he got her answer.

"Are you excited?" Dad asked in that annoying fake-eager voice he used in times like this. Like when she appeared for ten seconds as a cactus in that stupid third-grade play, or when he announced upcoming visits from relatives she'd never met.

"Whatever," Valorie said.

Dad glanced at her again in the mirror, the good humor disappearing from his eyes. "I thought you liked soccer."

She made a sour face. "It's pouring outside, and it's cold."

Dad laughed, that big, stupid laugh that meant he didn't really think it was funny. "You play in the rain all the time."

Yeah, she moped, but the rain made her clothes stick to her skin and showed her underwear. All the other girls' fathers would stare at her. Ick.

"Besides," Dad went on, "Your uncle is coming today. He's very excited. Don't you want to show him how good you've gotten? Maybe you'll score another goal."

She scoffed. "I doubt it. I got lucky last time."

Dad shook his head, stared at her in the mirror, then looked away so he could make the turn. He stopped at the far end of the parking lot. "You run on ahead while I park. I don't want you to be late."

She stared out the window at nothing.

"Valorie? Go on, now. What are you waiting for?"

She swallowed, or tried to. A lump of something got stuck in her throat. She wiped her nose on her sleeve, sniffled. "I don't want to play today."

"Valorie." Dad put the car in Park, but left the motor running, and turned to face her, as best he could with the seat belt still buckled. "Come on. You've missed two games in a row. It's your last chance to play this season. It'd be good for you. Please?"

"I don't feel well." She held her stomach, which hurt all of a sudden. Tears warmed her eyes, and she blinked super-fast to keep them from falling.

"Again?" Dad frowned, disbelief written all over his face. "It's because you're not eating. Here, I packed you an extra chewy granola bar. Chocolate chip, your favorite. Eat it up and you'll feel better." He handed her a brown paper bag, which probably contained three pieces of fruit and all kinds of other healthy stuff.

Valorie moped and took the bag. "I'm not hungry."

He frowned. "What's the matter with you lately? You're so quiet, you're not eating right, you don't even brush your hair some days. Has something happened at school, or between you and Beth?"

She shook her head, stared into her lap.

"Look," he said, "you don't have to play, but unless you tell me what's wrong—"

"I gotta go." Valorie pushed open the door and ran across the field, clutching her soccer ball and a bag of snacks against her sides. Thank God for the rain cooling the hot tears splashing down her cheeks. Nobody would know that she was crying.

Coach Katie Skinner, a thirty-something blonde-haired woman with boundless energy, smiled at her when she joined her teammates in the sideline huddle. "Just in time!" she said. "But you'll need to warm up before you play. Beth, will you practice with Valorie? Amy, you'll start at sweeper. Okay, girls, get out there, and have fun!"

Beth hugged Valorie, nearly breaking her neck. The girl didn't know her own strength sometimes. "I'm glad you made it," Beth said. "I was beginning to wonder."

"Yeah, me too." Valorie trotted a few yards away and passed a ball to Beth. The two girls kicked it back and forth several times, extending the distance each time. When they were 20 feet apart, Beth boomed a kick past her, into a crowd of adults watching the game. It bounced off a man's legs, and he picked the ball up.

"Thanks," she said, reaching for it, glancing up at the man's face—

Valorie froze.

Uncle Milt stood staring at her, gripping the ball in his hands, wearing that awful, sleazy smile. "Hello, Valley Girl," he said. He held the ball closer to his chest. "Is this yours?"

Dizziness swept over her, and her stomach buckled. Breathing became impossible. Nausea bubbled up inside her, and she crumpled to her hands and knees on the wet grass. What was he doing here? When Dad said "her uncle," she'd thought he meant Uncle Val. Not this weirdo. Oh my God oh my God oh my—

"Valorie?" Beth came up behind her, the earth shaking with every stomp of her running feet. "Are you okay?"

"I'm...I don't know..." Valorie choked on whatever fought its way up her throat. She gasped air through her mouth.

"She's fine," Milt said. "She just needs a little air."

A heavy hand rested on her back. Too big to be Beth's. She looked up, and the bulk of Milt's huge body blocked her view, on one knee in front of her.

He was near her. Touching her!

She dropped to her knees and vomited, hot acidic liquid shooting out of her mouth onto the grass. No solids, as she hadn't eaten squat in days. It burned her insides and tasted horrible. But Milt's hand stayed on her back, and she erupted again.

"Is she okay?" someone asked—a grown-up. "I think she's sick," said another.

"Give her some room!" Another man's voice broke through the buzz. A voice kind of like Dad's, but not. "Are you sick, Valorie?"

Uncle Val!

Uncle Val pushed Milt aside and sat next to her. Right on his butt, in the wet grass. "Breathe," he said, "nice and easy."

"I'm okay," she said. "I just—I'll be fine." She did as he instructed, though—sucked in a long, easy breath, then exhaled. Then again.

"Good girl." Uncle Val kissed her forehead, then stood and growled at Uncle Milt. "What the hell are you doing here?" He pushed the big man with a flat palm in his chest, knocking him back a step. "You've got a lot of nerve. Get the hell away from her, you piece of shit, before I kick your balls into next week."

"What'd I do?" Milt protested in a weak voice. "I was just standing here, minding my business, and—"

"If you aren't out of here in three seconds, I swear I will rip your goddamned head off and shit in the hole!" Uncle Val shouted.

Milt opened his mouth to protest, but before he could utter a syllable, Uncle Val grabbed Milt's jacket in his massive fists and lifted him to his tip-toes. With a mighty shrug, he tossed Milt onto his back on the ground. Before Milt could recover, Uncle Val karate-chopped Milt's throat, then knelt on his shoulder and chin, pinning him to the turf.

Excited voices exclaimed vague phrases of surprise and wonder. "Is he hurt?" someone asked. "What a punch!" said someone else. "That guy's a cop, isn't he?" said a third.

"Your three seconds are up," Uncle Val said in a low voice to a struggling Milt. "This girl told me what you did to her, and I will investigate. If I find a single solitary shred of evidence backing up her story, I will lock you up for the rest of your goddamned life, which I hope is as short as your worthless dick. Do you understand me?"

Milt squirmed on the ground, and a slew of grunts and unintelligible syllables emerged from his mouth. Valorie stumbled to her feet, and rested in the arms of Beth, who pulled her away from the quarreling men.

"Val? What's going on?" Dad raced up from the parking lot. "Who's that on the—Milt? Jesus, Val. What the hell are you doing?"

"Getting rid of some scum." Uncle Val ground his knee harder into Milt's face. "Now get out of here. Do you hear me?"

Milt managed a tiny nod, and Uncle Val removed his foot from Milt's face. Milt rolled to his hands and knees, breathing hard. Dad's gaze swiveled back and forth between the two men. "Would someone please explain—"

"He slipped," Uncle Val said. "Didn't you, Milt?"

Milt nodded, staring at the turf, and shook himself to his feet. Without looking back, he pushed his way through the crowd of onlookers and walked through the rain to the parking area. Moments later, a dark red Buick rumbled out of the lot.

Ms. Skinner appeared, gazing in wonder at the assembled crowd. "What happened?" she asked.

"Valorie and Beth, are you all right?"

"We're fine," Beth said. "Right, Valorie?"

Valorie nodded, shivering in Beth's arms.

"Are you two girls ready to play?"

Valorie shook her head and sank deeper into Beth's embrace.

Dad glared at Uncle Val and Valorie, with equal measures of bewilderment. "I'm very confused," he said.

"Are you okay, Valorie?" Uncle Val said.

Valorie shook her head again and left Beth's arms to be swallowed up in Uncle Val's bear-like hug.

"Katie," Uncle Val said, "I'm sorry, but I'm afraid Valorie's soccer season is over. Mike," he said, turning to Dad, "you and I need to talk."

Chapter Twenty-Five

Val stumbled into the kitchen late the next morning, her eyes barely open, in dire need of caffeine. To her surprise, a full pot waited for her on the counter with a puzzling note from Beth: "Save some for Val."

Then it hit her: the coffee wasn't for her.

"Hey there, sunshine," Josh said from behind her, walking in the front door with a carton of creamer and a dozen eggs. Despite the cold December morning, he wore only a hooded sweatshirt, gym shorts, and running shoes without socks. "I'm in charge of breakfast today. Cheese omelet okay?"

"Yeah, fine." She poured them both coffee and sipped hers in the living room while Josh cooked.

"So, why'd you go to Hartford last night?" he asked over the clanging of dishes and pans.

"How the hell did you know I went to Hartford?" she asked.

He laughed and held up his phone. "It's in the news."

"It's in the *what*?" She accepted the offered gadget and sat down to read. With a groan, she recognized the website: *Clayton Copwatch.*

Clayton Cops Take "Talents" to Hartford
By Paul Peterson

Clayton police, despite being unable solve our own town's growing crime problem, have decided to branch out into neighboring jurisdictions. Their tactics, and low success rates, seem to be rubbing off.

Two of Clayton's finest were involved in a bungled stakeout at—get this—Hartford's Silver Fox strip club last night. The result? A top fugitive, a man who attempted to murder a Clayton police officer several weeks ago, escaped into the wind.

Hartford police had maintained an ongoing stakeout of the

suspect's residence for several days. Yet they pulled sentries from that perfectly sensible location, where they could have arrested the suspect with relative ease, and attempted to surround him in a dimly lit, unsecured, two-acre parking lot.

Surprise, surprise. In spite of having extra staff on hand (imported from our own dear city), the fugitive escaped—again.

Did I say "surprise?" I meant to say, DUH.

And did I say "in spite of?" I meant to say, *because* of.

The Clayton officers involved include a certain female rookie cop who owes her employment solely to her family connections. The same rookie was responsible for the fatal shooting of an unarmed Asian man last month in Upper Abernethy. She and her partner have also been linked to bribes and corruption in multiple internal investigations. Investigations that, sources say, were quashed by powers-that-be so as not to embarrass the department.

"What a load of bullshit!" Val threw the phone down before remembering it wasn't hers. It bounced off the throw rug, against the thick wooden leg of the coffee table, and clattered back onto the floor. The device's various components flew in all directions.

"Hey!" Josh carried three plates of eggs into the room, his mouth agape. "Damn, girl. That phone cost me eight hundred bucks!"

"I'm so sorry," she said, red-faced. She picked up the pieces and reassembled the phone, then pressed the power button.

Nothing.

"It sometimes takes a minute," Josh said, doubt in his voice. "Beth, breakfast is ready!"

Val pressed the power button again, held it. Several moments later, she sighed and collapsed onto the couch. "I'll replace it," she said. So much for Christmas shopping this year.

"I kinda needed that today," he said. "I have a job interview. Over the phone. At two."

Crap. What a lousy way to spend a day off.

***

The following Friday night, Gil and Val walked the beat at an extra fast pace, partly in the hope of closing in on Harkins, and partly to stay warm. No amount of coffee could stave off the deep bone chill of the frigid night, however. Her fingers went numb within an hour, even wearing gloves.

They'd just decided to take the chill off in a local cafe when a shout sounded from up the street. A young African-American teen waved and ran toward them.

"Dog?" Val said in wonder to Gil. "Running *toward* us?"

"Copsky," Dog said when he drew near, out of breath. "Pope wanted me to tell you. That white dude you're looking for? He's back."

"Harkins?" Gil leaned over and held Dog by the shoulders. "Where? When did you see him?"

"With that lady and girl over on Greenfield Street," Dog said, still panting. "He's got a gun, too. Thomas saw him buy one at a pawn shop today."

"Call for backup!" Gil took off before she'd even unclipped her radio mic. "SWAT team, too. Do it!"

She called in the request while trailing him. Dog chased after her.

"What are you doing?" she said to him. "You can't come with us!"

"Pope said to collect his five hundred," Dog said.

"How the—! Dog, go tell Pope I'll pay him once we confirm he's there. Now get lost!" She raced away. He continued to run after her. "Dog, for God's sake, you're going to get yourself killed!"

He kept running. Almost keeping up with her. Dammit!

She stopped, faced him. "Dog, listen. I don't have it with me. But I'll bring it tomorrow. Okay? Now scram!"

Dog nodded and ran off in the opposite direction.

She passed Gil after another three blocks and arrived a block ahead of him at the intersection. A cruiser pulled up at Antoinetta's house a moment later. Two officers jumped out and hid behind it, guns drawn.

"Stay down!" one of them hissed at Val, a young red-haired officer named Shaughnessy. "Armed and dangerous!"

"We know," she said, tumbling into a crouch next to them. "We're the ones that called it in."

"Which house?" asked the other officer, an older African American named Jameson. Val pointed to Antoinetta's house, dark on both floors. "Who else lives here?" Jameson asked.

"Two females," she said. "Adult and young teen."

"I see movement on the upper floor," Shaughnessy said, peeking through field glasses. "Looks like it's one of the girls."

"One's a *woman*," Val mumbled. Freaking guys.

Gil joined them, out of breath, moments later. "Harkins has Antoinetta and her mom, or maybe her aunt, inside," she told him.

Gil nodded. "Dispatch said we've got two uniforms staking out the neighbor's yard and two more to the south," he said, still breathing hard. "They can watch the back door and the driveway from there."

Radio static echoed somewhere south of them. "Greenfield Units, please turn your damned radios down," Jameson said into his mic. "Unless you want to broadcast our every move to the son of a bitch!"

Gil gritted his teeth and glimpsed over the hood of the cruiser. "Once the SWAT team arrives, he ain't going anywhere, unless—"

Gunshots rang out, splitting the night with ear-shattering reports, accompanied by the tinkling of glass cascading down the roof over the front porch. Curtains sailed in the wind from an upstairs window.

"Jesus!" Shaughnessy said. "What's he firing, a cannon?"

"Sounds like a .44," Jameson said. "The real question is, what's he firing at?"

Another explosion, this time followed by a loud, close collision of metal on metal. The body of the cruiser vibrated against Val's hand.

"Us, that's who he's firing at!" She flattened herself to the ground, and another shot shattered the pavement in front of the vehicle.

"We've got to wait for the SWAT team," Shaughnessy said, fear quaking in his voice. "No way we can take this guy ourselves."

Jameson radioed in for more backup, and the four of them huddled behind the cruiser.

Gil peeked again over the cruiser's hood. "I see movement in the living room," he said. "He may be making a move."

"Something, or someone, is running around upstairs,

where the shots came from," Shaughnessy said. "He might have help."

Quiet reigned for several moments. All four officers checked their weapons. Val's heart raced, the danger of the situation colliding with the possibility of nailing Harkins. If it was Harkins. Please, please, she begged the universe, let it be Harkins.

A woman appeared in the bedroom window to the right, her hands on her head, elbows splayed to either side. She stood there, unmoving. Val couldn't tell if it was Camila, Antoinetta, or Rosa, her mother.

"He's got to have a gun on her," Jameson said. "Where the fuck is he?"

"It looks like she might be blindfolded," Shaughnessy said, again viewing the house through the binoculars.

More movement inside. A young girl appeared in the picture window in front. Val borrowed Shaughnessy's binoculars and looked through. "That's Antoinetta," she said. "She's blindfolded too. And her hands are tied."

"Think he has help in there?" Gil said.

Val shook her head. "He's always acted alone before."

"Alone or not, we need to stay put until he makes a move," Jameson said.

Another cruiser pulled up and parked behind them. Two more uniforms got out, guns drawn.

"Could you be a little more obvious?" Jameson said in a hoarse whisper to them. "Turn those stupid lights off!"

"Movement in the rear of the house," a male voice barked over someone's radio. "Door's opening—"

A shot rang out, echoed over the radio, followed by swearing. "This fucker's crazy!" the radio voice shouted. "Holy shit, he's out, he's on foot, he's coming around...he's on the north side, coming toward you—"

Val caught Gil's eye. "He's mine, remember." She unholstered her weapon. "You promised."

"Dawes," he said. "In a normal situation, yeah, but this is different. We—"

Another explosion, and a bullet whizzed past over their heads. Val peeked through the car windows, then swung her arms over the hood, aiming her weapon toward the north of the house.

"Get down, Dawes!" Gil shouted at her.

She ignored him. Where was Harkins?

A flash of light, and a shot slammed into the car's front grille, spraying shards of metal and glass everywhere. Bits of everything sprayed her face, drawing blood. Luckily nothing hit her eyes. She dropped to her belly and rolled toward the front of the car, again aiming at the shadows on the house's north side.

"Dawes! Get back here!" Gil hissed.

Something moved in the darkness on the side of the house. She'd never get a shot at him from behind the car. "I can get a clear shot from those hedges over there," she said.

"Don't even think of it," Gil said. "That's suicide!"

Another gunshot. The windshield of the cruiser behind them shattered onto the sidewalk. "We're sitting ducks here!" Shaughnessy said. "We've got to do something!"

"I smell gas," Jameson said. "Shit, look! One of those shots must have hit the gas line. If he gets lucky, we'll all go up in a goddamned fireball!"

She swore and raised herself into a sprinter's crouch. She took in a breath—

A rough hand drew her backwards, and she tumbled onto the ground, bits of broken glass pricking her skin. Gil sprawled backwards, landing in front of the car. His backside, then his head, hit the pavement, and he lay still.

Unprotected, in full view of the house.

Another gunshot, and asphalt exploded on the opposite side of Gil. He raised his head, shook it, as if dazed. His weapon lay a few feet from him, farther away from the shelter of the cruiser, and he leaned over to reach for it.

"Kryz!" Jameson shouted. "What the hell are you—!" Another shot drowned out his remaining words.

"He's concussed. He needs help!" Val tried to crawl over to him, but a pair of large hands held her in place.

"Don't you go out there too!" Jameson shouted in her ear. "Kryz, get back here!"

Val struggled against Jameson's grip, but she couldn't shake herself loose. Then another shot rang out, and Gil's body convulsed.

He did not fire back.

He did not move.

Val screamed in rage, throwing Jameson's arms off of her. "Cover me!" she yelled over her shoulder and scampered on her knees toward Gil, weapon drawn. Out of the corner of her eye, she noticed movement—a dark figure, Harkins-sized, near the house. She fired at it, splintering the siding on the corner of the house, and the shadow disappeared.

She reached Gil's side. More gunshots rang out, and bullets whizzed around her. She ignored them. Gil wasn't moving.

"Gil!" she shouted. "Gil, are you all—"

Then she noticed the blood, drenching his right side, in the gap where the kevlar vest ended above the hip. The torn fabric. How still his body lay.

"Officer down!" she heard herself shouting. "Goddamn it to hell. *Officer down!*"

PART 3

Partner Trouble

Chapter Twenty-Six

The cops went into ape-shit mode, as Harkins expected, as soon as the big guy went down. For a moment he feared that the woman cop—probably the same one who'd tried to arrest him at Rosa's last time, and at the Silver Fox—would take a shot at him, but she went just as ape-shit as the others. Dawes had frozen in Hartford, and she'd frozen in the house the first time they'd met. He filed those facts away for future reference. For now, he had to move.

He hid in the overgrown bushes that lined the edge of the property, an evergreen variety that provided lots of cover. They'd grown up against the siding of the house, forming a waist-high tunnel under the thick canopy, camouflaging him in the dark thicket. He crab-crawled toward the back yard, but stopped when footsteps and rustling noises emerged ahead. The two cops guarding the rear, he guessed, were heading his way.

He squeezed through a gap among the trunks of the shrubs, counting on the cops' racket to cover the noise he made. After scooting the ten feet of open space to the neighbor's house, Harkins ran to the far corner where a network of plank and chain-link fences joined behind a leafless, sad-looking maple tree. He used the tree's branches to help him scale the fence, the way he'd seen Antoinetta and her friends do it, and slid down the other side to the spongy turf.

Harkins stayed low and followed the cedar plank fence away from the chaotic scene at Rosa's house. A couple of kids ran by, chattering in Spanish, too excited to notice him. Still, he crouched in the shadows until he could no longer hear them, exhaling steamy breaths into his jacket. He listened for the footsteps of adults large enough to wear blue uniforms, or who would report a suspicious-looking gringo to the cops. But none came.

He scanned the yard, looking for a path to escape—anything except the brightly lit street. Just his luck, this neighbor kept their front yard's flora tidy. But one of their kids had left a full-sized bicycle laying on the ground, unlocked.

Five minutes later, chilled by his own sweat in the frigid air, he abandoned the bike at a nearby park. He boarded a city bus and crouched in the back row, behind a group of rowdy black teenagers with multiple gold earrings. One of them made eye contact with him, and he glared at the kid until he looked away. Still. Not good. His heart rate jumped up, and he started to sweat again.

Harkins got off the bus two stops later and pulled his jacket close, his upturned lapels warming and hiding his face, and walked, head bowed, until he spotted Raven's Jeep outside her sister's place. He had it hot-wired in under a minute. He had everything he needed to get away...except somewhere to go.

No matter. He drove. Worry about those details later.

***

Val dragged Gil to safety behind the parked cruiser and stayed with him, applying pressure to his wound with a bandage she improvised from a section of Gil's shirt. She checked his heartbeat and breathing several times—still there. Meanwhile, Shaughnessy and Jameson set the perimeter as the SWAT team arrived. An ambulance pulled in a few minutes later, or a few hours, she couldn't tell. The medics took years to secure him to the gurney, then hoist him in the ambulance, and then, in an instant, the vehicle peeled away, siren blaring.

"Go with him," Jameson said. "We've got this, and you'll be useless to us until you know he's all right. Go on, get out of here."

Val stumbled away, upright, but only got a few steps before Shaughnessy pulled her to the ground. "You got a death wish?" he said to her. "Stay low until you get clear of the site. Where's your vehicle?"

She stared at him, not recognizing him for a moment, or

the words he spoke. When it sank in, she sat on the ground, numb, tears etching a salty path down her face. She had to do something—what was it? Right. Find their cruiser. Head to the hospital. "Where'd they take him?" she mumbled.

"Mercy General, I think. They're the closest ER." Shaughnessy squinted at her. "Are you okay to drive?"

Val nodded, aware that he knew she was lying. What could he do? He had to stay at the scene.

She rolled to her hands and knees and shuffled over to a thick patch of hedges that shielded her from sight, then got to her feet. She walked at a slow pace at first, directionless. At the end of the block she realized she was closer to home, and her own Honda Civic, than to the cruiser. She broke into a run, then stopped, realizing that she still had her gun drawn, safety off. When had she pulled it out again? She wiped blood off of it, onto her already-bloody uniform, and re-holstered it. She took in a deep breath, exhaled. Focus. What's next? Oh, right. The car.

Val sprinted past houses and intersections and stop lights, all a hazy blur to her. She reached her Honda in five minutes, Mercy Hospital in another ten. She parked in a patients-only spot and raced to the emergency room's double glass doors. They opened automatically, but not fast enough. She pushed them open faster with a grunt and lurched into the room.

The receptionist glanced up from her computer screen and gasped. "Officer, are you hurt?" he asked.

"What? Me? No." Val examined her condition. She looked like a gunshot victim herself, other than the fact that she could, obviously, run. "An officer was just brought here by ambulance. Gil Kryzinski. Where is he?"

"He's being prepped for surgery." The receptionist pointed to a set of swinging doors. Val pushed through them and followed the signs to the surgical ward. Another receptionist waved her over and informed her that Gil had just gone under anesthesia. "Are you in any pain?" she asked Val, her eyes wide.

Val shook her head, numb, and sat in a hard, metal-framed chair to wait.

Blake and Gibson showed up fifteen minutes later, along

with a couple of bureaucrats who took care of the paperwork related to Gil's admission and treatment. "Any word?" Gibson asked.

"Still under the knife," Val said. Her voice broke, and she failed in her attempt to rise out of the chair.

The men sat on either side of her, and Gibson rested a hand on her arm. She resisted the urge to pull away. He cleared his throat to get her to look at him. "What the hell happened out there?" he asked.

"Harkins opened fire and pinned us before the SWAT team got there," she said in a dull voice. "I came up with the dumb idea to change position and get a better angle on Harkins. Gil tried to stop me, and..." A sharp pain knifed through her chest. Breathing became difficult. Words, impossible.

"Take it easy, Dawes," Blake said. "Take a breath."

Val fought tears, holding her sides. Gil had taken a bullet. *Her* bullet. And now he might die. "Did they get him?" she asked in a weak voice. "Harkins, I mean."

Blake and Gibson exchanged glances. "We're still looking," Blake said.

"What? You mean he got away?" Val's anger flashed, then sank under the weight of the sadness that swept over her. "What will it take to get this guy?"

They sat in silence for a few moments, nobody having an answer.

"We hoped you could give us an idea of where he might have gone, or who to talk to," Blake said. "Seeing as how you've made him a project of sorts."

Val leaned back, still forcing the tears not to leave her eyes. She wished she had an answer for them—for Gil. But if he was in Clayton, and no longer at Antoinetta's, she had no idea. That saddened her, and she gave only a muted choke in response.

"Let's give her a minute," Gibson said. "Dawes, maybe you should go clean up?" He squinted, concern on his face. "You might want to get looked at—"

"I'm fine," she said, her voice sharper than intended. She wiped her eyes with her hands. "I'll wait here, in case there's news."

"Let's get her a fresh shirt, at least," Gibson said to Blake. "Dawes, you need to have a doctor look at you. I can see bits of glass in the cuts in your face. I insist."

Val touched her face and winced in pain as her fingers pressed tiny shards of shattered windshield into her skin. Between that and the blood on her blouse, she must look a fright. "Okay," she said. "But if there's any news—"

"We won't let them tell us until you get back," Gibson said with a hint of a smile. "Now, go."

A young female intern cleaned her cuts and picked out the glass bits in a cramped, antiseptic treatment room. Someone knocked on the door, and moments later Brenda Petroni entered with a clean blouse, sweater, and a pair of jeans.

"Are you okay?" Brenda asked her. Val stared at her in a fog. "Yeah, uh...what time is it?"

Petroni's face curled into a puzzled frown. "What time...? Val, did you get hit in the head? You're behaving oddly."

"No, no," she said. "It's just all too much. I'll be fine."

Brenda nodded, but her expression remained skeptical.

Back in the waiting room, they exchanged office gossip until the receptionist directed a tall, ginger-haired woman in her thirties over to them. She wore fashionable black slacks, a crisp white blouse, and impeccable make-up. Definitely not an on-duty doctor or nurse.

"Lieutenant Gibson?" she said when she neared them.

Gibson stood. "That's me. And you are...?"

The woman extended a well-manicured hand. "I'm Jessica Swan. Gil Kryzinski's fiancée."

If Val had not still been seated between Petroni and Blake, she would have fallen to the floor. The others stood to express their concern to the woman, but the room swirled around Val, rendering her immobile. From her seat, she gazed up at the newcomer, an archetype of femininity, with her flawless skin, long red hair, huge green eyes, and a slender but proportional figure. Despite her emotional state, Val detected confidence, intelligence, and alertness that would carry her in a crisis like this. No wonder Gil loved her.

Val, not so much.

"How did it happen?" Jessica said in a broken voice.

"Dawes?" Gibson asked. "Can you provide some details?"

Val steadied herself on the arms of her chair and pushed herself to her feet. She extended a handshake, her fingers trembling. "I'm Val Dawes."

"You're Gil's partner." A statement, not a question. Jessica Swan's voice grew icy, her eyes distant. "I've heard about you." She turned away from Val to face Gibson. "If you don't mind, I'd rather hear the *official* version of the incident."

"Ms. Swan," Val said, "I'm very sorry for—"

Swan whirled to face her. "Not sorry enough to keep him from possibly getting killed!" Her lip trembled, and she glared at Val another moment before turning back to face Gibson. Her voice calmed again. "Now, Lieutenant, what information can you share with me?"

"Excuse us, please." Gibson furrowed his brow and shook his head at Val. He pulled Swan aside and spoke to her in a low voice.

"Since when does Kryz have a fiancée?" Brenda asked Val and Blake. "And where does he hide her? She looks like a runway model!"

Blake shrugged and waited for Val. "News to me," she said. "He told me he wasn't seeing anybody. Not since he left New Haven."

Jessica strode over to within a few feet of Val and crossed her arms. Her voice shook. "Yes, I'm the one Gil left behind in New Haven. We've resumed our relationship in recent weeks, long-distance." She cast Val a withering glance. "We were *supposed* to get together this week, but he had to work on his day off."

"Gil and I are just friends," Val mumbled, her heart racing. "You have nothing to worry about from me." She wanted to believe that. But the words sounded hollow to her.

Swan addressed Gibson again. "If you check your HR records, you'll see I am still Gil's emergency contact and am authorized to make medical decisions on his behalf. I understand that you approved surgery for him?"

"It was an emergency, and our lawyers—"

"I appreciate that," she said, calmer. "But I'll take it from here, thank you." She strode away from them and spoke again to the receptionist.

Gibson heaved a sigh and they sat down in uncomfortable silence. Brenda patted Val's arm, sitting next to her. For once, she didn't feel revulsion at the intimate human contact. She rested her hand on Brenda's and lost herself in fearful musings about Gil's wounds and surgery while Blake sauntered off to get everyone coffee.

Two hours later, a gray-haired woman in clean scrubs approached them. "Ms. Swan?" she said to Val. "I'm Dr. Vargas, Officer Kryzinski's surgeon."

"Over here," Jessica said, huffing in exasperation. "How's Gil?"

"Gil's resting and in stable condition," Vargas said. "The bullet damaged some muscle tissue and tore the wall of his large intestine. It also grazed his pelvis, enough to scatter fragments of bone into his abdomen, causing significant internal bleeding and contusions on the outer walls of his small intestines. We saw no damage to other organs, but we'll monitor him for several days to make sure."

"What's the prognosis, then?" Blake asked. "I mean, is he...will he...?"

"He's not out of the woods yet," Vargas said, her tone grave. "He lost a fair amount of blood, and suffered shock, both from the trauma of the wound, and from surgery. But he's showing great signs. I like our chances."

Our chances. Val bit her lip, hard. When doctors talked about "chances," that meant they didn't know for sure. She discovered Brenda Petroni's arm supporting her around the waist, and she sagged into her. The rest of the group remained quiet, absorbing the news. Jessica Swan stood alone, her eyes shut, her body shaking.

"When he recovers, and I say *when*," Blake said with false bravado, "what's he looking at? Will he walk again?"

Vargas nodded. "Yes, but it takes time," Vargas said. "The intestinal damage, and the risk of infection, is our most immediate concern. The damage to the pelvis, though, will take much longer to heal. Pelvic bone is very thick and provides core support to the entire body. He'll need to be immobile for a few weeks. After that, he'll be in considerable pain and won't be able to walk under his own power for several weeks."

"Will he require further surgery?" Jessica asked, her eyes still pressed shut.

"Not immediately," Vargas said, "and it depends on how his pelvic bone heals." She turned to Gibson. "I'm afraid you'll be without his services for the foreseeable future. Months, perhaps longer."

"Or forever, if I have anything to say about it." Jessica opened her eyes again and pushed long red hair out of her tearful eyes. "And I expect that I will."

Chapter Twenty-Seven

On Monday morning, Dr. Chris Cyrus waved Dawes inside his office with a forced smile. "How was your Thanksgiving?" he asked.

"Fine." She brushed past him and took a seat on the edge of the sofa. A handful of half-healed scrapes on her face presented the only outward evidence of the trauma she'd experienced in recent days. Dressed in jeans and a blouse, her short, light-brown hair pulled back in a headband, she looked less like a cop who'd just seen her partner shot and more like a college kid focused on passing final exams.

Cyrus pushed his black-rimmed glasses onto the bridge of his nose, waiting for more. None came. He sighed. Something about this woman disturbed him. Not her cockiness, a trait she shared with her male counterparts—in lesser amounts, if he told himself the objective truth—nor, even, her reticence to share her innermost thoughts and feelings. That, too, her male counterparts shared, many exhibiting even greater reluctance than Dawes. Nor even her open resentment at having to go through psychological evaluation again, for the second time in less than two months—another trait the men shared.

No, something else bubbled inside this one. Something made Valorie Dawes extra angry, more mistrustful of the world, even more than male cops twice her age who'd earned their cynicism. Something that, someday, might manifest itself in a way they would all regret.

But for now, Cyrus had no actual evidence of her being disturbed. For now, it was just a feeling. And feelings didn't justify negative evaluations.

"My condolences to you and your partner for this tragic turn of events," Cyrus said, stalling. Maybe a little empathy would open her up.

"He's not dead, for God's sake," she said, her voice hoarse. "But I'll pass on your good wishes when I see him."

Cyrus drew a deep breath. Take it slow. "Have you seen him since..."

"He's been under heavy sedation, in intensive care. I'll see him as soon as he's able to receive visitors." She made a face, as if remembering something distasteful.

He thought about asking why, then figured it was obvious. "And how are you feeling?" he said. "Your cuts are healing?"

She scoffed and shook her head, staring at the floor. "Yeah, it took two or three band-aids and a whole squirt of Bactine to put me back on my feet." Dawes fell silent a moment, then met his gaze. "I guess I'll live, too."

Cyrus nodded and made a note of her surliness—again— on his notepad and smiled. "I'm glad you're okay, physically. I hope your mental and emotional state are equally strong. When officers witness their partners getting shot, even non-fatally, it can be a traumatic experience."

"You can say that again." She exhaled, hands folded across her knees. "So, what do you need to know?"

He coughed into his palm, surprised by her directness. She'd been so evasive on prior visits. "Are you sleeping well?" he asked.

Dawes shrugged. "Hard to say. It's only been two nights. I stayed up all Friday night waiting for him to recover, then took a few naps on Saturday. Worked out at the gym yesterday, trying to wear myself out."

The doctor pursed his lips, evaluating her response. "You didn't answer my question."

She blew out a burst of air, as if exasperated. "Six hours a night, maybe five. I'll sleep better once Gil comes out of the ICU. Sound normal?" Her voice rose, then tightened, under her conscious control.

Cyrus shifted in his seat. This woman clearly wanted to strangle him. Yet, he had a job to do. She wasn't making it any easier. Perhaps she'd appreciate an approach as direct as her own.

"Do you blame yourself for Officer Kryzinski's injury?" he asked.

"He took my bullet." Her voice remained calm, matter-of-fact. "Of course I'm responsible."

Cyrus leaned back in his seat, weighing her words. "I wasn't aware of that detail," he said. "Did he say why he did that?"

Dawes rolled her eyes. "No, he was too busy bleeding and passing out," she said. "But I'll ask him when he wakes up, for your files. Jesus!" She stood and paced across the room, her back to him.

He let her blow off some steam, wandering about, scanning the various diplomas, certifications, and commendations framed against the dark walls of his office, taking her time. After a few moments, though, Cyrus grew self-conscious. He'd earned his degrees from smaller, less-famous schools, and earned his few commendations over a decade ago. He imagined her judging him, not favorably. "Miss Dawes?" he said when his nerves could take no more.

She returned to the sofa, her face calm. "Did you have anything else to ask me?"

"How do you feel about the man who shot your partner?" Cyrus asked. "I understand you've been in pursuit of him for some time now."

Dawes barked out a sharp laugh and gazed at the ceiling. "Richard Harkins is human garbage who has abused countless women and children, shot two police officers, and God knows what else. We need to stop him before we have to bury his next victim. Which I would like to help with, in every fiber of my body. But where am I going to be while you 'evaluate' me? Tied to a telephone in a precinct office, listening to angry neighbors complain about stray cats and errors in their tax bills. Does that make sense to you, *Doctor* Cyrus?"

The force of her words pressed him back into his chair, his shoulders hunched around his neck. He cleared his throat, forcing calm into his voice. "It makes sense that we ensure our peace officers are not acting out of anger or revenge when they apprehend a suspect," he said. "Surely you agree that taking a moment to determine your emotional state—"

"Look," she said, leaning forward on the sofa, her voice tense but even. "I get it, okay? You don't want me shooting first, asking questions later. So listen, Doc. Since I started this job three months ago, I've pulled my weapon out three times, and fired once—in self-defense. Each time, I filed a mountain of useless, unread paperwork, which alone ought to be enough to discourage anyone from even thinking about unsnapping their holster. I'm not running amok out there, okay? I'm exercising restraint, and I will continue to do so. It's how I was raised, it's how I was trained, and it's how I've conducted myself on the job.

"As for my emotional state, I want to kick the shit out of that son of a bitch," Dawes went on. "But I won't. When I do find him, I will drag him by his long, greasy hair straight into a jail cell, and testify at his trial to make sure the judge and jury throw away the key. Write *that* down, submit your report, and let me get back to doing just that. *Please!*"

Cyrus exhaled, realizing he'd held his breath during her entire speech, and licked his lips. Part of him agreed with her about the futility of the department's policy of requiring psych evals following partner shootings. Officer Samuels' partner, Lopez, said almost the same thing a few weeks back, although he hadn't spoken with the same level of passion. He'd sent him back out without a second thought.

Maybe that's what Cyrus had sensed earlier. Her passion. That wasn't such a bad thing. He'd seen cops go bad out of cynicism and frustration with, as they put it, how the department and city council tied their hands with red tape. None went awry out of passion for protecting the citizenry, in his experience.

He stood and ambled toward the door, signaling for her to follow. When she met him at the door, he smiled at her. "I should have my report filed in a day or two," he said. "In the meantime, I recommend you take time off, visit your partner in the hospital, and try to relax. I can prescribe sleep medication—"

"Not necessary," she said. "What will your report say?"

He paused, reading her eyes. He saw eagerness, and— what? Just the passion, or was it something more? He couldn't tell. Meanwhile, she waited, unmoving.

"I'll recommend that you return to patrol duty," he said in a rush of air and words.

"Thanks, Doctor." She gave his hand a perfunctory shake and strode out the door.

He watched her go, and second thoughts about his decision crept into the back of his mind before she left his sight.

***

Val took the bus from Cyrus's office to Mercy General and learned that the doctors had moved Gil from intensive care to a private room. Shedding her jacket, she roamed the hospital until she located his room, where two uniformed officers stood at attention outside his door. The larger of the two she recognized. "Are we expecting an attack on Gil's strategic location, Pops?" she asked him with a wry smile.

Pops scowled at her and exchanged glances with the other uniform, a quiet guy named Rico Lopez, whom she recognized as Samuels's former partner. "Standard procedure after an officer shooting," Papadopoulos said. He blocked her attempt to open the door. "He's got company already."

"So?" She took a step back, as much to escape the smell of garlic emanating from his every pore as to acknowledge his guardianship. "How small a room is it?"

Pops shook his head. "One visitor at a time. The fiancée's in there right now. Good-looking gal with red hair. Have you two met?"

Val's heart sank. "We have." Of course Jessica was still there.

Pops shrugged. "I'll let her know you want to visit. Better wait over there for now. It'll give you time to react if she goes ballistic." He laughed and slapped his partner's arm. Lopez rolled his eyes but said nothing.

Pops hitched up his belt and waited, his eyes resting on Val. About chest level, to be exact. The one time she wore a form-fitting top, too. She moseyed over to the waiting room and remained standing while Pops entered Gil's room. He exited moments later, a satisfied smile on his face, and he made his way over to her.

"She says she'll be just a few minutes, then he's all yours," Pops said.

"Is he awake?" Val asked, hopeful.

"In and out," Pops said. "He's pretty doped up, but he

seemed happy to hear you wanted to see him."

Val sat on one of the metal-framed chairs and stared at the muted TV, trying to get comfortable, without success. She brought out her phone and caught up on email, which took only a few seconds, and struggled to remember her Facebook password, eventually giving up.

Minutes ticked by. Nobody emerged from Gil's room. Damn Jessica! She was playing with her, hoping Val might give up or create a scene. The latter option tempted her, but that wouldn't help Gil any. She drew deep breaths and continued waiting.

A half hour later, the door opened, and the tall, ginger-haired beauty swished past the two officers. Val stood and half-ran to Gil's door.

Jessica stopped and held up an open palm. "Could you wait before going in, please?" she said. "I need to speak with you, but I need a moment to collect myself."

"I just want to say hi," Val said. "I have to leave soon. My shift starts at five."

"I'll just be a moment. Please." Jessica disappeared into the ladies' room. Val sighed and returned to her seat.

Jessica, true to her word, emerged a few minutes later and ambled over to Val, taking the seat next to her. She seemed lost in thought at first, and Val opted to wait her out. After a moment, Jessica cleared her throat. Val braced herself for the verbal onslaught.

"I want to apologize," Jessica said, "for being a perfect bitch to you the other day. I was upset and worried, but I shouldn't have taken it out on you. I realize you were also worried and upset about Gil's condition, and I only made an emotional situation even more difficult."

Val, stunned, searched for words. "Thank you," she said. Relief flowed through her. She'd braced for a fight and hadn't even realized how tense her body had become. "I understand. It's a terrible situation."

"I...how can I say this?" Jessica looked away, her hands bundled together in her lap. "I blamed you," she continued in a soft voice. "For Gil being shot. The other night, I mean. I don't feel that way now." Her voice dropped to a whisper, and she clenched her eyes shut.

"I blame myself, too," Val said. "Finding this guy Harkins

has become a fixation for me, and Gil has kind of…adopted the cause, so to speak. When I suggested we get more aggressive, Gil preempted what I was going to do, and… and…that's when he got shot."

Jessica opened her eyes and wiped tears from her cheeks, smearing mascara onto her face. "He has a bit of a hero complex," he said. "That's one reason we broke things off years ago. I couldn't bear the worry anymore, of wondering whether he'd be coming home each night, or if I'd end up in a place like this…or worse." The tears flowed again, this time in torrents, accompanied by loud, mournful sobs.

Val watched her a moment, unsure of what to do. The poor woman was a wreck, in need of a comforting hand. But providing comfort had never been one of Val's strong suits, and memories lingered of how Jessica had treated her two nights before, despite the apology. She hesitated, hoping the crying would stop on its own, somehow.

It didn't. Jessica cried harder, wrapping her arms around herself in a self-hug, rocking from side to side.

Val's throat constricted. Her hand hovered near Jessica's shoulder, shaking. Almost close enough to touch her. Almost.

She recalled her own pique of sadness, two days before, and how comforting Brenda had been, just sitting with her and holding her hands. How grateful she felt. Why couldn't she do the same for this woman, who was so important to Gil?

Jessica's body rocked harder, and her shoulder brushed against Val's hand. To her own amazement, Val didn't pull it away. Instead, she extended both arms and wrapped them around the sobbing woman's shoulders, drawing her in, holding her, rocking with her to Jessica's own internal rhythm. At some point, Jessica returned the hug and rested her forehead on Val's shoulder.

Minutes passed, maybe hours. Days. Val's body ached from holding the woman in the awkward position. It ached more from the inside, though, as Jessica's grief crept into Val's own heart. Grief for Gil that she shared, fear for what might happen to him now, and compassion for what this poor woman must have felt upon hearing the news. Her own body shook almost as much as Jessica's.

How odd, that she only allowed herself to feel this in the arms of a stranger, and only through another woman's grief. How cold she'd become!

After several minutes, Jessica's sobbing slowed, then stopped, as did her rocking. She pulled back and wiped her eyes, then looked at Val and smiled. She reached out to touch Val's face and wiped wetness off of Val's cheeks. How her cheeks had gotten wet, Val had no idea. Must have been Jessica's tears, dripping onto her, somehow, from below.

"Thank you," Jessica said. "Thank you so much." She handed Val a tissue from her purse and used another to wipe her own face. "I must look a wreck." She emitted a short, sad laugh. "How do you keep your mascara from running?"

Val dried her cheeks with the tissue. "I don't wear any," she said in a small voice. How stupid that sounded. How unfeminine, especially compared to this beautiful creature.

"Your eyes are that pretty naturally?" Jessica said with a sad smile. "I'm jealous."

Val's head spun. This gorgeous woman, with perfect—oh, everything—was jealous of *her*? Words would not come.

"Well," Jessica said, "you'd better get in there while he's still awake." She gave Val a quick, firm hug and sat in the hard metal chair nearby.

Val trudged over to Gil's room. Pops looked down his long nose at her, clucked, and pushed open the door.

Gil lay flat in the bed, a myriad of tubes and wires running from his body to a slew of machines beeping nearby. His skin, what little she could see through the blankets and bandages, had paled, almost as white as the sheets. She drew to the bedside and rested a hand on his arm. He opened his eyes.

"Dawes," he croaked, and the hint of a smile turned up the corners of his mouth. "Thanks for coming."

"I'm so sorry," she said. A lump rose in her throat.

He waved his hand a few inches over his chest. "Not...your fault."

"You're right," she said, forcing a grin. "You stole my idea."

Gil half-laughed, half-coughed. "One of your worst ones," he said through heavy breaths. "Shit, this hurts." He shifted in the bed, maybe a millimeter, and winced in pain. He turned his head toward her. "Harkins got away, huh?"

Val's eyes misted over, and the lump in her throat doubled in size. "We'll get him. Don't worry."

He nodded. "I know. You will." He smiled and coughed, wincing again. "Fuck. That. Hurts."

She blinked. Gil was always so stoic. For him to admit it out loud, his pain must have been extreme.

"I mean it, Gil," she said. Heat rose in her voice. "I'll make it my mission. And when I catch him, he will be sorry he was ever born." Her own vehemence surprised her.

He closed his eyes tight, grunting. He spoke with great effort, a heavy breath punctuating each word. "Don't. Become. A. Four."

"A Four? What the—Oh, right. Type Four. An Avenger, right?"

Gil nodded, drew a heavy breath.

Val squeezed his arm. It felt...okay. Which, itself, felt weird—to touch a man without fear or revulsion. She set that thought aside and remembered what Gil had said about Avengers. They'd do anything to get their man, including break rules, get violent, and take shortcuts. They get tunnel vision, he'd said: all that mattered was getting their perp.

"I think I'm still a Two." Her voice squeaked, and she realized that even she didn't believe what she'd just said. She wasn't a Savior anymore. Not with how she was feeling. Nor was she a Survivor, like Pops. "Maybe I'm becoming a One?"

Gil gazed at her a moment, then shut his eyes. "Don't be. Soldiers...end up...like me." He grunted louder with each word. "Shit." He pressed a button on the side of his bed, and the machine beeped.

"You need something? What can I do?" she asked.

He shook his head. "Pain meds button," he said. "I'll be fine." His head lolled back and his breathing grew heavy.

Dammit! She'd made his pain worse. Her chest tightened and the lump returned to her throat. "I should go." She waited for Gil to respond. He didn't. She patted his arm. Still nothing.

She sighed. So much she wanted to say to him. To ask him. Not least, whether the red-haired beauty crying outside was really his fiancée, and if he'd really given her decision-making control, and—

Something started beeping, and a gray-haired nurse in light blue scrubs entered moments later. "What's up with our hero?" she said. "Oh, boy. Heart rate's up, as is his temperature. His pain must be spiking." The nurse fiddled with a dial and wrote on his chart while Val backed away. "I just increased his morphine flow. He'll be out of it again for a while," the nurse said. "Visiting time's over for our boy here, I'm afraid." She fussed with Gil's blankets, then glanced at the displays of his machines.

Val exited to the hallway, ignoring the curious stares from Pops and Lopez. Jessica was nowhere in sight. Val trod toward the hospital exit, Gil's words still rumbling around inside of her head.

An Avenger. Gil had said these were the worst kind of cops. And that she was becoming one.

What's more, she really couldn't argue with him. Val wanted Harkins so bad she could taste it, especially after seeing Gil.

She thought of Gil, and Samuels, and Antoinetta. No, she insisted to herself. Gil was right the first time. It's for them. She was still about the victims.

She exited the hospital, not yet convinced of her own argument.

Chapter Twenty-Eight

Val took only one day off, and spent the night covering her ears to muffle the sounds of Beth and Josh in seemingly endless passionate bliss through their apartment's thin walls. She returned to work the next evening, harboring thin hopes of Cyrus submitting his report early or Gibson changing his mind about assigning her to desk work. But the posted duty roster dashed her inflated expectations the moment she arrived. The next two nights she answered phone calls from irate citizens and followed up on cold leads for hours on end. Her boredom and depression hit new depths. She felt certain she'd gained a pound per hour from eating crap and missing out on the exercise she'd enjoyed walking the beat.

Late in the second evening of such drudgery, the phone rang just as Lieutenant Gibson's imposing figure cast a shadow over her. His booming voice shook her out of her lethargy. "Dawes. My office."

She looked up from her desk, receiver pressed against one ear, scribbling on a notepad to keep up with a litany of complaints being lodged by an angry citizen against his neighbors. "Yes, they should keep their dog inside if it's going to bark," she said into the phone. "Yes, I have your number, and we will follow up and call you back." Still the man ranted on about his neighbor's barking dog, their rude children, their overturned garbage cans, and their inattention to the upkeep of their house and yard. She lodged the phone between her ear and shoulder and held out one finger toward Gibson's amused face.

"Absolutely. I'm not sure when, sir. That depends...No, we won't forget...We rarely arrest people for overturned trash cans, but it's reasonable to expect—yes, sir, I will *personally*—of course. Dawes. D, A—yes, sir, that's me. What's that? Oh, thank you, sir, I appreciate that...Yes, it's difficult sometimes. We don't like to use deadly force, if we can avoid it..."

Gibson motioned to his office, mimed hanging up the phone, and turned away. Val stood and held out her hand, imploring Gibson to stay. "Sorry, Mr. Parks, but urgent police business requires that I—What's that?...No, I hope not sir. Thank you, Mr. Parks. Yes, you're welcome. Goodbye." She hung up the phone with a loud sigh. "Lieutenant?" she called after him, but he'd disappeared into his office. She hustled to his open door and peered in, finding him already engrossed in work at his desk. "You wanted to see me, sir?"

"Having fun on the phones?" Gibson said with a smirk and pointed to a chair.

"Loads." She slouched into a seat. "If it were up to Mr. Parks, I'd be filing use-of-weapon reports daily, just to combat the litter epidemic."

"You're a natural," Gibson said, enjoying himself a little too much. "Maybe I ought to transfer you to Dispatch."

"I'll quit!" Val blurted without thinking, then blushed. "I mean, whatever you think is best, sir."

Gibson laughed. "Lucky for you, Cyrus's evaluation has come in."

"And?" She sat up in her seat, almost on the edge, her back straight.

"The report says you're not completely crazy." Gibson grinned, glancing at a document on his desk. "Just crazy enough to do police work."

She sighed in relief. "So, what does that mean?"

"Normally, in cases like this," he said, "I'd insist you go through more psych tests, the whole nine yards. But I'm short too many men—er, *officers*—so I can't afford it. So, I'm putting you back on patrol. Same beat, new partner."

She leaned forward. "Thank you, sir. But, who?"

"Alex Papadopoulos."

Her breath caught in her throat. She couldn't imagine a worse fit than the creepy, condescending Pops—except answering phones. "Isn't he on guard duty at the moment?" she asked.

"He'll rotate off tomorrow. Pops is too experienced, and

expensive, to play kindergarten cop at the hospital. Besides, you need to see a different style than Gil's. Pops is a little more low-key, but you two will work well together."

"Sure." She could think of only one trait they shared: the color of their uniforms.

Gibson grimaced. "You don't sound convinced."

Val took a breath, exhaled. "He's a little, um, old school."

Gibson nodded. "Yup. You have a lot to learn from each other." He held her gaze for a moment. "I mean that, too, Dawes. *Each other.* Naturally I expect you to take notes on what a more experienced officer can teach you. But he hasn't exactly kept up with the times, as you say. So, I want you to teach him a few things, too."

She grinned and stood. "I'll do my best, sir."

"I mean it, Dawes. Get him off his ass. He needs to get with the program—walk a beat, not drive it, and get familiar with people out on the street. The whole community policing package. There's nobody better to teach him that than you."

"Thank you, sir."

"Don't thank me yet. Give it a few weeks, then we'll talk."

Val left Gibson's office with a skip in her step. Back on patrol! And with a vote of confidence from the boss—a request to shake Pops out of his old school ways. It'd be a challenge, but one she embraced. Anything to push the good-old-boy mentality out the door and into the dustbin worked for her.

And now she could get back to the job she relished: getting crazy, violent trash like Harkins off the streets. For good, she hoped.

***

Val arrived at the hospital the next day as Brenda Petroni and Shannon O'Reilly exited through its double glass doors.

"He's all drugged up again," Brenda said. "They needed to run some sort of test that would put him in a lot of pain."

"Doc says he'll be out until tomorrow morning," Shannon added. "I must be bad luck. I have yet to get here when he's conscious."

"Stay the hell away, then," Val said, then covered her mouth. Shannon's shocked, sad expression told her that her joke landed on a sore spot. "I'm sorry," Val said. "That was in poor taste."

"Make it up to me with a spiced latte," Shannon said. "I've wanted to catch up with you anyway."

The three women met at Friendly's and sat in a back corner booth, sipping sweet, hot coffees while Christmas music chimed over scratchy loudspeakers. The smell of French fries permeated everything, from the duct-taped vinyl bench seats to the sticky plastic covering the faded menus crammed behind 50s-style metal napkin holders. A framed poster on the wall boasted of an "upcoming" concert at Tanglewood—from 1993.

"Word is you're getting a new partner," Shannon said after taking a long hit on her drink. "Lucky you."

"How do you feel about it?" Brenda asked. "I understand you and Pops have butted heads a few times already."

"I'm sure I'll learn a lot from Alex," Val said without conviction.

Brenda and Shannon laughed. "Good thing you're not trying to sell me a car," Brenda said. "But I can't say I blame you." She exchanged wary glances with Shannon, who pretended to read the Christmas message on the side of her drink's paper cup.

"I've never had a good poker face," Val said. "So, help me out here. What's the best thing about working with Alex?"

"Going home after your shift is over," Shannon muttered. Brenda snort-laughed with a mouthful of coffee and made a mess of the table.

"You have personal experience?" Val asked.

Shannon grimaced and checked with Brenda before answering. She sighed when Petroni nodded and waved as if to say, "After you."

"We were partners for a year," Shannon said. "If you leave aside how many times he propositioned me, put his hand on my leg in the car, told jokes, and took credit for my collars, it was an outstanding educational experience."

"Yeah," Brenda said. "She learned what an asshole he is."

"And how much the department will back up a sexist jerk when it's *his* word against *hers*," Shannon said, heat rising in her voice. "The first time he touched my leg, I let it slide, like an idiot. The second time, I complained. You know what they said? 'If you're so upset, why didn't you complain the first time?' And they said—get this—'Next time, grab his balls. That'll stop him.' As if I'd want to touch that sleazy pig, for any reason!"

Val shivered, and not from the cold. She'd been nervous around Gil, who'd acted like a perfect gentleman. Now they'd confirmed her worst fears about Pops.

They sipped their coffees in silence for a few minutes. Then Brenda smiled and patted Val's hand. "In a way, it'll be good for you. A new partner will expose you to a different style of policing, different approaches and attitudes. Not everyone's a prince like Gil Kryzinski."

"This is good, how?" Val said in a sour voice.

"You'll appreciate the good ones more," Shannon said.

Brenda squeezed Val's arm. "Be careful," she said. "Pops also has a reputation as a bad-mouther."

Shannon blew air between her lips. "To say the least. I got my worst evals ever when I worked with him. Remember, anything that goes wrong is your fault."

"Jeez," Val said. "Does he have a good side? I mean, he's not going to side with the crooks and child molesters, is he?" She imagined him making excuses for Harkins, not wanting to keep up an aggressive pursuit, and shuddered.

"No, no," Shannon said. "He's square, as far as that goes. Never went on the take, anything like that. Although I wondered at times if—no, forget it." Her eyes drooped and focused on something miles away to Val's left. Brenda looked away as well.

"What?" Val said. "You guys know something? What did you wonder about? Come on, tell me!"

"Sh!" Brenda patted the air with her hands. "Keep your voice down."

"Tell me what I'm getting into, here," Val said, lowering her voice. "Please."

Brenda and Shannon exchanged glances. Shannon cleared her throat. "A few times, Pops arrested some street kids, and I thought, What's he up to here? The kids weren't doing anything wrong. But sure enough, he searches them, and turns up some contraband or a weapon in the kid's pocket. You know what I mean?"

"He planted it?" Val asked in a squeaky whisper.

"That's what the kids always said," Shannon said, hiding behind her coffee cup. "But that's what perps do, right?"

"Pops wouldn't be the first cop to do it, nor the last," Brenda said with a shrug.

Val sat back in her chair, stunned. Of course she knew that bad cops existed. She had a harder time understanding how casually Brenda and Shannon accepted it. Business as usual.

"Again, we have no proof," Shannon said. "Be on the lookout for it, though."

"But we were talking about Alex's good side," Brenda said. "I will say this: he's not likely to put you—or himself—in harm's way. You'll always have plenty of backup around before you rush onto any crime scene."

"That sounds more like a criticism of Gil than praise for Pops," Val said, her eyes stinging. How could Brenda be so indelicate?

"Sorry," Brenda said. "I don't mean it that way. All I'm saying is, you might need to get used to a more cautious approach with Pops than you had with Gil."

Val nodded. She understood Brenda's point too well. If she wanted to pursue Richard Harkins, she couldn't expect much help from Alex Papadopoulos.

Chapter Twenty-Nine

Val squirmed in the passenger seat, putting as much distance as possible between herself and her new partner, Alex "Pops" Papadopoulos, driving the squad car down Broadway Avenue. His long but rotund frame took up half of the bench seat of their new Crown Victoria, which, he'd reminded her, she had dented on her second day on the job. He hadn't yet brought up the incident at the firing range. But he'd have a hard time spinning that story in a way favorable to him.

"So, Alex, tell me about yourself," she said, trying not to breathe in through her nose. Anything to minimize the aroma of garlic and stinky cheese that seemed to comprise half of his diet—the half not consisting of coffee and rich pastries. That reinforced her urge to sit as far away from him on the seat as she could, still mindful of Shannon's warnings about his wandering hands.

"Not much to tell." Val hadn't noticed this before, but when he wasn't insulting somebody, Pops plodded through words so that even a short sentence droned on. "Been on the force half my life, since the day after my twenty-fourth birthday. Most of it downtown and South End. Grew up in Granby. Married nineteen years, and Betty and I are still as much in love as the day we tied the knot. I guess that's sort of special, huh?"

"That's sweet." Val smiled. "Any kids?"

"Two," Pops said, scratching his teeth while waiting at a red light. "Alex Junior is twelve, Hannah is fifteen, almost sixteen. Already dating boys. Can you believe that? I never dated until I was a senior in high school. Even that was a blind date, to my senior prom. But things sure are different these days."

"That's for sure." Val gazed out the passenger side window. "Does your wife have a job?"

"Full-time homemaker. And she does a great job. A *super* job. Betty sacrificed a lot to stay at home and raise the kids. Heck, we both did, living on just my salary. But neither of us would trade it for anything." He stared ahead into the night and scratched a fingernail on his front teeth again. After a bit he shrugged. "Otherwise," he said, "pretty much what you see is what you get."

Which wasn't much. Brenda Petroni had used generous terms to describe him: "deliberate" in nature, and "somewhat out of shape." She'd use the term "roly-poly." Pops wore a thin crown of short black hair around the bald top of his head and kept black horn-rimmed reading glasses stuffed in the front pocket of his uniform. Val suspected he might benefit from bifocals, judging by the way he squinted to read passing street signs.

"Sounds like the all-American life you've got there." Val put on a rueful smile. "Pretty different from mine."

"You can say that again." He sniggered and slowed to a stop at a yellow light.

She turned toward him, warming under the collar. "Excuse me?"

He said nothing, just hummed something resembling a Christmas carol.

"Alex? Would you care to explain that remark?" Val kept her breathing steady, through her mouth to avoid the onslaught of his recent gastronomic exploits.

"Nothing," he said. "Just agreeing with you, sport. Oh and call me Pops. Everybody does."

She waited for the return interrogation, got none. He drove well under the speed limit, deep in thought, and stopped at all yellow lights. She wondered if his teeth-scratching habit was a nervous tic or an economy measure to save on dentist bills. He slowed down whenever they passed young men on the street, particularly dark-skinned men, something she'd never notice Gil do. After he'd done it a few times, she asked him about it.

"No, I don't," he said. "Not consciously, anyway."

"It seems like you do. Just wondered if you had a particular reason." She wondered why Brenda and Shannon never mentioned his racial profiling. Maybe that's what they meant by "old-school."

"Just to get familiar with the faces. This being a new beat for me, and all."

Ah! Opportunity. "That would be easier if we got out and walked," she said.

Pops shot her an irritated glance. "We will," he said. "But I want to get a feel for the neighborhood first."

"Okay, that's fine." She tried to strike a more placating tone. "Why don't we find our local crime watch group and say hello—"

The crackle of the radio reported that the owner of a nearby store wanted a group of loitering youths removed from his premises. "That's close by," she said. "I'll call it in."

"Is that a black area?" he asked after she notified dispatch.

She frowned. "Half of Liberty Heights is African American. Why?"

"I just want to know what we're up against." He pressed the switch to turn on the blue-and-white lights, but kept the siren off.

"Their skin color tells you that?"

He grimaced at her. "Maybe that upsets your liberal sensitivities, but too bad. I call 'em as I see 'em, and in my experience, skin color is useful information." He sped through an intersection, beeping the siren despite the green light facing them.

"Okay." Val took a deep breath and tried a more conciliatory tone, the way she imagined Gil doing. "So what do you know about the situation we didn't know before?"

Pops gave her a knowing look. "That they don't trust two white cops?"

She snorted. "I know that without knowing what color they are."

He laughed. "You're funny, Dawes." A few minutes later he pulled into the store's tiny parking lot and turned off the engine. "Okay, here we are. Normally, as the senior partner, I'd take the lead, but you know these people a little better. So why don't you take the lead this time?"

"Sure." Val suppressed the urge to roll her eyes at the way he said "these people," opting to remain as positive as she could. She approached the dim light of the building, Pops following. At least one of the fluorescent bulbs lighting the doorway had burned out. Three black youths loitered outside the store's all-glass front and at least two more moved around inside. She ignored her partner's "ahems" and addressed the teens standing in front of the store.

"Night, guys."

"Hey." They glanced over their shoulders into the store.

She focused on the tallest one, who had two gold loop earrings in his right ear. She recognized him as a Disciple, and one with a little authority. "Trap, isn't it?"

"Yo, Copette." Trap waved and looked away. His buddies laughed.

"Got plans tonight, Trap?"

"Not a lot." More laughter.

"You all been hanging out here a while tonight?"

"Yeah. S'nice here. S'got a nice *am*-biance."

"Ambiance!" his buddies repeated between guffaws. "Good one."

"Yeah, well, Mr. Tanner would rather you move along."

"Who's Mr. Tanner?" Trap asked.

"The store's owner, who has the right to ask you to move along, if you're not shopping."

"I already done my shopping. We just waiting on Gunner and Pip. They inside."

"Okay, look. I'm going in for coffee," she said. "When I come out, I want you guys to have made a choice as to where you're going next."

"Hey, we gotta wait for our homies," one of the other boys complained. "They inside getting some smokes."

"They'll be out in a moment." Val turned to Pops. "How do you like your coffee?"

"Black, three sugars."

"I'll be right back." She turned to the boys. "I'm serious. I want you on your way."

"Isn't this a school night?" Pops asked. "Don't you boys have homework to do?"

"Homework?" they screeched amid peals of laughter. "Oh, man. That's a good one."

Val sighed and made her way into the store. Sure enough, two black youths stood at the check-out counter, pointing at their favorite brand of cigarettes. The shorter, husky boy with a scraggly beard and a single gold loop earring she recognized as Gunner. The second youth, though taller, looked younger, perhaps about fourteen, with no earring. Must be Pip. A new recruit.

She headed straight to the coffee counter, but kept an eye on the group outside. Pops had struck up a conversation with them. She winced, imagining him uttering a racist remark to rile them, giving him an excuse to arrest them all.

"Five dollars? For one pack?" Gunner shook his head. "Man, that's a rip-off. Last week they was four dollars."

"They've been five dollars for two years now," said the cashier, a rotund, middle-aged white man with a crown of salt-and-pepper hair. "Come on, you want 'em or not?" He picked up the pack as if to put them back.

"Damn, man," Gunner said. He dug change out of his pocket and dropped it on the counter. Several coins rolled off the edge and onto the floor.

The cashier counted the remaining change. "You're fifty cents short," he said.

"No, man, two quarters dropped on your side," Pip said.

"I didn't see any quarters drop," the cashier said. "Come on. Pay or get out."

Val approached the counter with two coffees, waiting behind the youths.

"This dude's ripping me off," Gunner said to her. "You oughta arrest him."

"Mr. Tanner?" Val said. "I thought I saw some coins drop. You want to check?"

Tanner growled at her and bent over for a moment. When he straightened, he held sixteen cents in his hand. "You're still thirty-four cents short."

"I'll cover the difference." Val slapped three one-dollar bills on the counter. "Have a good night, guys."

The two youths stared at her, then at each other, then grabbed the cigarettes and ran out of the store.

Tanner leveled her with a long, hostile glare. "That was fucked up," he said.

Val stared back at him. "What's fucked up about it? Seems like everything came out even."

Tanner fumed and rang up her purchase. "I called you guys to help me get rid of these kids, and—"

"And that's what I'm doing." Val pushed the money toward him. "Keep the change." She allowed herself a smug smile and pushed her way outside—

Where she found Papadopoulos cuffing Gunner on the ground, his knee planted in the kid's back.

"What the hell are you doing?" she yelled.

"Arresting this punk," he said. "Didn't you see him? He tried to steal a pack of cigarettes!" He held up the pack of Kools, then shoved them into his pocket.

"Dammit, Pops, he paid for those," she said. "Let him go."

Pops finished cuffing the kid and stood. "He what?"

She shook her head. "Go on inside, ask Tanner. He'll tell you. He paid."

Pops's face darkened. "Yeah? Then why did he run?"

Val shrugged. "Who the hell knows? You can't assume—"

Pops waved her off. "Doesn't matter. I got him on possession." He reached into his pocket again and pulled out a bag of weed. "Over an ounce, I bet. This kid's a dealer."

"What?" Gunner, still on the ground, twisted his neck to look at them, fear and alarm on his face. "I didn't have no–"

"Tell it to your lawyer," Pops said. "You're under arrest."

Val started to protest, then remembered Brenda's and Shannon's cautions about Pops throwing partners under the bus. She'd have to deal with this a different way.

Chapter Thirty

Val took her mid-shift meal break at the precinct station at 9:00 p.m. while she waited for Pops to book Gunner on the drug charge. She'd convinced him that the kid had paid for the cigarettes, but he insisted on booking him on the possession-with-intent-to-sell rap, despite her reservations. "The dope fell out of his pocket," Pops said over and over again. Val hadn't seen it, so she couldn't say either way.

She'd just opened an email invitation from Beth to a dinner party when her phone rang, and Chad's image popped up on Caller ID.

"Happy birthday!" Chad said in his ever-cheerful voice. "I hope you're out doing something fun."

"Working," she said. "You know I haven't celebrated my birthday in...ten years." She groaned. Val preferred to avoid even oblique references to those unhappy days surrounding her thirteenth birthday. She'd refused to celebrate the day she "became a woman," as Milt—and clueless Dad, copycatting Milt's creepy phrase—had put it. Birthdays came with too many awful memories.

***

Ten Years Earlier: Valorie's 13th Birthday

A knock came at the door. "Valorie, are you in there?" Her mother's voice.

Valorie huddled under her blankets, curling into a fetal position. If she stayed quiet enough, maybe she'd go away.

"Dinner's almost ready," Mom said. "Uncle Milt wants to see you. He has a present for you." Impatience, bordering on annoyance, tinged the edges of Mom's slurred speech.

Valorie's insides lurched, bile rising in her throat. She took the covers off of her face so she could breathe better. Several silent seconds passed.

"Valorie, you're being rude." Now the annoyance. She needed to defuse Mom's anger before things got out of hand.

"I don't feel good." She moaned as loud as she could and held her stomach, which really did hurt.

The door handle turned. "Do you need me to—"

"No!" Louder than she'd intended. "I'm not dressed." She'd changed into her pajamas right after school.

"Well, get dressed and come say hello. He came all this way." More silence, then a heavy huff, then footsteps fading away down the hall and stairs.

When the sound ceased, Valorie climbed out of bed and set Mulligan, the stuffed bear with the little bell around his neck, against the bedroom door. Of course, she wouldn't need the bear's warnings if her parents had installed the lock she'd asked for ages ago. Oh, how many problems that would have solved!

For the past few weeks, she would lie awake in her bed for hours after turning out the light, not letting herself sleep until the house grew quiet. That morning her parents told her they'd invited Milt over for her birthday dinner, over her protests. When they asked why, in their permanent state of clueless surprise, she couldn't tell them. Not without TELLING them.

Which she couldn't do. Milt had forced her to promise not to tell and warned her of what would happen to her if she ever broke that promise. Terrible, horrible things. Worse, even, than what he'd already done.

Uncle Val said he'd help her with that. He had to work until eight o'clock, but promised to stop by for dessert. By then, she'd feel better. Not until. And if he saw Milt there, maybe he'd arrest him this time.

She turned out the light and closed her eyes. She needed her strength for when Uncle Val arrived.

The sound of clinking plates, voices, and laughter told her they'd sat down to dinner. Later the television came on, and every so often, somebody laughed—most often, Dad or Uncle Milt. After another hour, the phone rang. A loud, dull thud of the front door closing sounded a few minutes later. Hope rose in her chest. Uncle Val had arrived early!

More footsteps, this time getting closer. Then Mulligan's bell rang. Valorie's eyes sprang open. The door swung wide—

"Are you feeling any better?" Mom sat on the end of the bed. The aroma of whiskey or something equally foul wafted over her.

"My stomach still hurts." She held her breath. Mom wore so much perfume these days to cover the stench of the whiskey, but it didn't work. It all just smelled stronger and more terrible. "Is Uncle Val here?"

"No, dear. He got held up at work. There's some sort of problem at a shopping center. But he promised to swing by soon."

Valorie sat up onto her elbows. "I thought I heard the front door."

"Uncle Milt had to leave. He was very disappointed that you didn't come downstairs." Mom swayed from her perch on the bed. "He asked that you wait to open his present until he could be here."

"Pfft." Valorie lay back down, shutting her eyes again. Hell would freeze over first.

"Now, Valorie." Mom sighed, and the scent of whiskey filled the air again. She lay a heavy hand on Valorie's side, as if steadying herself rather than trying to comfort Valorie. "You've been so quiet lately."

"I said I'm fine."

Mom's hand stroked her back. Valorie wiggled away. Mom gave her shoulder a little shake. "If something's bothering you, we need to talk about it."

Valorie rolled over, facing away from her mother. No. She would not talk about it. Not alone. Maybe not ever. Even thinking about it made her sick to her stomach. Made her insides hurt, and made everything else hurt, too. It was all so confusing. Made her ashamed of herself. What "we'd" done, he said, as if she'd been part of it. She'd let him do it, he said. Pain seared her stomach, and her body heaved, the bile surging up her *throat again.*

"Valorie, are you going to—"

"There's nothing to talk about." She huffed into her pillow to stifle the ugly boiling in her gut and absorb the hot tears flowing onto her cheeks.

Mom sighed, her eyes unfocused. She burped, and her body convulsed enough to shake the bed.

"Mom, are you okay?"

Mom jumped up, hand covering her mouth, and rushed out the door. A door slammed. The muted sounds of puking drifted in.

She rolled over, hoping tonight she'd sleep. With Milt gone, it might be possible.

But not until Uncle Val arrived.

***

Several hours later

Valorie woke up to loud knocking on the bedroom door, her room still pitched in blackness. "Valorie!" Chad shouted. "Let me in. Please!"

She sat up, alarm bells ringing. Chad's voice sounded raspy, like he'd been crying. But he was sixteen. He hadn't cried in years. Not even when he'd broken his arm a few weeks back.

"It's open," she said and checked to make sure her PJ's covered everything. To be safe, she pulled the covers up to her chin.

Chad burst through the door and flicked on the overhead light. Tears flooded his red, puffy cheeks. He collapsed at the side of the bed, but flung an arm over her. "Oh, my God, Valorie," he said. "It's horrible, horrible!"

"What's horrible? Chad, what's happened?" Tears welled up in her eyes. She'd never seen her brother like this.

"It's Uncle Val," he said between sobs. "He was at the shopping mall—there was a shooter—he tried to—and then they—oh, shit, it's horrible!" He broke into sobs again, and he clutched her in a tight hug.

Her heart pounded and fear gripped her. "What,

Chad? What happened? Was he hurt?" Tears splashed her cheeks. Movement over his shoulder drew her attention. Dad stood in the doorway of her room, his face as white as Mulligan's belly. Tears lined his stubbly face.

"Did Chad tell you?" Dad asked in a raspy voice.

"He hasn't been able to," Valorie said, holding her brother's shaking body. "What is it?"

"Your Uncle's been shot," Dad said. "A mass shooting at the mall."

Valorie burst into sobs, matching Chad's intensity. Her heart ripped in half, her chest heaving, and dizziness enveloped her. Not Uncle Val. Please God, no. "Is...will he be all right?"

Fresh tears flowed over Dad's face, and his body collapsed against the door frame. His gaze dropped to his feet, and he wagged his head. "No, honey," he said in a whisper. "He's...he's gone."

***

Chad's voice jarred Val back to the present. "So, happy ten-year suck-a-versary." He'd coined the phrase on her fourteenth birthday in solidarity with her not-celebrating and reprised the term every year. "How's life at 23?"

He laughed, and she tried to chuckle along, but as always, no humor would come. Not about that. Still, Chad meant well.

Val cleared her throat. "Beats being dead, I guess. Anyway, I only have a few minutes left on my break, so..."

"I'm sorry about your partner getting shot," he said after a brief pause. "Is he going to be okay?"

She drew in a slow breath. It hadn't occurred to her that Gil had gotten shot on the ten-year anniversary of Uncle Val's death, almost to the day. Her heart grew even heavier, her voice tight. "We think so," she said. "If by okay you mean not being able to walk and having to eat and breathe through tubes. Yeah, he's rocking this getting shot thing."

"Okay, Miss Grumpy." Chad's heavy sigh sounded in her ear. "So, Val, are *you* okay?" he asked. "The papers didn't mention any other injuries, and nobody called, so—"

"A few cuts and bruises, and deeply hurt feelings," she said. "He got shot trying to protect me, so, I guess I also have some guilt over it." What an understatement. Val shook her head, squeezing her eyes shut to force back tears. "How are Kendra and Ali?"

"That's the other reason I called. Ali insists that we invite you for Christmas. Kendra and I would love it too," he said, his words rushed. "Can you make it?"

She thought about it. Seeing Ali would lift her spirits, as would seeing Chad and Kendra. But there was something else she had to ask, somehow, without coming across as an ungrateful jerk. Maybe he'd just volunteer the information, if she waited...

After ten seconds of silence, she sighed and summoned her courage. "Will Dad be there?" she asked, her voice weak.

"He...hasn't answered my invitation," Chad said. "He no-showed the past few years. I'm not sure he's been sober enough to drive, or even realize Christmas is coming."

"That's kind of important to know," she said.

"I know. I just don't have an answer for you."

Val tapped her pen on the desk, thinking. "I'll make it to your house at some point," she said. "When he's not there."

"Fine." Chad sounded frustrated, but too bad.

"So. What do you want in your stockings? And by you, I mean Dar and Ali." She laughed. "You get coal, as always."

"Awesome. I bought energy stocks." Chad laughed again. Good. "Let's see. Kendra, as always, asks for donations to the homeless shelter in lieu of gifts, which I will again ignore. Dar's too young to care, but Ali's in full Auntie-Val-worship mode, so anything cop-related for her. She has a uniform and toy gun, all that crap, already. She'd love something 'authentic'. Like a police radio, or a remote-control cop car."

The hairs on Val's neck bristled. "Kendra's okay with that?" she said. "Last time I was there, she made it clear she'd hoped Ali would grow out of this cop fantasy."

Chad sighed. "Me, too. But it would break Ali's little heart if we didn't let you do *something* 'coppy'. But no guns, okay?"

"In light of recent events," Val said, "I'm not a big fan of guns, either."

Unless the weapon was aimed at Richard Harkins. Especially if she was the one holding it.

Chapter Thirty-One

Val stewed in a cubicle for the next hour, taking phone calls and searching the database for any updates on Harkins. She looked up when a broad figure cast a faint shadow over her desk, expecting to see Pops. Instead, Travis Blake took the guest seat in the cube.

"Talk to me about Gunner," he said. "That kid a dealer?"

Val searched the vicinity for signs of eavesdropping ears, found none. "I don't know him well," she said, "but I've never known that to be true. Why do you ask?" She kept her eyes low, not wanting to give her suspicions away.

"He's got a short rap sheet," Blake said. "A few petty larcenies, a car break-in, an unregistered gun possession. No drugs. Not even a public intoxication charge. Weird, huh?"

"Yeah, that is weird," Val said, her heart racing. Her first day with a new partner and already she didn't trust him.

"And," Blake said, "nothing in the last six months. Kid was a week away from getting off probation. Now he's looking at two-to-five for what, a bag of weed? That add up to you?"

She shrugged. "None of what these perps do makes sense." Her face burned. She realized what Travis was after. Could she do it? Bust her own partner?

"Did you see Pops find the evidence?" Blake asked.

"I was still inside," Val said, shaking her head.

"That's right," Blake said. "You saw the kid pay for the butts. Weird, huh? He's nearly broke, had four buddies with him, and could have overpowered the old man in two seconds. Yet he counts out exact change to buy smokes for the whole group."

She opened her mouth to speak, had nothing.

"And guess what? His attorney finds it strange, too. Did you know that The Disciples keep a lawyer on retainer? She didn't get four feet inside the building before claiming the evidence was planted."

Val met Blake's eyes, saw the anger there. The disgust. The hope. Or was that her, projecting onto him? "Have you checked the baggie for prints?"

"It's in the lab," Blake said. "What do you expect we'll find?"

"Not much," she said, still meeting Blake's gaze. "You might ask them to weigh it, too. It looked small—less than an ounce. Maybe we shouldn't charge him for intent. Maybe simple possession."

"Now you sound like his lawyer," Blake said with a half-smile. He leaned closer. "Keep an eye on Pops, would you? Give me a heads-up if anything else strikes you as, ah, *funny*." He nodded once and patted her arm.

She steeled herself at his touch, fought hard not to pull away. "I will."

"And, Dawes? We never talked." He stood, turned—

And nearly bumped into Alex Papadopoulos, walking into her cubicle.

"What's up?" Pops glanced from Blake to Val. "What are you guys talking about in such low voices? You two making out in here?" He guffawed and slapped Blake on the back. "You dog."

Blake glowered at Pops, then said to Val, "Give my best to Gil next time you visit." Blake strolled off, rounding the corner without so much as a glance back.

"Let's roll," Pops said. "Lots of criminals to go catch."

"Let's walk for a while," Val said as they approached the car. "I can introduce you to some people."

"Nah, too cold out." Pops shivered, zipped up his jacket, and got in on the driver's side.

"Mind if I drive, then?" she said, but Pops closed the door as if he hadn't heard.

Val climbed in the passenger's side. "What was that crack about back there about me and Travis?" she said with an edge to her voice.

Pops shrugged. "I was only joking."

"It's not funny," Val said, "and people might take it wrong, you know?"

"I doubt it," Pops said. "You and Travis? Come on, that's

not even thinkable. And at work? He's not that stupid." He shook his head, laughing. "I mean, how low would that be? Travis hitting on you, with Kryzinski in the hospital?"

She spun to face him, her seat belt slicing into her neck. "What the hell do you mean by that?"

A sly grin creased Pops's face. "I'm just saying. Even the randiest of operators wouldn't think of moving on a gal with her boyf—I mean, *partner*, laid up in a hospital."

Val gritted her teeth, fists clenched. "Pops, let's get something straight. Gil and I are *not* involved, have never been, and have no intention to be. He was my partner—as a cop. That. Is. It. Understood?"

Pops stared at her, eyes wide. His glance dropped to where her fist had balled up a significant fraction of his jacket. When had she grabbed him?

"You say so." He pried her hand off.

"Is that what people in the department think?" Val asked, seething.

He shrugged. "It's common knowl—uh, yeah, lots of people think it. After all, you're both single. You're no dream, but not bad looking, alright? A little scrawny for my taste, but–"

"I don't give a rat's ass whether you find me attractive," she said, spittle flying. "In fact I'd rather you didn't. And those rumors are utter bullshit. Got that? Gil and I are not a couple!"

Pops cocked his head, let out a slow breath. "Okay, you're not a couple." He rubbed his face with his palm. "Tell that to the gorgeous redhead in the hospital. I bet she thought you two were knocking boots."

"I don't care what she thinks, or you," she said, although only that half of that statement was true. Val didn't want Jessica Swan as an enemy and vowed to straighten that out with her the next chance she got. "Stop spreading those lies. In fact, I want you to set people straight. Pro-actively. Am I being clear?"

He scowled at her. "First," he said, "I'm not the one spreading the rumor. Only telling you what I've heard. Second, you don't give me orders. I'm the senior partner here. Is *that* clear?"

She huffed back into her corner of the bench seat. "Screw

you. When it comes to my reputation, I'm in charge. If you can't accept that, we're done as partners. Just stop the car and I'll walk back to the precinct."

"Whatever." But he kept driving.

A half hour of tense silence later, he pulled into a 24-hour bakery. "Break time," he said.

"I'll pass," she said. "You go ahead."

Pops laughed. "You don't get it, do you, rookie?" He handed her a five-dollar bill. "Black coffee, three sugars, and a cinnamon Danish. Keep the change."

"Excuse me?" Val pushed the bill back to him. "You want Danish, you go get it. I'm not hungry." She crossed her arms and stared out the window.

A broad, pudgy hand entered her lower peripheral vision. As if in slow motion, the hand approached her body at leg level, mid-thigh. It slowed to a stop, hovered over her leg. Frozen, she watched the hand drop downward. Touch her. Push the bill between her legs. It lingered there a moment.

Just as slowly, she turned her head toward the body connected to the hand. A large man, older than her. Bigger. Stronger. With power, and authority.

Touching her.

Between her goddamned legs!

The man stood over her, grinning, breathing hard,
reaching out—

Val willed her body to react, but it refused. She sat, rigid, frozen, her legs burning where his hand pressed between her thighs. The burning shot outward, down to her toes, but also upward, fusing in almost unbearable pain inside of her, where another man had violated her so horribly once before. A larger, older man who had no right, no business doing—

The burning sensation ebbed as the pressure on her thighs lessened. Her mind unfroze. She realized he'd finished stuffing the bill between her legs and had lifted his hand up. That it was Pops, not Uncle Milt, touching her. That she was a grown, strong woman, trained in 27 ways to incapacitate a man with her bare hands—yet she had done nothing to thwart this violation.

And that she wanted to kill this rotten motherfucker.

Exercising as much restraint as she could muster, she slapped his arm away. "What—the—*fuck*?"

Pops scowled and turned away. "Three sugars, Dawes." He drummed on the steering wheel.

Val slapped the money to the floor. "I'm not your fucking waitress!"

He heaved a loud breath, unbuckled, grabbed the bill off the floor, tossed it onto her lap. "Rookies, men and women, do what their senior partners tell them to," he said. "If I tell you to go get coffee, you get coffee. If I tell you to suck my cock, you suck my damned cock. You get it? Now go. Three sugars, Dawes!"

She glared at him a long moment. With one quick motion, she could drive two rigid fingers into the soft spot under his chin, leaving him at her mercy, gasping in pain, unable to breathe. She relished the prospect of teaching him a painful lesson in where, and how, not to touch her. Ever.

Val took the fiver from him, rage boiling inside her. She breathed in, fighting for self-control.

"That's better," he said, smiling. "Now, what do I want?"

She opened the car door.

"You'd better undo your seat belt, or you're not getting very far," Pops said, chuckling.

She held the money in her right hand, extended out the door. Crumpled the bill into a ball and dropped it on the pavement.

"You want fucking Danish," she said, her voice hoarse, "get it your own damned self."

***

Val paid Gil a brief visit the next day, although the painkillers reduced much of their exchange to winces and grunts on his part, cheerleading and platitudes on hers. His only lucid moment came toward the end of their chat.

"Any...leads on...Harkins?" Gil asked, his words punctuated by painful grunts.

"No sign of him since..." She let her voice trail off. How to reference that awful night? "Your shooting" seemed too blunt. "That night" seemed too oblique. And "the incident" was, well, *taken*.

He reached out a hand, and she held it in hers. "You'll...
get him," he said. "Wish I...could help."

"You've done plenty," she said. "The best thing you can do
right now is heal."

"Val," he said, "I want to...thank you."

"Thank me?" She shook her head. "I figured you'd want to
kick my ass for putting you in here."

Gil's face relaxed into a wry smile. "Yeah. And that." He
leaned toward her, lowered his voice to a whisper. "In case...I
don't...uh...you know," he said, wheezing, "I just..."

"Don't even think that," she said, grabbing his arm.
"You're going to be fine."

"Sure," he said. "But...in case. Thanks for...telling me.
About...you." He gasped, then groaned, and the machine
beeped several times. The nurse rushed in and administered
more painkillers. Val exited the room, shaken, and Jessica
Swan met her in the waiting area.

"You look troubled," Jessica said as they walked toward
the hospital exit.

"He just looked so much worse than I expected." Val folded
her arms across her chest. "I expected him to be getting
better. What happened?"

"The tests they ran revealed internal infections, and
they've flooded him with antibiotics." A worried expression
crossed Jessica's face. "He didn't react well. And if the drugs
don't work, he may need more surgery."

Val stopped and turned toward her. "If so, I want to be
here," she said. "Even if it means missing my shift." Anything
beat sitting in a car with Pops for nine hours.

Jessica stared at the floor. "Gil is lucky to have such a
strong community here," she said. "Back in New Haven,
we..." Her voice broke, and she waved the rest of her sentence
away.

"He's lucky to have you, too," Val said after a moment.
Despite Pops's claim, Jessica seemed far from jealous. More
proof that his instincts paled next to hers. "Is there anything
you need? Any way I can help you?"

Jessica rubbed her eyes. "I'm...fine. I'm not sure how
long—I mean, I need to get back to work, and my dog, and—
I just hope he bounces back from this. It's so..." She shook
her head, squeezed her eyes shut.

Val stood in front of her, silent, fear and sadness welling up inside. Almost as much as Gil, Jessica needed her support. A helping hand. Someone to spend time with her, listen to her.

A hug, maybe.

She edged toward Jessica, the taller woman's body stiff, her head bowed. No response from Jessica. She seemed so alone. So vulnerable. A feeling Val knew well.

Val's fingers twitched at her sides. Then, of their own volition, her hands raised up, hovered beside Jessica's arms. Achingly, slowly, they inched toward Jessica until they rested on her skin. Jessica leaned in, ever so slightly. Val did the same. Their bodies touched. She patted Jessica's back, then let her hand rest there. A moment. Two.

Jessica stepped back, sniffling. "Thank you, Val," she said in a low whisper. "My God, look at me, I'm a wreck." She smiled at Val through tears. "I judged you too harshly when we met. You're really very sweet, and…a good friend to Gil."

Val shuddered out an unsteady breath. "I want you to know, there has never been anything between us. Romantically, I mean."

Jessica smiled. "I know. But, thank you. And I'm grateful to you. Gil was lucky to have you as his partner."

Val started to smile back, but then realized the import of Jessica's words. "*Was?*"

Jessica cocked her head to one side. "The doctors have made it clear: his injuries are too severe. Gil can't ever go back. He'll be medically discharged from service. Didn't he tell you?"

Val stepped back in a numb haze. She'd known the injuries were serious enough to keep him out of action a while, but always expected he'd return, notwithstanding Jessica's earlier oath to prevent it. But if the doctors said he couldn't…

Despite the hospital's bright lights and bleach-white walls, in that moment, the world became a much darker place.

Chapter Thirty-Two

The short visit with Gil left Val with plenty of free time, so she showed up early for work, hoping to chat with Lieutenant Gibson about her partnering assignment. She'd had it so good with Gil, and too late, realized how much she'd taken him for granted. She'd likely never get another partner that good. And if he didn't return, her assignment to Pops could become long term.

She cursed as she changed into her uniform. Anybody but Pops.

On her way to see Gibson, Travis Blake stopped her and waved her into his office. "Got an update for you on that Gunner kid," he said, sliding an evidence report across his desk. She scanned it and choked when she read its conclusions.

"Gunner's prints were on the baggie?" Her mouth dropped open. "How is that possible?"

"You said you didn't see Pops take it from him," Travis said, "but you didn't see him *not* take it, either. There's a little surprise on the kid's personal possessions list, too."

Val flipped the page, scanned down, and let out a low whistle. "Twelve hundred in cash?"

"In small bills," Blake said. "And another detainee ID'd him as his supplier in exchange for a plea. Still think he wasn't dealing?"

She crumpled in the chair. No way Pops planted a thick wad of street cash in Gunner's wallet. "So that big scene in the store, counting out pennies..."

"An act. Or maybe he's just a runner and he needed to give the cash and the drugs to someone higher in the organization." Travis grunted. "In the eyes of the law, it's still dealing."

Numb, she set the reports back on Blake's desk. "I guess I jumped to conclusions."

Blake shrugged. "Doesn't mean Pops won't try it on someone else. Keep your eyes open, Dawes."

Gibson was in a meeting, so Val trudged off to an empty cubicle and logged into the crime records database. A half hour of searching turned up a long list of Disciples with records for dealing drugs, mostly small quantities of pot, crack, meth, and ecstasy, including two others in the past month. Notably, Pope's name never appeared on any of the lists.

Val turned her search to Harkins, hoping to find leads to his current location. She started with Clayton and Hartford, then expanded the geographic reach to the entire state. An hour later, she'd come up with nothing. She was about to log out when an unexpected item caught her eye. A stolen vehicle report from the Silver Fox, from the day after she and Gil had staked out Harkins there. An old Jeep, owned by one of the Fox's dancers.

Coincidence? Doubtful. She called Hartford P.D. and asked for Jalen Marshall.

"Dawes!" Jalen's hearty baritone sounded friendly. "I hope you're calling with good news on Gil. I'm planning to come visit him in the hospital my next day off, but I'd rather visit him at home."

"Sorry," Val said, her heart heavy. "Gil's had a setback. Infections, and still a lot of pain. But we're keeping our fingers crossed."

"Dammit." Jalen sighed into her ear. "Rumor is, the shooter was that guy we let slip at the Fox. True?"

Val's turn to sigh. "Afraid so. That's why I'm calling. An employee of the Fox reported a stolen vehicle. Asheeda Wilson."

"Raven. She's a dancer," Jalen said. "Think it's connected to Harkins?"

She shrugged. "Worth a quick ask."

"I'll follow up. Good work, Dawes."

"Thanks," she said. "Keep me posted. And when you come to visit Gil, call me. We can get a cup of coffee."

Jalen went silent for a few moments. "Yeah, okay," he said, "I'll do that."

Her ears burned, and her pulse quickened. What had she

done this time? "Is something wrong?" she asked.

"No, no. Mind if I bring Ben along?" he asked, his voice cautious.

"I guess so," Val said, although seeing anyone named Peterson remained near the bottom of her social calendar. "Why?"

"Well," he said, "I just...don't do social one-on-ones with women. My wife gets jealous sometimes."

"Jalen," she said with a nervous laugh, "I'm not asking you out on a date. I was hoping we could brainstorm on how to nail Harkins." She held her head up with her open palm, suddenly weary.

"Great. Yeah, that works. Let's do it. I'll leave you a message at the precinct before I come." He rang off, saying he needed to get out on patrol.

She sat for a while in the cubicle, massaging her temples and reflecting on Jalen's awkward response to her invitation. Even the good guys, it seemed, struggled with how to act around women. Gil had had his moments, and now Jalen. Soon she'd be on patrol again with Alex, who was definitely not among the best of guys.

No. Not acceptable. That situation *had* to change. She jumped to her feet and headed down the hall toward Gibson's office.

***

"I'm sorry, Dawes," Lieutenant Gibson said in his office five minutes later, "but I have no one else I can assign you to." He removed his glasses and rubbed the bridge of his nose, something she'd noticed he often did when stressed. "Besides, you've only worked a couple of shifts together. It's early yet. Give it time. You guys will work things out."

"He put his hand between my damned legs!" she said, her voice on edge. "And basically said that he owns me, in very crude terms. *Very* crude." She worried her fingers together, trying to imagine any other way to interpret what Pops had said. She couldn't.

"Cops are crude people sometimes," Gibson said. "And hell, Dawes. If bad language upsets you, you won't get along with very many of us."

"It's not about him saying naughty words!" Val strained to

keep her voice under control. "He's downright misogynistic and belittling. If I told you what he said, you'd probably suspend him. I mean, it's a basic violation of our code of conduct." She stopped, realizing how lame her protests must sound. 'Violating the code of conduct.' Yeesh.

"What were his exact words?" Gibson asked. He paused, waiting, as patient as Job.

Val hemmed and hawed a moment. "He said, if he told me to, um, suck his—"

"Shit." Gibson threw a pencil onto his desk. "That asshole. Okay, that's serious. So, do you want to file a formal complaint?" Gibson said. "It won't be easy to prove—your word against his, blah blah—but I'll back you if that's what you want." He waited, tapping his fingers on his desk, his eyes locked on her.

Val considered it. She couldn't allow Pops to get away with treating her like that. And if he treated her that way, it meant he treated all women that way. On the other hand, he'd been careful to call her "Rookie," and that "men and women" rookies must do what their partners tell them to do. He could claim he meant it as a hazing ritual, something he might have said to a male rookie. True or not, she'd be hard-pressed to refute it.

She also didn't want to earn a reputation as a thin-skinned snitch who couldn't take a joke or the rough-and-tumble life of a cop. Men like Pops already believed that women weren't tough enough for the job. The last thing she wanted was to give them fodder for their backstabbing attacks and make life worse for other women like Shannon O'Reilly and Brenda Petroni. Or, more likely, future recruits.

"Not...yet," she said in a rush of air. "But I don't want to let this go, either. Not entirely."

Gibson shrugged. "Tell you what. There is something else we can do. It's called a 'Note to the File.' You document what happened in a memo. I put it in his job performance file, instead of his H.R. record, and a copy in yours. It becomes a performance review item. I'll have an 'informal' chat with him about it, too. See if I can't coach him a bit. Sound useful?"

Val smiled. Gibson was a crafty old bureaucrat when he wanted to be. "Sure. Baby steps."

Gibson stood. "All right. We'll call this a teachable moment for Pops. You know, when I said I wanted him to learn a few things from you, I didn't realize that I'd have to include 'How to treat a female colleague' on that list. Besides," he said, "I don't have other options. Not many other people want to work with him either. Or..." He cleared his throat. "Ah, yeah. That's all."

"What?" Alarm bells rang in her head. "What were you going to say?"

"Nothing." Gibson rubbed his nose again. "Are we done?"

"No, we're not done!" Val stood and stepped closer to Gibson. "People don't want to work with him, and...what?" She searched his eyes for a clue, and he looked away.

Realization struck her like a baton to the face. Her jaw dropped, then closed. In a weak voice, she said, "They don't want to work with me, either, do they?"

Gibson glanced at her, said nothing.

"That's it, then." She collapsed into her chair, deflated and hurt. "Can I ask why?"

Gibson strolled around his desk and sat on the edge, right in front of her. His expression went grim. "You have a rep for being a touch...*reckless*." He held out his hands to dampen her protests. "Earned or not, it's out there. And this did *not* come from Kryz. But." He took a deep breath. "The fact that Gil is spending his days at Mercy Hospital getting his insides stitched back together doesn't help your cause."

"I am *not* reckless!" Heat rose in her face, and her voice swelled to nearly a shout. "Where the hell did that come from?"

"Call it water cooler talk," Gibson said. "I think it's bullshit. But you did run head first into a few situations over the past few months where a wait-and-see approach might have been the more prudent course. Gil has always stood by you, but other people form their own opinions. Okay?"

"No, it's not okay," Val said, seething. "I take risks, like any other cop, but I don't put my fellow officers in harm's way. I mean, hell, we didn't create that stand-off on Greenfield. Harkins did!"

"I agree," Gibson said, his voice low and calm. "But people talk. Now you know what they're saying. That information gives you the power now to take steps to correct that impression. Right?"

She sank into her seat. At that moment, she felt anything but powerful.

***

Richard Harkins left the girl whimpering on her bed, her scrawny fifteen-year-old body curled into a fetal position in the corner. He zipped up his pants and threaded the black fake-leather belt through the loops of his slacks. He'd barely broken a sweat this time. Barely felt the release when it happened. Stupid bitch. Almost a waste of damned time.

The girl, Kayden, covered her body with the filthy pile of blankets he'd ripped off her moments before, using it to wipe her face and muffle her sobs. He had no use for her tears, and she knew better than to yell for help. He'd taught her that lesson the first time around, with the aid of that same belt. Now all he had to do was loosen the buckle and she knew what to do. And what not to do.

Harkins trudged to the john, took a long leak, thought about what to do next. His growling stomach answered for him: Dinner. He left the toilet seat up, the bowl unflushed, his hands unwashed—like the rest of this disgusting dump— and made his way to the kitchen. Found some leftover chicken and fried potatoes in the fridge, nuked them in their takeout container and cracked open a beer. Must be something good on cable. He clicked on the TV, scrolled to the adult channels. Found a movie rated NC-17. That'd do. He pressed "Select" on the remote—

And then his head exploded in pain. He screamed and grabbed the top of his skull, smearing his hair with chicken grease, and rolled off the sofa. He scrambled to his feet and looked up, just in time to dodge the business end of a cast-iron frying pan. It swished an inch from his nose, held by the girl's scrawny brown arm. Kayden swung at him again, accompanying her attack with a throaty, wild roar. He smacked her arm on its way past, knocking the pan into a cheap metal lamp, which crumpled to the floor, leaving only the twenty-seven-inch TV to illuminate their struggle.

She grabbed the broken lamp and tried to hit him with it, but the cord jerked it back into her, cutting her face with the jagged remains of the light bulb. She cried out and ran from the room. "Help! Police!" she yelled. Loud enough for the neighbors to hear, dammit!

Harkins followed her into the kitchen, shielding his eyes from the bright overhead lights. He tripped over a chair, hit his head against an open cupboard door. The girl disappeared out the back door before he could catch her, a cell phone pressed to her ear. Fuck! He couldn't let her get through to the cops. He chased her out the door, but night had fallen, and his eyes were slow to adapt to the darkness. "Kayden!" he yelled. No response. He searched the yard, searching for the glow of the phone, listening for her crying, her breathing, her voice. Nothing. A cold wind whipped at him, splattering misty snow into his face. She couldn't have gone far. He scanned the neighbors' yards on all three sides, identical 100-foot well-lit suburban squares. Nothing.

A car engine started in the driveway. Raven's Jeep! He almost laughed out loud. She wouldn't get far in that piece of shit. Probably didn't even know how to drive. Harkins ran toward it, but the wheels spit smoke and ice as the car lurched out onto the street. He cursed himself for having parked it face-out, keys beneath the seat as always. He'd prepared for a quick getaway, as usual, but this time that tactic had worked against him. The car's tires squealed, the girl's frightened face visible behind the wheel with the light of her cell phone.

Damn her!

Harkins returned inside. Grabbed his coat, made sure the .44 was still in the right pocket. He snagged an envelope full of cash he'd discovered a few days before, taped to the back of the fridge. The mother's emergency fund. Well, this constituted an emergency.

Minutes later he checked out of a corner store with a stash of beef jerky, two 40s of malt liquor, and a burner phone. He walked toward the center of town and dialed Candy from memory.

"Where *are* you?" she asked. Sounded like traffic in the background. "And where have you been? The cops have been looking for you!"

"Still?" He swigged the beer, chewed on the jerky. "Look, I need a place to stay."

"Not here," she said. "The pigs are everywhere. You won't get within a hundred feet of this place. Where are you now?"

"New York," he lied. "Heading south. You know how I hate the cold." His breath puffed white clouds in the frigid air.

"Where down south?" she said. "How about I, um, join you?"

Something about that bothered him, and he stopped walking. "Join me?" he said. "What about work? How will you make money?"

"They got strip clubs down south," she said. "How are you getting there? That Impala won't make it back to Louisiana."

"I, uh..." Dammit. Caught. "Well, maybe we can go together. How's your car doing?"

"It's in the shop," she said. "Maybe...we could use Raven's Jeep."

"No," he said, too quickly. "We'll think of something else." Headlights flickered around the bend behind him. After ensuring that it had no blue-and-whites on top, he stuck out his thumb. It whizzed past, never slowing down. Bastards.

"Why?" she asked. "What happened to it? You 'borrowed' it, didn't you?"

"How the fuck do I know what happened to it? And what the hell kind of question—" Realization struck him too late, and he dropped the phone to the ground, crushed it under his heel. Fucking Candy was working with the damned pigs. Goddamn her! Thirty bucks, wasted.

An eighteen-wheeler slowed to a stop and the passenger-side window lowered. Harkins pulled his coat over his face and leaned close, wiping wet snowflakes from his brow. "Was that your Jeep, broken down on the road a mile back?" the driver asked.

"Yeah," Harkins said. The truck's warm air melted the snowflakes on his nose, and he caught a faint scent of whiskey on the man's breath. "Out of gas. Can you help me out?"

"Happy to," the driver said. "There's a gas station a few miles up."

Harkins smiled and got in. Felt the cold metal in his pocket. He didn't need the Jeep any more, and at this point, it was probably a liability, anyway.

Chapter Thirty-Three

Seconds passed like hours that evening, patrolling the streets in the cruiser with Pops. In addition to everything else that bugged Val about him, he'd come down with a cold. His intake breaths sounded like a drowning man, and his exhalations whistled out of his snout like a freight train. He blew his nose every five minutes and littered the seat with soggy, mucous-filled tissues.

"Why didn't you take the night off?" Val asked him at one point.

"I used up my sick leave already this year," he explained, "taking care of my wife when she had her hysterectomy."

She sank lower into her seat, putting as much distance between them as she could. The frigid temperatures outside made it a certainty they'd spend the entire night in the car, breathing in his contagious air. On the plus side, he talked less, and kept his hands away from her.

"Ready for a break?" Pops asked two hours into their rounds. He sneezed all over the steering wheel and wiped it off with his sleeve.

Val shook her head. "I ate a half hour before our shift."

He sighed and drove another few minutes in silence. The radio crackled a few times with calls in the south end of town, nothing that concerned them.

"It's just that usually I stop around now for coffee and a donut or something."

Air hissed between her clenched teeth and she drummed on the armrest. Noise, any noise, to keep her from succumbing to the urge to snap back at him. She clenched her jaw, expecting him to ask her to get him a Danish again. He'd have the excuse of being too sick to go inside. Whatever. If he touched her again, she'd break his damned fingers.

"What's the matter with you tonight? Wrong time of the month?" He glared at her.

"That's a rude question. And watch where you're going." Val turned up the volume on the scanner.

Pops faced forward, muttering to himself. "You sore at me because of that drug dealer thing?"

"Gunner? No. I'm not mad at you." She straightened up in her seat, got eye-level with him. "I was just surprised. I didn't think you had a strong reason to stop him. But live and learn, I guess."

His smug smile made her sick to her stomach. A few seconds later Pops turned into Java Joe's parking lot.

Val's jaw clenched. "What are you doing?"

"Getting a snack." He parked and turned off the engine. "What do you want?"

"Nothing."

"Figures." He pulled cash out of his wallet. She tensed, but he unbuckled his seat belt and popped open his door. "After last time, I ain't even gonna ask you to fetch me anything."

Relieved, she smiled at him. "Hey, leave the keys, would ya?"

He paused, the driver's door half-open. "Say, what?"

"Standard operating procedure, right? I'm staying here, so you need to leave the keys in case we need to respond quickly."

Pops wrapped his fist around the keys and held them in front of his face. "Nah. I wanna be certain the car will be here when I get back."

Val's jaw dropped. "You think I'd drive off and leave you?"

"I'll hang onto 'em, just the same. You want to write me up, go ahead."

She sighed. "Pops, you ought to know better than that by now."

"Then don't quote chapter and verse from The Book at me. And another thing. We ain't stopping again for a while, so if you want a break, this is it."

"If we don't stop again tonight, it's fine by me," she said. "You're the one that panics if he isn't eating every fifteen minutes. So go have your damned coffee and let's get back to work."

He glowered at her, got out and slammed the door. Clearly she'd pissed him off, but she didn't care. If something didn't change soon, she'd have to look for a new line of work anyway.

That sentiment surprised her. Not that she'd thought it, but that it came so easily. Her whole life she'd wanted to be a cop—never anything else. To follow in Uncle Val's footsteps, continue his work. She never imagined that she'd have to put up with this kind of treatment, day after day, year after year. Plus the corruption, the cynicism, the glass ceiling—it all seemed much uglier up close.

Things had been different in Uncle Val's day. Fewer rules and less bureaucracy, it seemed. Cops were tough, aggressive, smart—like Gil, and Uncle Val. Not like lazy, lumpy, and bigoted Alex Papadopoulos.

Pops took a seat in Java Joe's behind a tall, steaming Styrofoam cup and a stack of powdered donuts. She would have laughed—he was such a caricature of himself and every bad TV cop show—but her frustration mounted with every passing second. He took his time, dipping the chewed edge of his donut into the cup a quarter-inch at a time and nibbling the soggy end as if he had all day to do nothing.

"Dammit!" She leaned across and beeped the horn. He gave her a half-puzzled, half-annoyed grimace. She waved at him: come on, come on. He waved back: Hello, I'm ignoring you. "Fuck," she said, spraying spittle on the dash. She scrunched down in the seat. It was shaping up to be a long, long night.

The radio crackled three donuts into Alex's coffee break. "Reported disturbance on Albany and MLK, Jr. Boulevard," the dispatcher said. "Unit A-22, are you in the vicinity? Please confirm."

"Five minutes or less," Val said into the mic. "Will report again when closer." She dashed into Java Joe's, heading straight for Papadopoulos. "Wrap it up, Pops," she said. "We've got a call."

He grimaced at her, glanced down at his half-finished meal of sugar and caffeine. "Give me a sec. I need to get a lid for this." He ambled over to the fixings bar, taking his sweet time.

Val fumed, ready to punch him, until she noticed

something important: Pops had left the car keys on the bar.

She grabbed them and ran out the door, jumped in on the driver's side, and started the engine. After backing out of the spot, she stopped at the cafe's exit, passenger side toward Pops, who lumbered out with goodies in each hand. She leaned over, pushed open the door. "Get in," she said. "Eat fast."

"Wait until I get buckled in, at least," he said, but she ignored him. Coffee spilled on his shirt when she raced around a corner, tires squealing and siren blaring.

"Dammit Dawes," he yelled at her. "Don't get us killed just so we can be late to a gang war."

"Let Dispatch know we're there," she said, turning south onto Albany. But the intersection came into view before he'd even set down his donuts. She screeched to a halt at the corner of the parking lot and barked their location into the mic. "That's them," she said, pointing to two groups of heavily armed young men. The Disciples lined up along the back wall, with Pope standing in front. A group of Asian toughs entered the lot from the street. Angry shouts filled the air. She needed a strategy to defuse the tension. What would Gil do?

He'd take action—in a way that kept his fellow officers safe.

She opened the door.

"Where the hell are you going?" Pops asked.

"This is our call," she said. "We need to put a stop to this before someone gets killed. Are you coming to help me, or not?"

"Not without backup," he said. "And neither are you." He grabbed the mic and spoke in a low voice to dispatch.

"Dammit, Pops!" She kicked her door out wide and slid out of the car. "If we roll six more cops in here, waving guns, we'll be fighting a whole different war—them against us. Or we'll be sweeping bodies off the gravel—possibly a few of our own. Let's go!" She unsnapped her holster and rested her hand on her baton.

Pops sneered at her. "You wonder why people say you're reckless?" He shook his head. "I'm staying here. You want to get yourself killed, go ahead." He gazed out the window at the gangs, paused about thirty feet from each other, staring at Val and Pops.

"Fine." Val closed the car door and approached the space between the two gangs. "Evening, gentlemen."

Pope stepped forward, flanked by Cardinal Thomas, Dog, and another familiar face. One she'd seen at the precinct house the day before.

"Gunner?" she said. "Surprised to see you here."

Gunner smiled, hands on his hips. "I got me a good lawyer. Appears your fat-boy partner didn't do his job right. He coming out, or is he gonna hide in the car now?"

"He's calling in backups," Val said. "In about two minutes, we'll outnumber you all here, unless I can convince them you're here to celebrate my birthday. What ya say, Pope? And you guys?" She faced the Asian gang leader, a short, muscular Japanese man in his early twenties, wearing a sleeveless T-shirt despite the bitter cold. His long black hair swayed in the breeze from a light-blue headband. The men behind him also wore T-shirts, no coats, and headbands of various colors.

"You the cop that killed Kuku?" the Asian gang leader asked with an angry edge to his voice.

"Kuku?" Val blinked, then her brain made the connection. "You mean Alfred Takura?" Her heart pounded, but she stood tall and faced the man. "I returned his fire. Unfortunately for him, I'm a good shot under pressure." She rested her hand on the handle of her weapon.

The gang leader stepped back. "We're not here for you." He indicated his fellow gang members with a shake of his head. "He wasn't part of the Dark Dragons."

Val shuddered. The Dark Dragons, the New York chapter of the Nakaguchi Syndicate, had taken over from the Setting Sun gang after Takura's death. Even more ruthless and violent than Setting Sun, reports of their internal battle were anything but bloodless.

"We're here to politely ask The Disciples to stop harassing Dragons for no reason," the gang leader said.

"Bullshit," Pope said. "Tell her, Dog. What you told me." He pushed Dog forward, and the youth lowered his gaze.

"Two Dragons pulled guns on me on Abernethy yesterday," Dog said with a quick glance up at Val. "Told me we had to back off of this territory if we wanted to live to Sunday."

"That's a lie!" the Dragon leader said. "It's The Disciples who've been threatening us and our families, telling us where we can and can't go. That's bullshit, man!" He pushed forward toward Pope, whose hand disappeared behind him. Probably grabbing a pistol out of his waistband.

"Jesus, guys, knock it off!" Val shouted. "The cops are here, remember?" She stepped between them and waved them apart.

Pope glared at her, then backed off a step with a noisy cloud of steam emerging from his lips. "Dragons are asking for trouble, coming here," he said. "They gonna get it, too. I'm just saying."

She turned to the Dragon leader. "What's your name?"

He stared at her, a smile frozen on his disbelieving face. "My name?"

"Yeah. Your name. What your mommy calls you when she kicks you out of bed in the morning."

He scoffed. "Lady, my mother booted my ass of the *house* when I was thirteen. And what she called me, I can't say in front of a girl." He laughed and looked to his gang for support. They laughed along, obligingly.

Val faced him square on. "Try me, motherfucker."

Exclamations of surprise escaped both gangs, amid bursts of laughter. "Bitch got her a mouth!" someone said.

The Dragon leader nodded at her, smiling. "Okay. Call me Fumi...*Officer* Dawes." He pointed to a few others. "That's Ito. Kimura—he goes by Kim. Over there, that's Ishi."

"You're in charge?"

Fumi emitted a nervous laugh, then collected himself, put on a false bravura. "For now."

She noted his uneasy stance, his uncertain tone. Fumi hadn't been the leader of this gang for long. Which meant, he still had something to prove. An explosive situation, for sure.

"Okay, Fumi," she said. "Here's what I'm going to do." She glanced up and spotted two Clayton P.D. squad cars pulling in. Alex crouched behind their cruiser's open door, gun drawn. The gangs clutched their weapons, and many crouched into a fighting stance. She turned back to Fumi, keeping Pope in her field of vision. "My friends in blue are about to crash this party. So, unless you boys break this thing up right now, you're all going to spend the night in cold, cramped, smelly jail cells downtown. You can ask Gunner here how comfy they are."

"I've had the pleasure myself," Fumi said. He eyed Pope, then glanced at his lieutenants, bobbed his head. He took a slow, careful step away from Pope, hands outstretched to his sides. Ito, Kim, and Ishi did the same, with the remaining Dragons retreating a few steps behind them. "Their turn," Fumi said.

Pope, shook his head, a look of cold amusement in his eyes.

"You, too," Val said. "Or do I call my friends over?"

"You something else," Pope said. He sized her up, took a deep breath, and signaled to Thomas with his finger. A moment later, Pope, Thomas, Gunner, and Dog stood in a row opposite the Dragons. The remaining Disciples crowded behind them.

"Come on, back it up," Val said.

"Our fucking turf," Pope said with a snarl.

Heavy shoes crunched on gravel behind Val. Glancing over her shoulder, she verified that the footsteps belonged to well-armed, uniformed cops. The gangs stood, unmoving.

"Do it, Pope!" Val snapped at him. "Now!"

The gang leaders stared at each other. Footsteps continued approaching from behind Val.

"Well?" Fumi said after an eternity. "Your move, Pope."

Footsteps pounded closer. "Everybody back off and drop your weapons!" a male voice shouted. Not Pops.

Val held up her hand behind her, and the footsteps stopped. "Get the hell out of the way, Dawes," Pops shouted at her. She gave him the finger, then resumed her "stop" sign. A few gang members chuckled.

Val lowered her voice so only Pope, Fumi, and their lieutenants in front could hear. "They won't wait there long, so if you hope to walk away from this, do what I say," she said. "On the count of three, both sides, take two steps back."

"Fuck that shit," Pope said.

"We ain't moving unless they do first," Fumi added.

"Or else," Val said, her voice growing louder, "I'm going to let my senior partner and his pals take over with, shall we say, more traditional policing methods. *Capiche*?"

The leaders eyed each other, said nothing.

"Dawes! Get out of there!" yelled an authoritative male voice she didn't recognize. "Now!"

"One." She glanced at Pope. His eyes remained locked on Fumi's. His, likewise. "Two—"

"No sense going to jail over your dumb yellow ass," Pope said.

"I'll kick your ugly black ass later," Fumi responded.

After a moment, Pope snapped his fingers twice. The Disciples, en masse, took two steps back. Fumi waved at his group, and the Dragons retreated the same distance.

"Again," Val said.

After a moment's hesitation, the two groups pulled back to opposite edges of the lot.

"Gentlemen," she said, raising her voice so her everyone could hear, "I trust you all have better places to be this evening?"

After a brief huddle, the Dragons stole away, leaving the lot to The Disciples.

"What the heck happened?" Pops asked at Val's elbow moments later. "Five minutes ago they were going to kill each other. What'd you tell them?"

"I told them they could either do it my way or your way," she said with a smirk. "And they chose mine."

"You let them off easy," he said. "Not that it matters. We can lock 'em up every day and their smart-mouthed lawyers will put them right back on the street again. You saw that Gunner kid's already out on some technicality?"

"Yeah, lucky him." Bitterness crept into her voice. "Until the next time you screw with him."

"Oh, cry me a river!" He walked back toward the car. "Don't you realize how messed up that was? You could have gotten yourself killed. And a lot of other people!"

"You're confused," she said, following him. "If I hadn't intervened, people would have died."

"You're the one that's confused!" He paused at the side of their cruiser, his loud voice drawing stares from the other officers returning to their vehicles. He glanced at them and lowered his voice, pointing at The Disciples gathered around their trash can fire. "You think you saved them from something? Well, you didn't. Tomorrow night, these guys will be back at it, cutting throats, shooting each other and selling crack to ten-year-olds. So will all the other gangs. As soon as one goes down, another will take their place. But these men here—" He waved an arm toward the officers, standing outside their cruisers, doors open, frozen in place. Pops fought for words, fuming at her. "Let's just say I care a whole lot more when you put one of us at risk."

She waited a beat, taking a deep breath. "That's why I didn't put you at risk," she said. "That's why I handled it myself. Did I follow established protocol? No, probably not. But it worked. For tonight, at least, nobody died." She opened the passenger side door, held it there a moment. "And unlike you, Pops...for me, their lives count, too."

She started to climb into the cruiser, then stopped. No way she could sit inside the car with him right then. She slammed the door shut. "And now it's time for *my* break."

She turned her back on him and walked past the dumbfounded officers still standing at their cars, up Albany Street, in a state of mind she knew all too well: angry, and alone.

Chapter Thirty-Four

Val walked the streets for the better part of an hour, checking in with various small shop owners and street regulars and responding to the occasional complaint. Pops passed her in the cruiser once, slowed to a stop and called out to her, but she ignored him and strolled past. He burned rubber pulling out from the curb, and she laughed. Let him pout if he wanted. She couldn't get back in that car yet. Maybe ever..

She and Gil had never experienced such problems. Val missed his patience, intelligence, and strength, and most of all his intense desire to connect with and understand his fellow human beings. She'd been lucky to have him as her first partner. Now, it seemed, she'd be stuck with much lesser men—Pops, or others like him—for the foreseeable future. How depressing.

Val's radio chirped with her call number—meaning, someone wanted her, personally. She clicked the mic. "Dawes here."

"Officer Dawes, please return to the precinct immediately," the dispatcher said in a neutral tone.

"What's up?" Her hands shook. Recalls in mid-shift were never good.

"Report in to Lieutenant Gibson when you arrive. Confirm, Officer Dawes."

Her breath caught in her throat. Pops must have written her up, the asshole. "Confirmed. I'll be there in twenty."

"Negative, Dawes. Give me your 10-20 and we'll send a cruiser."

Her heart racing, she gave Dispatch her location. Not good.

Ten minutes later, she waited in an uncomfortable chair

outside Gibson's office while he concluded another meeting behind closed doors. When the door opened, Travis Blake waved her in. He paused in the doorway and leaned close. "Say as little as possible, but tell the truth. Got it?"

Val nodded. Travis gave her a reassuring nod and stepped aside. Pops sat in the guest chair to the far right. A large blue windbreaker, probably Blake's, claimed the center chair. She stood next to the third until Gibson, seated at his desk, motioned for her to sit. Blake shut the door and remained standing behind her.

"Officer Papadopoulos described a curious, and if he's right, serious sequence of events from your shift together tonight," Gibson said. He rubbed his eyes and took a sip of coffee. Dressed in plain clothes, he looked like he'd just woken from a bad dream.

Then she realized: he'd come in on his day off. She really was in trouble.

"Tell me, in your own words, what happened," Gibson went on, "and what compelled you to abandon your partner in the middle of your shift."

"Abandoned?" Val glared at Pops, who smirked and looked away. "Sir, with all due respect—"

"Perhaps Officer Dawes is unclear what part of the evening you refer to," Blake said, pacing behind them. "I'd hate to waste time getting off on a trivial tangent here."

Gibson's eyes narrowed, following Blake across the room. He grimaced, then held up an open palm to Pops. "Alex, give us the nickel tour."

Pops shook his head, disgust all over his face. "Fine," he said. "Dawes here left the security of the squad car, in contravention of my direct orders, to confront two rival gangs about to engage in a street brawl." Spittle landed on the floor in front of him. "She narrowly escaped inflaming them into armed conflict and putting myself and four other officers at great risk of bodily injury. She refused to debrief with me afterwards, instead going AWOL, patrolling alone, on foot, in direct violation of department protocol. Then she refused—"

"That's enough for now." Gibson shushed him with an open palm. "Dawes?"

Blake strolled over to the side of the office, leaning against the wall in full view, and nodded to her.

She swallowed hard, her mouth dry. "I did intervene in the gang dispute, but it hadn't yet escalated into actual, visible fighting," she said.

"Bullshit!" Pops said. "She—"

"Shut it, Pops," Gibson said. "Go on, Dawes."

Blake smiled and nodded. That made her feel better.

Val took a deep breath before continuing. "In the situation described, I applied lessons learned about conflict de-escalation in college, the academy, and Sergeant Kryzinski's training to *prevent* actual combat. In particular, I engaged with the gang's leaders, establishing the rule of law and outlining the negative consequences of a brawl. I put no officers at risk except myself."

Blake winced at her final remark. Oh, well.

"What about ditching him afterwards?" Gibson asked.

She glanced at Pops again, who huffed and crossed his arms. "Officer Papadopoulos chewed me out for 'putting him at risk' and said his life, and those of the other officers, were the only ones that mattered," she said. "I lost faith in his commitment, at that point, to carry out his oath to protect and to serve our citizens. I thought a break from each other might heal our *mutual* anger." She glared over at him, still seething in his chair. "Apparently, I was mistaken."

"Can I talk now?" Pops said, rising out of his chair.

"No," Gibson said. "Sergeant Blake, you talked to the other officers at the scene?"

Blake nodded. "Their accounts square more with hers than his."

"*What?*" Pops landed back in his chair with a thud. "That's crazy! I want to talk to them. I want—"

"I want you to shut up," Gibson said. "Travis, find Alex something to do to finish out his shift. Dawes, you stay here."

Pops stood again, his mouth agape. "This is such baloney. I'll appeal to the union. I'll—"

"You'll shut up and leave my office, as ordered, or get written up yourself," Gibson said. "Travis?"

Blake escorted Pops out of Gibson's office, grinning at Val as he closed the door behind them.

"Dawes, Dawes, Dawes," Gibson said a moment later. "What am I going to do with you?"

***

Gibson answered his rhetorical question of Val less than an hour later, appearing at the cubicle she'd holed up in with Travis Blake at his side. "You two will ride together the rest of the night," Gibson said. "I'll figure out something more permanent later."

Val jumped up, eager to get off phone duty and its endless litany of crank calls and noise complaints. "Thank you," she said, pulling on her jacket. "Does this mean that Alex and I—"

"Like I said, I'll figure that out later," Gibson said with a growl. "This is temporary. And, Dawes?"

His ominous delivery froze her, one arm halfway through the sleeve. "Sir?"

Gibson leaned in and spoke in an icy tone. "Let's be clear. Sergeant Blake's your boss. You do what he says, no matter what." His dark eyes shone with fierce intensity.

She gulped. "Yes, sir." Val shrank back into her chair, feeling like a misbehaving school girl again.

Gibson shoved off down the hall. Blake smiled at her. "Don't let him spook you," Travis said. "I don't eat my young, and last time I checked, I only had one head."

Val laughed, nervousness cascading off of her shoulders. "Verified, sir."

Blake waved his giant paw at her. "Cut the 'sir' crap, at least for tonight. We're partners. Call me Travis, or Blake, or TB. You prefer Val, or Dawes?"

"Val, sir—I mean, Travis." She reddened.

Blake belly-laughed. "This is gonna be fun. What say we go check on those two gangs and see if your little chat had any lasting effects?" He tossed her the keys. "Get the car. I'll be along in a minute."

When she reached their cruiser, the legs of a large, apple-shaped man extended out the driver's side door. The door pushed further open, and the rotund body of Alex Papadopoulos sat up, red-faced from exertion. His face registered surprise and embarrassment.

"Forget something in the car?" she asked.

Pops stood, shoving something into his belt or back pocket. "Yeah, just, ah, looking for my wallet. Got it." He displayed a saccharine smile, closing the door. "All yours, princess."

Val's temper flared, but she held her tongue and allowed him to pass. She glanced at his back after he slid by. The handle of a cheap pistol showed above the top of his belt.

"Expecting to bust some gang members on desk duty tonight?" she muttered under her breath.

"What's that?" Pops whirled to face her.

"Have a good night," she said, smiling. Pops narrowed his eyes with suspicion, but stalked away without replying.

Blake insisted that she drive, something Pops had refused to *let* her do, and they arrived at the Disciples' favorite corner minutes later. A small group warmed their hands around the garbage can in the center of the otherwise empty parking lot. Val recognized Dog, Gunner, Thomas, and Pip standing closest to Pope, seated facing the fire.

Pope glanced at Val and Blake as they approached, then lit a second cigarette from the smoldering tip of his first and tossed the butt into the flames. "You come to pay up?" he asked when they closed within speaking distance.

Blake shot Val a quizzical glance. She hadn't confided her five-hundred dollar bounty offer for leads on Harkins to anyone other than Gil and had let it slip her mind. "Payday is Friday," she said. "That soon enough?"

Pope shrugged. "If we both make it to Friday." He inhaled, blew smoke out of his nose. "I ain't here, you give it to Dog. Cool?"

A few gang members muttered surprise. Dog's eyes grew wide, and he shrunk back into the crowd.

Val nodded and glanced at her partner. Blake's face showed confusion and concern, but he remained quiet, his eyes fixed on Val. She understood: this was her show. He'd chime in later.

"Are we going to have more trouble with you and the Dragons?" she asked, edging closer to Pope.

The gang leader coughed around another deep drag of his cigarette. "That's on them. This is where we live. They want trouble, they know where to find it." Pope coughed again and tossed his cigarette into the can. "Fucking cancer sticks. They gonna kill me if Fumi don't." The Disciples around him laughed.

"I'd rather not have to step into the heart of another meeting like you had today," Val said.

"Then fucking don't," Pope said, laughing. He stood and warmed his hands at the fire. "Listen, Copette. I'm cool with you checking in, doing your cop thing. I get it. It's your job. And, assuming we settle our business on Friday," he said in a more serious tone, "I dig what you're doing. You did right by Dog and Gunner. Ain't no other cops around treat us fair, or even talk to us like human beings, 'cept you and Copsky. You're all right." He glanced at his buddies. "Am I right, Disciples?"

"Yeah, she's all right," a few of them mumbled. Gunner gave her a thumbs-up. Blake's face darkened, and he crossed his arms. Still, he stayed in the background.

"Let me be clear," Val said. "I had nothing to do with Gunner's release. I didn't know he was out until we saw you earlier tonight."

Pope chuckled. "You say so." He stared into the fire. "You going to talk to the Dragons now, keep them on their side of the playground?"

Val sighed. "Care to tell me where to find them?"

"That'll cost you another five." Pope laughed. "Nah, I'm only joshing ya. They hang out by the Y in the old mill district. Long as they stay there, we're cool. Dig?"

"Yeah. Dig." Val couldn't keep the sarcasm out of her voice. She signaled Blake, and they headed toward the cruiser.

"Yo, Copette?"

Val paused, exchanged a glance with Travis, and faced Pope. "Call me Officer Dawes, if you don't mind."

Pope, still standing, shrugged. "Yo. I heard what happened to Copsky. I just wanted to say sorry. That sucks."

The comment caught Val off-guard, and she stammered before replying. "Thanks. I'll tell him next time I see him."

Val and Blake returned to the cruiser. Pope's expression of concern for Gil occupied Val for several minutes, distracting her from Blake's tight-lipped, tense brooding. After they'd driven a few blocks in silence, she said, "Something on your mind?"

Blake cleared his throat. "Yeah, that business with the five

Franklins," he said. "You're seriously paying them cash for some leads on a case or something?"

Val's heart rate quickened, her ears burning. "I offered a reward for information leading to that child rapist, Harkins," she said. "They gave us the tip that led to the shootout where Gil, er—"

"Holy shit!" Blake wagged his head and exhaled a burst of air, clouding his passenger side window. "I couldn't think of a worse idea. You know what they do with that money, don't you?"

"I can imagine," she said. "It was an impulsive decision."

"You can't do it," he said. "Even if you could afford it, which I doubt, on a rookie's pay."

She stared at him. "I have to do it," she said. "I made a deal."

"A dumb deal," he said, throwing his hands up in the air.

"If I go back on my word, they'd never trust me again."

"Bullshit!" Travis gripped the armrest on the passenger door. "Besides, you haven't caught Harkins yet. We can't even be sure he's the one who shot Gil that night. You've got no proof they gave you good information."

Val considered that and kept her voice calm in response. "Fair point. But we're ninety percent sure."

"Even if you were a hundred percent," he said, his voice rising, "every penny of that money makes our jobs harder. It's another gun on the street, another needle in a twelve-year-old's arm. Can you live with that? Do you want to be the one shot by that gun?"

Her arms shook on the wheel, frustration and guilt rising to storm levels inside her. The vision of Gil lying in the hospital, the victim of a thug's bullet, tore at her insides. Samuels, too, had taken one from a thug. How many others?

But the thug in both cases was Harkins—whom The Disciples were trying to help her catch.

"Besides," Travis went on in a calmer voice when she didn't respond, "it strikes me, they owe you. At least for Dog, whatever the hell that's about. You're right about Gunner—the prosecutor let him walk because of Pops's sloppy arrest. But they don't need to know that. I'd say your accounts are settled for now."

Val swallowed hard and focused on driving. It was the one thing she could do on the straight and narrow at that moment.

Chapter Thirty-Five

Val found a note pinned to her bedroom door when she trudged in late that morning. Oversized girlish curlicues piqued her interest with the words, "Big news! Lunch at Claytown Café?" A noontime meeting meant getting less than eight hours of sleep. Not good, but she'd neglected her lifelong friend lately, and longed for meaningful conversation with someone she trusted. Besides, some old-fashioned girl talk would cheer her up. She scribbled "YES!" on the back of the note and shoved it under Beth's door before collapsing into bed.

Val arrived early and nursed a cappuccino to jump-start her waking-up process. Beth, as usual, slid into the booth twenty minutes late, nearly colliding with the pink-haired waitress who'd come by to refill Val's water glass.

"I've only ever been here for breakfast," Beth said, shivering inside a fluffy winter coat. "How's the lunch menu here?"

"Like, the best ever," Pinkie said, hovering nearby. "Bagel sandwiches, frittatas, and, like, a killer omelet, the Freaky-Greeky. Totally vegan, except for the eggs and the feta cheese. You want a cappuccino too?"

"Regular black coffee's fine," Beth said, and leaned across the booth to hug Val.

"So, what's the news?" Val asked when Beth settled back into her seat. "New car? Job? Boyfriend?" *Please*, she begged the universe, let it be a new boyfriend.

"None of the above." Beth's grin burst off her face. "In fact, you might say I've lost a boyfriend." She slid her left hand to the center of the table. It took Val a moment to notice the glistening diamond cluster lighting Beth's ring finger.

"Beth, I'm so...happy for you!" She hoped that sounded

more convincing than it felt. She hugged Beth across the table, shouting congratulations and spilling the salt and pepper shakers. She waved Pinkie back. "This calls for a celebration!"

After a round of mimosas, the two friends settled down to lunch and serious talk. "I didn't realize the relationship had gotten so serious," Val said. "A month ago, you weren't even sure you wanted to keep seeing Josh."

Beth sipped her drink. "True. But we've talked a lot since then, and he is so sweet. He really loves and respects me, and that's more than I can say about ninety percent of the guys I've dated."

"But do you love him?" Val asked. "Last time we talked, you were only lukewarm on him. All your life you've talked about hooking up with an athlete, and, well, Josh is kind of..."

"He's no Adonis," Beth said. "But I don't care. I've had my fill of those self-centered guys. A skinny, nerdy guy who wants to raise my children and treats me like a queen beats those empty-headed assholes any day."

Val forced a wry smile. "I'm glad for you," she said, trying to mean it. "You look happy, and that's what counts."

Beth gushed about her wedding and honeymoon plans for the next half hour. Val tried her best to show enthusiasm, but her heart wasn't in it, and that only intensified her sense of guilt. She couldn't decide on the culprit for her dour mood—she had too many options. Jealousy over Beth's romantic bliss? Unease over Beth settling for the wrong guy? Her guilt over Gil's condition? Perhaps it was her rising sense of desperation over the dimming prospects for finding Harkins. Or her general sense of frustration with her failures as a cop. She decided on All of the Above.

"What about you, Val?" Beth asked, finally running out of details to share. "Any new guys in your life?"

"No." Val's smile turned wry. "I fill my life with other things. Work keeps me busy, and I spend as much time as I can with my niece. Hell, Ali's doing better than I am. She has a boy interested in her, and she's only five!"

Beth laughed. "I'm sorry, Val," she said, "but that's funny. Well, maybe you can meet someone at my wedding, if you haven't by then. You're welcome to bring a date, of course."

"Well, I doubt I'll meet anyone by then." Against her will, her mind flashed to the man she most admired, lying in his hospital bed because of her. "Besides, it's boring to be the date of a bridesmaid."

Beth's expression made Val blush and caused her heart to sink. "Uh, oh." Heat rose in Val's cheeks. "I just assumed— I shouldn't have."

"I'm sorry," Beth said. "We're keeping the wedding party small—just a maid of honor and best man—my sister, his brother. Oh, Val, I'm so sorry. I didn't mean to hurt your feelings."

"No, no, forget it." Val faked a sneeze and dabbed her nose and eyes with a napkin. She took a sip of mimosa to help her swallow the lump in her throat. "At least I can't say, 'Always the bridesmaid, never the bride.'"

Afterward, Val sank into a deep funk on the bus to the hospital. Until Beth's announcement at lunch, her lack of a romantic or social life hadn't bothered her. Suddenly, though, she felt lonely. Beth was her only real friend, and she knew from experience—her growing distance from Chad sprang to mind—that Beth's engagement and marriage would drive them apart, too. She'd made only one true friend on the force, and look what she'd done to him.

On the other hand, her limited dating experience was almost universally bad. Not all as bad as Josh's Neanderthal friend Brent, but close.

She choked when she realized that Brent would probably be at the damned wedding. Oh, great, she chided herself. Way to ruin even *that* with negative thinking.

Val tried, and failed, to remember the last time a decent guy had asked her out. She rarely even drew a second glance from men, other than the leers from creeps like Pops. Being a cop didn't help. But then again, she didn't even try to attract men. She kept her hair short, rarely applied more than a trace of makeup, and when not in uniform, she dressed casually—Beth would say "frumpy," and sometimes, "like a tomboy." But she was not unattractive. Due to regular workouts, her body stayed fit and thin—okay, perhaps too thin. Her breasts could be bigger, and maybe she should invest in something other than an unflattering sports bra one of these days. Guys sometimes checked out her butt, thinking she hadn't noticed. Guys other than Pops. Like that cute-ish guy in the second row of the bus...who got off on the very next stop. With his wife or girlfriend.

The problem wasn't looks. Hell, Beth was no looker, but she fought the boys off with sticks. But Beth was interested in meeting men and showed it. Val wasn't, and didn't. Guys could tell before asking she would say no.

"And why is that?" she asked aloud to the nearly empty bus.

Stupid question. She knew the answer. She slouched down in her seat, covering her face with the lapels of her overcoat.

Thanks a lot, Milt. Thanks a whole fucking lot.

***

Hospital staff welcomed Val with good news upon her arrival. The doctors had upgraded Gil's condition to stable and lowered his morphine dose so he could more or less function again. A more puzzling revelation greeted her at the door to his private room: the return of Pops standing guard.

"Surprised to see me?" Pops said. "You shouldn't be. You're the reason I'm here."

Val tried to hide her elation. "Believe it or not, your own behavior might have had something to do with it," she said. "On the plus side, Gil's getting better, so you'll be back on donut duty soon. Hopefully with a new partner."

"Stuff it, Dawes." Pops sneered at her, blocking the door. "Or would you rather I exercise my discretion and not let you in? It's up to me, you know."

"Why?" she said in an innocent tone. "Do you suspect I'm packing an illegal .22 somewhere?" She adopted a wide stance and held her arms out, daring him to frisk her. Please, please, she said with her eyes. Give me an excuse to level you.

Pops glared at her, lips curled, and stood aside. "Get in there before I change my mind," he said.

Upon entering, Val found Gil awake and watching a sports talk show on TV. He'd lost the ghostly pallor, but dark circles remained under his eyes. When he spotted her, though, a huge grin spread across his face. "Hey, partner," he said in a tired voice. After muting the TV, he held out his hand. Without thinking, she grasped it in both of hers. She noticed how clammy her hands were, and queasiness rose in her gut. She tried to let go, but he held on, drawing her closer.

"N-no Jessica today?" she asked.

Gil shook his head. "She went back to New Haven for a few days," he said. "Sit, stay a while." He nodded toward a guest chair.

Relieved to have an excuse to escape his grip, she pulled the chair close and rested her hands on her lap. "Jessica's great, Gil. You're lucky to have her."

"Yeah, she's—wait." Gil fixed her with a puzzled frown. "What do you mean, 'have' her?"

Val's mouth stopped working for a moment. Or her brain did. In any event, words wouldn't come. She coughed and patted her chest to buy time. "Uh, you know. As a fiancée."

"As a *what*?" Gil's frown deepened from puzzlement to pure confusion. "Did she tell you that?"

"Uh...yeah...she said you two had gotten back together." Val's ears burned, and guilty feelings swelled in her chest. "Don't you remember?"

Disgust replaced confusion on Gil's face. "Oh, Lord. Jessica's telling her damned stories again." He blew out a gush of air, closed his eyes a moment, then opened them and faced Val again. "Jess and I *were* engaged—ten years ago. And I did call her a few days before, uh, all this happened." He lowered his eyes and looked away. "I was lonely, I guess. Hearing her voice cheered me up, but we did *not* 'get back together'. At least, not in my mind."

Val covered her broad smile with her hands and pretended to cough again. Not engaged! She should feel sorry for him. And for Jessica. But she didn't. No matter how inappropriate her feelings were for her partner, they would not go away. "You two need to chat," she said after an eternity.

"We will. Damn, I don't look forward to that conversation." He chuckled. "I'd rather face Harkins again. He doesn't scare me half as much as her."

Val laughed. "Well, your sense of humor is back." In a more serious tone, she continued, "I'm glad to see your condition has improved. You had us worried there."

Gil waved that sentiment away. "I ain't going anywhere. Not as long as I have these fancy accommodations." He gazed around the room and his face lit up with another tired smile.

"You've got quite the armed guard outside your door," she said. "Clayton's finest."

"Yeah, that's weird," he said. "I seriously doubt Harkins is showing up here. Besides, I thought Gibson assigned Pops to you?"

"We, uh, didn't work out too well." Val heaved a deep sigh. "You're a tough act to follow."

He turned toward her, still smiling. "I miss working with you."

His directness caught her off guard. "I, uh, miss you too," she said. "Working with you, and...everything." Sweat collected on her scalp, and she could hear her heartbeat. She'd never told anyone that, other than her brother. What was it about Gil that made her blurt out such things?

"Speaking of work," he said. "Any new developments on Harkins?"

"He apparently stole a Jeep from one of the strippers," she said, happy to switch gears in the conversation. "I'm supposed to meet with Jalen Marshall to follow up. Has he been by?"

"Jalen's supposed to visit today. I actually expected him when you showed up." Gil adjusted his position in the bed and grunted. "I'm going to have wicked bedsores before I get out of here."

Seeing his pain and hearing his complaints, guilt washed over her again. "I'm so sorry I did this to you. I feel so awful."

"Don't!" Gil reached out again. After several moments of pretending not to notice, she pressed her hand into his again, and he enclosed it in a firm grip, sending a tingling sensation up her arm. "Listen to me, Dawes. You didn't do this. Harkins did. Nobody else. And it's my fault for being careless, not yours."

"You took my bullet," she said. "I—"

"Bullshit!"

"I'm the one fixated on this case—this guy," Val said. "It's my fault we chased him, and that led to the standoff. And you were trying to protect me that night, and instead—"

"Instead I fell on my ass and he shot me," Gil said. "None

of that is your fault."

Val drew a deep, unsteady breath. "I guess we'll have to agree to disagree."

"We do agree on one thing," Gil said. "You're obsessed with finding him—understandably so. It makes sense given the type of cop you are, and your personal history. And because the guy's a damned feral animal. But it's important to me, too, Val. To the whole department—hell, the whole city. Or should be."

"Yes, but it's not worth losing y—uh, good cops like you over." Her lip trembled, and tears welled up in her eyes.

"You haven't lost me yet." He glanced at the heart monitor behind him. "At least, last time I checked."

She laughed, and tension flowed out of her. "You need to check the machines to be sure?"

Gil laughed too, then winced again. He squeezed her hand harder. To her amazement, no more tingling ran up her arm, and the clamminess had disappeared.

She had one more thing to say to Gil, but the words stuck inside her. She owed him more details about what had happened with Uncle Milt, and she'd waited long enough. Gil may no longer have been her partner, but he was still a friend—besides Beth, her closest friend. She couldn't wait for another close call, or worse. She cleared her throat and composed her message in her mind—

A knock on the door interrupted. A moment later, Jalen Marshall entered, carrying a sheet of plastic rolled up in his hand.

"Kryz, you old dog!" Jalen bopped the metal rail at the end of the bed with the plastic roll. "How many women you got coming to hold your hand every day?" He laughed and slapped Val on the back. She pulled her hand from Gil's grip, reddening.

"I'll give you two some time," she said, moving toward the door. "Jalen, can we catch up when you're done?"

"Meet me and Ben in the cafeteria in twenty minutes. But first, stay for the ceremony."

Val and Gil exchanged glances, eyes wide. "Ceremony?" she said.

Jalen stood erect by Gil's bed and unrolled the plastic

sheet, exposing a bulls-eye bearing the caption, "Slowest-moving Target Award. G. Kryzinski, 2018." She stared at it, her feelings of guilt doubling. Jalen, oblivious to her humiliation, burst out in laughter. "If you want, Gil, I can make a T-shirt for you!"

"You're an asshole!" But Gil laughed along with Jalen and accepted a massive bear hug from him.

Great. Not only can Jalen get away with bringing inappropriate gallows-humor gifts, but he had no problem giving Gil hugs, the lucky bastard.

Val slipped out the door, her shoulders shaking, fighting to keep her emotions in check. But Pops's disdainful grimace broke the dam, and as she fled down the hall, hot tears flowed like rain.

Chapter Thirty-Six

Val had no interest in hanging out with Ben Peterson while she waited for Jalen Marshall, particularly in her emotional state. Instead, she found an empty waiting room in the hospital's pediatrics wing, set the alarm on her phone, and zoned out to a travel show on a muted TV.

Five minutes too early, her phone roused her from an unplanned nap on the rock-hard chairs. The Caller ID brought a smile to her face.

"Chad! So sorry I haven't called you lately," she said without a hello. "Work has been awful, and—"

"Don't worry, I'm not calling to chastise you," he said. "Dad isn't coming for the holidays. He's ill and isn't up to traveling."

"Ah. Is he, you know, sick-sick, or cold-and-flu sick?" Another thing to feel guilty about. Dad lived ten minutes away, yet she got news of him through her brother.

"Neither. He's going back into rehab." Chad's voice grew sullen. "He's been hitting the juice hard lately, I guess."

"Oh." She supposed she should feel bad about that. "So, when do you want me there?"

"Can you come a few days early and stay the weekend?" he said. "Kendra's playing with the orchestra in a concert on the Friday before Christmas. If there's any chance you could make it..."

Val sighed. She hadn't seen Kendra perform in years, and Christmas concerts always gave her a big lift. "I'll try. That means taking Friday through Tuesday off, at least. As a rookie, I'm not sure how that'll fly." Her phone chimed again—her alarm. "I gotta go. I'll let you know as soon as I can."

She rang off and hustled down the hall, following signs

through the maze of corridors to find the cafeteria. She arrived a few minutes before noon—rush hour. Small groups of sad, nervous people jostled in long lines and huddled around Formica-topped tables, filling the space with noise, heat, and sweat. After a quick scan of the room, she spotted two men sitting together, both around her age. She navigated toward their table, then stopped in her tracks.

The man facing her resembled Ben, but differed in appearance, too. She recognized his familiar face with a start: Paul Peterson, Ben's cousin.

Paul appeared agitated, jabbing his finger at Ben while he spoke. Ben shook his head, his gaze lowered, his hands raised as if to shield him from his cousin's verbal onslaught. Paul's expression showed frustration, which shifted to surprise when his eyes met Val's. His lips moved: *Uh-oh.* Ben spun around, spotting Val, and mouthed: *Shit.* The men muttered something to each other—terse goodbyes, Val guessed—and Paul hustled out of the cafeteria without a backward glance.

"Did you have a nice chat with your cousin?" Val asked, pulling up a seat across from Ben.

"Yes, we were, uh, making holiday plans," Ben said in an innocent tone. "The whole fam damily gets together Christmas Eve. How about you?"

"How lovely. I look forward to his post-holiday blog," she said. "I'm sure I'll learn more about how bad a cop I am."

"Those stories don't come from me," Ben said through clenched teeth. "If you want to find out who's feeding him, you ought to look closer to home." He looked up and waved. "There's Jalen."

Marshall's imposing figure appeared by their table, and he sat alongside his junior partner. "Good news," Jalen said. "The stolen Jeep showed up a couple days ago near the New York border. Abandoned, with Harkins's prints all over it."

"But where's Harkins?" Val asked. "In two days, he could be anywhere."

"There's more," Jalen said. "A young girl filed a complaint, saying a guy matching Harkins's description molested her—more than once. He was shacking up with her mother out there."

Val's stomach heaved. Another victim! All because she'd

let him slip away again. "Holy crap," she said. "This guy's out of control. We have got to track him down. Organize a manhunt or something."

"We've sent an APB with photos and fingerprints to law enforcement throughout the region," Jalen said. "By nightfall, his face will be on every TV, airport security gate, train station and post office bulletin board in the Northeast. If he's on the move at all, we'll find him."

"Not if he's left the area," Val said. "We need a national search."

"Whoa, slow down, cowgirl," Jalen said, and Ben, who'd remained quiet, chuckled. Jalen went on, "First, we don't have the resources. Second, Harkins doesn't know that we're onto him. Third, I think he's staying close. Last time we thought he was running south, but then he popped up again in our own backyard."

"Sooner or later he'll run out of girlfriends with young daughters," Ben said, smirking.

Val glared at him, but then sighed, and nodded. "I agree. He's running out of options here. He'll dash, sooner rather than later, and we need to get aggressive to find him."

"We?" Ben looked from Val to Jalen. "Whose case is this?"

"S'matter? You tired of this case?" Jalen said and frowned.

Ben shrank in his seat. "How many cops need to get shot because of this guy?" he said. "I say, if he runs to New York, he becomes New York's problem."

Val stared at him, open-mouthed, and shook her head. "You remind me of my ex-partner, Pops," she said. "It's all about you, isn't it?"

"Ex?" Jalen sat back in his chair. "Already?"

Val grimaced. "We didn't last a week, but it seemed like years."

Jalen laughed. "I feel your pain. So, who are you with now?"

"Nobody, at the moment," Val said. An idea came to her, and excitement built in her voice. "How about we team up on this case? We both have warrants out for him, and it solves my boss's problem of finding me a partner."

Jalen rubbed his chin and nodded. "Nice idea. You need a partner, and we need each other's help. Let's pitch it to our bosses as an inter-city task force. What do you think, Ben?"

"Two's company. Three's a crowd," Ben said in a dull voice.

"Then try to stay out of our way," Jalen said. "Let's do this, Dawes!"

***

The night grew wintry toward the end of their shift. The icy drizzle turned to a steady downpour of freezing rain, raising the prospect of a bone-chilling walk home through the dark city streets. Val parked the cruiser in the garage and rubbed her hands together, shivering.

"Well, Val, we survived another one," her partner said with a weary smile, surprising her by using her first name. Despite his exhaustion, his face radiated energy and kindness. He extended his hand, and Val shook it, then hugged her body for warmth. He cocked his head. "You walking home?"

"I'll call Uber." Her teeth chattered, and she laughed. "One with central heating, I hope."

"Nonsense," he said. "I'll give you a ride. It's the least I can do."

She relented. This one time, she could let someone do something nice for her.

After they clocked out, he waited for her in his SUV, motor running. When she clambered in, hot air blasted her face. Even the seat felt warm. "I got the winter package with this beast," he said with an easy grin. "In Connecticut, I have to use it half the damned summer." His strong arms rested on the wheel, a safe distance away from her. By the time he parked outside her place, she'd unbuttoned her coat and removed her gloves, but she was still hot. "Sorry," he said, turning down the heat. "I guess I overdid it."

The wind gusted and the clouds opened up. Torrents of rain splashed the windows. "I'm going to drown just getting inside!" she said with a nervous laugh. After a brief pause, she asked, "Would you mind walking me to the door?"

A massive golf umbrella covered them both as

they ran up the walk to the building's entrance, but they got soaked anyway. Val inserted her key into the lock, but the old mechanism refused to turn.

"Can I try?" he said. Gripping the handle, he gave the door a mighty shove. It burst open and he tumbled through the doorway onto the floor. Horrified, she covered her mouth—until she heard him laughing.

"What a klutz!" he said. "Oh, crap. That hurt."

Val took his hand and pulled him to his feet. He weighed next to nothing. His dark brown eyes riveted on hers the whole way up.

"Well, I appreciate the ride," she stammered. "I hope it didn't take you out of your way."

"Not at all." He smiled. "Okay, that's bullshit, but what am I supposed to say?"

She laughed again. He was still holding her hand. Or was she holding his?

"Anyway, I should thank you," he said.

"Me? What for?" Their hands still touched. She should let go. Or he should. But they didn't.

"You've made police work fun again for me," he said. "Your curiosity and enthusiasm, the way you pick everything up so quickly. It reminds me of when I first started." His eyes twinkled, radiating a smile that arose from deep within.

"Oh...uh, thank you," she said. "You've made learning to become a police officer an absolute pleasure." They stood in silence a moment, eyes locked. This is when Val should say goodnight. Thank you again for the ride. See you tomorrow.

"Would you like to come inside to get warm?" she said instead.

He nodded. "I'd love to." His voice floated in a smooth, baritone wave around her. Like velvet. Or chocolate. Or...something.

Val led him inside, locked the door behind them, and put a finger to her lips. "My roommate might be sleeping," she whispered.

"Might be?" He giggled. "At 3:00 a.m.? Who'd be

asleep at this hour?" He pretended to sleep-walk
through the living room, arms outstretched, but he
looked more like a zombie, and it made Val laugh.
That made him laugh too, and they tried not to laugh
out loud but they couldn't not make noise, which
only made it funnier. She finally made it stop by
looking away from him. Which sucked. Even with the
five o'clock shadow, he had a nice face, framed by
that wavy dark hair. And his smile could melt the ice
frosting her giant living room window.

Wait. Since when did her living room have a
picture window?

Music played from somewhere, a ballroom piece
her dad used to like. Weird. Beth and Josh must be
awake after all, picking out a wedding playlist.
Hopefully they'd stay in her bedroom.

Val glanced at him, astonished to discover him
dressed in a tux, complete with black tie. And
completely dry. So was she. "May I have this dance?"
he asked, bowing.

She laughed again. "Shouldn't I be wearing a
gown, or something?"

"What you wear doesn't matter," he said. "You're
beautiful."

Val blushed, but he took her hand in his and
waltzed with her across the floor. She stared at her
hand, enveloped in his, wondering why it didn't hurt,
or tingle, and why it stayed dry instead of getting all
clammy like it did on dates. And why his hand on
her waist felt so gentle and reassuring, rather than
scary-creepy-awful.

She looked back at his face and had her answer.
It was a face she liked. Admired. Trusted.

"Gil," she said. "This is amazing."

The music swelled, and he lifted her up, swirling
her around and around until she got dizzy. His arms
must be getting tired. Had to be. Hadn't he gotten
injured? But he held her steady, twirling them both
in slow circles to the ancient tune, her feet in the air,
as if she, too, weighed nothing. It felt like flying.

Val looked down and discovered that his feet, too,

had left the floor. They floated near the ceiling, arms around each other's waist, their faces close, eyes inches apart, bodies touching, his skin pressed against her thighs and abdomen, and *holy shit we're both naked.*

Exactly when their lips met she couldn't say, but it was soft, and sweet, and both gentle and strong. Gil's hands caressed her back, her hips, her legs, in a way that was loving and beautiful.

She remembered to touch him, too, appreciating his muscular arms, his broad shoulders, his strong back. He pulled her close and lifted her again, like a groom carrying his bride across the threshold, and beyond. Five seconds he carried her. Ten. And not walking but racing across the room, the breeze blowing her hair into her face. Thirty seconds, a minute, across the entire apartment. Just when she thought to warn him they'd run out of room, the apartment exploded with light and the tinkling of shattered glass. They'd crashed right through the big picture window, into the rain, and in a moment they'd land on the frosty grass outside, bruised and full of regret.

But they did not. The tiny shards of glass turned into a cloud of mist, gentle and warm on her skin. Instead of frozen turf and concrete, a giant canyon opened beneath them, layered with red and yellow strata reaching back into the millennia of existence. Rather than falling, they floated above it all, clutching each other and gasping in awe at the view. He kissed her again. Their bodies joined, and for the first time in her life she experienced the joy of a man giving himself to her rather than taking what he wanted, and it felt blissful.

In that instance, all the cold and wind and rain outside disappeared, as did Harkins, Pops, and the whole damned world except for Gil. All that mattered, all that existed, was him, and her, in a moment that could not last long enough.

PART 4

Manhunt

Chapter Thirty-Seven

Val lay in bed for hours after waking from her dream, reality splashing her face like the nasty weather pounding the window of her darkened bedroom. Part of her wanted to go back to sleep, to resume that amazing fantasy. But she couldn't command that dream to return. And would she, if she could? It felt so good while it lasted, but now the prospect of being touched by a man once again brought only fear and revulsion.

Besides, she couldn't have Gil. He and Jessica weren't engaged, but they still had something going. Plus, he'd made it clear: she was too young for him. And he was her partner. Or was he? No. He had to leave the force. Jessica told her so. The doctors had ordered it. But maybe Jessica had gotten that wrong, too.

Val showered for eons and would have stayed longer had she not remembered that Beth and Josh needed the bathroom soon, and hot water, and what the hell was she doing up at 7:00 a.m., anyway? After pulling on a pair of jeans, she yanked them off and changed into nicer slacks, a real blouse, and one-inch heels, the tallest she had. She even put on makeup.

She took herself out to breakfast at The Claytown Café, ignoring Pinkie's crazy chatter, nursing free coffee refills long after her toast had gotten cold. The café filled with customers until a line formed, waiting for tables to empty. But Val remained rooted in her chair by the door, needing even more caffeine, to make up for the sleep the night had denied her. Visiting hours at the hospital opened at 10. She had time.

The queue of shivering customers-in-waiting grew, with people standing in small groups between tables to get out of the icy rain. A young couple chatted while surfing on their phones, their voices cutting through the clatter.

"They shouldn't let gangs off the hook like that," the woman said, brushing black curls away from her face. "Cops who do that are criminals themselves, if you ask me."

"What's the difference?" the man with her asked, stuffing his free hand inside the woman's coat. From her furtive, evasive movements, he wasn't just warming his hand in there. Ew. "The gangs will kill each other off, anyway. The sooner the better."

The woman wriggled away from him, to Val's relief. "That's so sick. Besides, they don't just kill each other. What if they hurt someone we know? What if it's one of us?"

"We don't go where they go," the man said. "We're safe."

"The article says they were on MLK," she said. "Close to here."

Val's ears perked up, her face warming. This sounded far too familiar.

"They probably had guns, and God knows what else," the woman said. "And that cop just let them walk!"

That did it. Val could sit still no longer. She tapped the woman's arm. "Excuse me. What is that you're reading?"

The woman blinked at Val, as if she hadn't noticed her before. She showed Val her phone. "It's this crime blog I'm hooked on. This guy's got the inside scoop in the police department. Amazing stuff. It's totally going viral right now."

"Half of it's crap," the man said with a laugh. "I don't believe most of it."

"Let me see that," Val said. The woman handed the phone to her.

Just as she suspected. Paul fucking Peterson. She scanned to the post's concluding paragraphs:

> The officer in question, oddly enough, inherited her job rather than earned it, trading on the legacy of her forebears—true heroes, who died while in the City's service.
>
> Her rash, irresponsible behavior has made her a pariah of the Clayton P.D. Already one of her partners fights for his life in a hospital bed. Unsurprisingly, none of the other officers on the force will serve with her.

The comments at the bottom of the blog were no friendlier:

> Clearly, the officer in question is not fit for the job. Fire her! Better yet, let the gangs have her!
> - **ClaytonLifer**

> She's impulsive and dangerous, a threat to public safety, and a disappointment to her family's legacy. This is why legacy hires should be banned.
> - **CopStalker79**

> She's a menace!
> - **JQCitizen**

Val handed the woman's phone back to her, hands shaking.

"See what I mean?" the guy said. "Inflammatory crap."

"I think it's great," the woman said, but her smile faded when her eyes met Val's. "I take it you don't agree."

A thousand pointed remarks came to mind, but Val swallowed them all. "Let's just say, I agree with your boyfriend." She threw cash on the table and stood to leave.

"Hey, score! A table!" the boyfriend said.

"I hope you're not leaving because of us," the woman said, her tone belying her words.

"No," Val said. "That officer that was shot? Friend of mine. I'm going to visit him in the hospital."

"That's awesome," the woman said. "Cops like that guy are heroes. Tell him I said so, okay?"

Val frowned at the woman, a swirl of emotions battling for control. In a hoarse voice, she said, "I'll do that." She pushed her way out of the restaurant.

***

Val sweated off her frustration, and the extra calories from her carb-loaded breakfast, with a vigorous workout at the department's aging but under-utilized gym. She spent extra time on the rowing machine, facing away from the room while wearing noise-canceling headphones and pumping up her pace with Jimmy Eat World, Linkin Park, and Green Day. A perfect morning.

Val had just finished her third set of two hundred reps when, despite the headphones, someone tapped her on the shoulder. She turned to glare at the unwelcome intruder and prepared some choice leave-me-the-hell-alone invective, but the sweaty face greeting her reversed her grimace into a smile.

"Shannon and I are going for a run," Brenda Petroni said. "Care to join?"

Despite the rubbery state of her legs, she agreed, and minutes later the three women jogged abreast on the pedestrian trail overlooking the Torrington River. At first their slow clip frustrated Val, but after the second mile, her prior workout caught up with her, and she struggled to keep pace. Their breaths puffed out in white clouds as they chatted. Or, in Val's case, mostly listened.

"Come on, keep up," Shannon teased her another half-mile into the run. "Weren't you a track star at UConn?"

"That was...an entire...year ago," Val said between gulps of air. "Working with Pops...all we do is drive. I gained five pounds... in less than a week. All on my butt."

"Welcome to the club," Shannon said. She didn't struggle to breathe one bit.

"Oh, quit your bellyaching, both of ya," Brenda said, panting, and gestured at her own thick torso. "The two of you together couldn't fill a doll's dress. Besides, aren't you done with Pops?"

"We'll see," Val said. "I don't have a new partner yet. Are either of you free?"

"Love to help, but not if it means working night shift," Shannon said. "My husband would kill me."

"The old guard won't pair up two women, regardless," Brenda said. She slowed to a walk, and the others did too. "They think we need a man to 'protect' us. We're so small and frail, you know?" She spat on the sidewalk. "If only they knew."

"It's ridiculous, especially in your case," Shannon said. "Aren't you a black belt in jiu jitsu? And a great shot with a firearm. You're more likely to save their ass than the other way around."

"Lieutenant Gibson never gave me the impression that he thinks that way," Val said. "Nor Travis."

"Yeah, but Gibson thinks—probably correctly—that there's more to gain by having men and women partner up," Brenda said. "Teach the guys like Pops how to act around us."

"The problem is, you started with one of the best," Shannon said. "Frank, my first partner, was more worried about retirement than doing the work required to earn this week's pay. And the humming! Constant frigging humming!"

Brenda wagged her head and led them to a park bench. "My first partner, who shall remain nameless, refused to respond first to any crime scene," she said. "The biggest risk he'd take is chasing pickpockets, blasting his siren at street fights, and following up on petty theft not worth filing the paperwork over. I almost quit after a week."

"I don't expect to get someone as great as Gil," Val said, sitting between them on the bench. "Just give me a guy who doesn't pick at his teeth and fart in the car all the time. And one who gets out of the damned cruiser once in a while."

Brenda laughed. "As a rookie, you're going to get a senior cop—guys at least my age. In our day, the Academy taught old-school policing. That's what they know."

"Uncle Val gave me a different impression," Val said. "All the cops he worked with seemed so diligent and courageous."

"Your uncle brought out the best in people," Shannon said.

For a few moments, they sat in silence, and Val's companions exchanged guilty glances. "What's up?" Val asked. "What are you not telling me?"

Shannon looked away. "This one's yours, Bren."

"Well," Brenda said, taking a deep breath, "thanks to Pops and that idiot blogger Peterson, the whispers among the guys around the water cooler are that you're a loose cannon. It's bullshit," she added, "and when I've pressed them for details, they tell me things they praise their male counterparts for. But in a woman, to the good old boys, it comes across as rash and dangerous, because of that 'we have to protect her' mentality."

"What a crock!" Val jumped up from the bench and paced the sidewalk, hands folded behind her. "Why do they think I became a cop? To answer phones and type reports while they chase the bad guys? Or, like Pops, sit in the car and eat donuts? Should we just wait for the rapists and gang members to enter twelve-step programs?"

Brenda laughed out loud. "Sorry, Val, but that was funny."

Val's own wry smile faded. "I wish I could laugh about it. Lately, I've been wondering...maybe I'm not cut out for police work."

"That's crazy!" Shannon and Brenda said at the same time.

Brenda stood and held Val by the arms. "I know you're going through a rough patch," she said. "We all go through it. But please don't give up. We need you in Clayton."

"I sure don't feel needed these days," Val said. "How did you get through times like this?"

"The same way you will," Brenda said. "Just keep on being the best cop you know how—and Val, you're a *damn* good cop—until the situation improves."

"So, I just wait? Pfft." Val broke free of Brenda's loose embrace and stepped away from them. She drew a deep breath, exhaled. "I've got a possible Plan B. Can I run it by you?"

"Shoot," Shannon said, standing.

"All ears," said Brenda.

Val faced them square-on again. "Jalen Marshall from Hartford is going to propose I work with their team on this Harkins case. Part of a multi-city task force. Think Gibson will go for it?"

"The child rapist guy?" Shannon's brow furrowed. "Didn't he run off to New York or somewhere?"

"Marshall thinks he's still in Western Connecticut," Val said. "I'm hoping he's right."

"To be honest, I doubt Gibson will say yes," Brenda said. "Harkins is still out of our jurisdiction, and with Gil and Samuels out, we're already short-handed."

Shannon nodded. "While I love the idea, I agree with Brenda. Sorry, Val."

Val stewed on it a moment, then remembered Ben Peterson's reluctance. That gave her an idea. "What if, instead of lending me out, we made a temporary trade?" She paced again, rubbing her hands in excitement. "Jalen's partner is a rookie out of my class in the academy. Kind of an even exchange, at least on paper. Right?"

Brenda's lower lip bulged, and one shoulder rose and fell. "Might sell."

Shannon grinned. "It'd sell better if we each put in a good word. Come on, Bren. Let's use our standing with the boss to help Val out. What do you say?"

Brenda smiled and nodded. "I'm in," she said. "What have we got to lose?"

"I'll tell you what you can lose," Val said. "Last one back to the gym buys lunch!" She dashed down the trail, laughing at their howls of protest, then slowed to allow them to catch up. Let them win this one. If they convinced Gibson to say yes, she owed them a lot more than lunch.

***

Val ran her modified version of Jalen's plan past Gil over a game of gin rummy on her next visit to the hospital. His reaction lifted her spirits even more than Brenda's and Shannon's support did.

"I love it," he said with a grin. "This is what you're born to do, Val. Detective work is in your blood. Gin." He laid out his cards and laughed when Val swore good-naturedly at him. "That's four beers you owe me."

"Three!" she protested. "I won the first game."

"She can run, fight, and shoot, but she can't count," Gil said in mock condescension. "Typical athlete."

Val gave his arm a playful smack and gathered up the cards to reshuffle. "So, do you think Gibson will go along?"

"He might," Gil said. "I'll call and urge him to do it sooner rather than later. We need to get this guy, and you're the one to do it."

"Gil," she said, slowing her shuffling, "I can't tell you how much it means to have your support. I only wish you could be out there with me."

"I know," he said, his expression turning sad. "I miss it. But it's hard to catch crooks when you can't even walk."

"What's the prognosis on that?" she said, keeping her tone casual.

"Too soon to tell," he said. "I keep asking, but the doctors don't have an answer yet."

An awkward moment of silence passed between them. Every time she looked at him, Val's subconscious reprised her dream of them flying and making love—so far from any reality she could experience. Yet here they sat, so close to one another, almost touching, sharing stories, talking like old friends...

Except that they weren't. Old friends shared secrets, confided in one another. They didn't hold back the most pertinent details of their lives from each other.

"You gonna deal those cards at some point?" he asked. "Or should we save time and just declare me the winner?"

"Brat," she said with a wry smile. She set the deck down and sat facing him, hands in her lap. "Gil, when you say I'm the one to get Harkins...are you saying that because... well...of my history?"

His face fell into a sad frown. "I said it because you're tenacious, smart, and motivated as hell," he said. "Your past may have something to do with that last part, but you were born with the rest. That's why you're such a great cop."

Val sighed. "That shrink, Cyrus, feels I'm on some sort of vendetta."

Gil's eyebrows arched high on his forehead. "Why?" When she didn't reply, his expression hardened. "They didn't catch the guy, did they?"

She took a sharp breath, eased it out of her lungs, and shook her head no.

"Shit," he said in a whisper. "I guess I always assumed that your uncle locked that fucking pig away for life."

"He gave him a good beating." Val forced a smile, but it faded. "He wanted to put Milt—that's the guy who raped me—away in prison, but Uncle Val got killed right after I told him. Mom and Dad didn't believe me at first, and even after they did, I always thought they blamed me. God knows, I blamed myself." She wrapped her arms around herself, suddenly very cold.

"God, that's awful." Gil's voice shook. "I hope you had someone there who did, who supported you."

"I didn't tell anyone else. Not for a long time. Not even my brother. I was...too ashamed..." Her voice broke, and no more words would form.

"Hey, now." Gil held out his hand to her. Val stared at it. She should accept his gesture of friendship and caring. Let him in a little more.

But her arms stayed wrapped around her own body, frozen. She couldn't. If she did, that awful feeling would return: the clamminess, the tingling that turns into pain, the numbing that would travel from her fingers to her heart—

"Val, you've carried this inside for so long," he said. "A heavy burden."

She glanced up—when had she looked away?—and found painful understanding in his eyes, tears burgeoning on the brink of falling onto his cheeks. In that moment she knew he really cared, that it meant more to him than just liking his partner. Val meant something to him. Something more than friends, and something far better than a Brent or even Josh, who only cared about scoring a piece of ass.

The dream came back to her again—this time, not the crazy naked flying and kissing and lovemaking, but rather the sense of safety she felt with him, and confidence, and trust. The emotions that, she realized, did not crash from her dreams into real life. They crossed *from* real life *into* the dream. Sentiments that made dreams like that possible.

The tears fell from his eyes, splashed down his cheeks. He didn't wipe them away. Instead, he let them fall. His hand remained outstretched, toward her. Compelling, but not commanding. Open. Inviting.

Val lifted her hand and moved it toward him. It hovered over his for a moment, then glided into a soft landing. He closed his fingers around hers. She waited for the tingling jolt of electricity to sting her arm, numb her body.

But she felt no pain. Instead, it felt...nice.

She let it rest there for a long, long time.

Chapter Thirty-Eight

Val got stuck on desk duty for the next several days while Gibson and Travis sorted out their staffing decisions. She and Travis made occasional forays into the field when his schedule permitted, but those reprieves from the cube farm came too far apart for her taste. Every time someone closed the door to Gibson's office, she suspected they were talking about her. But then another day would pass, and nothing changed.

She spent as much time as she could searching for more clues of Harkins's whereabouts, but once again, he'd vanished into the wind. Stakeouts at his known haunts such as the Silver Fox, Candy's house, and Antoinetta and Rosa's neighborhood turned up dry. He avoided bus terminals, train stations, and airports, while his Impala and Raven's Jeep remained impounded as evidence. Where had he gone? And how did he get there?

One night, toward the end of her shift, Gibson's imposing frame cast a shadow over her cube. "All right, Dawes, we've decided on your next assignment." He pulled up a chair and sat close to her, keeping his voice low. "You're an enigma, Dawes. I mean, on the one hand, you've got talent—lots of it. You're innovative, resourceful, courageous as hell, and tough as nails." He shook his head in wonder. "And tenacious. Your persistence in going after this Harkins asshole is commendable."

"And?" she said after an eternity of waiting. "Or should I say, 'But'? What's in 'the other hand'?"

"But," he said, nodding, "your mistakes sometimes are dumber than dumb. Paying off that gangster, for example? Holy crap on a cracker, Dawes. That shit's nuts."

Val opened her mouth to argue, thought better of it.

"Meanwhile, half this force thinks you go off half-cocked,

risking life and limb over a parking ticket," he said. "The other half thinks you're fragile as a champagne glass, and they need to protect you."

"The men think those things, you mean." She set her lips in a line, her heart pounding.

"Yes. The men, or most of them. But have you noticed, Dawes? Most of this department is men. I'm trying to change that," he said, waving off another protest from her, "but progress is slow. I don't agree with it, nor does Travis. But neither of us can be your partner." He sat back and looked her in the eye. "You've got supporters, too, though. Petroni and O'Reilly, of course, but also Travis, Gil...and me. And, Jalen Marshall."

Val's ears perked up, as did her hopes. They must have spoken to him about the task force. She leaned toward him, straining to hear Gibson's every word.

"Marshall wants to work with you on an intercity team to track down Richard Harkins," he said.

She gripped one hand in the other, squirming in her seat. Please, please, say yes!

"He's offering to 'trade' some numb-nuts named Benjamin Peterson for you in the meantime," he said. "What do you know about him?"

Val cleared her throat. "Ben and I went to Academy together," she said. "He's...okay."

Gibson's face curled up in puzzlement. "Seriously? Word is, you kicked his ass in the martial arts demo, and he's hated you ever since."

She reddened. "Yeah, well. He wasn't top of class."

"No, Dawes. But you were. So it's a shitty trade."

Her heart fell. Damn it. Working on the task force would have given her work new direction and meaning, but now—

"However, keeping you tied to a desk is a complete waste of your talent. So I'm gonna approve this crazy scheme," he said with a sigh. "I want you to focus on that case exclusively. Turn over every stone—"

"Thank you, thank you, thank you!" she said, jumping out of her seat. "That's so great! I can't wait to get started. Should I work here, or in Hartford, or—"

"Easy, easy," Gibson said. "The downtown detective squad will take the lead for Clayton, but you'll work with them, under their supervision. Take good notes, Dawes. This will be a great experience and will mean a lot for your career down the road. And, do me a favor, Dawes?"

The sudden gruff tone dulled her enthusiasm for a moment. "Yes, sir?"

Gibson's expression softened, and he patted her shoulder. "Get that son of a bitch!"

***

Val paced the floor of her apartment, waiting for someone to pick up the phone at Chad's law office. As a junior associate, he and a dozen other lawyers shared a secretary, and getting through often meant multiple redials. She had her finger an inch from the "End Call" button when a voice answered, "Milbourne Kaplan O'Sullivan, can you hold, please?" Smooth jazz interrupted her reply.

She plopped onto the sofa and rehearsed how she'd break the news to her brother. Perhaps leading with the exciting new assignment, to buy him in, then when he asks her what it means—

"How can I direct your call?" asked the brusque female voice.

"Chad Dawes, please," she said.

"Charles!" the secretary called out without covering the phone. "It's your sister."

"Hey, Val," Chad said a moment later. "Just running between client meetings. I hope you're not calling to tell me you can't make it for Christmas. Ali hasn't stopped talking about you this week."

Val sighed. "Damn you, Chad," she said. "Sometimes I wonder why I bother to even call. How did you know?"

"Because you never call with good news," he said, sending a heavy sigh back to her. "Dammit. Ali will freak."

Her heart split in half at the idea of disappointing Ali. She curled into a fetal position on the couch. "I got assigned to a new inter-city task force to nab this child molester. It's a huge opportunity, but it means I don't get any days off. Please tell Ali, I'm so sorry."

"Not even Christmas morning?" Chad asked, incredulous. "Or Christmas Eve?"

"I'm on twelve-hour night shifts," she said, becoming even

sadder. "I won't have time to drive to your house and back on Christmas Day. Believe me, Chad, I would if I could."

He sighed. "First Dad, now you. What a Christmas this is going to be." The phone went silent for several moments.

"Well," he said, "it sounds like a fabulous career break for you. Look, don't worry. We'll be fine. You get that guy, and then we'll celebrate together, okay?"

Val pressed the phone hard against her ear. Chad's understanding only made her feel worse. "Yeah. Sorry. I really wanted to see you."

"Me too." After a long pause, he added, "There is another option."

She sat up on the sofa. "Such as?"

"We could all celebrate Christmas at Dad's place," Chad said in a quiet voice.

She bolted off the love seat and paced the room, her brain racing. With Dad? How could he suggest such a thing! Val's heart pounded, occupying the long silence between them. Words, Val. Speak.

"Then Ali could see him, too," Chad said, filling the awkward silence. "She barely remembers him, and he hasn't even met Dar yet."

"You can't fix this, Chad," she said. "Dad and me, I mean. It goes deeper than a gift exchange and a round of Christmas carols."

"I know," he said, his voice soft, almost inaudible. "But it's a start."

"There's nothing to start. Anyway, doesn't Kendra have a concert?" She regretted her sharp tone, wished she could take it back.

"Yay, you remembered," Chad said, his words edged with sarcasm. "So, yeah, we'd have to come the weekend before."

"Wait, you mean *this* weekend?" Panic replaced disappointment. "You mean, like, two days from now? No, Chad. Shit! Listen, I haven't even started Christmas shopping, I'll be working double shifts, and I—I—I'm not ready!"

"Well," he said, "it's our only option. Do you want to see the niece that idolizes you, or not?"

"Chad, that's not fair—wait a minute." Suspicion swelled up inside her, piled on top of everything else. "You'd already planned this before I called, hadn't you?"

A jumble of voices rose on Chad's end of the line. "I...have to duck into my meeting," he said. "Let me know what you decide. Okay? Gotta run." He hung up.

Val sank back onto the sofa, still gripping the phone, her knuckles whitening. Christmas with Dad, in Clayton. If that didn't give her incentive to catch Harkins, nothing would.

***

Val's new assignment began two days later, on Friday, and it meant making adjustments to her work routine. First, she reported to work four hours earlier to better align with the schedules of her new team. Second, it meant working indoors, instead of walking the beat. Third, rather than walking from home to the Liberty Heights station, she had to take the city bus to police headquarters in downtown Clayton.

To make up for the reduced physical activity, she took the stairs to the fifth-floor office. Someone had taped a makeshift sign reading "Intercity Task Force" on the frosted glass panel of a heavy wooden door. Val pushed it open, spotted the familiar-looking detective seated behind a 70s-era gunmetal desk, and grinned. "Shannon! How did you—"

"And you thought I was only lobbying for this task force because of you?" Shannon stood and waved her over. "I saved you a good seat, next to mine. Awesome digs, eh?"

"Are you in charge, then?" Val asked while Shannon gave her a quick tour. "Where's everybody else?"

"I'm second in command of the unit," Shannon said. "Detective Grimes and his partner, Woodson, are pursuing some leads. Jalen Marshall has an equal-sized team in Hartford, and there's another one in New Haven. Now, how familiar are you with the statewide database?"

"Pretty well, thanks to a recent overdose of desk duty," Val said. "Whatcha got?"

Val dove in to her assignment, creating a map of alleged Harkins sightings. She developed a color-coding system of high, medium, and low-likelihood sightings, and within a few hours had put together a rough itinerary of his recent travels.

"Very impressive!" Shannon said to her when Val finished. They spread the map out over a long black meeting room table. "What do you make of it?"

"Harkins seems to be drifting south on smaller state and county highways along the western edge of the state," Val said. "After he left Warren, he appears to have hidden out in Kent a few days, then New Milford, Waterbury, Southbury, and Newtown."

"He doesn't stay anywhere long, based on your data," Shannon said.

"He does plenty of damage, though," Val said. "Reported rape in Warren. Likely assault in New Milford. Potential stolen car in Waterbury, abandoned in Southbury, where he robbed a convenience store—and assaulted another teenage girl. He's a one-man crime wave!"

"We need to project where he's heading next and alert the locals," Shannon said. "And if I were to guess, I'd say his next stop is Danbury."

Val froze, staring at the map. Shannon was right. Of the major towns in southwest Connecticut, Danbury sat next in line along Harkins' current trajectory.

Where Chad, Kendra, Dar, and Alison lived.

Chapter Thirty-Nine

Richard Harkins sipped his coffee in the corner booth of a local egg-and-pancake joint he found in the suburbs on his way to Danbury. It looked like a worn-down Denny's, with half of the harsh fluorescent lighting, double the food portions, and a lot less customer traffic. Perfect: he avoided the big chains, wary of their friendly relations with state and local police, and their internal networks that shared warnings of suspicious-looking types like him.

Today, he did look suspicious. He hadn't showered in two days, and he still had the stench of that ugly red-haired bitch from Southbury on him. Thank God for the crushing aromas of bacon and burnt coffee permeating the air.

A young family of four, if you count their loud-mouthed baby who never stopped crying, occupied a table to his right. Their charming little girl almost made up for how insufferable the rest of them were. The mom, a real looker in her late twenties with auburn hair and perfect skin, spoke in soft, melodious tones in a failed attempt to make the little brats behave. She tried to discreetly breast-feed the baby, but Harkins knew what she was doing. Lucky brat.

"Dar's had enough," she said to her husband, a brown-haired dork with glasses. "He needs changing."

"I'll do it. Ooh, he *is* stinky," the dork said, taking the baby from her. Baby poop odor drifted over to Harkins's booth. Why, oh why, couldn't they have changed him first?

"Let's go, little guy." Dorky Daddy carried the baby into the men's room.

The little girl tugged on her mother's arm. "Mommy, can I ride with you the rest of the way?" she asked. "I want to play the license plate game."

"Daddy will play it with you," the woman said.

"Daddy never lets me win," the girl said.

"A true Dawes," the woman said with a sigh.

Dawes! A name that made Harkins' skin crawl. Probably a coincidence, but—

"Auntie Val lets me win at Candyland," the girl said.

Val Dawes! That woman cop that had almost nailed his ass in Clayton—twice. And "Auntie." An opportunity, perhaps, for revenge.

"Dar's done feeding, so I suppose it's all right," the woman, smiling. "We'll have some girl time on the way to Clayton."

Clayton. Wrong direction, but it had its advantages. Familiar territory, and plenty of young meat there. Antoinetta, Raven's kid, and, more important, the chance to pay back the Dawes family for some long-festering wounds. Maybe end this battle, once and for all.

"Let's trade cars," the man said, reappearing with a much fresher-smelling baby. On closer inspection, he bore a familial resemblance to the woman cop. "You take the Volvo, I'll drive the CRV. That way we don't have to switch the kids' car seats. Come on, let's get going."

Harkins ducked his head as they left the restaurant. Sure enough, they loaded up into two separate cars, parked close to the entrance. He set his coffee down, but a middle-aged man dressed in black slacks, a short-sleeved white shirt, and a name badge blocked his exit from the booth. The stupid waiter.

"Sorry," the waiter said, scooting out of his way and smiling behind his bushy, salt-and-pepper mustache. "Was everything to your liking?"

"Yeah, fine," he said. "Good coffee."

"Great." The waiter slapped his bill onto the table. "Where are you headed?"

He decided. Smiled. "Jersey Shore." No longer true, but whatever. He glanced out the window. The parents had loaded the kids into the cars, turned on their engines. He fidgeted in his seat. He had to get rid of this guy.

"This time of year? You must be a glutton for punishment." The waiter smiled and took away his empty plate.

"You could say that. I'm visiting family." Another quick peek. The Volvo, driven by the pretty wife, inched backwards out of the parking space.

"Will you need a refill on the coffee?" the waiter said. Fucking jerk. Would. Not. Leave.

"No, no. All done." The Volvo finished pulling out, then waited for the Honda.

"I can take that whenever you're ready." The waiter smiled again. The tips of his mustache hairs disappeared inside the guy's mouth. Gross.

"Good to go." Harkins slipped a precious ten-dollar bill onto his check and skidded out of the booth. "Keep the change." Which, after his breakfast-all-day-with-unlimited-coffee plus tax, amounted to about a dollar. Last of the big-time spenders.

He made it outside just in time to see the Honda exit onto the highway. The Volvo pulled forward into the parking lot exit, then stalled. It made a whirring sound, that of an engine trying to start but not turning over. It happened again, then a third time, before the headlights went out.

Harkins smiled. What incredible luck. He walked over to the Volvo and tapped on the driver's window. The woman lowered it halfway.

"Car trouble?" he asked.

"It won't start," she said. "So weird. It's never done this before."

He nodded, put on the all-knowing face of the Guy Who Can Fix Things, like all men do in this situation. "Pop the hood, let me see what's up," he said.

"Oh," she said. "Thank you so much."

The hood clanked up an inch. Harkins pressed the release and propped up the hood. Pretended to check things—touching this, wiggling that. Returned to her window, rubbing his hands as if cleaning them off. "Try it again," he said. She did, producing the same whiny sound as before, with no success. As expected, since he'd loosened the battery cable even more. "I think it's your starter," he said, "or your alternator."

"Is that bad?" she said.

"It's not going anywhere tonight," he said. "Put it in neutral and I'll push you out of the way here."

He got her into a parking spot, taking advantage of the downward slope of the ramp. "Can I give you a lift somewhere?" he asked.

"I'll just call my husband. Thank you." She pulled her cell phone out of her purse.

Harkins smiled. "I'll wait, just in case." He smiled at the little girl in back, gazing at him with gigantic brown eyes, with auburn hair like her mother. She said nothing. Just scowled at him.

A gentle tune began playing. The woman cursed and picked up a second cell phone from the console next to her. "Dammit, Chad!" She hung up her own phone, and the tune stopped. "My husband left his cell phone! It's his car, you see. Now I have no way to reach him. Dammit!"

The little girl made a face, her mouth shaped in an "O." She wagged her finger at her mother. "Mommy said a bad word."

The woman laughed. "Yes, I did, Ali. I'm sorry." She shook her head. "What am I going to do?"

Harkins took a moment, as if uncertain of the offer he'd been dying to make since the Volvo's engine first choked out. "Did I hear you say you're going to Clayton?" he asked.

"Yes," the woman said in a cautious tone.

"Well," Harkins said, "I'll understand if you don't want to, but I'm heading to Clayton, and I have plenty of room." He gestured toward a Toyota RAV-4 he'd come to possess three hours before, courtesy of a trusting and now-unconscious plumber in Newtown. By now, the cops would be looking for it, though. Still, he needed to play this through. He clicked the fob, and the car's lights blinked.

"I'll just call Triple-A," she said. "Thank you, though."

Harkins shrugged. Perfect. "Sure," he said. "Of course, this time of night around here, it could take them a while. An hour or two, if you're lucky."

The woman paused with her phone in hand, as if contemplating the offer again. "Yeah, that's okay," she said. "My husband will figure out that I'm not behind him and come back for me." She tried the engine again. Nothing.

"Let me take another peek under the hood," Harkins said.

She popped it open. He strolled to the front and re-tightened the battery cable as best he could. "Give it another shot," he said.

She did, and it worked. "Thank you!" she shouted.

Harkins lowered the hood, circled around to the

passenger's side, tapped on the window, held up an index finger. She lowered the window, a quizzical expression on her face. He reached in, unlocked the door, and climbed in.

"What—what are you doing?" she asked.

Harkins grabbed the cell phone from her hand, and her husband's off the center console, and shoved them in his pocket. Then he pointed his .44 at her and said with a sneer, "Drive, *Mrs.* Dawes."

Chapter Forty

The woman's hands shook on the wheel, her bright green eyes welling with tears. "Please, mister," she said. "You can have the car, my money, anything. Just leave my daughter alone!"

"I don't want your piece of shit car!" He seized her purse and emptied its contents onto the floor. "But I'll take your cash. How much you got in here?"

The little girl burst into tears. "Leave my mommy alone!" she yelled.

"Shut the hell up!" he yelled back, raising an open hand, threatening to slap her. The girl cowered and stopped screaming. "Now drive, bitch!" Harkins waved the gun at the woman. "Like you mean it!"

She put the car in gear with shaking hands, then inched it forward. Her left hand drifted to the center of the steering wheel.

Harkins smashed the back of her hand with the butt of the gun, and she screamed in pain. "Touch that horn again and your daughter's a fucking orphan," he shouted. "Now, for the last time, *drive!*"

Her jaw quivered, and tears ran down her cheeks, but she placed both hands on the rim of the wheel and pulled forward to the exit. "W—where to?" she asked.

"Clayton, of course," he said, disgusted. "Weren't you listening?" Stupid bitch. The pretty ones always were.

"W-why Clayton?" the woman asked.

"Never you fucking mind," he said. "Just drive."

The little girl in back gasped and covered her mouth. "Uh-oh," she said. "You said a naughty word. You're going to get in trouble!"

Harkins twisted in his seat, raising his hand again to strike. "If you don't shut your fucking mouth—"

"Leave her alone!" The mom glared at him a moment, taking deep breaths. "She's only five years old. And she doesn't need to hear language like—ow!"

Harkins' hand stung from the slap, but it shut her up. "One more word, and I'll cut out your fucking tongue!" He spun back to the little girl. "That goes for you, too!"

The girl glowered at him, venom in her eyes, but she kept quiet. He faced front again and lowered the passenger-side sun visor so he could watch her in the mirror. She stuck her tongue out at him. He laughed. Kid had spunk.

A light rain sprinkled on the windshield, mixed with wet snow. They drove for a half hour, the wipers keeping a steady rhythm above the engine and highway noise. Harkins used one of the woman's phones to send a text message to a number he recalled from muscle memory. The reply pissed him off: *Ninguna manera.* Loosely translated, *No Fucking Way.*

A warm bed, denied. Fuck! He needed a Plan B.

But he always had a Plan B.

***

Val grabbed a quick dinner of greasy takeout and reported back to headquarters in time to greet Jalen Marshall exiting a cruiser driven by Ben Peterson. Peterson glared at her and burned rubber in his haste to depart.

"What's his problem?" Val asked.

"Ben wanted no part of this deal," Jalen said, "and blames you instead of me for being 'stuck in Clayton,' as he puts it."

Val laughed and shook her head. "Kids these days."

They rode the elevator this time, which took nearly as long as the stairs. Jalen gave her as much space as humanly possible in the tight quarters.

"Great work on tracking Harkins's trail," Jalen said once they'd rejoined Shannon in the office. "Any new reports since I left Hartford?"

"Possible sighting in a greasy spoon outside Danbury," Val said. "Unconfirmed. Almost a half hour ago. Nothing since."

"We're not sure which direction he went from there, either," Shannon said. "But get this: Danbury P.D. picked up a stolen Toyota at the scene, reported missing in Newtown. So we think he's continuing southwest, toward New York."

"I just hope he doesn't stay in Danbury." Val sat on the edge of her desk. "I have family there."

"There are families everywhere," Jalen said, grimacing. "I don't want him near any of them."

"Detective?" A young plainclothes officer, Dion Woodson, held a phone out to Shannon. "Call for you. Says it's urgent."

Shannon grabbed the phone and a pen, scribbling notes on a pad on her desk. "O'Reilly. Who's this? Oh, hello, *Señora.* What've you got?...I see. When was this? What's the number?...Thank you. And yours? Hello?" She swore and hung up, then smiled. "Good news. Harkins is heading our way."

"To Clayton?" Val jumped up and pressed closer to Shannon. "How do we know?"

"That was Rosa Martinez," Shannon said.

"Antoinetta's Mom?" Val said. When Shannon nodded, Val explained to Jalen, "She was one of his victims here—the one where Samuels got shot."

"Where you all met," Jalen said with a touch of irony.

"Harkins got in touch with her tonight, looking for a place to crash," Shannon said. "We have the number of the phone he used."

"We should be able to trace it and track his whereabouts," Jalen said. "That's a huge break for us!"

"I'll do it!" Val took the notepad from Shannon to copy the number. Before writing a single digit, her whole body went numb. In a whisper, she asked nobody in particular, "Why the hell is Harkins using my *brother's* cell phone?"

***

Harkins eyed the woman, who kept surprisingly calm and drove in the right lane at a few miles under the speed limit. Her delicate face had no scars, no wrinkles, no blemishes except where tears had streaked her light makeup. He imagined her slender form naked, bending to his will. Doing nasty, wonderful things to please him. Pretending pain, but she'd love it, secretly craving more. They all did.

"Mommy," the girl said, interrupting his daydream, "I have to go potty."

"Just hold it," Harkins said. Stupid kid.

"Hold on, honey," the woman said. "We'll find a bathroom

for you soon."

"We're not stopping," he said.

"But I have to go!" the girl said.

"Piss on the seat," Harkins said. No way he'd let them stop. Too risky. He turned back to the girl, remembered her parents addressing her in the restaurant. "Your name is Ali, right? Is that short for Alice?"

The daughter shook her head. "Mommy says not to talk to strangers."

"How do you know her name?" the woman said.

"I'm a good listener," he said with a harsh laugh. He stroked her thigh. "So, what's *your* name, sweetness?"

She slapped his hand off. He grabbed her leg again, gripped it tight. "Keep your mitts on the wheel, bitch!"

Something thumped the back of his head. Multiple times. Harkins swung an arm back, blocking a Dr. Seuss book from smacking his skull again. He snatched the book, lowered the window, and threw *The Cat in The Hat* onto the wet roadway.

"Hey!" the girl said, crying. "That was mine!"

"Now it's nobody's." He powered the window back up, leaned over the seat and grabbed her wrists, shaking her. "If you so much as move one inch for the rest of this ride—"

The car swerved, tires screeching. Harkins slammed against the passenger side door. His head hit the glass, and he saw stars for a moment. The car veered again a few times, but he braced himself and grabbed the steering wheel with one hand, the woman's hair with the other. "Do that again and you spend the rest of your short life in the trunk!"

The woman cowered and slowed the car, but kept driving. After several seconds, she nodded, tears flowing again. He let go and relaxed into his seat. Once again, the car went quiet.

"My auntie's a cop, and she's going to arrest you," Ali said.

"Ali!" the woman said.

Rage boiled inside Harkins. He pulled out his gun, spun to face the back seat again. "You think so?" he shouted. "Is that what you think will happen?"

Ali stared at him, defiant. "Yup. You broke the law."

"Hush!" the woman said, but both he and the girl ignored her.

"Oh, did I?" Amusement replaced some of his anger. The girl had chutzpah. "What law is that?"

"You stole my book," she said, matter of fact. "And you didn't buckle your seat belt. You can go to jail for that."

"Is that so?" Harkins laughed and lowered the gun. "Well, Ali, guess what? You only go to jail if you get caught. And I'm not."

"Is this necessary?" the woman asked, her voice shaking.

"Yes, you are," the girl said. "My auntie will catch you."

Harkins laughed. "I can't wait."

"Be quiet, Ali," the woman said. "He asked us not to talk. We don't want to make him mad, do we?"

"That's right," Harkins said. "You sure don't." He grabbed the woman's thigh again. "Remember that."

The kid shut up, finally, thank God. The woman glanced at him, her lip quivering, but said nothing, and let his hand remain on her leg this time. He slid it into her crotch, squeezed, then continued up her torso and cupped her breast.

"That's very...rude. And distracting," she said, choking.

"I can imagine." He squeezed her breast harder.

"As in, dangerous," she said. On cue, a car passed way too close on the left, its horn blaring.

"We may need to pull over, then," he said, "to relieve the tension." Harkins laughed and dropped his hand back to her leg. More meat there. Her boobs were too tiny.

"You wouldn't..." She licked her lips, not looking at him. "Not with her right here. You *couldn't*."

"Oh, I don't know," he said. "Maybe she'll learn something."

"That's disgusting!" She glared at him. "You pig. I know you're just trying to get a rise out of me. Well, it worked. Good for you. Okay? Now, we're ten minutes from Clayton—"

"Take the next exit," he said.

"But—"

"Do what I tell you!" Harkins poked her in the ribs with the .44. "Now, answer me this time: what's your fucking name? And don't lie!"

"K-Kendra," she said.

"Well, Kendra," he said, "we're going to have ourselves a little party. And you're going to like it."

Chapter Forty-One

Val's first instinct was to call Chad's cell, but Jalen warned her off. "Harkins might turn the phone off, and then we can't trace it," he said. "Worse, we'd tip him off that we're on his trail. We're better off staying quiet."

Shannon obtained a data dump from the local cell towers and requested access to the state's Stingray tracking system, but the usual bureaucracy intervened, forcing them to wait. "It's amazing we ever catch crooks," Val complained after Shannon shared that unfortunate news.

"Patience," Shannon said. "Harkins will make a mistake, and when he does, we'll be ready."

Val's cell phone rang, and the Caller ID made her head go numb. "It's my father," she said. "He hasn't called me since I graduated high school."

"Answer it," Jalen said. "He might have word on your brother."

She did. "Hello, Dad."

"Val. It's me, Chad. Is this a bad time?"

"Chad!" Val crossed to a freestanding whiteboard and uncapped a dry erase marker. "Where are you? What happened to your phone?"

"Guess I lost it," he said. "Val, Kendra and Ali have gone missing!"

"What? How? When?" Heart pounding, she scribbled "Wife & daughter missing" on the whiteboard.

"We got separated after we stopped for dinner," Chad said, worry etched in his voice. "I kept expecting her to catch up with me on the highway, but she never did. I've waited at Dad's for a half hour, but she hasn't shown up. She's not answering her phone, either. This isn't like her, Val. I'm worried."

"Where did you last see your phone?" Val asked, jotting

notes on the whiteboard. Nervousness grew inside her. The timing of Harkins having his phone and Kendra going missing struck her as much more than coincidental.

"Never mind my damned phone! Help me find her. What should I do?" His voice climbed a register above his usual tenor, almost a shriek at the end.

"Which car was Kendra driving?" Val asked.

"The Volvo," Chad said. "Should I go looking for her?"

"She's probably broken down somewhere on the highway," Val said to reassure him. "I'm sure she called Triple-A."

"Then why won't she answer her phone?" The worry in his voice doubled.

"Maybe it's dead, too."

"Then she couldn't have called Triple-A! Val, I've got to go find her!"

"Don't do that," Val said. "Give me the license plate number. I'll ask the highway patrol to look for her." After writing down the digits, she performed a quick search of the state trooper's online logs. Nothing.

"Chad, listen. Stay put at Dad's in case she calls the landline. Now, don't panic, but a criminal we're tracking on I-84 is using your phone. He must have found it or stolen it from you when you stopped for dinner. Give me the whens, whats, and wheres of that and we'll—"

"Do you think this has something to do with Kendra and Ali going missing?" Chad asked, his worry escalating into panic. "Oh, shit, Val, I just realized. He didn't steal it or find it. I left it in the charger in the Volvo! He has Kendra and Ali!"

"We don't know that," Val said, scribbling notes for Shannon and Jalen. But in her heart, she agreed with him. "Listen. Can you go online at Dad's and trace your phone?"

"If I can remember my password," he said, calming. "Hold on." Tapping noises and occasional beeps drifted in over the phone. "Well, that's weird."

"What's weird?" Val asked. "Did you find it?"

"According to this," Chad said, "my phone is right here in Clayton. Downtown, at the old public housing complex— Torrington Meadows. I thought that place had shut down?"

Val scribbled the tenement's name on the board. "I'm just a few blocks from there," she said. "We'll check it out. Stand by the phone!"

"I'll send some units into the area," Shannon said.

"I'm going, too," Val said.

"Me too," Jalen said. "O'Reilly?"

"I'll coordinate from here," Shannon said. "You go on ahead."

Val took the stairs while Jalen and Woodson waited for the elevator. Reaching the lobby about a minute later, she glanced at the elevator's indicator lights. Sure enough, they hadn't yet started their descent. Protocol demanded that she wait.

Screw protocol.

She dashed outside and ran at top speed toward the old apartment building, abandoned two decades before after several failed health inspections. Numerous proposals to demolish and redevelop Torrington Meadows had foundered under the weight of extraordinary debt, grand-standing politics, and regulatory red tape. Instead, the site had become a hotbed of gang and drug activity, crumbling inside a wire-link fence that kept out anyone without a death wish, or a way of delivering on one.

A patrol car pulled up as she arrived. The passenger side door opened, and Rico Lopez climbed out. "You coming, Pops?" he called into the vehicle.

Val pulled up to a stop next to Rico in time to hear the end of Alex's response. "...To secure the perimeter," he said. "We can do that from here and stay in the loop over the radio."

"Pops," Rico said, "the guy's not going to come out and knock on our door." He rolled his eyes and gave Val a "What can we do?" look.

"Never mind him," Val said. "What's the latest? Have they tracked the phone?"

"What phone?" Lopez said.

"My brother's," Val said. "Long story." She gazed up at the six-story building, occupying the entire city block. She guessed it once housed five or six hundred people. An interior search would take hours, if not days.

Jalen and Woodson pulled up in a cruiser moments later. "Another half-dozen units should be here within the next five minutes," Jalen said. "We can wait him out, if need be."

"And let him rape my sister-in-law? And, God forbid—" She couldn't bring herself to say it. She fumed. No way she would let anything happen to Ali.

"We're not even sure he's here," Jalen said. "If he is, he's armed and dangerous. We need a plan—and running in headlong doesn't count."

With no better suggestion at hand, Val agreed. She paced around the perimeter of the building while additional cruisers filed in and took their positions. After turning the third corner, she spotted the familiar face of an African American kid. She approached him, waving an open palm in the air.

"S'up, Copette?" Dog said when she came within earshot.

"Have you been out here long?" she asked in a friendly tone and accepted his high-five.

"Hour or so. You still looking for that white dude?"

Val started. "Harkins, yeah. Have you seen him?"

Dog pointed at the building. "About twenty minutes ago, in a green car. One of those boxy Euro jobs the white ladies in the burbs drive."

"A Volvo?" Tension danced in her voice. "Was he alone, or did he have anyone with him?"

"Had a white woman and a little girl with him," Dog said. "Funny, man. The little chick, she like, five? And she's wearing a cop uniform. I near to died laughing."

"Did they go inside? Where's the car now?" Val knew she shouldn't pepper him with too many questions at once, but the emotion of the moment got the better of her.

"They parked in that lot there." Dog pointed to a surface lot across the street. "See that hole in the fence on the end? That's where they went in. Dude was yelling at them and shit—uh, sorry. *Stuff.* Like he was mad at 'em."

"Would you be able to stay here for a bit?" Val asked, her voice cracking with excitement. When he made a face, she pulled out her wallet. "I'll pay you. A dollar a minute. Ten bucks now, ten more in twenty minutes. All you have to do is watch this side of the building until our other units arrive. If he comes out again, you come around front and let me know which way he goes. Deal?" She waved a ten at him.

Dog glanced at the bill with a skeptical eye. "Did you ever pay Pope the five hundred?" he asked.

"Dog, I'm paying you half up front," she said, exasperated. "Come on, you owe me. Remember that time I could've busted you? Please?"

He shrugged and snapped the money out of her fingers. "Aright. But I gotta let Pope know." He tapped a message on his cell phone and gave her a thumbs-up.

She ran around to the front and found Jalen, chatting with Pops and Lopez. "One of the Disciples saw him going inside," she said in a rush. "We can guard the exits, then sweep the building bottom to top until we find him. But we've got to get moving, before he hurts either of them!"

Pops shook his head. "Too risky. He's armed, and if he chose this spot, it means he knows it better than we do. He could escape, ambush us, or for all we know, finish his business long before we ever spot him. I suggest we wait for reinforcements."

Val shook her head in disgust, unable to form words. Lopez snorted and spat in the dirt, but said nothing.

Jalen scowled. "Pops, even for you, that's too conservative," he said. "We've got enough manpower—er, people here to stop him before he hurts someone else. I say we go in."

"You're out of your jurisdiction," Pops said. "As the ranking officer on the scene, I say we wait."

A squad car pulled up with two more uniforms inside. Brenda Petroni and a thirty-something male cop hustled out to join them.

"I think you're now outranked," Jalen said to Pops with a nasty grin.

Val summarized her strategy to Brenda as another car arrived with two more officers, including Ben Peterson.

"Good plan," Brenda said. "Who's going in?"

"I'm in," Val said.

"Me, too," Lopez said.

"I'll take Dawes up the back way," Jalen said. Val nodded and released the snap on her holster.

"Rico and I will take the front," Brenda said. "We'll do the odd floors, you take evens. Pops, you take charge of the scene here and cover the exits. Let's sweep this place clean!"

Chapter Forty-Two

Harkins locked the deadbolt of the disgustingly dirty, abandoned apartment and forced his captives to the rear bedroom. He pushed the woman into the corner and shoved the girl on top of her. The brat hadn't stopped crying since they'd parked the car, and she'd lost the little-girl charm she'd shown earlier in the evening. Now the woman was bawling, too.

"Quit your belly-aching!" Harkins raised his hand, threatening to strike them. "You're killing my buzz." He chuckled at that notion. Nothing could kill this buzz.

"My auntie's going to come here and shoot you," the brat said, sitting up. "You'll be sorry because you'll be dead—Ow!" His slap dropped her back to a lying position on the filthy carpet, crying louder than ever.

"Don't touch her!" the woman said, seething. She gathered her daughter in her arms and kissed her head. "She's just a girl. Don't you have any decency?"

"I'm much more than decent," Harkins said with a sneer. "I'm fucking amazing. Literally." He laughed. "Which you're about to find out."

"Don't you hurt my mommy!" Ali shouted. "Or me. Go away!"

"Shut up!" He raised his hand again, and the girl cowered into her mother's protective arms, crying again. The kid would make him crazy with that bawling. "Don't you move," he said, jerking his hand as if to hit them. "You so much as budge and I'll really give you something to cry about."

He backed out of the room, watching them, then rushed to the living room, where he found an old sweater and a free-standing lamp. He cut the cord with his pocket knife and returned to the bedroom. The girl and her mom hadn't moved.

"Let the kid up," he said.

"Please don't—"

"I said let the kid up!" Harkins whipped the woman's legs with the cord, and she yelped in pain. He grabbed the girl by the arm, yanking her to her feet. He cut off a section of the sweater, shoved it into the girl's mouth, and tied another piece tight around her face. "Say your name," he ordered her.

"All-ss-shmm," the girl mumbled, and gagged.

"Good. Now hold still." He tied her hands behind her back with the sweater's sleeves, then pushed her onto her butt against the wall. He turned to the woman, seated against an adjacent wall. "Hands behind your back."

"No!"

Harkins swatted her with an open palm, knocking her down. He sat on top of her, turned her face-down, and grabbed her arms. She bucked and wiggled, but he overpowered her. He bound her wrists with the lamp cord and tested to make sure she couldn't get free. Then yanked her slacks to her knees.

"Stop, please," she said. "For the love of—"

He swatted her again. "Shut the hell up." She continued crying, but at least she stopped her damned yapping. He stood, unbuckled his belt, unzipped his pants. "It's time," he said, "to give your daughter a lesson on the birds and the bees."

The woman rolled away from him, but she ran into the wall, and he cornered her there, straddling her and tearing at her clothes. Tiny bound fists pecked at his back. He turned, grabbed the brat by the collar, and threw her to the floor. "Stay there!" he yelled at her. Dammit. He should have tied her feet.

"Run, Ali!" the woman yelled. "Get help!"

"No!" Harkins raged at the kid. "Don't you dare move!"

But Ali listened to her mother, not to him. She scooted toward the door. Harkins swore and ran after her, catching her in the living room. He grabbed her by the hair, eliciting a high-pitched howl, and dragged her back toward the bedroom. He needed to find something to tie her up better. A peek into the bathroom and spare bedroom yielded nothing.

Siren sounds filtered in, getting louder. He dragged the girl to the window. Police cars surrounded the building, with uniformed cops guarding every exit. Time to move.

He couldn't run with both of them. But the little one, he could manage.

"Looks like your auntie's friends are here, kid," he said. He dragged her back to the living room and out the door, leaving it ajar. Voices and loud footsteps echoed from the stairway. They sounded close. So much for escape.

Plan C. He kicked open the door to the apartment across the hall and pulled the kid inside. He closed the door, readying his .44.

"Come on, Dawes," he said under his breath. "Come to Papa."

***

When Val and Jalen rounded the corner of the crumbling tenement, the street was empty, save for a pair of officers crouched beside their cruiser. Dog was gone, probably scared away by the police presence. Val shrugged it off and led Jalen to the gap in the fence Dog had pointed out earlier. Long threads of fabric blew like banners in the wind from the jagged wires around the opening.

"Those look fresh," Jalen said. "Looks like your gang friend had it right."

They bent the wires back further so they could squeeze through without ripping their clothes and ran to the rear entrance. The thick metal door lay ajar, its handle smashed and hanging loose. The inside reeked of urine, smoke, and rot. Brenda's voice echoed in the distance, along with heavy footsteps. Val and Jalen dashed up the stairs to the second floor.

"We go door by door," Jalen said. "You cover me." Val crouched by the first apartment's entry, and Jalen pounded on the door. "Police! Open up!" After ten seconds of silence, he kicked the handle off. The door swung open.

"They don't build them like they used to," Jalen said, deadpan. They entered and spread through the apartment, completing the search in seconds.

"One down, two hundred to go," Val said when they met again at the entrance. They repeated the process at each apartment, every time coming up empty.

"Oh-for-thirty," Jalen said after they'd searched the last

apartment on the floor. "I hear Petroni and Lopez upstairs. Let's head up to four."

Val reached the top a good ten steps ahead of Jalen, who, unlike her, finished the climb out of breath and sweating. "You gonna be all right?" she asked him.

He nodded, but held up a hand. "Wait. A. Sec." He panted, bent over at the waist.

"No time to wait," she said. "People's lives are in danger."

"So's mine," he said. "From a heart attack. Wait ten seconds." True to his word, he calmed his breathing in a few quick beats and they turned the corner into the hallway, just after hearing a door slam.

"Was that on our floor, or downstairs?" Val asked, halting her steps.

"Sounded like it came from down the hall," Jalen said in a whisper, pointing ahead of them. "Let's go listen."

They crept down the hallway, one on each side, and listened at each door. At each stop, Val imagined Harkins inside the apartment, doing horrible things to Kendra, and—no. She couldn't even imagine him touching innocent little Ali. Not Ali!

About a third of the way down, Jalen signaled for Val to halt, and he pressed his ear against the door. He nodded and waved her over. She crossed in silence to the hinge side, weapon at the ready. Jalen stood and kicked at the handle. This time, it didn't give. He backed up and took some air, smashing it with his right foot, then collapsed to the floor in pain, howling, as the door skidded open.

"Shit!" Jalen gripped his leg with his free hand. "I think I broke my fucking ankle!"

"Wait here," Val said unnecessarily, and slid into the apartment. The faint cry of a woman seeped out of a partially-open bedroom door. Val scooted down the hall and peeked inside. Kendra lay on the floor, her slacks at her knees, hands tied behind her back. Val raced to her, scanning the room to make sure Harkins wasn't lying in wait.

"Kendra! Are you okay? Where's Ali?" Val lifted her sister-in-law to a sitting position and pulled her slacks up, then untied her hands. Disgust with seeing what Harkins had done to Kendra mixed with relief that he'd gotten no further—and panic that Harkins and Ali were both missing from the scene.

"He took her," Kendra sobbed. "Just a few minutes ago. I don't know where. Find her!"

"Jalen!" Val shouted toward the open door. "He's somewhere close—"

A cry of pain drowned out her words—Jalen! A moment later came a thump, the sound of a body hitting a hard floor. Then footsteps, running away.

Val ran to the door and spotted Jalen's unconscious body sprawled across the doorway, his forehead bleeding from a fresh gash near his hairline. Val checked his pulse and breathing. Unconscious, but alive. She leaped over his inert body into the corridor. An explosion echoed in the hallway, and something tore a gaping hole in the door frame. At the end of the hall, Harkins crouched behind a young girl wearing a police uniform, one arm around her waist, the other pointing a handgun at Val's face. Ali, bound and gagged, squirmed in his arms, a look of terror on her face, but otherwise she looked unharmed.

Harkins aimed the weapon at her. Val dove into an open doorway a moment before a second explosion sent a bullet buzzing by her, inches from her head. She crept to the doorway, stealing a quick glance down the hall again. Another shot splintered the door frame, and Val jumped back in surprise.

"Suspect located on north end of the fourth floor of Torrington Arms," Val barked into her radio, her heart pounding. "One officer down. Suspect has a hostage—a five-year-old girl—and has opened fire. All units, respond!"

Ali let out a muffled yelp, and from the sounds that followed, Val guessed that Harkins had pushed her down and gone down the stairs. A quick glance in their direction revealed Ali lying in a heap against the wall, crying, with no Harkins in sight. Val calculated the risks in a flash: Harkins might be using Ali as bait to draw Val out of hiding, or he might have shed the extra baggage to aid his flight.

If she chased too soon, her guess could prove fatal. But Harkins had shown no limits to his cruelty. If she waited, he might up the ante by hurting or killing Ali.

At Antoinetta's, he'd run. But he'd also shot Gil.

Gil's voice echoed in her head. "What kind of cop are you?"

he'd asked. Survivors would stay put. A Soldier would return to Jalen's side. Saviors would rush to the aid of the victims—Kendra and Ali. An Avenger would chase after Harkins.

Val took a deep breath, readied her weapon, and barrel-rolled into the corridor.

***

Harkins tossed the girl to the floor and ran down the stairs. He hated surrendering his hostage-slash-shield-slash-ultimate insult to Dawes. But the other cops were closing in, and she'd slow him down too much.

When he reached the second floor, pounding footsteps approached from below, and he ducked into the hallway. Two cops in uniform thundered up the staircase past him. He padded down the hall, southbound, hoping like hell the other cops would stay focused on the north end of the building.

Voices echoed in the floors above him. The cops were taking their time. The guards outside had probably reported that nobody had exited, so they knew he was inside. That gave him an idea.

Three-quarters of the way down the hall, he entered an open apartment he'd used before for parties like the one he'd planned for Kendra. It still had running water and electricity—perfect for the distraction he had in mind. He plugged the bathroom sink and turned on the faucet. In the kitchen, he flicked on the oven and tossed a fistful of loose paper and rags inside. The building's smoke alarms would take care of the rest.

He descended to the first floor via the south stairway and peered out the exit door's window. Two cops stood guard in a cruiser on the street, twenty feet away. Exiting here would mean certain death. He needed to reach the break in the fence at the north end. Dammit. The cops would have that exit guarded too, but its proximity to the hole gave him a better chance.

So did his .44 Magnum. But his magazine had only five rounds left, and he had no spares with him. Harkins would have to pick his shots and hope his second-floor distraction would draw their attention long enough for his planned escape.

Chapter Forty-Three

V al rolled into a crouch in the hallway and raised her weapon in the direction Harkins had taken Ali. A young girl's scream pierced her ears. In horror, Val realized she'd pointed the weapon at her niece! She lowered her weapon and raced down the hall to Ali, curled into a ball in the corner. She removed the gag and untied her. "Ali! Are you all right?" She tried to keep the panic out of her voice, but it didn't subside until Ali nodded and wrapped her in a tight embrace.

"Let's go check on your mom, okay?" Ali nodded again, but maintained her death-grip on Val's shoulders. Val carried her back to the doorway of the apartment where Jalen sat in a half-conscious daze.

"Did that son of a bitch get away again?" Jalen asked in a dull voice.

"Not yet," Val said. "He ran down the north stairs. Can you radio that to the team?" She hoped that Jalen's injuries weren't serious and that he'd recovered enough to fulfill that simple task.

"Ali!" Kendra appeared from the hallway, and Ali slid out of Val's arms to run to her mother's arms. "Oh, my sweet girl, I was so worried about you," Kendra said through a veil of tears.

"I was brave, Mommy," Ali said. "I think my police uniform scared him."

Kendra laughed and hugged her closer. "Thank you, Val," she said. "Where is the creep now?"

"Somewhere in the building, still," Jalen said, re-holstering his radio. "But we have the place surrounded. He can't escape."

Val shook her head. She'd felt that way about Harkins before. "I should rejoin the search team," she said.

Jalen nodded. "I'll keep guard here, in case he comes back."

Val gave Kendra and Ali one final hug each and rushed out of the apartment. Only after she'd descended a full flight on the north stairwell did she realize what her decision meant for her in Gil's taxonomy of cop types.

She was an Avenger—the most dangerous kind of all.

***

Harkins hustled down the hallway, back to the north end. The footsteps on the stairs paused, but the jumble of voices continued. At the end, he could make out the words, "I'll check it out." A woman's voice. Hopefully not Dawes. He wanted her close, and alone.

He paused for breath and peered out the door's tiny window. Nothing. Good. He readied his weapon, yanked open the door, and ran toward the opening in the fence.

"Freeze!" someone yelled. A fat older cop and a young, skinny guy crouched behind a police cruiser. The fat one raised himself up, extended his arms across the hood, a weapon shaking in his hands. Harkins dove for the turf, rolled, came up firing. The shot skimmed the car's hood and hit the big guy in the side, spewing blood and spinning him to the ground. "I'm hit! I'm hit!" he screamed.

Harkins aimed a second shot at the skinny guy, missed. The kid disappeared behind the cruiser, screaming in panic.

Harkins ran to the hole in the fence, which somebody had kindly widened for him, and thrust himself through. He landed hard on the sidewalk and found it hard to breathe for a moment. But a gunshot, followed by the shattering of pavement a foot from his face, drove him back to his feet. A glance to his right revealed the two cops at the building's south end, crouching behind their cruiser and taking aim. He fired wildly in their direction, and they ducked for cover.

He found himself only a few feet away from the cruiser. A gun lay in the gravel. The fat cop must have dropped it when he'd gotten hit. He snagged it on his way past, shoving it into his jacket pocket.

Harkins ran across the street, down an alley, and the stench of human waste and rotting garbage engulfed him. Loud voices shouted after him. Bullets skidded across the pavement and ricocheted off the walls of the nearby buildings. Two young black men ran away from him down the alley. Not cops. Street kids. Panicked women screamed from overhead. Doors and windows slammed shut, and the tires of a vehicle squealed to a stop. Halfway down the alley, he came upon steps that descended into a basement, the door ajar. He fled down the steps, pulling the door shut behind him.

A single, bare bulb lit the dank basement, lined by coin-operated washing machines and dryers, smelling of detergent and mold. Harkins smashed the bulb and tossed someone's basket of laundry in the doorway, a trip hazard for whoever followed him. He exited into a storage area of the basement and up the stairs, out the front door, hung a random right into another alley. Sirens blared, with blue-and-red flashers flickering off windows and parked cars, but for now, the cruisers giving chase remained out of sight.

But running footsteps and bellowing shouts told him he hadn't yet lost his pursuers.

At the alley's dead-end, a fire escape led to an open sliding door on the second story. Harkins climbed up, yanked the ladder up behind him, and turned into another unlit hallway. "He went inside!" a man's voice shouted. One of the cops, or a snitch. Whatever. An enemy. They were all enemies now.

He found a side door that opened into a row of smelly garbage bins and ducked between them to rest. His lungs burned, and his legs felt like lead. He couldn't outrun them, especially not the young Dawes. He recalled news reports lauding her for being a star athlete in college. She'd run that Japanese gang member down, a guy fifteen years younger than Harkins. No, he'd have to take her down with a bullet to beat her.

Harkins smiled. Maybe he could have a little fun with her first. Make up for missing out on Kendra.

"Check every alley," a woman's voice shouted off in the distance. Official-sounding. Cops closing in. He had to move.

He slithered to the end of the alley, peering out. The coast looked clear. He shuffled down the street, walking at a normal pace. A young couple emerged from a bar and turned away from him, walking twenty yards ahead in the same direction. He recognized the street. It led to Upper Albany, a gang-banger neighborhood. They wouldn't expect him to head there. He pulled up the hood of his jacket, close to his face, as if bundling up to fight off the chill. He might get out of this after all.

***

Alarms clanging and smoke filling her lungs, Val exited the north end of the building. Outside the fence, Ben Peterson bent over a large, inert figure lying on the ground.

Peterson looked up at Val, his face as pale as alabaster. "The bastard shot Pops!" Peterson said, panicked. "Help us out here!"

Val dashed to the fence and slipped through. Gunshots drew her attention across the street, where a large figure ducked into a dark alley. Had to be Harkins. Two uniformed officers pursued him, weapons drawn. She glanced back at Pops. A wound on his right side bled profusely. A bare bone, probably a rib, poked through the tear in his jacket.

"Go get bandages from the first aid kit from your cruiser," she yelled at Ben. He stared at her, a numb expression in his eyes.

"I've got some!" Brenda Petroni shouted, rounding the corner with Rico Lopez. She hustled over to Pops and waved Val and Rico away. "Go! Peterson and I got this. There's nothing you can do here."

Val didn't wait for a second invitation. She ran toward the alley where Harkins had disappeared. But before she reached it, her radio reported that Harkins had entered the basement of the building to her left, with her colleagues in hot pursuit. She'd seen the building's front entrance on her dash over from headquarters. Maybe she could beat him there. She kicked it into high gear and circled the building.

At the corner, she spotted Harkins running down another alley across the street. She gave chase, radioing in her position. More footsteps and shouting joined in pursuit behind her. Sirens revealed that other cruisers were closing in to offer aid.

She reached the alley and ran to its dead-end. No Harkins! But how?

"He went inside!" Rico shouted, pointing to a fire escape ladder one story up. Val jumped to yank it down, but it was out of her reach. Rico's too.

"Surround the building, and close off all the exits," Dion Woodson said. "Dawes, you're the quickest, so you take the front exit on the other side. Rico, go left. Steve, right. I'll guard this one and radio in."

Val sprinted around the building and noticed multiple dead-end alleyways with emergency exits. "Check every alley!" she barked into her radio. It would slow them down, but they couldn't risk letting him escape again. "We need more backup," she added. The dispatcher responded with a call for all available units. Val raced on. They were counting on her to secure the front exit.

Val reached the doorway, which opened onto a high-traffic downtown street. All quiet. Harkins either hadn't yet left the building, or she'd already missed him. She had no way to tell.

She radioed in and waited.

***

Harkins spotted a police cruiser turning onto Abernethy Street and ducked into a convenience store, shuffling over to the coffee stand. The shopkeeper, a subcontinental man in his early 30s, greeted him. "Welcome, sir," he said. "Can I help you?"

Harkins replied without turning. "Just need a cuppa Joe."

"We kindly ask patrons to please pay for their purchase prior to pouring coffee," the man said in a polite but firm tone. A sign over the coffee pot reinforced the request.

"Sorry." Harkins continued to fuss with the coffee, taking his sweet time until the cruiser passed by the window. Took forever, too. Must be scanning every face on the street. Finally, the vehicle slid past.

"Guess I don't need coffee after all." Harkins shuffled toward the door.

But the shopkeeper blocked his path. "You must pay for that coffee you poured," he said. "I cannot serve it to another customer." He smiled, but he showed no signs of moving.

Harkins read the man's nameplate. *Taufiq Sharkar.* "Well, Taufiq, it's like this," he said, keeping his voice friendly. "I don't really care for your coffee." He picked up the foam cup and threw the scalding liquid in the man's face.

The man screamed, and Harkins punched him in the

temple. The man collapsed in a heap. Harkins stepped over him and resumed his walk up the sidewalk, as if he hadn't a care in the world.

Which he wouldn't, soon. Oh, so soon.

He reached the end of the block. Another cruiser headed away from him. He turned and headed toward Martin Luther King Boulevard. A small theater loomed ahead, with a parking lot next door. Time to do some car shopping.

Chapter Forty-Four

Minutes ticked by. Val grew anxious at the front door of the apartment building. Several people had exited, but none of them resembled Harkins or had seen him. A crowd gathered across the street, speculating about the scene but staying out of her way.

Val's radio coughed with a report of an assault at a convenience store. She recognized the address as Taufiq's Quick Mart. Then came Shannon O'Reilly's voice: "Dawes! The description of that assailant matches Harkins. Are you close by?"

"Less than two blocks away!" Val said. "I'm on it!" She took off at a run. Moments later, she found a wet and groggy Taufiq leaning on the counter of his store, tended by an elderly woman bearing an expression of concern.

Val showed Taufiq the picture of Harkins. "The man who hit you," she said. "Was it him?"

Taufiq nodded. "He knocked me down, then went that way." He pointed to the right. "I think."

"Thank you, Taufiq!" Val shouted and dashed out of the store. She ran to the corner. No one in sight. Which direction had he gone?

Footsteps pounded the street on her left, and Dog ran into view. "That white dude," he said, his chest heaving, "is at our meeting place." A gunshot from the same general area punctuated his breathless announcement.

"Thank you, Dog!" Val left him there, catching his breath, and radioed in as she ran.

**

Harkins crept among the few parked cars in the theater parking lot, checking the oldest models for unlocked doors or signs of prior tampering. Older vehicles lacked the advanced security systems so many drivers opted for in recent years. Most were a cinch to get started, once inside.

He found a late-90s Honda Civic deep in the corner of the lot. Twin clean-swept arcs on the windshield indicated someone had driven it recently. Probably that morning, during the rainy commuting hours. Perfect.

Harkins darted to the driver's side, which faced away from the street, and pulled a jackknife from his pocket. He'd broken many a lock with it before, including Hondas. He jammed the blade into the keyhole and jimmied it in a circular motion.

"The fuck you doing?"

Harkins turned to find two black men hovering over him with gold rings piercing each ear. The larger one, built like a football player, sported three rings in each lobe, and brandished a nasty-looking knife. The other, younger man stood a step behind him, arms crossed, a single earring in his right lobe.

"I, uh, lost my keys," Harkins said, standing.

"That ain't your fucking car," the younger man said. Three-Rings glanced at him, signaled him to shush. Harkins slid his left hand behind his back, reaching for the .44 tucked into his waistband.

"Keep your fucking hands where I can see them," Three-Rings said.

"Sure, sure." Harkins froze his position. "I was just getting my wallet, so we can settle this like gentlemen." He cocked his head as if to ask: okay?

Three-Rings scowled. "I said, hands where I can—"

Harkins whipped the weapon around and fired, but too soon. His shot went wide, blasting a hole in the wall ten feet away. The younger man dove to the ground, but the larger man swung a fist at Harkins. He dodged the punch, suffering only a glancing blow off the side of his head. He aimed the gun again at the big man's chest. Three-Rings ducked, but he remained a huge target. Harkins pulled the trigger.

Click.

Nothing! He'd miscounted his rounds, or something malfunctioned, but the .44 no longer served its protective purpose. He reached his left hand into his pocket for the cop's .38, but the big man charged him. Harkins spread his legs wide, grabbed the man's charging shoulders, and drove his weight onto him. Three-Rings hit the ground with an audible grunt and tried to roll free. Harkins smashed the butt of the .44 onto the top of the big man's skull. Three-Rings collapsed, unconscious.

Time to go. Harkins headed toward the street, then stopped. To his left, a gang of black youths marched toward him, joined by the kid with the single earring. To Harkins's right, a lone figure approached, running fast. A policewoman, talking into her radio with her left hand, holding a gun in her right. He recognized her: Valorie Dawes.

Their eyes met.

**

Val spotted Harkins ahead, right where Dog said he'd be. He froze in his tracks for a moment. From the far end of the block, a dozen or so Disciples approached in a V-formation. Pope and Trap led the march, angry determination lining each man's face.

She spoke into her mic: "Suspect in sight!" She put the radio away and ran even faster toward him. "Hands up, Harkins! Don't move!"

As unpredictable as she'd found Harkins in the past, he remained predictable in one essential respect: he never did as he was told. He darted into the street, but cars blared horns at him from both directions, tires squealing. More cars followed. He leapt backwards, then dashed back into the parking lot. A mistake. He had no way out except back into the busy, wide-open street.

Val pressed her back against the building bordering the lot. "Where's my backup, Dispatch?" she muttered into the mic.

"On its way," came the static-laden reply. Which could mean twenty seconds or twenty minutes. The latter meant she'd either have to face Harkins alone, or let him escape. Again. The sirens that had filled the neighborhood air for the last several minutes seemed no closer.

Val took a deep breath. She couldn't let him escape. But protocol demanded she wait for backup. She searched ahead for a patrol car, then behind her—

Piercing pain shot through her skull—the pain of metal

smashing into bone. She fell to her hands and knees. Something wrapped around her throat, a wire or cord of some kind, cutting off her breathing. She flailed her arms, but couldn't reach her assailant. The cord grew tighter around her neck. She couldn't breathe.

Val's self-defense training kicked in. The first rule of survival: Don't panic.

She pointed her weapon behind her and fired, apparently straight into the ground, as gravel exploded around her. Something smashed against her right hand, and she dropped her .38. But the cord loosened around her neck, allowing her to sneak a hand under it and yank it off. She elbowed her attacker in the ribs, and he loosened his grip. Reaching behind her, she grabbed his hair, dropped to one knee, and twisted her body forward, expecting him to land hard in front of her. But she'd rushed the move, and they rolled together, crashing into the side of a pickup. Val's head hit the wheel, and for a moment she saw stars.

She recovered and lurched to her feet. Harkins lunged at her, knocking her flat on her back next to the truck. He pinned her elbows with his knees and punched her face, splitting her lip. Blood spewed from her nose into her mouth. She tried to wriggle free, but his weight crushed her ribs and elbows, and she had trouble breathing through her bloody nose.

In his right hand, Harkins held a .38, identical to her own. He pressed his weight onto her and ground his groin into her chest, then laughed and aimed the weapon at her head. "Goodbye, Valorie Dawes," he said. "Another dead hero for Clayton."

In a flash that felt like forever, memories and regrets flooded Val's mind. So, this was it—the end of her life, and her short career. Lofty ambitions to rid the world of scum like Harkins would die with her. She'd never see her friends and family again, never see Ali's cherubic smile again, never know true love. Nothing. Never make up with her Dad, as Chad had begged her to do, as deep down she'd hoped would be possible someday.

At least Ali and Kendra were safe. Chad, too, she guessed. He'd always remember that she'd kept his family safe. He'd be proud of her.

But Gil wouldn't. Val had done what he'd warned her against. Became an Avenger, putting lives in danger—this time, her own—to nail her perp, no matter the cost. She'd never be able to see him again, explain to him why she'd done things this way. Never see his eyes twinkle when he smiled, hear his reassuring voice. Never know what it would be like to hold him.

She gazed up at the heavy-set man on top of her. Shadows darkened his face as he pinned her to the bed, forcing himself onto her, dominating her—

No, no, not *him*, not Milt. Harkins. And he was going to kill her, any moment now.

"It would be such a shame," Harkins said in a husky voice, "to waste an opportunity like this. I bet you have a pretty little pussy, don't you?"

Hot bile surged up her throat. She glared up at him, struggled to wriggle free. He leered at her, joy in his eyes—yes, joy, the sick bastard. He loved this. Loved the sight of her, helpless and afraid beneath him.

Harkins ground into her harder. "Yeah, that's nice," he said. His foul breath swept over her face, gagging her. He shifted his weight, pressing his hand onto her chest, groping for her breast through the thick Kevlar vest. He swore and reached back, groped her thigh, moved it up toward her crotch.

That took some pressure off her elbows, and she shook one free. Val punched him under his left eye, whipping his head back. She bucked up and shoved him, and he toppled off her, dropping his weapon. She rolled away, onto her feet, and reached for his .38, but he batted it away. She spotted her own .38, five yards away. She chased it down and turned back to face Harkins.

He reached his weapon and pointed it at her. She scrambled to her left before he could fire. He ducked behind a Subaru split-seconds before a shot ricocheted off the brick wall behind him. Men shouted: "Get him, Dog!" "I got him, Pope!" "Watch it, Trap!" The owners of the voices, members of The Disciples, crouched behind cars parked along the street, pointing probably illegal weapons at the Subaru shielding Harkins.

More shots rang out. Bullets hit the dirt and plunged into

the sides of the Subaru, creating dark craters and flattening its tires. One of them missed Harkins by inches. The Disciples had spread out, improving their shooting angles, pinning Harkins in.

Val crept to another vehicle, searching for a better shot without exposing herself to stray fire from the gang. She peeked around the car's bumper.

No Harkins. Where had he gone?

Gravel crunched to her left. Harkins sprang out from the vehicle's front end. He ran at Val, screaming, pointing his weapon at her. Val crouched and aimed her weapon at his torso, as she'd been trained.

But at the last moment, she lowered her aim, ever so slightly, and fired.

Harkins' body flew backwards, as if he'd been rammed in the midsection, and blood spilled over his crotch and legs. He landed flat on his back, arms splayed, and his weapon skidded away from him. His head hit last with a loud, sickening thud, and he lay spread-eagle on the gravel, bleeding.

Val lowered her weapon, watching Harkins for signs of life. His chest remained still as redness enveloped his midsection. Voices blended together around her, unintelligible words that sounded like praise or awe or at least not anger. She stood and approached the body. Checked for a pulse, found a faint one, and equally weak breathing. She held her radio mic close to her mouth.

"This is Dawes," she said. "Subject is down. Repeat. Subject, down!"

Try as she might to maintain a professional demeanor, she could not keep the jubilation out of her voice. She did, however, suppress the strong inclination to dance on Harkins's inert body.

The figure of Pope appeared before her, arms crossed. "This the guy that molested those young girls?" he asked.

Val nodded and surrendered a tiny, relieved smile. "Guess I still owe you five hundred dollars."

Pope shook his head and raised his hand for a high-five. "Copette," he said, "let's call it even."

Chapter Forty-Five

The architects who designed the public meeting room in Clayton police headquarters never anticipated more than a few dozen people to show up for the dry, low-key ceremonies often conducted there. But media attention surrounding the dramatic chase and take-down of Richard Harkins filled the space to overflowing. Newspaper, TV, and radio outlets flooded in from cities as far away as Springfield, Boston, and New York. Seated on the dais between Jalen Marshall and Shannon O'Reilly, Val stared wide-eyed at the legion of cameras and microphones, searching for familiar faces behind them. The ceremony was supposed to begin in five minutes, but most of the people she'd invited remained absent.

"You've got fans," Shannon said with a smile. "I hope your autograph pen has lots of ink in it."

"Do I have anything stuck in my teeth?" Val asked without looking over at Shannon. Not that she'd eaten anything all day. Her nerves barely permitted her to slam a cup of coffee that morning.

"You look great," Shannon said. "Your face even looks normal, almost."

"Bullshit," she whispered back. Harkins's punch had cracked her nose and given her a huge bruise on the cheek. Beth had offered to lend expensive foundation to cover it, but Val had refused. "Let the world see what he did to me," she'd insisted. And to all of his other victims, she could have added.

As if summoned, Beth pushed her way into the room, with Chad, Kendra, and Ali in tow. Ali, dressed in her favorite outfit—her police uniform—waved at her, and they found seats in the back row. Val smiled at them, then spotted Brenda Petroni and Travis Blake mingling with a few other sergeants on the side aisle. Good—some friendly faces. But still a few hadn't yet shown.

"Let's get started," Gibson said, tapping the microphone at the podium. "Ladies and gentlemen, I am pleased to announce that last Friday, Clayton Police apprehended a violent fugitive, Richard Harkins, who had wreaked havoc in recent months on several communities in the region. Mr. Harkins resisted arrest and opened fire on our officers, wounding Sergeant Alex Papadopoulos, who is being treated for gunshot wounds at Mercy Hospital. Alex, I'm pleased to say, remains in stable condition at this time. Mr. Harkins also attacked Officer Valorie Dawes, who discharged her weapon in self-defense while attempting to capture the suspect. Mr. Harkins remains in critical condition and will stand trial as soon as he is able."

Gibson turned to acknowledge her with a quick nod, and Val smiled back, appreciating his supportive words. For a change she allowed herself a moment of pride. Harkins had victimized so many women, girls, and even armed police officers, like Gil, Pops, and Samuels. But no more.

"Today," Gibson went on, "I would like to commend the Inter-city Task Force for a job well done in removing a menace from the streets of not only Clayton, but the entire region. Would the members of the Task Force please step forward?"

Shannon stood and waited for Val, who remained rooted in her chair. "Get up!" Shannon whispered. "You have to stand for this."

Val glanced around and noticed that Jalen had also stood, as did the handful of Task Force members in the second row. She swallowed hard and pushed herself to her feet. Bright lights shone in her face, reporters and news cameras scurried into position to get the best shot of them, and the room got scorching hot all of a sudden. It reminded her of why she always hated award ceremonies, even after her victories at track. The fuss, the speeches, and the poses struck her as fake and beside-the-point. Let her accomplishments speak for themselves.

"I hate the idea," she whispered, "of getting a medal for shooting a guy in the balls."

"You're the hero of every divorcée in town," Shannon said,

deadpan, and Val nearly laughed out loud.

She glanced away from the cameras and bright lights, and spotted one of the faces she most wanted to see: Antoinetta, standing with her mother, Rosa, in the rear of the room. Val grinned at the pair, and Antoinetta waved back. Okay. She'd accept the award for Antoinetta, and Kendra, and Ali, and all the women Harkins had terrorized. Let them see what it means for a woman to win.

Gibson stepped in front of her, holding a gold pin in his hand. Val braced herself: to fasten it to her uniform, he'd have to touch her, close to her chest. She held her breath and met his eyes.

Gibson smiled at her, handed her the pin, and shook her hand, then moved on and repeated the gesture with Jalen, Shannon, and the others.

Val sighed with relief. Of course protocol would demand a more discreet ritual, particularly in a sex abuse case!

The subsequent press conference went by in a blur. Gibson and Marshall answered questions from the media and kept their remarks brief, citing legal reasons for not providing more information. After Gibson thanked the attendees for coming, Val followed the others off the podium and headed straight for her brother.

Ten feet away, she stopped in her tracks. Behind Chad stood the gaunt figure of Michael Dawes, crammed into one of the dark suits he'd favored during his successful career as a manufacturing executive.

"Dad?" She blinked and cleared her throat, not knowing what else to do. "I—I didn't expect you."

Dad gave her a crinkly smile. "Chad invited me. Is that okay?"

She shot Chad a dark stare, took a breath, and smiled at her father. "Of course. I'm glad you came."

His hug was unexpected, as was the aroma of musk and peppermint that permeated him. Usually he reeked of alcohol. Rehab must be working. Dad ended the embrace and held her hands in his. "I'm proud of you," he said. "You did good."

Val searched for words, her mouth dry. Nothing came.

"I need you to know," he said. "I believe you. And I'm sorry. About...about everything. I just—"

"Dad," she said, taking hold of his shaking hands, "I'm sorry too. We'll talk later...alone. Okay?" She met his gaze, and the tears flowing down his cheeks nearly broke her heart.

But he nodded, and smiled, and stepped behind her brother, whose sudden embrace felt incredibly warm and reassuring.

***

Val had hoped Gil would have recovered enough to make it to the ceremony, but his doctors had refused to release him. Travis Blake drove her, Shannon, and Brenda to Mercy Hospital in a cruiser. Gibson drove another group over in a van for a planned late-morning award ceremony for Pops, still laid out in his own hospital bed. "I didn't realize Pops was hurt that badly," Shannon said on the drive over.

"He was, and he wasn't," Brenda said. "That .44 round is a beast, but it more or less grazed him—broke a rib and tore a lot of skin and muscle. No doubt it hurt like hell, but it wasn't life-threatening."

"Enough for him to get medical disability," Travis said. "Given how close he is to retirement, I doubt we'll see him back in uniform. But you didn't hear that from me."

Val zoned out of the conversation, and after a few minutes, her phone buzzed. A message from Beth read, "Check it out!" with a link to a website. She tapped it, and her mouth opened wide in surprise.

One Scum Down, Thanks to Clayton Police Heroics
By Paul Peterson

Clayton Police have rid the city of a violent scumbag, a man single-handedly responsible for a regional crime wave of sexual assaults, police shootings, and other crimes.

Clayton P.D. officers shot the man after an armed standoff and a destructive chase through the city. Officer Alexander Papadopoulos, wounded in the assault, will be among those awarded today with medals of honor.

"Pops?" Val laughed. "He's the hero?"

"What the hell prompted that remark?" Blake asked.

"Dawes is reading that trashy Clayton Copwatch blog again," Shannon said, reading over her shoulder. All three of Val's companions groaned. Val ignored them and scrolled farther down the page.

> Papadopoulos had help in taking down Harkins. Readers of this site will note that we have been critical of a certain rookie policewoman for her reckless behavior that often put citizens and fellow officers at considerable risk. But sources indicate that in this instance, Valorie Dawes lived up to her family legacy and did the city a great service. For today, at least, Dawes performed the way a Clayton police officer should: with intelligence, bravery, and professionalism.

Val set the phone down and realized she'd been holding her breath the whole time she'd been reading. She exhaled, but the tightness in her chest wouldn't subside.

"Geez," Shannon said, still reading over her shoulder. "What's gotten into Paul Peterson? That's almost complimentary!"

Val smiled. She hated to admit it, but Peterson's grudging praise pleased her.

The department borrowed a chapel in the hospital for the award ceremony, attended by a small gathering of officers and higher-ups. Moments before it began, orderlies rolled in another bed, occupied by a smiling Gil Kryzinski. He looked energetic and alert, his skin color back to normal. Elated, Val hurried over to stand next to him.

"I was coming to see you next!" she said in a hoarse whisper.

"You'd better," he whispered back. He winked at her. "Nice medal." She rolled her eyes.

Gibson kept the ceremony brief, and Pops made it official: in his thank-you speech, he announced his impending retirement. Alex's wife Betty, a rotund, smiling woman with gray-flecked brown hair, beamed with pride at him. Afterwards, flanked by two bored teenagers who looked just like her, Betty pushed Pops in a wheelchair along the lineup of attendees for perfunctory handshakes, with Val and Gil at the end.

"Congratulations, Pops," Val said after the briefest,

limpest handshake of her life. She stammered, struggling for something to say. "And, um, thanks for your help in nailing Harkins. We couldn't have done it without you." Behind Pops, Shannon covered her surprised grin with both hands. Blake mugged and looked away with an embarrassed, toothless smile.

"Dawes," Pops said, "I just wanna say, I'm glad I got to work with you. I know it wasn't always easy."

"I learned a lot from you," she said. Like, never take crap from one's partner, she added to herself. Gil fake-coughed and covered his mouth.

"Have they given you a new partner yet?" Pops asked.

"Not yet," Gibson said, stepping toward them. "That might take a few days. I've already got a half-dozen requests for you, Dawes. How about we sort through those in my office, this afternoon?"

Val grinned so hard it hurt. "Lieutenant," she said, "I wouldn't miss that meeting for the world."

***

Val accompanied Gil back to his hospital room while the others extended polite congratulations to Pops in the chapel. A nurse hooked him back up to the monitors and exited with promises of lunch within the hour.

"No meds?" Val asked, sitting in a chair beside the bed.

Gil grunted. "The doc cut me off so I don't get addicted. I'm feeling much better, anyway. I'll be out of here in a day or two and start rehab next week. Doctors say I'll be walking, with assistance, soon after New Year's."

"That's amazing!" Val said. "I'll help any way I can. How about I show you the technique that won me gold in the 400-yard hurdles?"

Gil laughed. "You're on. And when I come back to work, you can train me in self-defense, too."

Val's response caught in her throat. "When you...? Did you say—I thought—"

"What, that I'd follow Pops' lead and take medical retirement?" Gil mock-frowned at her. "No way. You're not getting rid of me that easily."

"But Jessica said—"

"Jessica doesn't speak for me," Gil said. "Nor do the

doctors she conned. In fact, Jessica and I...well, safe to say, we're back to 'ex' status."

"Gil, that's wonderful! Wait, not the 'ex' status part," Val said, reddening. "I meant that you're coming back. I can't wait!"

"Which brings me to an important point." He fixed her with a level gaze, all seriousness. "When you meet with Gibson later today, tell him the new partner assignment is interim. I want you back, Val." He reached out and squeezed her hand.

Warmth flooded over her. "I want the same," she said. A smile teased out of her. "Are you sure you can stomach being partnered with an Avenger-type of cop?" she asked.

Gil huffed. "Whoever called you that?" He pulled her closer with a firm grip. "Val, you're a cop's cop. Don't let anyone ever tell you different."

Her hand shook inside of his, and she wondered if she should pull away. Her heart pounded at the intimate touch, and his kind words. "But I—"

"Saved a lot of lives," Gil said, "and, from what I heard from Petroni, you made sure your team members were safe before taking Harkins down. I couldn't be prouder of you."

She stared at him, her heart bursting. "That means so much," she said. "All I've ever wanted was to be with you. As partners, I mean," she said, and her face grew ridiculously warm.

Gil laughed. "I've never seen you turn to red," he said with delight. Then, more seriously, he added, "To be honest, Val, it's a verbal slip I could have made myself."

Val's spine seemed to melt, and her hand got clammy. Still, he held tight. "Gil," she said, "are you saying...I mean, did you think I meant...what did you—"

"Just between us, I like you, Val," he said. "In a...more than professional way." He looked away, and his voice grew dry, catching in his throat. "I've thought a lot about this, and...it complicates things."

She sighed and nodded. Took a deep breath, let it out slowly. "Gil," she said, "we can't be partners, and also see each other. For starters, it's against policy."

"Screw policy." Gil's voice cracked. "We need to do what's right for us. Both of us." He returned his gaze to her, his eyes moist.

Val let out a slow, unsteady breath. "I agree. But Gil...we can't. And we both know why." She gripped his hand tighter. "While it's tempting to want both, it never ends well."

"So, we have to choose." His eyes met hers again, pain evident in his face. "And I take it, you've already chosen."

"I can only choose for me," she said. "But if you feel differently, I'd like to know that."

Gil stared at her for several seconds that felt like hours. "It's a tough choice," he said. "So, for me..." His voice trailed off, and he looked at her with a touch of sadness in his eyes. "If I must choose, I would never give up the opportunity to work with you. I respect you more than any other cop I've ever worked with."

"Gil, that's so...Wow. Thank you." Val sat up straight again, and the frayed nerves and uncertainty flowed out of her: they had made the right choice. For both of them. "Likewise," she said. "On all counts."

They sat together for a long moment in silence, still holding hands. *Holding hands!* She realized with a start they hadn't let go of each other the entire time. She was touching a man, and he was touching her, and it didn't feel strange or painful or frightening.

It felt perfect.

From The Author

Thank you for reading *A Woman of Valor*. If you enjoyed reading it, won't you please take a moment to leave me a review at your favorite retailer? And please, tell your friends!

Questions to consider when posting a review

What made me first decide to read this book was...

As I started reading, the first thing that drew me into this book was...

What I liked most about the main character was...

What I liked most about the plot was...

What I liked most about the author's writing style was...

My favorite part of the story was...

Compared to other books in this genre, this book was...
  __ Among the best __ Better than most
  __ About average __ Not as good __ Among the worst

I would / would not recommend this book to a friend because...

ACKNOWLEDGMENTS

My father, Donald Corbin, first dreamed up the basic story of *A Woman of Valor*, and I loved it from the start. We completed the first rough draft together, but we weren't able to get it into publishable shape before he lost his battle with lung cancer in 2006. It was only years later that I was able to get past the emotional wall that kept this project tucked away in a drawer for so long. I hope, Dad, that the result does you justice.

Several members of the Hartford Police Department assisted me in my background research for this book, and helped ground this fictional story in reality. In particular, Detective Buyak and Officers Mulroy, Kent, and King gave generously of their time, expertise, and personal perspectives, and I thank you all. *A Woman of Valor* would not have happened without you.

Many other friends, colleagues, and family members—too many to count or even remember—have contributed ideas, feedback, critique, encouragement, and love. I thank you all.

Special thanks goes out to Randal Houle, Rankin Johnson, Kate Kort, and Joe Walters, whose scene-by-scene critiques improved this story on a weekly basis.

Thanks also to my Beta Readers—Judith Bottorf, Sam Donavon, Danielle Faucheux, Richard Gray, Nicole Sherriffs, and Patsy Silk—who gave me invaluable late-in-the-game feedback.

No writer can survive without a great editor, and I have two. The keen eyes of Laura Lee Bennett and Patsy Silk caught many errors long after my own eyes glazed over. If errors remain, they are my fault, not theirs.

I can never give kudos enough to Steven Novak, whose creativity and patience with me once again yielded an amazing cover design.

Nobody contributed more to my writing career than my dear mother Patricia Corbin, who awakened in me the love of books and reading, and always encouraged my love of writing.

But most of all, thanks to Renée, the kindest, most patient, most beautiful person I've ever known, whose smile lights up the darkest night and brightens the sunniest day. Your support makes all of this possible. I love you.

Book Group Discussion Questions

Characters

1. What do you think of Valorie? What terms would you use to describe her?

2. Do you think you would like Val if you met her in person?

3. Which of the other police officers did you like? Which did you dislike? In each case, why?

4. What do you think happens between Val and Gil after the end of the story?

5. Do you think that the author – a middle-aged white male – portrayed Val, a young woman who struggles with her memories of abuse by older men – authentically and sympathetically?

Scenes and plot

6. Which scene or scenes stood out to you? Why?

7. Were you satisfied with the conclusion of the story? How would you describe the state of Val's healing at the end of the book?

Personal connection

8. For the most part, what emotion(s) did the story evoke in you as a reader?

9. Did you identify with Valorie? Any other character? How did that affect your enjoyment of the book?

Writing

10. *A Woman of Valor* crosses genres, blending some character-driven aspects of literary fiction with the plot-driven aspects of

police procedurals and crime novels. Did this work for you, as a reader?

11. If you could change something about the book what would it be and why?

12. Describe what you liked or disliked about the writing style.

General

13. Name your favorite thing overall about the book, and your least favorite.

14. At what point in the book did you decide if you liked it or not? What helped make this decision?

15. If someone asks you what this book is about, how would you answer them?

ABOUT THE AUTHOR

Gary Corbin is a writer, actor, and playwright in Camas, WA, a suburb of Portland, OR. His creative and journalistic work has been published in *BrainstormNW*, the *Portland Tribune*, The *Oregonian*, and *Global Envision*, among others. His plays have enjoyed critical acclaim and have been produced on many Portland-area stages.

Gary is a member of the Willamette Writers Group, Nine Bridges Writers, the Northwest Editors Guild, PDX Playwrights, and the Bar Noir Writers Workshop, and participates in workshops and conferences in the Portland, Oregon area.

A homebrewer and home coffee roaster, Gary is a member of the Oregon Brew Crew and a BJCP National Beer Judge. He loves to ski, cook, and root for his beloved Patriots and Red Sox. And when that's not enough, he escapes to the Oregon coast with his sweetheart.

Connect with Gary Corbin

Keep up to date with the latest at
http://www.garycorbinwriting.com

Follow me on Twitter: http://twitter.com/garycorbin

Follow me on Facebook:
https://www.facebook.com/garycorbinwriting

Follow my Amazon Author Page (and review this book!)
http://smarturl.it/GaryCorbinAuthor

Favorite me at Smashwords:
https://www.smashwords.com/profile/view/GaryCorbin

ALSO BY GARY CORBIN

The Mountain Man's Dog

In the small town of Clarkesville, in the heart of the Oregon Cascade Mountains, Lehigh Carter, a humble forester, stumbles into the complex world of crooked cops and power-hungry politicians...all because he rescues a stray, injured dog on the highway.

The *Mountain Man's Dog* is a briskly told crime thriller loaded with equal parts suspense, romance, and light-hearted humor, pitting honor and loyalty against ruthless ambition and runaway greed in a town too small for anyone to get away with anything.

ISBN: 978-0-9974967-1-0

Available in hardcover, paperback, audiobook, and all eBook formats at garycorbinwriting.com, and at your favorite local retailers.

The Mountain Man's Bride

In this thrilling sequel to *The Mountain Man's Dog*, the murder of popular Acting Sheriff Jared Barkley. The murder puts Lehigh and Stacy's plans to marry on hold when Stacy is arrested for committing the crime.

But evidence of a secret affair makes even Lehigh wonder if he should fight for her freedom against the corrupt local machine that accused her.

ISBN: 978-0-9974967-3-4

Available in hardcover, paperback, and all eBook formats at garycorbinwriting.com, and at your favorite local retailers.

The Mountain Man's Badge

Appointed to fill out the unexpired term of disgraced sheriff Buck Summers, mountain man Lehigh Carter investigates the murder of sleazy businessman Everett Downey, murdered in a forested area frequented by off-season hunters and poachers.

As the evidence mounts, pointing to Stacy's father, George McBride, Lehigh battles the mistrust of the entire sheriff's department as well as the District Attorney, the County Commission Chair and his own wife—until he finds shocking evidence of the killer's true identity.

ISBN: 978-0-9974967-7-2

Available in hardcover, paperback, and all eBook formats at garycorbinwriting.com, and at your favorite local retailers.

Lying in Judgment

A man serves on the jury trying a man for the murder that he committed!

Peter Robertson, 33, discovers his wife is cheating on him. Following her suspected boyfriend one night, he erupts into a rage, beats him and leaves him to die...or so he thought. Soon he discovers that he has killed the wrong man—a perfect stranger.

Six months later, impaneled on a jury, he realizes that the murder being tried is the one he committed. After wrestling with his conscience, he works hard to convince the jury to acquit the accused man. But the prosecution's case is strong as the accused man had both motive and opportunity to commit the murder.

As jurors one by one declare their intention to convict, Peter's conscience eats away at him and he careens toward nervous breakdown.

Lying in Judgment is a courtroom thriller about a good man's search for redemption for his tragic, fatal mistake, pitted against society's search for justice.

ISBN: 978-06926426-8-9

Available in hardcover, paperback, audiobook, and all eBook formats at garycorbinwriting.com, and at your favorite local retailers.

Lying in Vengeance

Two months after serving on the jury trying a man for the murder that he committed, Peter Robertson's worst nightmare comes to fruition: Christine, his beautiful and charming fellow juror, knows his dark secret and uses it to blackmail him.

The price of her secrecy: Peter must kill again, this time to stop Kyle, the man who torments Christine and threatens her very existence.

Their sizzling nascent romance gets interrupted when Kyle kidnaps her. Peter's daring rescue provides him the opportunity to commit the awful deed. Peter refuses, however, only to discover that his best friend Frankie may have committed the act in his place. Or was he framed?

Peter's relentless search for evidence to clear his lifelong pal forces him to confront his demons and risk his own freedom—and his life—as he battles the ruthless, manipulative, and resourceful woman who always seems one step ahead and knows his every move.

ISBN: 978-0-9974967-5-8

Available in hardcover, paperback, audiobook, and all eBook formats at garycorbinwriting.com, and at your favorite local retailers.

FORTHCOMING

A Better Part of Valor

The exciting sequel to "A Woman of Valor"

When Valorie Dawes discovers the body of a young girl who had also been sexually molested, Lt. Gibson assigns her to assist the detectives investigating the case. Then Clayton Mayor Megan Iverson, candidate for governor of Connecticut, ties her political fortunes to the case, vaulting herself into the lead in all of the major polls with her law-and-order campaign.

Iverson's meddling in the case costs them dearly when key evidence disappears and other evidence, withheld for strategic reasons, gets leaked to the press. The pressure intensifies when a former campaign aide, Val's childhood friend Amy, becomes the next victim.

Can Val find and stop the killer before he strikes again?

Expected release: Spring, 2020

Check the free sample chapter from this book
in the following pages!

EXCERPT FROM

A Better Part of Valor

by Gary Corbin

Chapter 1

The sun sank low over the Torrington River, peeking below the angry storm clouds threatening to ruin the last mile of Valorie's evening run. Dressed in running shorts and a gray cotton sweatshirt with "Property of Clayton P.D." stenciled across the chest, she'd keep warm enough if the rain held off. But late March storms in western Connecticut often turned brutal. She picked up the pace and considered the bright side. Maybe she'd even beat her best six-mile time.

She passed a pair of twenty-something men dressed in expensive name-brand running outfits and ignored their catcalls. Why men her age lacked the ability to keep rude comments about her ass to themselves, she might never know. She dialed up the music volume and pushed a loose earbud back into her ear canal to drown out their lewd shouts.

Approaching the pedestrian bridge over the river, she slowed to allow a mother pushing a stroller to exit going the other direction. The two men behind her gained enough ground to return within earshot, and one of them said something to the effect of thanks for reconsidering his offer. She sprinted onto the bridge without looking back. Reconsider this, butthead.

Halfway across, lightning flashed, followed a second later by loud thunder, and the skies opened up in a torrential downpour. The metal grates beneath her feet grew slick, and she debated slowing her pace, but the risk of lightning striking the steel structure outweighed the danger of a slip or a twisted ankle. The high-pitched shrieks of dismay from the men behind her almost made her laugh. Such tough guys.

Lightning flashed again as she approached the end of the

half-mile crossing, accompanied a few seconds later by a loud thunderclap, startling her. She stumbled and caught herself on the side rail, breathing hard. The last thing she needed was to fall into the frigid current of Berkshire snowmelt thirty feet down—or worse, the jumble of rocks that lined the embankment. Slowing her pace now seemed a much better idea.

Val took a few deep breaths and pushed herself away from the rail to resume her run, then stopped. Something caught her eye along the rocky shore of the river below. A pile of clothing—no, not a pile. A parka, backside-up, arms outstretched, with gloves protruding from them. Slacks extended from the bottom of the parka. And bare feet.

A body—from what Val could tell, a woman's body— appeared to have gotten snagged in the rocks on the shore, pushed there by the river's relentless current.

The two men caught up to her and slowed to a stop. An athletic white guy in matching Adidas shorts, shirt, and shoes shared a sweaty grin and wiped his brow. "Hey, gorgeous," he said. "Want to join us for an after-running drink at—"

"Call 9-1-1," Val said. She ran ahead, veering off the running path onshore toward the riverbank.

"Something I said?" the guy asked. His buddy, a taller, skinnier black guy in Nikes, laughed and slapped him on the back.

Val picked a path among the rocks toward the body. Before she could reach it, the current shook the body free, and it floated downstream, rocking in the river's wake toward the bridge. If she hesitated, the current would wash the body away from her, and it would be lost downstream.

Brushing rain from her face, she waded into the water. The river's icy cold shocked her skin, and her teeth chattered. She slipped on the slimy rocks on the riverbed, and the strong current threatened to knock her down. She paused to regain her footing, shivering, rubbing her arms for warmth. The body drifted further away, picking up momentum. She reached for it, missed the woman's arm by inches. Another step closer...her foot skidded out from under her and she fell onto her butt, the water splashing up to her armpits and onto her face. So. Fucking. Cold!

Above, Mr. Adidas shouted down to her, still holding a cell phone to his ear. Val couldn't make out what he said and didn't care. "Send an ambulance!" she shouted back.

She rolled forward onto her knees, reaching again for the body. Almost. She crawled toward the woman, scraping her knees on the rocky bottom, frigid waves soaking her hair and neck. But her face stayed above water, and now she could reach the body. She grabbed the parka's arm, stopping its journey into the center of the river. The current tugged back, nearly knocking Val over, but she held firm, and dragged the body back to the shore.

The other runner, whom Val had nicknamed Nike-man, met her on the rocks and helped her pull the body to the grass alongside the running path. Val thanked him and then checked the body for signs of life.

"Do you think she's dead?" the guy asked, wide-eyed.

"I don't feel a pulse, and she's not breathing," Val said. "Do you have a phone? Mine just got soaked."

The man nodded and unlocked an iPhone, then handed it to her. "I never touched a dead body before," he said, then ran ten feet away and fell to his knees in the grass.

Val sympathized. She'd never forget the first dead body she'd ever touched. Then again, it was only five months ago. It was also the first person she'd ever killed, a gang member who'd shot at her first, whom she'd stopped from raping a teen-age girl. A day she'd never forget—but not one she could dwell on now.

She dialed her boss's number from memory. "Clayton Police, Blake here," her sergeant answered. "How can I help you?"

"Travis, it's Dawes," she said. "I just pulled a body from the Torrington River, on the east side of the ped crossing. A young woman, possibly a teen-ager. White, about five-five, one thirty, dark hair. Dressed for winter, other than being barefoot. I'm guessing she fell or jumped off the bridge."

"Or got pushed," Blake said. "But no shoes, huh? Any signs of foul play?"

"Some bruises on her face, but that could be from the fall. Is anyone missing that meets her description?" Val's teeth chattered. As the excitement of the moment abated, bitter cold crept deeper into her bones.

"I'll check missing person reports," he said. "Dawes, are you okay?"

"I got a little wet," she said. "The sooner you get someone out here, the sooner I can change into dry clothes."

"On it," he said. "Actually, it looks like someone called it in already." Sirens sounded, as if on cue. "Shouldn't be more than a minute. I'll send fresh clothes out to you ASAP."

Val waved thanks to the white guy, still leaning over the rail on the bridge overhead and talking on his cell phone. She strolled over to his buddy, still puking on the grass. "You going to be okay?" she asked him.

He rolled over to a sitting position on the wet grass, rain splashing his face. Lightning lit up the sky again, and thunder rumbled in the distance. "I guess I need to get used to this," he said with a sheepish grin. "I'm going to UConn Med School in the fall."

"It gets easier, I'm told," she said. "What's your name?"

"Diego Collier," he said, taking a deep breath. "Up there, that's my friend Kent Mercer. Sorry about what he said to you earlier. He can be kind of a jerk sometimes."

Val waved it off. "Thanks for your help tonight, Diego. Can you stick around for a few minutes? Detectives will want to ask you a few questions."

"Sure," Diego said. He pointed to the logo on her sweatshirt. "But aren't *you* a cop?"

Val sighed. "Believe it or not, this is my day off."

***

Rico Lopez, her patrol partner since the first of the year, met her in the break room at the start of their 5:00 shift the next evening. "I heard you had a fun day yesterday," he said, pouring them both a mug of coffee. He handed her one and leaned his compact, muscular frame against the counter, facing her. He rubbed the white scar that ran across the light brown skin of his forehead, a souvenir of a domestic violence case six months before that put his partner, Brian Samuels, on long-term disability with a gunshot wound.

Val toasted him with her mug and took a sip. "Any word from the M.E. on the victim's identity or how she died?" she asked.

"Drowning," intoned a deep baritone from the break room

door. Sergeant Travis Blake, a 6'5", barrel-chested white man in his early 40s, took up the entire doorway, and his voice occupied any space his body didn't. "No opinion yet as to how or why."

The room fell silent, each officer paying their own private tribute to the woman. After suffering rape at the hands of a so-called family friend at the age of twelve, Val had struggled with occasional thoughts of suicide, temptations she resisted with therapy and the unflagging support of her older brother, Chad. She stuffed the unbidden memories and brought her thoughts back to the present.

"What else do we know about her?" Val asked. "She had no ID on her when she washed up on the riverbank, no phone, nothing."

"Her name was Susan Lambert," Blake said, waving Rico aside so he could access the coffee pot. "We matched the body to a missing persons report this morning, and the family ID'd her a few hours ago. Seventeen years old, a junior at Liberty High School. Varsity volleyball, honor roll, student body treasurer. Volunteered on weekends with the mayor's reading-to-poor-kids program. Oldest of three girls, parents still together."

"Why would a girl like that kill herself?" Rico mused aloud. "She had the world by the ass on a downhill pull."

"Don't be so sure," Val said. "You never know what a teenager's going through. Boyfriend troubles, school, acne, almost anything can trigger depression."

"Scratch the boyfriend angle," Blake said, stirring four scoops of sugar into his coffee. "Her parents said she wasn't dating, and her sister confirmed it. Apparently she was too busy with all of her extracurricular activities. Oh, and it ain't school. On top of everything else, the girl had a 3.8 grade point average."

"Sergeant Blake?" An African-American woman with gray-specked curls and oversized red-framed glasses poked her head in the door. Val recognized her as Yvonne Conrad, executive assistant to precinct commander Laurence Gibson. "Oh, and Officer Dawes, good, you're both here. The M.E. report on that drowned girl came in, and there's an emergency meeting at City Hall to brief the mayor on it. Lieutenant Gibson wants you both there." She handed Blake a sealed manila envelope with his name scrawled across it.

"The mayor?" Blake frowned. "Why would Megan Iverson give a rat's ass about this case?"

"Don't shoot the messenger," Yvonne said. "Meeting's in twenty minutes. You'd better get a move-on. Traffic's a mess out there." She scooted out of the room, humming an old-time blues tune Val couldn't quite name.

Lopez rolled his eyes. "I bet I know why. Iverson's considering a run in the next governor's race, running on a law-and-order platform. She's looking for a headline to ride into the primaries."

"Whatever the reason, we'd better get on the road," Blake said. "Rico can drive us over while we read this report."

"Beats desk duty," Rico said. "I'll get the car."

Val and Blake scanned copies of the report while Lopez fought Clayton's clogged city streets at rush hour. He blipped the sirens a few times to scoot past some of the uglier backups, but they remained stuck in traffic at 5:30 when the meeting was supposed to begin.

Val didn't mind. She appreciated the opportunity to dive deeper into the report's details. The M.E. had declared drowning as the cause of death, but hadn't ruled out suicide, homicide, or accidental death. But a possible explanation for why the girl would take her own life emerged deep in the report's background pages—an explanation that left Val numb and silent for several moments.

"Look at this," she said when she could speak again. "Bruising on the thighs in various stages of healing—some fresh. Scar tissue and traces of semen in the vaginal canal."

Blake stared at her, recognition dawning. "And our all-American girl allegedly has no boyfriend."

Val nodded, a lump rising in her throat. "No boyfriend," she said, exhaling a long, uneasy breath, "but she does have a history of violent sexual abuse." Her throat grew tight, and she turned her gaze out the window, unable to focus again on the report's details.

Blake let out a long, low whistle and dove back into the report. For the rest of the ride, only Rico's muttered curses at Clayton's idiot drivers broke the somber silence.